THROUGH THE THORNS

THROUGH THE THORNS

M. WARREN ASKINS

First Edition: 2024

ISBN: 978-1-7341200-5-9 (paperback)
ISBN: 979-8-8742153-4-7 (hardcover)
ISBN: 978-1-7341200-4-2 (e-book)

For Mom

The hillside overlooked a vibrant forest, spanning endless to the horizon. A warm breeze gently tussled Jonas' hair, encouraging his entry.

"Can't hurt to check it out?" said Jonas to himself. As he prepared his first downward step, screams issued from within the forest. Then the sharp peal of steel clashing upon steel, like swords in combat, complimented the screams. A movement to his right shifted his attention.

"Jonas!" A man exclaimed, hurriedly limping toward him. He wore a gray mantle overtop a set of medieval armor. "I found you!" His gait was impeded by an arrow jutting from the back of his leg and the tips of his hair dripped beneath his drawn cowl.

The man now stood before Jonas, and though Jonas did not know him, recognition bloomed on the stranger's crimson face. It was not rainwater that had soaked the man's hair. Then the wound to his leg became too much to bear, and the man dropped to a knee. Almost instantly, pressure clamped around Jonas' fingers, squeezing them into a tight bundle. A tug brought him to a knee.

Jonas peered into the man's eyes. "Dude, who are —"

"War has reached the Riverlands!" the man interrupted. "You will be called and you must answer!" The man shook Jonas. "Please! Find the Joiner. Before it is too late!" The man returned his grip to Jonas' wrists. "You must —" A hoarse whisper on the wind bit off the man's words. His grip loosened, and Jonas took advantage, springing to his feet.

The streaks banding the skyline hardened, and the forest turned a darker hue. It became haunting and unwelcome, and from its depths the whisper had come. Suddenly creatures burst from the spaces between the tree trunks. Perhaps thirty or more, and after making their way onto the hillside, they paused, swiveling their heads as if tracking a lost scent.

"The Hylda have caught up already..." The man hesitated. "No matter." He met Jonas' eyes. "Find the Joiner. You're a true Valorous. Like your father." With that, he set his jaw and rolled onto his back. The Hylda had focused their direction and were now overtaking the ground. Like an emboldened sickness, they hurtled for the stranger.

Confined in this nightmare, Jonas screamed himself awake.

His eyes snapped open and he scrambled back against the headboard, kicking free of the blankets that threatened to strangle him. He recalled those horrid creatures, the *Hylda* that had just latched onto that man's throat. The headboard cracked against the wall, snapping free. Now unhinged, the bed listed sharply, jolting Jonas onto his side. He frantically burrowed his fingers into the mattress, the rusted springs preventing him from spilling out.

"Phew," he breathed, puffing a lock of hair from his eyes.

I hope that didn't wake Mom.

Frail ribbons of moonlight filtered through his window's bent slats, dousing the rumpled blankets with a pallid glow. The rest of his bedroom was dark and creased with shadows. When he reached for his glasses, he could still feel that man's iron grip on his wrists. While his right hand fumbled with the wire rims on his nose, his other hand scoured the space above his nightstand for his lamp. He could not help but stare into the chasm of darkness that his bedroom transformed into after night fell.

Once his glasses were on, the fuzzy contours of the room snapped into focus. The clarity was calming, but his fear had already taken hold. Jonas' breathing became harder, a wheeze.

A shadow from the closet was rising. It unfolded, expanded. There was a density to this shadow. The moonlight arrested on its surface.

Jonas had never seen a shadow like this one before. Was he still dreaming? When he exhaled, a wheeze rattled through his teeth.

"Leeeeeeds..." The shadow hissed, elongating the word, drawing closer. A fan of spittle struck Jonas' glasses. A dreadful, distorted face hovered in the meager rays of moonlight. "Devil," the monster concluded, slavering hungrily.

The springs of his bed screeched in protest as the monster placed clawed hands upon the mattress, leaning in, incrementally. Saliva began to flow like a lanced blister.

Jonas could not even gasp.

No longer able to maintain its integrity underneath such weight, the bed frame began to snap. Finally, a harsh crack issued from the footboard and the mattress caved onto the floor. Upon impact, the saliva-soaked mattress emitted a mist, further drenching Jonas' t-shirt.

The overhead light flicked on.

"Jonas!" Jonas' mother, Sandy, stood in the doorway. Light from the hallway streamed around her, sending more shadows to flight. When her eyes settled upon the familiar lemon tinted puddle spreading upon the mattress, her expression softened. "What happened?"

The monster had evaporated, returning a shred of normalcy to the room. With hands still fused to the mattress, Jonas gaped at his mother. The stain had nearly overtaken the bed. He looked at his damp clothes and a tremor of embarrassment rushed over him. From the initial tilted angle of the bed, a vast swath of drool had pooled over the groin of his basketball shorts.

"Oh, Jonas!" Sandy said, folding her arms. She bit her bottom lip, surveying the swampy devastation.

"It's not!" Jonas sputtered. Suddenly his big toe discovered a patch of drool. "Gah!" He sprang to his feet, holding his chest.

Sandy recognized that pose. "Where is your inhaler?" she prompted, wincing.

Jonas waved her question away. "That's not pee!" He managed to gasp, pointing at the substance that looked exactly like pee. "I'm sixteen, Mom! I haven't wet the bed in forever!"

Sandy nodded like a doctor prepared to relate ill news. "Of course not," she said, bending toward the splintered wooden frame. Doubt lingered in her eyes. Whether the doubt was from his statement, or the gratuitous amount of yellow liquid dripping all over the place, he could not tell.

"No more Mountain Dew before bed," she said. "And take your inhaler." Indicating his nightstand with a pointed finger.

Jonas took a puff. "Mom, I'm not lying," he said, the tightness in his chest alleviating. Where he expected to see his mother's relief, a haunted expression lingered. "What is it?"

She covered her mouth. "Your wrists!" she shouted.

First-degree burns with a solid crimson filament through the center wrapped around each of his wrists. As he rotated his hands, he discovered distinct finger impressions closing around his tendons. In horror, Jonas reeled and gulped a few more hits from his inhaler.

"Get closer to the light!" urged Sandy, tugging Jonas toward the lamp. She surveyed the burns with narrowed eyes. "This looks *weird but* doesn't look *too* bad. Did you sleep with your arm on the heat register or something?"

"I don't think so," said Jonas, pulling away. "And it doesn't hurt."

"Why don't you go run some cold water over it," advised Sandy. "And I'll clean this mess."

"No, no," said Jonas, eyeing the closet where the monster had first appeared. "I'll take care of this, you can just go back to bed. I'll crash on the couch."

Sandy wavered. "Alright," she relented with a sigh, making for the hall. "But if that burn looks any worse tomorrow, we're going to get it checked out."

"Okay," said Jonas. "Goodnight, Mom."

Sandy spoke from the hallway as the door closed. "First thing tomorrow, we're going to find you a new bed." Then continued in a whisper, after the door clicked shut, "love you, Jonas." She placed a solemn hand to the wooden surface. *Oh, Sebastian, he's looking more like you every day.*

CHAPTER 2

"Who knew beds were so expensive?" voiced Sandy as she and Jonas exited the furniture store. The parking lot was empty, save for their tired, old minivan. It was late in the day, and just shy of closing time for the shops along Main Street. On Saturdays, the local stores closed a few hours earlier.

"Everyone but us, I think," replied Jonas, his foggy winter breath enhanced by the lamplight. He wanted to say something to cheer her up, but he was feeling just as disheartened. While perusing the beds, she did not say it, but Jonas could tell from her expression that everything was beyond their budget.

It was their life story; everything was always *just* out of reach.

"Huh." Sandy paused, shivering. "You can sleep in my bed tonight, I guess. It's my turn on the couch."

"No, I'll take the couch again. It's not so bad." Jonas' teeth chattered. The last thing he wanted to do was draw that shadow monster into his mother's bedroom. "C'mon, toss me the keys, you said I could drive us home."

"Did I?" said Sandy brightening. "Twenty bucks and they're yours."

"I'll give you twenty-five, if you throw in this rust bucket," replied Jonas, patting the driver side door. Powdery snow fell onto his wrist, sending a chill all the way to his molars. His mystery burns had not quite healed.

"Deal," laughed Sandy, under-handing the keys into her son's chest.

The wintery winds were defeated once they eased inside.

When Jonas turned the ignition key a hesitant yelp issued from somewhere within the vehicle's guts. "C'mon, c'mon, you know I didn't mean that whole rust bucket thing." A familiar gagging whir issued from the depths, and the engine grumbled to life. The apology seemed to work.

Hopes and prayers, along with Sandy's innate understanding of machinery were all that kept the minivan running. Well, *running* was perhaps an overstatement. *Limping* was a better word.

"Tomorrow is Sunday," said Sandy. "The shops will be closed."

Jonas snorted. He hated Sundays. Hated the looming dread that swelled as the hours passed, reminding him that Monday was right around the corner. Good thing Christmas Break started this Monday.

The minivan nearly bottomed on a pothole, interrupting Jonas' moment of relief.

"That was a deep one!" announced Sandy. "Didn't see it, did ya?"

As Jonas shook his head, a building caught the corner of his eye. He had been on this route thousands of times and had never noticed it before. He slowed to catch a better glimpse.

The place looked like an old and weathered depot torn out of the Old West. A dimly lit sign graced the storefront, resting above the porch. It was open for some sort of business. Maybe it sold straw for thatch-roofed cottages, or whalebones to repair worn out corsets?

A single word upon the sign caused Jonas to gasp and mash the brakes, sending the minivan into a fishtail. In the passenger seat Sandy cursed and stomped at her imaginary brake pedals.

Luckily, Jonas had been driving slowly, so the minivan came to a safe, gradual stop on the shoulder of the road. Several more feet though, and they would have needed a tow.

"You don't stop for potholes!" said Sandy, pinching the bridge of her nose in irritation. "That'd be an instant fail on your driving test."

"That store!" Jonas fought with his seat belt, rotating in his seat to point behind him. "Have you ever seen it before?"

"What store..." Sandy followed her son's flailing index finger. "That store?" Her tone flattened. "That old place. Yeah it's been there for ages."

Jonas continued to stare, dumbstruck. "I've never seen it before."

"Well, it'll be there tomorrow," said Sandy.

"I think it's still open!" Jonas slapped the minivan into reverse.

Sandy turned as the entrance rushed toward their back bumper. "Just because the lights are on, doesn't mean they're open."

"What's the worst that could happen?" said Jonas.

Sandy nodded. "Like we have anywhere else to be?"

The minivan ambled down the driveway, bathing the store's sign in clear light.

"M.T. Joiner," said Sandy, reading the sign's inscription. She leaned forward and squinted, deciphering the smaller words beneath. "Antiquities and antiquity repair."

Within Jonas' memory, the dream stranger reared his head. *"Find the Joiner."*

This *had* to be a coincidence.

"Before it is too late."

Funneling from the parking lot, the shoveled footpath gave way to a saloon-style porch where several rocking chairs and rocking horses were frozen to the planks. They all seemed to have been struck by a freeze ray at the same time, halfway through a teeter.

Scattered salt crunched beneath Jonas' boots as he stepped onto the porch. The interchangeable sign on the front window displaying its "OPEN" side did not inspire confidence.

"It's too quiet," muttered Sandy. "I don't think anyone's home."

"The lights are on," said Jonas, "and the sign says they're open."

"I don't know, Jonas," said Sandy with a cross-armed sigh, cracking salt as she shifted her weight. "Maybe we should —"

The sharp bark of a large dog cut off Sandy's words.

Jonas placed a hand on the knob. "See," he said. "Somebody is home."

Sandy tugged his elbow. "What makes you think they'll have a bed in there that we can afford?" She released her grip and winced into her shoulder. She went out of her way to avoid mentioning their finances. It was her burden alone. "And we don't know that dog! It could be vicious!"

"I dunno," said Jonas, unconvinced. "That bark sounds friendly."

"How can you tell?"

"Well, there's no growl."

Sandy adjusted her scarf. "That doesn't mean anything," she stated. "It sounds *vicious* to me."

A voice called out from somewhere within the shop. "Cucumbers! What is it boy?"

Sandy glared at Jonas, daring him to laugh.

Jonas returned his hand to the knob. "Ah, yes, *Cucumbers*," he said. "The lesser known, but shaggy fifth Horseman of the Apocalypse." The knob was feather-light when he gave it a turn.

"Oh, whoa!" A sweatered man had been opening the door at the same time. He steadied Jonas at the shoulders, saving him from a fall.

The overwhelming warmth of the shop was welcoming and stifling all at once. Jonas' glasses fogged up instantly, disorienting him. "Your sweater is so soft." He grappled blindly as he cut past.

"Easy now," said the man, stepping aside. "Would you like a cloth for your specs?"

"No," replied Jonas. "Thank you though." He nudged the bridge of his glasses up, tilting his head back to peer through the slits developing along the lower rim. "They're pretty scratched and I don't want to make it worse."

The man nodded in Jonas' direction. His hair fell past his shoulders, tucked behind his ears. A curvy shadow of stubble filled out the rest of his face. On the beard spectrum, it leaned toward ruggedly carefree. Jonas could not help but envy this guy's facial hair prowess. No matter how hard he tried, the best he could grow was a pathetic shadow over his top lip. In the Big Leagues of Mustaches his would just be pretending to play t-ball.

"Welcome to the shop," said the man half-heartedly. "My name is Tasso."

Jonas jumped when an invisible nudge was suddenly deployed to his ribs. The tips of his fingers happened through a coarse patch of fur as he recoiled.

"And that's Cucumbers," Tasso continued with a chuckle. "He's friendly to strangers, but not usually that friendly."

A creature torn from the pages of Dr. Seuss stood before him, cocking its head playfully. Furry endless legs sprouted up from the center rectangle of a Persian carpet, bringing the animal's snout all the way up to Jonas' sternum.

"W-what is he?"

Tasso's chuckle grew into a laugh. "He's a pain in my neck."

"I mean, the breed."

"You've never seen an Irish Wolfhound before?"

"That sounds made up."

"Well, there's one actually staring at you right now."

Jonas rubbed his chin. "Learn something new every day."

"That's how it goes." Tasso raised his eyebrows. "So, are you here for a pick-up?" He turned to look at Sandy.

Since entering, Sandy had been staring at the man. "Have," she said at length with eyes to the floor, "we met before?"

Tasso scowled with one eyebrow remaining arched. "Don't think so," he replied, shaking his head. He strode toward the back of the foyer. "What's the name for the pick up?" he asked, disappearing through a door.

"We're not here for a pick up," Jonas replied for his mother. He looked her way and mouthed the word *"what."* Her eyes darted to him and she dismissed him with a quick shake of her head. "We've been bed shopping all day," continued Jonas, "and we haven't had any luck. We spotted this place on the way home, and figured why not give it a shot?"

"Huh," called Tasso from out of sight. From wherever he was, something metallic tumbled onto the floor. "I don't get too many shoppers, though we have plenty for sale." He sounded pre-occupied. "Most of my earnings come from the basic woodworking classes I teach on weekdays. The schedule is on the hallway by the door. And of course, repairs." He re-emerged smelling of chemicals and was scouring his hands with a soiled rag. "Tipped over some varnish," he explained. "Bed shopping is it? Why don't you have a look around while I tend to my lake."

Cucumbers activated when Jonas took his first step, pressing tight to his side. "Okay, okay," Jonas breathed. For his size, the dog was far more agile than Jonas thought possible. "Let's see what we can find, eh Mr. Cucumbers?"

To their left a doorway opened into a room chockful of furniture. Sofas, couches, and easy chairs were lined up in three separate rows, thoughtfully spaced for easy perusal. Rimmed around the furniture were glass-paned cabinets and bookcases spanning from wall to wall. With a meticulous eye for symmetry, an arrangement of clocks and lanterns had been pinned to the walls, overlooking it all. Jonas smiled at an old airplane propeller with a clock face fashioned to its central hub. Antiques and oddities were not really his thing, but he knew that his mother would freak out at some of this stuff. Especially the clocks.

"Where are the beds, Mr. Cucumbers?" Jonas inquired of his new companion. He weaved through the paraphernalia, passing by a circular table adorned with a clan of sock monkeys admiring a bowl of wax fruit. "Tasso's kids must get pretty bored hanging around here."

Standing beside the table he could make out a series of ornate wooden bollards sticking up from behind a horizon of gigantic picture frames. "Jackpot," whispered Jonas, ruffling the fur between Cucumber's ears.

A pair of dusty bed frames were leaning against the corner. Sturdy and amazing, they appeared to have been crafted from Redwood.

Inside Jonas disappointment welled. There was no way these frames would make it into his room without knocking down every wall along the way. Also, it went without saying, his mother could not afford them.

The accompanying mattresses were leaned in the same nook, still wrapped in clear plastic.

"Maybe, we won't leave empty handed after all," said Jonas looking intently at the price tags. He made his way to the corner and hurriedly flipped the tag over. To his disappointment, in tiny print just right of center sat the number *1000*. "Aw, dang," he groaned. He had hoped to have walked away with a mattress at the very least. The mattress alone would have been so much better than the couch, even without a frame or a box spring.

Why was everything so expensive?

When Jonas' chin wilted to his chest, Cucumbers whined and ducked down to nose at the teenager's fallen hand. In truth, he was tired. This "M.T. JOINER" place turned out to be a waste of time. He had found the *Joiner*, but to what end? Another letdown? It turned out that the dream stranger was simply that: a dream. Nothing more.

Once Jonas finally lifted his face, he discovered that his mother had only made it a few steps into the room. Her winter cap was in her left hand and she was inclining her head against a grandfather clock.

"Oh, boy," said Jonas. "Here we go."

Sandy did notice Jonas' approach. She was busy persuading the clock's glass door open. "It's a triple chime," she said.

"What did you say?" Jonas asked, standing behind her.

Sandy reeled. Luckily her hand was free of the fragile door. "Don't do that!" she said, clutching her collar. "What have I told you about sneaking up on your poor mother?"

"I see you found a friend," said Jonas, leaning into the clock's exposed guts. "He doesn't seem to be doing very well. What's the diagnosis?"

"Could be anything," she replied, bending down next to Jonas. Her eyes grew distant. "This old timer seems to be standing fairly level..." And just like that, she was lost to her thoughts. Jonas had seen this hundreds of times. His mother had entered her *state of diagnosis*. When this happened, it was best to just step back. She could return in a matter of minutes, or a matter of hours.

"Is everything all right?" Tasso asked. "Thought I heard a shout."

"We're fine," replied Jonas.

Sandy did not react. She was stone-faced, analyzing the moon dial and muttering about suspension springs.

Tasso entered the room. "Oh, I see that you found the Howard Miller," he said crouching beside Sandy. "I managed to spruce up the planton and bonnets, and the levelers were a smidge off so I shimmed them a bit and now the old guy sits plumb *and* level."

To Jonas' surprise, his mother snorted. In the past when she was zoned out like this nothing registered.

"A customer inherited this piece from a dead uncle, I think," Tasso explained. "It was in rough shape when she brought it in. I managed to restore it back to a semblance of its former glory, but unfortunately, as you can tell, the clockwork doesn't, well... work."

Sandy snorted again.

"Uh, yeah." Tasso scratched the back of his neck and sighed. "That was about three years ago, and the owner hasn't picked it up. And per our shop's repair contract, anything that sits for six months becomes our property." He shifted his stance and folded his arms. "I've been meaning to look up a clock repair guy to see if we can get it functional again, but honestly, I just haven't gotten around to it. And here it sits. Not too many people have use for a clock that doesn't tell time, ya know?"

"Oh, I am grossly aware," murmured Sandy, slipping from her trance.

Cucumbers whined and Jonas settled a hand on the wolfhound's head.

"It's a spectacular conversation piece," continued Sandy, easing the glass door closed. "But there's something about a clock that doesn't tick. Almost like a skeleton on display. The soul is gone, the essence — its purpose, its meaning — just isn't there. It lacks a certain... a certain..."

"Destiny?" offered Tasso.

"Yes!" Sandy pointed steepled fingers at the man. "A destiny!" she agreed, skimming a thumb across the clock's pronounced overlay. "You get it."

For several moments Tasso and Sandy just looked at one another.

Jonas was growing uncomfortable.

"Are you sure we haven't met before?" Sandy asked a second time.

Jonas coughed into his fist.

"I don't get out much," said Tasso, turning his attention to Jonas. "We don't have a lot in our bedding department. Does anything we have strike you?"

With eyes downcast, Jonas replied with a shake of his head.

"Probably for the best," said Tasso. "If you were planning on leaving with a bed tonight, you'd be out of luck. I'd need some time to rearrange the room, and we'd need one more person to get one of those frames out of here. As capable as old Cucumbers is, I don't think he'd be of much help." Then an idea suddenly dawned on the man's face. "Unless..." he trailed off, wagging a finger as he exited.

The old wolfhound muffled a bark and padded toward the hallway, then stopped at the threshold and looked back over his shoulder at Jonas.

"I think he wants us to follow him?" said Jonas, exchanging a shrug with Sandy.

Cucumbers led them down the hallway to the room that Tasso had disappeared into earlier. Upon entry Jonas felt as if he had just walked into the massive cabin of a tremendous pirate ship. A pirate ship manned by master carpenters.

Jonas' eyes traced the vaulted ceiling that molded the room into a dome that flung light into the farthest corners and rooted out all the shadows. He liked that. The less shadows the better.

The place smelled like shop class but was nothing like it.

"Welcome, welcome," Tasso called. "Come on, I want to show you something." The man was standing beside a semi-circle of glazed wooden furniture. The crème de la crème of his shop. He wiped his brow and gestured for them to approach.

"It was pretty heavy, but I managed to get it clear for you to check out."

Just what Tasso was talking about instantly became clear.

Tasso folded his arms across his chest. "I think you'll dig it."

Reclining at center stage was an immaculate gothic bed frame. Chills climbed up Jonas' neck.

The headboard pitched up into a quarter-length canopy, and each columnar supporting it looked like human skeleton bones. The posts, the feet, the frame, all of it resembled human bones. It was remarkable, and scary. But the most striking part, to Jonas, were the curved metal cylinders that sprang up from the sides of the bed, clearly meant to resemble a rib cage.

Jonas could not pull his eyes away.

"It's like you're the beating heart," said Tasso, tugging at one of the taller ribs. "When you're sleeping in it. Pretty clever, huh? Though it's a bit of sport getting in and out."

"What size mattress fits inside that... *thing?*" asked Sandy, clearly not nearly as enamored with it.

"It's between a twin and full. Kinda small, but perfect for a bachelor such as your son. Sturdy aged mahogany. The holder has yet to claim it and they have about..." He rolled up his sleeve to glance at his watch. "Three hours before it's officially forfeit."

"That's *something* for sure." Sandy withheld bolstering her son's excitement, presuming a staggering price tag.

"Mom," said Jonas in awe. "Do you see this?"

"Yeah," replied Sandy, leveling a side eye at her son. "I do. It's a wonder." She turned to Tasso. "And just out of curiosity, do you think the owner will be back before the three-hour deadline?"

The craftsman's mouth jutted to the corner as he shook his head. "Don't think that'd be possible."

"How's that?"

"The owner is deceased."

"Huh." Sandy blinked. "Surprised he didn't want to be buried with it."

Tasso laughed.

"Didn't think it was that funny," said Sandy to Jonas.

"It was that funny," said Tasso seriously before directing everyone's attention toward the headboard. "I thought about planting button tufts here to soften the mood a bit but decided against that. When you've gotten there, you may as well lean into the full Tim Burton."

Sandy's shoulders rose. "This bed looks incredible," she admitted through a sigh. "You do excellent work."

"Honestly, I didn't do too much."

"Either way." Sandy turned to Jonas. "As neat as it is, I think it's out of our price range."

"I understand," said Tasso. "Tough days, I get it."

"Thanks for your time." Sandy returned Tasso's frown. "And thank you for showing us this beautiful *whatever* it is."

"Nice meeting you, Tasso," said Jonas.

"Likewise."

When he turned to leave the disheartened expression on Jonas' face broke Sandy's heart. This world only seemed to be getting tougher.

"Good night," said Sandy with a farewell nod. Then added, "I'd look into replacing that crutch post."

As they walked away, Jonas thought he heard Tasso mutter, "Crutch post..." Then between their footsteps, Tasso spoke again but Jonas could not make out what he was saying. He was probably speaking to Cucumbers.

"Wait!"

He was not talking to his dog.

"You know clocks!"

Sandy was smiling.

"You're referring to the crutch post on the Howard Miller, right?" said Tasso, catching up with them. "Do you think you could fix it?"

Sandy shed her smile before she turned around. "I can," she replied.

Tasso was not hiding his smile. "Maybe we can work something out after all."

CHAPTER 3

Sandy and the Joiner had sealed the deal with a handshake, the terms fairly simple: Mom fixes the clock and Jonas gets the bed.

"You can even take it home tonight, if you're able," said Tasso to Jonas. "I'll throw in a box spring and mattress."

The words were not registering. Good things never happened. This deal seemed way too good to be true. That's when a beetle of doubt crept into Jonas' head.

Maybe this guy is just looking to unload this thing?

Tasso's face shifted into concern. "You okay?"

If that's the case, then why?

"No, no, I'm good." Jonas shook his head and turned to Sandy. "How are we going to fit it into my room?"

"Easy," replied Tasso, striding to the headboard. "Aside from the ribs, the whole thing breaks down." He gave the columnars that connected the canopy a tug, and the canopy folded into the frame. "Told you it was clever."

Sandy was impressed. "That is pretty clever," she admitted. "But it still won't fit in the minivan."

"I can take care of delivery," said Tasso. "Though I can't do it tonight."

The way Tasso just said *"I"* came off as odd. Jonas cocked an eyebrow at Cucumbers. *But then again, most everything about this guy was odd*, thought Jonas.

"The couch for another night?" asked Sandy.

Jonas shrugged. "Not so bad."

Along their path back to the minivan, the scattered salt had formed deep hollows in the snowdrifts. To Jonas they appeared as lunar craters.

"Feels like we're walking on the moon," said Jonas in high spirits. "Who'd have thought you could use your clock skills as currency?"

Sandy laughed. "It's quite a bargain," she agreed. "You want to drive this final stretch?" She flipped the keys back over her shoulder.

"I'm game," replied Jonas as he fumbled the keys and dropped them. "Now if only I can find these keys as easily as I found the Joiner," he muttered as he reached into the snowbank. He was up to his shoulder, fishing for only a few seconds before his fingertips glanced a brassy surface. "It is my lucky day," he said, shaking the snow from his arm.

Sandy was waiting inside the minivan, breathing warmth into her hands. "Glad you could join us," she said with a grin.

"Ha. Ha," returned Jonas, wrenching the seat belt across his chest. "Tell me, in all the years you've lived here, you've never once been to this place?" He scraped at the film of ice inside the windshield.

Sandy's smile leveled off. "A small wonder," she said. "Been past it a million times, but never darkened its doorstep."

"Tasso looks about your age," stated Jonas as he cranked the ignition. Without any coercion, the engine rumbled to life. "Do you think Gramps or Gram did any business with his parents back in the day?"

"Maybe?" replied Sandy.

The minivan crunched its way out of the driveway and loped out onto the road.

"So maybe you and Tasso met when you were kids, or when you were my age?"

"Maybe?"

"Maybe it was around the time you met Dad?"

Sandy grew rigid and said nothing. The Dad subject was touchy. She never spoke much about him. Whenever Jonas brought the subject up, her mind went elsewhere. Kind of like when she went into her state of diagnosis, only much sadder. As Jonas grew older, he had hoped that she would reveal more. Because before Jonas' arrival into this world, his father had departed it.

"I figured you wouldn't want to talk about him," said Jonas. "My bad."

Jonas' parents were young when they met, and it had been a whirlwind romance. His father had arrived in town, seeking fortune. His mother worked at the family clock shop, the shop she still worked to this day. Upon his venture, by the means of fate, he happened into the shop. And that's where their story began. It's also where the story ends, at least, as far as Jonas knew of it. There was more to it, but his mother was reticent to discuss it.

The minivan slunk down the street leading home. Jonas watched the familiar homes in the Historical District passing his window. Twinkly Christmas lights adorned their broad faces, broadcasting festive humors.

The minivan slowed and Jonas flicked the turn signal on. The gentle clicking filled the silence, and the blinking light illuminated heaps of snow piled on the curb. Just like the other homes in the Historical District, Jonas' home was large and interesting to look at. The second-story balcony doubled as the porch roof, supported by four thick columns. A circular window in the attic peered from high above the ground, just below the arch crested roofline. Some tinkerer had built the place back in the early nineteenth century. He had relegated the ground floor's front portion to accommodate a store front and workshop. And that very detail had caught Gramps' attention all those years ago.

The sign over the large bay windows read, "Porter Clock Repair." The lettering had grown dull and faded, and a casual passerby might mistake the sign's legitimacy for charming period adornment.

"Seems like I left a light on," said Sandy as she closed the passenger door. The front windows contained a dull glow.

"Seems so," agreed Jonas. "But what's that?" He pointed at a small unlit rectangle at the lower corner of the bay window. As Jonas stepped up onto the porch he discovered that the dark rectangle was a large, taped envelope.

"Maybe a customer left a note?" said Jonas, swiping the envelope and tearing it open. "Ah," he groaned crestfallen. "Nope."

"What's it say?" asked Sandy, accepting the letter. "Notice of Default?" she recited the heading with dismay. Her eyes scoured the remainder. "Don't worry about it," growled Sandy, somehow drafting a smile. "Looks like I'll finally have to sell the demagnetizer." She folded the paper and tucked it into her back pocket.

Jonas was holding the front door open. "I'm going to fix this," he told his mother as she entered.

Sandy unfurled her scarf and playfully slung it onto a hook. "How will you do that exactly?"

"Not sure," replied Jonas. "But it'll come to me. Don't worry."

"*You* don't worry," corrected Sandy. She waved a hand at a shop with less contraptions and devices than it had ever held. "I still have some stuff that holds value. And who knows? Business might pick up?"

"You sell that demagnetizer," began Jonas. He paused to tug off a boot. "And you may as well sell everything else."

"I'm freezing!" Sandy rubbed her hands together. "I'm going to head up to the kitchen and forage some hot cocoa, how 'bout it?"

"Mom."

Sandy shook her head. "No, we're not talking about the shop anymore today," she stated. "Instead we're going to discuss whether the perfect cocoa to marshmallow ratio actually exists." With that she skated on her socked feet toward the stairway leading to the upper floors.

"Mom," said Jonas unmoving. "'Notice of Default' means we're going to lose the house."

For the briefest moment, Sandy's smile flickered. "And hot chocolate means warm fingers," she stated. "Which is what I'm *way* more interested in right now. See you upstairs, kid." She disappeared up the stairs and out of sight.

"We should talk about this," said Jonas to himself. He could feel his asthma kicking in. "We should talk about this," he repeated louder, winding his way up the staircase.

"Jonas!"

His mother's scream did not come from the kitchen. She was in his bedroom.

A cold fear gripped him. Suddenly the shadow monster's face flashed into his mind. He bolted down the hall, ignoring the tightening inside chest. He nearly overshot his room, just barely managing to snag a hand to the doorframe.

A few steps inside, his mother was pressed to the wall, staring at something ahead of her.

"How," she began, her eyes darting to Jonas. "How did it?"

Bracing himself ahead of his overwhelming fear, Jonas crossed the threshold. During his short sprint down the hallway, he had been steeling himself for a hideous monster. And though there was no monster to be seen, what his eyes fell upon was just as troubling. For already nestled in the corner of his room was the Joiner's bed, complete with box spring and mattress.

Jonas wheezed and stumbled backward against the wall beside his mother.

"I know, right," said Sandy. "And it brought a friend." She inclined her head toward an oval cheval mirror that shared similar skeletal appearances. "Must be part of the set?"

In the mirror, Jonas watched his bewildered reflection brush at his cheek in disbelief. I think I'm ready for that hot chocolate now," he said calmly.

CHAPTER 4

Vampires sleep in coffins. Mummies sleep in sarcophagi. And Jonas was trying to fall asleep in a... giant skeleton. The ribs jutting around him was something he would have to get used to.

Despite the new mattress, he just could not fall asleep. He was worn out, not tired. There was a difference. And his head was spinning from the three hits he had just taken from his inhaler, which was not helping.

Someday, he told himself, *I will outrun my asthma.*

His eyes drifted inside the canopy overhead.

Someday we'll get out of this rut.

In the corner, a small face appeared within a shadow cast by the footboard.

"And someday I will stop seeing monsters in the shadows." A passing car pitched its headlights across the shadow, dispelling the creature. Jonas rolled onto his side, grinding his teeth against the pulsations in his wrists. This was going to be a long night.

After tossing and turning for what felt like hours, sleep finally took hold of him, and not gently. The initial tug at the scruff of his neck felt as a test, as if someone was testing the strength of a knot. Then the mattress evaporated and Jonas fell through the floor, through the shop beneath, then into the underground. Within moments the soil and earth gave way to a clear blue sky, and somehow through it all, he was unscathed.

This was an all too familiar dream, the classic freefall without a parachute. In a minute the ground would rush to meet him and he would wake with his heart lodged in his throat.

Wind whistled in his ears, and a sudden pressure gripped him at the nape of his neck, directing his fall, facedown. The force insisted that he speed up, causing the wind to shriek. As hard as he tried, he could not look away. When he closed his eyes they whipped back open, helplessly — he was only falling faster.

"Wake up!" he shouted, slapping at his face.

A green canopy stretched out beneath him, endlessly to the horizon. Forest and more forest, it seemed. Which meant branches and more branches.

Jonas braced himself.

Surprisingly, the fall through the canopy was not too bad. The branches hurt only a little bit, like the sting from a hard rain — there and gone — leaving little trace. Not like it mattered anyhow, he was just about to wake up.

Abruptly the force yanked back on his neck, stopping his fall. Jonas swung upward, his feet grazing the mossy carpet. For a few moments he pendulated there, suspended, before he was finally set down.

From the fringes of his vision, he spied something resting against the base of a tree. Immediately he recognized the shape as the shadow monster that had soiled his mattress the night before. In panic, Jonas scrambled for cover, his t-shirt bunching up around his shoulders when he sagged down.

"Help me!" he breathed through his fingers.

In the distance, steel clanged amid voices screaming.

Jonas nearly poked himself in the eye when he went to adjust his glasses. In shock he rummaged over his face. His glasses were gone and yet he could see clearly!

From the direction of the screaming, an explosion shook the ground, careening a shockwave through the forest. Surely the shadow monster had roused and moved. Pine needles sprinkled the crown of Jonas' head when he peered around for a better look. Between the leaves and loose-hanging branches cascading to the forest floor, the monster remained where he was.

Voices were drawing closer as the battle began to flow toward Jonas.

Another detonation erupted, ushering a cruel wave that blasted Jonas into the air. A series of hard roots painfully broke his fall, evacuating all the air from his lungs. Lying sprawled upon the ground, dazed and breathless, Jonas could do nothing but cover his head.

"Why won't you wake up?!" he gasped into the crook of his elbow.

The ringing in his ears gave way to the sound of voices. Voices close enough to be understood.

"I see him!" Someone called. "Over there!"

Jonas cracked an eye in the direction of the someone.

To his immense fear, the creatures from his nightmare advanced toward him — the *Hylda.* Now much closer, and in the daylight, he could clearly make out their appearance. Adorned in threadbare shawls, the Hylda were short, sickly thin women whose movements arrived unnaturally rickety and stilted. Everything about them, from their prolonged jaws to their inhuman gyrations, was horrifying. Jonas could not look away.

Wake up! Jonas relayed desperately to his subconscious. *Wake up, you idiot!*

His heart pummeled his sternum as his body crimped into the fetal position.

The Hylda were upon him.

Figments of his short life flickered in his mind. He tucked his chin and screamed into his knees. Where he expected sensations of intense agony, instead, he felt the gentle peppering of twigs.

It was then that it hit him, everything felt so real.

This was no dream.

With the sounds of battle nearing, the Hylda had formed a protective barrier around him. Jonas watched dozens of darkly calloused bare feet shift and move. Tattered cloaks twirled about their ankles, and Jonas feared to look any higher.

"I've found him!" Suddenly an armored human woman brushed through the Hylda, gripped Jonas' forearm, and hauled him to his feet. "We've got him!" She called in triumph, addressing the knights who rushed to gather before the circle of Hylda. "The Leeds forces have claimed the Devil first!"

Jonas forced a weak smile. "Hi, there," he said, feeling fool-ish, dangling there as a prized trout.

"*That's* the Leeds Devil?" one knight voiced in disbelief. "Captain," the knight addressed the woman gripping Jonas' wrist. "This can't be —"

"Luna Knights! The Terrens will not prevail this day! Bunker down and hold!" The captain ordered, spinning a closed fist over her head. All but two of the knights acknowl-edged her command and fanned out ahead of her. The captain spent a nod on the two that remained. "Vera, Greta, take the Devil to Brimon." Then with grim surety, she turned her back on Jonas. "We make our stand here!"

"No!" One of the knights argued, pressing through the Hylda. "We stay with you! We are too few as it is!"

The captain placed a hand on the knight's shoulder. "Vera, we knew most of us would not be returning," she stated. "The objective was to claim the Devil. If the prophecy proves true, then what we've done this day will assure the Leeds final vic-tory." She nodded at Jonas, released his wrist.

"But, Melindra —" Vera stammered.

The captain's hand glided from Vera's shoulder to her cheek. "Go. Now." A grim smile appeared on her face. "Make certain our sacrifice means something."

A tree exploded to their left and for the first time, Jonas saw the captain flinch. Jagged fragments pelted their sides and Jonas howled in pain. Somehow the Hylda heard Jonas' cries and sprung to his side. They circled as they had before, but this time they were pressing tighter against him. Most of their heads bobbed up to his chin, but the tallest were almost equal to his height. Confined within the barrier of Hylda, Jonas' nostrils were assaulted by the scent of bacon and unwashed gym socks. He felt a sudden urge to take a hundred baths. One of the shorter Hylda gripped him by the wrist and nodded up at him.

"Melindra!" Vera screamed as the captain rushed to join the luna knights.

The space between the battle and Jonas quickly diminished. Through the fog borne from the explosions Jonas watched a luna knight stumble backward, hands clinging to the pike that had passed clean through her belly.

Vera and Greta brusquely pulled Jonas up a hillock, the Hylda keeping up with ease. A pike struck the earth beside them. A Terren on the outskirts of the battle had drawn a bead, and was leaning back, preparing another.

Vera's eyes flicked to Jonas. "Devil!" She pointed off to her right with her sword. "Keep running! That way!"

"You got it!" replied Jonas. The further he ran from the explosions and the pikes the better. Pivoting hard, he sprang to his left and barreled toward the unknown, while his Hylda entourage joined in lockstep. They maintained their barrier, neither getting in his way nor slowing him down. It was as if they were in tune with some secret frequency broadcasting his movements ahead of time.

A high-pitched scream came from the forest behind him. Before the note concluded, a hundred more identical cries joined.

The Hylda drew closer.

Apparently the monsters making that sound were not friendly. As if anything in this forest could be considered *friendly*.

"Follow us!" said Vera. The two knights had caught up.

Jonas and the Hylda obeyed, joining the knights' rush.

"They gathered the Lancethanes!" Greta shouted at Vera.

Before long, they happened upon a clearing with a small cottage plunked in the center and a modest barn not far off. Jonas' legs began steering him toward the barn, seeking shelter. The cows inside lifted their heads and began to low at the Hylda. The closer they drew, the more frantic the cows became.

"Hey!" Vera called, noticing his change of direction. "Don't go in there!"

Jonas groaned as he turned, correcting his direction. *"Don't go in there,"* he scolded. The shortest Hylda who had clutched his wrist earlier, cackled back at him.

These knights and Hylda did not tire, and suddenly Jonas realized that he was not growing weary. And he was not wheezing! He had been running and running and his asthma had not kicked in once. For the first time, he rolled his shoulders and sucked in a deep breath. No rattle, no wheeze. In this world, not only could he see without glasses, but he could also run.

A Lancethane shrieked, announcing his presence, cutting Jonas' brief moment of elation short.

The knights hunched and halted, turning toward the shriek.

"How far until we are out of Terren territory?" asked Greta while she scanned the trees.

Vera placed a hand on Greta's shoulder armor. "Not far." She seemed distracted by something in the treetops. "I have an idea." Slowly she turned to Jonas. "I think we can make it." The way her lip curled made Jonas uneasy.

"Oh, no!" Greta slapped Vera's hand. "We'll never make it! The whole detachment gave their lives to give us this chance!"

"We can make it. Trust me," said Vera, "but we must move." She began counting, flicking her index finger against her thumb. "Devil," she said quietly. "See that thicket?"

Jonas turned and stared in disbelief. "It goes parallel to the Lancethanes."

"When I shout," Vera continued, ignoring Jonas. "I want you to run straight for it as fast as —"

The ear-splitting wail of a Lancethane interrupted the rest of what she was about to say.

"Now!" Vera screamed.

Greta backpedaled, fumbling at her satchel.

Jonas wheeled and hurtled as hard as he could for the thicket.

As he drew closer to the thicket, the Hylda shifted formation to fill his left flank, shielding him from the emerging Lancethanes. With the finish line only a few yards away, a jarring explosion forced him to stumble. Several hands pulled at him, correcting his stride.

A spear shot out from the forest, careening toward Jonas. Suddenly a Hylda leapt to intercept, and crumpled like parchment as she took the full blow. A host of palms pressed Jonas' back, keeping him upright as they left the shattered Hylda behind.

A shriek of frustration rent the air in response to the Hylda's sacrifice. Then an explosion diverted the dismayed Lancethane's attention.

Vera and Greta had cut a course toward the Lancethanes, bringing the battle to them. They cleared the charred fiery gap as debris harmlessly spattered their closed faceplates. At that moment Greta was looking down, reaching into her satchel to produce another bomb.

Fervent palms pressed Jonas into the thicket as he slowed to watch. The moment before his heels crossed over, one of Greta's explosions assured his entry. He tumbled and rolled and was hoisted back to his feet within the blink of an eye. Brambles, briars, and vegetation snaked around and overhead, blotting out the sun.

"Press on," a Hylda rasped into his ear. "Terrens can spell death."

"What?" asked Jonas, staggering onward.

The hands gently pressed the teenager into the snarl of thorns, decimating his t-shirt and sweatpants. All around he could hear the stretching and tearing of garments, the Hylda were not faring much better.

"Press on," said another Hylda, "this barrier will hamper the Terrens."

The Hylda inside the thicket flailed in alarm, hopelessly ensnaring themselves. Jonas lunged to help, but the Hylda that had already crossed stopped him, ripping him back.

"We can help them!" protested Jonas, swatting at their hands.

"No time!"

Jonas regarded the trapped, struggling Hylda. "I'm so sorry," he called. The freed Hylda forced Jonas away from that hellscape of a thicket, and soon Jonas was running through a meadow with a downward gradient. Varying shades of yellow and maroon blanketed the fields with a few sparsely placed trees interrupting the pattern.

A warm breeze passed between the torn slots in Jonas' t-shirt, and he glanced down, while maintaining a run, to take stock of his sweatpants. With relief he discovered that the garment, though torn into shorts, still protected his private bits.

From where he ran, the meadow shrugged along endlessly, with not a person in sight. And the meadow held a curious essence that persuaded his legs to keep running. Ordinarily, mists of pollen would trigger an asthma attack, but not in this world. With each footfall the distinct sound of rushing water increased in his ears. Intersecting the path ahead, Jonas and the Hylda came upon a very wide river, without a bridge nearby.

"We must cross," a Hylda advised. "Safety is just beyond."

Looking at the speaker, Jonas had to call in to question just what these disturbing creatures defined *safety* as.

"What is beyond —"

The shout of a familiar voice cut Jonas off. "Devil!" Vera had caught up, panting and clutching the collar of her chest armor. "Do not stop!" An explosion erupted from the foothills behind her.

From between ribbons of twirling smoke, Greta joined Vera's side. Her helmet was gone and the side of her face was scorched and blistered. "That was my last bomb!" she declared. "We have little time! The 'Thanes are right behind us!"

The knights turned for the river and bounded into a sprint.

Vera punched Jonas' arm as she passed. "We must cross the Taub!" she urged. "Come on! We'll be safe afterward!"

Jonas and his coven followed the knights down the hill to the bank of the river. "But how?" he asked Vera. He had to raise his voice to be heard over the roar of the water.

The knights had been unfastening their armor while they ran and were now hastily slugging it off. "Don't tell me," said Vera, bending to release her chest plate, "that you don't know what you are capable of?" She straightened and gazed at Jonas as if for the first time. "Just command the Hylda."

"How does one command a Hylda?" said Jonas.

Greta stepped in. "You're the Leeds Devil."

"I don't know what that means either!"

"Just tell them to get us across!" said Vera, gesturing to the Hylda.

Jonas' head was spinning.

"How will they get us across?" he said quickly as the Hylda hemmed his sides defensively.

"If what the diviners say is true —" Vera began but was interrupted by the bellowing of a Lancethane.

These cries were different. Jonas cocked an ear to the sound. The previous screams were not as low as these, nor as menacing. A strange feeling came over him, and he could almost understand what the Lancethanes were saying.

Jonas whirled on the Hylda. "Get them across!" he demanded, pointing at Vera and Greta. The Hylda obeyed, forming a horseshoe around the surprised knights.

"No! We aren't leaving you!" said Vera, trying to elbow through the Hylda. She was unsuccessful and soon her and Greta were ankle deep in the flowing water. "You must come with us!"

Vera continued shouting, but her words were lost to the river.

"Here we go," said Jonas alone, facing the hills.

CHAPTER 5

A hot breeze combed the tall grass and swept through his tattered sweatpants.

He could still hear Vera, but her voice was faint.

Jonas bent at the knees, waiting for the Lancethanes to finally show. His eyes shot to the crease of one hillock, believing that he saw movement.

"This is it," muttered Jonas. "If I'm supposed to wake up, now would be the perfect time."

Then the world seemed to grow silent and still, like the night air before snowfall.

A pair of cylindrical horns that curved into fearsome half crescents gradually rose into view over the hilltop. The horns concluded into a reptilian skull that shimmered in the daylight, as though it were composed of maille.

Jonas balked. "Lancethanes are..."

More of the Lancethane emerged, surveying the landscape.

"...dragons." Jonas concluded.

An armored figure was saddled behind the Lancethane's neck with a tree of a lance locked in his fist.

Jonas sincerely regretted sticking around on this side of the river. "Nope," he said backpedaling down the riverbank.

More Lancethanes joined the first, holding their position. At least a dozen appeared. Between every beat of Jonas' heart, another mounted dragon crested the hill.

"What are they waiting for?"

The Lancethanes parted, creating space.

"Oh," said Jonas, his heels finding a muddy recess, stopping him short. Another step and he would have fallen backward into the river.

The largest Lancethane assumed the center point of the hill.

"That's what they were waiting for."

This dragon was huge. If your average Lancethane was a velociraptor, then this guy was a T-Rex. But unlike the other riders, this fellow bore a tremendous longbow. The weapon curved well over his head and concluded down beyond his boots.

Jonas had seen enough. "Witches!" he screamed over his shoulder. "Hylda!" he corrected, and he heard the water splashing as the Hylda returned to him.

The Tyrannosaurus Lancethane reached across his saddle for an arrow.

"Get me across!" Jonas' voice rose shrill. "Get me across! Oh, man! Hyldas! Hurry!"

The moment an icy Hylda hand gripped Jonas' ankle, the massive Dragon leveled his snout and unleashed an ear-splitting roar.

The Hylda had created a bridge, standing with their feet locked to the riverbed, passing Jonas like a crowd surfing rock star. He craned his neck to his chest, training his eyes on the

Lancethanes teetering toward a downhill charge, waiting for their leader's signal.

Jonas made it to the other side, slipping and sliding his way to dry ground. "Why are they just standing there?" he asked, scuttling to his feet.

"I don't know," replied Greta. "But we're not hanging around to find out."

Jonas was as puzzled as he was relieved.

"Maybe they think we have more bombs?" said Vera, spinning Jonas around with a tug. "Who knows? We are three leagues shy from safety, so we must make use of this reprieve."

The Lancethanes' banners snapped in the breeze as Jonas gave them a farewell glance. "Well," said Jonas, jogging to catch up with the knights. "Is a Lancethane the dragon or the rider?" One by one the Hylda joined him, their numbers dwindling. It seemed that the river had claimed a few more.

"They aren't dragons," Greta answered. "They're drakes."

"But which one is the Lancethane?"

Vera stopped and pointed toward a series obelisks and statues ringed beneath a copse of sad, crooning trees. "We run through the graveyard. Right through its heart."

"Are you certain about that?" Greta did not sound pleased.

"I always thought that drakes were boy ducks," said Jonas.

"Vera," said Greta, shaking her head. "Do you think it's wise to cut through *this* cemetery?"

"It's still hours before dusk," replied Vera. "I don't think we'll encounter any imps." She turned to Jonas. "And Lancethanes are the drake and rider combined."

"Ah," said Jonas. "Cool."

Greta cleared her throat. "In *this* cemetery," she repeated with greater emphasis. "Imps are the least of my concern."

"I don't know where we're going," said Jonas. "But, that graveyard looks easier to cross than that forest."

"Yes, but" — Greta cocked her chin, addressing Vera — "*this* cemetery has other problems."

Vera's eyes darted between the diverging paths. "I don't know what..." Then a troubling look flashed across her face. "Ah, yes." She set her sights on the forest. "You're right, Greta. We should opt for the forest route."

"Wait, why," said Jonas as the knights sprinted for the trees. He looked to the shortest Hylda. "What's wrong?"

The Hylda only shrugged.

"Lots of help you are." Jonas smiled at the Hylda and the creature contorted its mouth back at him.

"Time is not our ally," called Greta from the treeline. As Jonas approached, she continued. "If we get separated, keep running."

"Gotcha," said Jonas.

After leaping hundreds of felled trees and steering beneath thousands of branches, the knights eventually drew up short before a barrier of ivy. Vera discovered a small opening, which granted single-file entry. Jonas followed while the Hylda bunched up tighter.

"There it is," revealed Vera, slogging an armful of vegetation aside. "Fort Brimon."

Once Jonas' eyes adjusted to the light, he took in an untilled field that stretched all the way to the gates of a fortified palisade. A village bustled within the walls, and soldiers in glistening armor formed battle lines.

"Wait here," said Vera, extricating herself from the vines. She stalked forward, staying within the grid of the forest's shadows.

"What is she doing?" Jonas whispered. "Why don't we make a break for it?"

"Can't be too careful," replied Greta.

"What else is hunting us?" asked Jonas.

"Not hunting *us.*" Greta's eyes settled on Jonas. "You."

Jonas did not know how to respond to that, so he peered around Greta to check on Vera. "Where did she go?" he asked himself. The knight was nowhere to be seen.

"We're good," said Vera suddenly beside him.

Startled, Jonas fell into the vines.

"Come on, let's go!" urged Greta, pulling him into the open. Jonas heard the Hylda scurrying through the foliage to catch up.

At first, the downhill slope made running easier, but soon Jonas was running faster than he could handle. "Oo-di-lolly!" he crowed before taking a nose-dive. A pair of Hylda, one to each elbow, hoisted the teenager back on his feet. After a quick dust-off, he took off again, this time choosing his steps more carefully.

Impressive, clean, and mighty, the walls of the palisade flared up before him. The final leg of this weird, scary journey was nearing its end. A vanguard of armored figures beckoned, straining to reach him, their belts tethered to the outer walls behind. With an air of urgency, they peered over Jonas' head.

Jonas was so tired, he was ready to lay down forever.

A column of archers clambered up the parapets, clutching longbows. Below them, a smaller side gate opened, adding more fighters to the field. Meanwhile the tethered soldiers had begun screaming, their gestures suddenly panicked. From inside their close-visored helms, their muffled voices were impossible to understand.

"The Ritts approach!" one archer screamed from overhead.

Suddenly the archers' bows swept upward.

Winged darkly ashen creatures descended from the sky, their wings flapping deathly silent. To Jonas, they appeared as gargoyle statues come to life. Except these creatures had razor-sharp claws extending from the backs of their hands. Then, one by one, the Ritts tucked their wings, preparing for an onslaught of nosedives.

Like owls to field mice, the Ritts tore the Hylda from the ground. Jonas ducked as the blackened bare feet of a Hylda kicked the air around his head. With each breath, he lost another Hylda. He gritted his teeth, continuing to run, expecting talons to sink into him at any time.

More arrows were spent from the fortress, coming into view before disappearing. The Brimon knights were close now. Jonas siphoned the reserves of his energy into his legs, bounding the last few steps safely into their midst. As friendly cold steel clasped his wrist, an overwhelming blow struck the back of his head. Pressure bit down on his shoulders, then released. Jonas managed to stagger one step before he fell, collapsing onto a knee.

Armored legs rushed past him, and Jonas turned to see a knight withdrawing his bloodied arming sword from a fallen Ritts' torso. Evidently the knight had rescued Jonas from an early grave by plunging his weapon into the creature's chest. Up close the Ritts did indeed look like a gargoyle, with frayed bat-like wings extending from its spinal column, and each of its vertebrae were as sharpened daggers.

The knight flicked the blood from his blade and shouted, "Get him inside!" Then Jonas was escorted by one contingent of knights, while the others remained on the battlefield. In Jonas' wake, he heard longswords scraping free from scabbards.

A tide of knights streamed past Jonas as he was rushed toward the main gate. Among their ranks, to Jonas' surprise, appeared to be minotaurs and werewolves interspersed with eyes set aglow by the gathering dusk. The archers on the parapets released volley after volley, darkening the remaining daylight.

Pain lanced Jonas' scalp, then the soldier on his left bundled the attacking Ritts to his chest. With his off hand, the soldier flicked a hidden dirk into his palm, then abruptly buried the blade in the convulsing Ritts' face. He dropped to a knee and face-palmed the sputtering gargoyle into the stone walkway.

Once inside the walls of the fort, the heavy door slammed mere inches behind one of Jonas' escort. He flicked his visor open and looked up as if to say, *"What gives?!"*

After a reluctant pause, an apology came down from the parapet.

"Keep your head down!" A knight placed a rough hand on the back of Jonas' head.

A Hylda did not care for this particular treatment of Jonas. She leapt, backhanding the knight's nose guard, spinning the helmet off kilter. The knight, startled and dazed, backed off and Jonas glanced around to see who remained of the Hylda and found only two.

While Jonas was ushered through the bailey, deeper into the fortress, he looked around hoping to spot Vera and Greta. Though he did not see them, he could not help but notice a mass of robed wizard-looking people making their way toward him. The foremost, a lanky tube of a man, doubled his steps to reach Jonas before the others.

"Command the Ritts!" shouted the lanky man. The eccentric goatee he sported twirled beneath his mouth. "I implore you, Leeds Devil! Compel them!" Then the man fell onto his knees. "Just as the Hylda, the Ritts will obey if you command them! Bring an end to this!"

Jonas shrugged. "Sure, guy," he said. "Easy enough."

CHAPTER 6

In a grim change of tactics, the Ritts had begun lugging Brimon soldiers into the sky and launching them onto the fort like torpedoes. Jonas ran over to a recently dropped soldier and knelt down to look into the dying woman's face. He was relieved to find that she was not Vera or Greta, and a pang of guilt struck him, stopping him.

"Devil!" With wide eyes, the lanky man shouted from beneath an overhang. "Find safety with us!" He flapped his arms, indicating the others huddled beside him.

"But," said Jonas, letting go of the soldier's hand. "I thought I needed to —" He bounded to his left as a soldier struck the earth beside him. The Hylda began circling, unsure about the best way to protect him from the sky.

As Jonas scanned for cover a hailstorm of bodies pelted the earth around him. A knight cowering beneath the lowest tier of scaffolding met Jonas' eyes and straightened to a full stand. With a resolute nod he broke from safety and crossed the perilous distance with a shield raised over his head. Once the knight joined Jonas' side he exhaled in relief and lowered his shield to speak.

"If we make our way to the gates, afterward you —" he began but was violently interrupted by a Ritts fastening its claws onto his shoulders and tearing him upward from the ground. The knight's legs flailed helplessly as he rose into the sky, powerless to free himself.

"To us, Devil!"

Jonas pulled his eyes from the skies to see three knights rushing toward him wielding tower shields over their heads. Quickly Jonas lunged beneath the shields, the Hylda tailing behind.

"Thanks, guys," said Jonas. "Can you get me to the gates?"

"That's the idea," replied one of the knights. Their surcoats were stained with mud and blood, and their breathing came ragged.

Jonas was not sure how to *compel* the Ritts, but when he compelled the Hylda, he had been looking directly at them. It stood to reason that the same logic applied, and the best view of the Ritts was from the main gate.

Around Jonas, the Hylda danced beneath the roving canopy. At intervals they peeked their heads out to see what was happening.

"We have to open the main gate," said Jonas to the nearest knight.

The knight turned mad eyes toward Jonas. "Is that necessary, Devil?" he spoke as one exhausted. "Whatever forces the Terrens have mustered will surely include a ground attack."

"Aye," said another knight, adding, "once the Ritts have thinned us, they will send in waves of ground forces."

"Have they attacked like this before?" asked Jonas.

"Nay," replied the same knight. "We have never experienced a Ritts assault."

"Then how do you know?"

The knight sniffed. "Because it's what we would do."

They don't know for certain, thought Jonas. *Maybe if we crack the gate open...*

"Hey! What are you doing?" One of the knights shouted. "Stay with us!"

Jonas had abandoned the shelter and sprinted toward the gate.

"Lift the gate!" he shouted with the Hylda scuttling behind him.

An archer took notice and obliged, heaving the gate upward just enough for only Jonas to roll beneath. The gate slammed down behind him, barring the Hylda.

Hurtling out into the open amid the soldiers fighting for their lives, Jonas took in as many Ritts as he could. Further beyond, enemy soldiers were streaming down the hillside.

Those must be the Terren ground forces, thought Jonas. *Those knights knew what they were talking about.* Jonas arched his back to the skies. *Let's see if I can end this.*

"Hey Ritz!" Jonas shouted and immediately felt a connection to the gargoyles. "Hold up!" he commanded, emptying his lungs. He dropped onto a knee and closed his eyes. He had never exerted so much energy before and required a moment to catch his breath.

Before he opened his eyes, the sounds of battle had come to an abrupt end. When he opened his eyes, the Ritts were placidly hovering over the battlefield.

"Put the soldiers back down!" Jonas commanded the Ritts, and suddenly a wave of fatigue washed over him. Fortunately the sensation came and went as quickly as it had arrived.

The Brimon forces had halted in disbelief, observing the Ritts leisurely delivering their fellow soldiers safely to ground.

A horn sounded in the forest, signaling Terren retreat, and the charge on the hillside reversed course. Which was peculiar, seeing as their numbers easily dwarfed the Brimon force.

Cheers swept from the battleground to the ramparts, and when the front gate reeled open, the noise from inside bellowed out. The Hylda bounded into Jonas, knocking him sideways. Something had changed in Jonas. Since he had dropped into this world he had felt different, but now he felt *something* else.

Is this what it feels like to have real friends?

This world he had fallen into was wonderful and terrible, all at once.

"Missed you too," said Jonas, and when he straightened, the Hylda seemed shorter. He was shocked to discover that he was now standing at equal height to the tallest knights. When he surveyed his arms, the deepest thorn scratches had healed. A crowd of knights suddenly gathered, clapping his newly broadened shoulders, expressing gratitude. Jonas was not sure how to respond, and simply shook a few of the outstretched hands.

As Jonas made his way toward the bailey, a throng of creatures insinuated themselves among the knights. Several among them he recognized as kin to the werewolves and minotaurs he saw earlier, but the others appeared ripped from fairy tales and puppet theaters. There were fairies hovering overhead on silent wings, fluttering so fast the eye struggled to perceive them. Jonas' right ear tickled sharp when one fairy called out his gratitude right into his ear canal. A satyr, at distance from the throng, applied his lips to a pan flute while pointy-capped gnomes and furry goblins danced and capered to his song. The creatures Jonas could identify at a first glance were few. The others would remain a wonderful mystery for the present.

"You're — You're welcome," stammered Jonas, awestruck, as a werewolf clasped his forearm and hauled him into an embrace. The sounds of elation throughout the fort steadily grew muffled, almost distant, as more werewolves joined in on the group hug. Jonas managed to free himself from the stifling warmth with a few firm yet friendly shoves.

"Devil!" A familiar voice pierced the crowd.

Jonas recognized to whom it belonged and changed course.

"Devil!" The lanky robed man repeated, forcing his way to Jonas.

"What's up?" said Jonas, while shaking the paws of a gracious fox-faced blacksmith. He turned while forcing a smile.

Out of breath, the man came to a teetering halt. His robed companions were fast on his heels and joined him as he spoke. "You broke from the shields," he panted. He fluttered a hand to the hills while his retinue bobbed their heads. "And ran out into the open, where you could have been struck down. You ought not do such a thing again." His face purpled from all the words, and he bent forward, gasping. The man was clearly not in the best of shape.

Jonas shrugged. "Sure thing, dude." Jonas disagreed. In the end, his decision had brought a swift end to the fight.

The lanky man heaved back to a stand. "Excellent," he said. The crowds had calmed. "Also, it should be noted, you do not need to raise your voice in order to command your passing spirits." With a sweeping gesture, he indicated the Hylda and the Ritts hovering over the battlefield.

A scurrying creature appeared and yanked at the hem of the lanky man's robes. The creature was short of stature, walking upright, and had a face resembling an anteater.

"Sage!" the creature squeaked, continuing to tug. "Guiltbrand!"

The sage named Guiltbrand sighed and scratched his goatee. "Yes?" His eyebrows crinkled. "What is it, Amos?"

Playing at the strap of his satchel, Amos looked away. "Letter for you," he said at length, offering a scroll. "I think it comes from Siegmund in the south."

Guiltbrand snatched the rolled parchment. "Away with you," he grumbled, squirreling the missive in his robes.

"Yes, yes." Amos bowed while backpedaling.

"Now where was I?" Guiltbrand tapped his front teeth. "Oh, yes! You may compel the Hylda and Ritts without the need to raise your voice in such a brackish manner. A connection should have been established between your souls, and shouting like that may cause irreparable harm to your throat."

Come join us, said Jonas in his mind, grasping his link to the Ritts.

Soon a thick veil of glowing red eyes alighted around the crowd. The Brimon folk shied away from the gathering Ritts, and the knights stiffened warily. Only minutes ago these gargoyles had been laying waste to their army, the bodies of those killed were yet warm.

"Ah, yes," said the sage. "Just like that! Well done, Devil!"

Like silent totems, the Ritts peered in Jonas' direction, but did naught else.

"Cool." Jonas flexed a bicep and looked under darkening heavens where the Brimon army was gathering their wounded.

The knights from the forest were piggybacking their comrades, while the ones who had fallen near the fort were carefully placed on litters. Aid to those too far gone was administered with curved daggers. The dying passed gently, finding a final reprieve from agony. Weary creatures plodded past the wreckage, relief evident in their bleary eyes.

"Devil," said Guiltbrand.

"Jonas," he corrected while holding his gaze on the knights. "My name is Jonas."

Guiltbrand's eyes tumbled. "Ah, yes, Jonas. My mistake." In hushed tones with a hand to the side of his mouth he spoke to a nearby sage. "Now," he began while the sage he had confided in began to scribble on a tablet. "If you would be so kind —"

"Wait," interrupted Jonas. "What did you just tell that guy?"

"My apologies, Jonas." Guiltbrand spread his hands in a gesture of self-importance. "I do not intend to keep *anything* from you. I merely instructed my scribe to make note of your name. We wish to make a record of this momentous day! The day my prophecy finally came to fruition!"

"Prophecy?" said Jonas. "Where have I heard that before?" Suddenly his wrist burns began to tingle and itch.

Guiltbrand noticed the young man's sudden discomfort. "Are both forearms afflicted with matching burns?" he inquired.

"Yeah." Jonas stretched his arms out. "Do you have any ointments or something? They're killing me, man."

Guiltbrand turned to the crowd. "He exists," he announced. "He commands the passing spirits and inlayed upon his wrists are burning shackles." As a showman, the sage held out his bony arms and clicked them together. "Thus proves the prophecy to be true!" He whirled on Jonas, fixing the teenager with his stare. "You have so much to accomplish! This is only the beginning, Jonas! The very, very beginning."

"This is a lot to take in, man," said Jonas, nervously scratching the back of his neck. "And I hate to leave a party early, but I think should go home."

"You what?" said Guiltbrand, deflating. He had been expecting a more heartfelt response. He drew uncomfortably close and inclined an inch from Jonas' ear. "I did not hear you?"

"A notice of foreclosure came today," replied Jonas, stepping back. "My mom needs me, so I can't be sticking around for the *very, very beginning* of anything. I'm sorry, I really am, but could we just fast forward to the end?"

Guiltbrand's robes billowed as he spun toward the crowd. "You are the Leeds Devil!" declared the sage, waxing theatric again. "The Evil Seed planted to eradicate the Terrens from this world, leaving the throne in Serpentfel empty! And thus allow the Leeds to claim their right as the true Lords of the Riverlands!" He tipped his chin and smiled at the crowd. "You good folk of Brimon, who have pledged your undying support for the Leeds family, would benefit greatly from this!"

"Stay with us!" The musical satyr called, and others repeated the shout.

"Yes!" A cloaked figure resembling a skeletal panther stood beside Guiltbrand, draping a bony hand over the sage's shoulder. "You must stay! Our region has not seen river trade in ages."

The sage scribe ceased her writing to bustle up next to the skeleton cat. "You are going to re-open the Riverlands to us again!" she said beaming. "It has been foretold!"

Jonas had always been overlooked for as long as he could remember, so it was tempting to give in and stick around. He was taller here, and much stronger. Also, he had a force of Ritts and Hylda that obeyed his every command. And it could not be overstated how much the people here actually *wanted* him.

Jonas heaved a sigh and looked at the expectant faces all around him. "It's been real, you know," he began. His tone betrayed where he was headed, and the skeleton panther's eyes drooped sadly. "I'm sorry, okay? I just can't stick around. Family comes first, and I can't leave my mom in the lurch."

Groans escaped throughout the crowd and bled up the street into the fort. All the elation was sucked from the air, pulling smiles into frowns. Yet somehow a grin was wreathed upon Guiltbrand's face, though his eyes disclosed disappointment. A Hylda blew her nose into Jonas' sweatpants.

"What sort of *lurch* is your mother caught up in?" asked Guiltbrand. "Perhaps we may alleviate any hindrances?"

"I don't think so," replied Jonas, pushing the other Hylda encroaching his leg. "Unless you have a ton of cash just lying around."

Guiltbrand scowled. "Cash?" he said. "No, I am not speaking of physical currency." He heaved a hopeful sigh and looked to the sages around him. "We need you here, and we would travel many lengths to make that happen."

One by one the folk of Brimon began to brighten at the sage's words.

"What do you mean?" asked Jonas.

Guiltbrand dabbed a finger at the crowd, selecting a particular individual. A fiendish creature nodded and skulked forward, moving with ease. This was a predator, wrapped in a hooded mantle. Brawny muscles showed behind his patchwork of tattered garb, attesting to a lean hunting lifestyle.

"Reveal to us what stands in your way," said Guiltbrand. "And Elias will take care of it."

Jonas imagined Elias cutting bloody swathes through the bank's corporate building. "No, no," he said, shaking his head. Killing debt collectors would not solve his problem.

Elias tensed at the dismissal; cutting a silhouette that was pure nightmare fuel.

"Not that Elias here doesn't look top notch!" said Jonas quickly to Guiltbrand. "It's just not that simple, and violence isn't the answer here."

"Who said anything about violence?" said Guiltbrand.

Jonas lifted an eyebrow. "You kinda did," he replied. "You kinda are."

"I am speaking about eliminating a problem," clarified Guiltbrand, holding his stomach and chuckling. "And murder does not *need* to be violent."

"See!" Jonas pointed at Guiltbrand. "That's what I mean!"

"More akin to the snuffing of a candle," said Guiltbrand, smiling.

Jonas pinched the bridge of his nose. "You can't just kill your way out of financial ruin."

Guiltbrand side-eyed Elias. "Methinks he does not understand what we are capable of," he stated to the fiend, then briskly turned to Jonas. "Ask yourself, how would one begin to prosecute a *monster* in your world?"

"Yeah, but..." Jonas trailed off. The sage made a fair point.

It's not as if the cops could trace it back to my doorstep, pondered Jonas. *What am I thinking?* Jonas snapped himself out of it and began to think of an alternative.

Guiltbrand tapped his foot. "Well?"

"Bear with me for a second," said Jonas. "My idea doesn't involve anyone dying or getting snuffed out." He raised his arms to flex his biceps. "Before I came here, believe it or not, I was scrawny and weak. Like, I would need my inhaler if I walked too fast or laughed too hard. But now, I'm pretty strong." The knights and creatures alike nodded, captivated, and Jonas continued. "I just ran like, what? Twenty miles? Something like that? And look at me now."

Guiltbrand was not nearly as enamored. "Your point being?"

"If I joined Scarberry High's track and field team, I would smoke our competition. And there'd be no way I'd go unnoticed by talent scouts. I'd get like a ton of scholarship offers, and then I'd get a free ride to a good school. After that, I would land a sweet job and pay off my family's debt." Jonas folded his ripped arms across his chest. "No one dies. No one gets hurt." He knew full well that his plan would not satisfy his family's present need for funds, but it was the best argument he could formulate in the moment.

"I see." Guiltbrand smoothed the ends of his goatee. "And where does that leave us? The Riverlands needs its Devil. This *trace and feel* does not sound like a viable solution."

"Track and field," Jonas corrected the sage.

Guiltbrand waved his hands. "Makes no difference what that is! Your plan will take too many cycles to complete! My plan would see your problems eradicated overnight!"

"Your plan kills a bunch of innocent people!"

"So?" Guiltbrand sneered. "What are a handful of lives compared to the value of thousands? Less than a beggar's pittance, I say."

"No! This is all wrong!" Jonas dug his eye with the heel of his hand. "I don't want any part in this!"

"You make your deals with green paper! We make ours with blood!" Guiltbrand gestured to the Hylda. "Either way the debts are quenched, satisfied."

A warm night breeze ruffled Jonas' hair as torchlight skipped across hopeful faces. The Riverlands would be fine without him, prophecy or no prophecy.

"I'm sorry, but my mother needs me," said Jonas with finality.

Bitter sincerity creased Guiltbrand's brow. "Farewell then, Jonas," he stated tersely. "May your reappearance into our realm be soon."

The congregation walked away sadly, leaving Elias with Jonas, the Hylda, and the Ritts.

"So," said Jonas, looking to Elias. "How do I get out of here?"

Elias contorted his neck as a serpent sizing its prey. "The Hylda will guide you," he revealed. "You must ask them."

CHAPTER 7

On Jonas' sixteenth birthday his mother shared an important story with him. It was not a fairy tale, or anything silly like that. Nor was it some repurposed fable geared for a modern audience. The story contained a certain truth that Jonas had never forgotten, and from that day forward, he sheltered the words close to his heart.

"Hic sunt dracones," Sandy had begun the tale in Latin. Then she had went on in English, explaining a bit of family history that set the stage for what came next: "Your grandfather's grandfather was a cartographer, a mapmaker, who explored the New World. He even claims to have run into Lewis & Clark once or twice! On some expeditions his team would explore new places in America, despite the Natives' warnings about certain spots, which they ignored, and they would often set foot in a forest or canyon, or cave, that hadn't seen a human being in a very long time. He told your grandfather that, regrettably, they went places that humans weren't meant to go. On more than one occasion. And they saw some scary things and lost valuable records, and people. So after all of the first losses, he had been instructed to write *hic sunt dracones* on the maps in those places to let others know that it was dangerous to go there."

"Are those places still dangerous?" Jonas had asked.

His mother's nod had been filled with decades of sadness. Anytime she spoke of her father, her tone was frosted with an ache. Jonas knew that his grandfather had left a heavy debt when he passed, but the details had always been a closely guarded secret.

"Wait," Jonas had said when his mother began collecting their cake dishes. "What does 'hic sunt dracones' mean?"

* * *

Elias stalked ahead with a lantern, parting the darkness clinging to the treebark. The taller Hylda walked with the fiend, apparently guiding him to the nearest portal. Jonas and the shorter Hylda trailed close behind. They had been walking for hours.

Flying overhead were five hand-picked Ritts, keeping watch in the gloom. Jonas had not deemed it necessary to bring the entire flock, and Elias had agreed and advised that they bring an odd number.

Morning would arrive soon and Jonas hoped that he would be home before then. He also hoped that time flowed the same in both realms. As cool as it would be to return to a future world with flying cars and laser guns, he would rather not. He barely fit in the current year.

"How much longer do ya think, Scary?" Jonas asked the short Hylda. "Not long?"

The Hylda replied with a grin. She liked her new name.

"I'll take that as a yes?"

Up ahead Elias had stopped, his lantern creating a frame of light. Beyond the glow, an unsettling quiet began spreading between the foliage. Furtively Elias waved a hand, signaling quiet.

"Don't move," he whispered before snuffing the lantern.

Everything fell to darkness and Jonas felt for the tree beside him. Without warning, Scary's hands crept up into his.

"Scary!" he whispered in near panic. "Don't do that!"

After securing himself behind the trunk, and collecting his nerve, Jonas exhaled a question. "What is Elias doing?"

"Doing what he does." Scary's reply was inside Jonas' head.

And I wonder what that could be? Jonas thought.

"Kill," replied Scary.

The distinct snapping of a twig interrupted Jonas' thoughts. Bracken swished against one another somewhere off to his right. A human shout was bitten off, followed by a struggle. Over his head a leathery slapping of Ritts' wings broke through the forest canopy, coalescing directly into the struggle.

"Call them off!" screamed Elias, sounding burdened. "Jonas! Call your Ritts off!"

"Hey! Ritz!" Jonas called. "Let them go!" Then transmitted a thought, instructing them to resume their flight pattern. They acknowledged with grunts, and just like that, Jonas discovered that he could telepathically communicate with both the Hylda and Ritts.

Elias' lantern flashed back to life right before Jonas. "Come," said Elias. Even with all the light, Jonas could not make out Elias' face buried in the hood.

As Jonas followed, he noticed that Elias' feet were not treading on the ground. He was performing what Jonas could best describe as a *slinking glide*.

A clearing soon opened ahead, guarded by a ring of thick underbrush. Two familiar knights were at its center, raising hands to dim the lantern light.

Elias lowered his lantern.

"Jonas!" exclaimed Vera. "Thank the depths we found you!"

"Vera! Greta!" exclaimed Jonas, elated to be reunited. He had lost track of the knights right before the battle, and he had feared the worst had become of them. A lot had happened in such a short span of time.

"With the Ritts protecting the Devil, you should have signaled your intent to join us," advised Elias. "Are you wounded?"

"We were about to signal," said Greta. "But then the Ritts attacked us." She raised an arm, displaying a thin scratch that curled up around her forearm. "And, yes, we're wounded, but it's not bad at all. Luckily the Devil called them off in time."

Elias cocked his head. "Why are you following?"

"Guiltbrand explained what happened," replied Vera, collecting the scattered items that she had dropped. "And a lookout gave us the direction you were heading."

"And we wanted to talk some sense into you," Greta added, stepping toward Jonas. "Before you made a mistake." She now had to look up to meet Jonas' eyes. If this troubled her, she did not make it known.

Jonas noticed for the first time that both Vera and Greta sported elongated canines. He pointed V-fingers at his own canines, then gestured toward the knights. "You have almost the same teeth as me..." he trailed off. In early childhood after his baby canines had dropped, what grew in their place were longer vampire-like teeth that served as source material for peer ridicule. And with his sudden new growth in this world, his canines had lengthened as well.

"Listen," said Jonas, shaking his head, returning to the argument. "I'm needed back home. And I'm sure Guiltbrand filled you in on my reason for leaving."

"Reason for abandoning your destiny," spat Greta.

Scary sidled closer to Jonas.

"He said it had something to do with your mother," said Vera, less irritated than Greta. "Family is a big deal to us too. I believe that it's one of the few traits our realms share. And we are standing here for that exact reason."

"Which is?" asked Jonas.

"Family," replied Vera. "Your arrival marked the end of an era. An era that had been filled with war and strife and sadness. And its ending would mean safety for our families." She cocked her head. "Do you see where I am going with this?"

Jonas shifted away from Scary. The Hylda's huddling had nearly abraded all the hairs from his leg. "That's a lot of mothers." He felt sympathy for these people, but dawn would be arriving soon and he wanted to be home to greet it. Jonas turned to Elias. "Can we get this show back on the road?" It pained him to behave so cold, but he knew no other way.

Greta grabbed Jonas by the collar. "I don't think you get it!" she growled. "This is —"

Before she could complete her statement, Jonas yanked her close. "You think I answer to you?" he seethed with surprising fury. He blinked and shook his head as if a spell had taken him.

Greta tried to pull away, but Jonas' grip was iron.

"I'm fine, Scary," said Jonas to the bristling Hylda, then he looked to the Hylda beside Elias. "You too, Posh. It's cool." He released his hold on Greta, and she backed away, rubbing her forearm.

"I am sorry about that," said Jonas. "I don't know what came over me."

"I was out of line," admitted Greta, bowing. "Forgive me."

Vera went to a knee. "We were out of line," she amended, signaling Greta to join her. "Please forgive us."

"No, no," Jonas interjected. "No one's kneeling. Please, stand." He thumbed the air. "No worries, everything's cool." He turned to Elias. "You ready to go?"

Elias adjusted his cowl. "Let's go."

The first rays of morning had introduced themselves to the horizon when Elias leapt from the path. His lantern bathed the bottom of a great tree, highlighting roots thick as saplings. A cavernous void was notched between the roots, receiving the lantern's gift but not giving any back.

"Here you go," said Vera, sweeping a few spindly tendrils aside. "This will lead you back to your world."

Jonas peered into the depths of the void. "I think I see a spider."

"Just the one?" Greta asked with folded arms.

"What happens if the Hylda were to come with me?"

"To clear out the spiders?" said Vera, sharing a smirk with her fellow knight.

Jonas snorted.

"Nothing ill would happen," replied Vera. "They would pass along into your realm unscathed."

Jonas rubbed his chin. "What if you came with me?" he asked.

"The same," replied Vera, looking away.

"I feel like there's something she's not telling me," said Jonas, turning to Greta.

"There is," offered Greta. "She would not be able to return."

"That's not entirely true," objected Vera. "I *could*, but I probably wouldn't survive."

"Perhaps one out of a million survives the Homecoming Sickness," Greta clarified.

Jonas looked to Vera, then to Greta. "And what's that?"

Greta closed an eye toward the path below. "It happens when we cross back over," she explained. "Your blood explodes inside your body. But you can avoid all that if you offer a sacrifice to the portal."

The shadow monster lying dead at the foot of the tree flashed into Jonas' mind. After drooling all over Jonas' bed, the monster had perished in its attempt to return to this world.

"Whoa," he said. "By sacrifice, do you mean like an arm or a leg?"

"Sometimes," replied Greta. "Or a wing, or even an unborn child. It's different every time."

"But what about the Hylda, what would happen to them?"

"Nothing," replied Vera, lifting her helm to scratch her ear. "They are passing spirits."

"Like me?" asked Jonas.

Greta laughed.

"Not even close," said Vera, shaking her head. "Your similarities begin and end with your ability to freely pass back and forth."

"Whoa."

"We have only just begun to scratch the surface of your power, Devil," said Vera.

Jonas placed his hands behind his back and gave the knights an awkward smile. "Well, anyways," he said after a breath. "I guess this is goodbye."

Scary tugged at Jonas' wrist, dropping his attention down to her.

"I'm sorry, I really am, but I have to go," he said. Though his fear had receded, he still recognized how terrifying the Hylda were up close. "You and Posh look out for each other, okay?"

Scary and Posh nodded. "Goodbye, Jonas," they said.

Greta and Vera stepped forward and bowed, bidding Jonas their farewell.

Jonas returned the knights a solemn nod, then looked to Elias with his dim lantern. "See ya later, Elias," he said, while wondering what that guy looked like under his hood.

Elias simply inclined his head.

Without losing more time, Jonas crawled into the void, where he found the soil remarkably soft. And at some point along the way the moss became a pillowy carpet. He would have been enjoying himself, if not for all the darkness everywhere.

"Stop thinking about spiders," Jonas told himself, working his way deeper. "Should have borrowed Elias' lamp." Inevitably he found himself in a horrible predicament; the harder he tried to force spiders from his mind, the more he thought of them. He hurried along, doubling his speed, his anxiety fueling him faster. Then suddenly an elephant trunk of a root blasted him square in the face, stopping him short.

"How long is this tunnel?" growled Jonas, rubbing his nose, feeling for blood. He decided to breathe for a moment, allowing the panic to dissipate. Once the star shards had finally faded along the edges of his vision, he decided to press on.

Soon the musty earth gave way to the familiar scent of his bedroom, and he found himself on his hands and knees, dirtying his bed linens with void grime. One second he was in a dank hole, and the next he was back home.

To his relief, his bedroom appeared the same as when he had departed.

"Mom!" Jonas shouted as he maneuvered out of the skeletal bed frame. The tear-off day calendar sitting atop his dresser displayed December twentieth, which did not help in explaining the actual date.

After exiting his bedroom he held his steps to listen for a response, but only heard furniture dragging downstairs.

How long have I been away? Jonas wondered as he pressed down the hallway. *I hope I haven't missed Christmas!*

While passing over the landing on the staircase, he heard the growl of a male voice in the shop below.

The police? His disappearance may have heaped more difficulties onto his mother's already overflowing plate. His heart raced, so he chased it down the stairs.

"Mom!" he said, bursting into the shop.

Every head snapped toward him.

The only face Jonas recognized was that of his mother's. The rest were strangers, not one cop in sight. Surrounding his mother at the front counter, burly men with shoulders where their necks should have sized him up. Almost immediately they determined that Jonas was not a threat, and as they turned their attention away one of the men muttered an audible "Meh."

In that moment, it struck Jonas that he was no longer tall, lean, and ripped. He was back in his old body.

Maybe it really had been a dream? He looked down and his tattered, stained sweatpants assured him otherwise. *What gives?* He wondered, looking back up.

The scene unfolding before him looked like a moving day. Two men were angling a large bench grinder through the front door while snow vented in around their ankles. It seemed that his mother had found a buyer for some of her equipment.

Sandy looked depleted, exhausted, but a wave of relief briefly passed over her face with Jonas' approach.

"Hey, Mom," said Jonas interrupting what appeared to be a rather heated conversation with a rickety old scarecrow of a man. He was ancient, perhaps eighty or ninety Jonas wagered. Off the rip, Jonas did not like him.

"Why don'tcha go back to bed, kiddo," the old man said. Purple saggy crescents ringed his eyes; the guy clearly needed more sleep. "Rough night, eh?" he asked, glaring at Jonas' torn clothing.

Sandy was about to say something, but the old man silenced her with a raised hand. "This is adult business, kiddo," he stated, working his jaw, and squaring his shoulders. "Run along now."

"Mom," said Jonas. "Who is this guy?"

"Back to bed, honey!" Sandy said quickly.

The old man faked a slap, causing Sandy to flinch.

Jonas had seen enough. Without sparing another thought, he bolted toward the old man. He did not care how old and feeble he appeared, nobody threatens his mother.

The placid look on the old man's face should have been a warning. Before Jonas could round the counter, one of the neckless juggernauts stepped forward to intercept. He delivered a downward weighty slap to Jonas' jaw, crumpling the teenager to his knees.

Jonas' head was swimming. He tried to stand, but his legs felt as wire filament.

"C'mon, kid," the colossus mumbled. "Just stay down. I barely touched you."

"Fabian," said the old man, flicking his chin toward the wall. "Get him away from me."

"You got it," replied Fabian, heaving Jonas up under his arm and carrying him as if he were nothing but a discarded towel. He placed Jonas on the floor against the wall, facing the cash register. "What's with his teeth?" Fabian asked, pivoting his stance toward Sandy. He pointed at his own canines. "They're all pointy, like a vampire, or a —"

Sandy cut the man off. "His teeth just grew like that," she explained. "And he's got asthma." Urgency abruptly invaded her voice. "He's having an attack, and I need to go and get his inhaler." She looked pleadingly toward the old man.

"He'll survive." said the old man, unconcerned. "You and I still have work to do. We need to develop a timetable here, Ms. Porter." He pinned a finger into the countertop, then swiveled around, using his finger as leverage. "It seems," he began, clearing his throat and gesturing to his men. "That clock repair is going the way of the Dodo. If you want my advice, I think you should explore a new career path." He knocked at the air as if it were a door. "Hello, it's 1997, not 1897. Maybe you should try Blockbuster video? My nephew Jakub just opened a new store not far from here, and he's in need of a manager..." The old man whirled and smacked the counter. "Blockbuster! Now that's modern-day job security!"

"The tape rental store?" Sandy was unamused. "Emil, please, I need to get Jonas his inhaler."

"Yes, the tape rental store," replied Emil. "And my nephew Jakub is, well, he's not too hard on the eyes either..."

Jonas tried to get to his feet but was pressed back down by the sole of Fabian's boot. The strangling *in* Jonas' chest combined with the pressure of the hard rubber *on* his chest caused his soul to begin clawing for escape. With a hard swallow, he gasped, vying desperately against the tunneling of his optics.

"Please! Emil!" Sandy was nearly running in place. "He can't breathe!"

Emil lifted a finger and ticked it back and forth, scolding the woman. "I have a long list to get through, Ms. Porter. I need you to focus. Your father accrued a fortune of a debt. His tab kept growing and growing, but he ignored it. Lucky for you, you had the good sense to start paying it back. *Start* being the key word here, but I need... what's the word..." he snapped his fingers, looking over his shoulder at Fabian.

"Continuance?" Fabian's unibrow creased like a second moustache.

"Yes!" Emil slapped the counter. "A continuance! Thank you, Fabian! We need you to keep paying!"

"I have been trying," argued Sandy. "But I'm juggling a lot of expenses —"

"Ah ha!" Emil sounded as if he had just discovered life on a moldy cracker. "So you have been paying *other* entities, eh?"

"Barely!" Sandy spat. "I have a son! And he takes priority!"

Emil launched forward in fury. "Proszę! My money takes priority! Ms. Porter! Don't you understand that by now?!"

"I'm losing my home!"

"Nie mój cyrk, nie moje małpy."

Fabian's shoulders trembled as he sheltered his laugh with a fist, returning his attention to the boy on the floor.

Whimpering, stirring, locking eyes with Fabian looming over him, Jonas moved to stand. The dim rattle that escaped his throat was the best challenge he could offer.

"Don't get up, kid," warned Fabian. "Don't do it."

Emil closed his eyes. "If you did not have a son anymore then I would be getting —"

With a feeble draw, Jonas gathered enough strength to slam his elbows to the wall and rise.

"What did I say?" said Fabian with rancor, viciously deploying the toe of his boot into Jonas' upper lip. The hardness of the wall was all that prevented Jonas' neck from snapping in half, the universe's version of a small favor.

Sandy could only watch her son drop onto his side.

Jonas' jaw felt unhinged, and he longed for air. A coppery tang flooded his mouth as he gulped back the blood he had snorted.

Emil returned his gaze to a frozen Sandy. "Then I would be getting my money," he concluded with a wink.

"Hic, hic," Jonas stammered, trying to rise. Saliva laced with blood brimmed over his bottom lip, unrestrained.

Fabian eased down to Jonas' eye level, his face twined with false concern. "What's that?" he asked. "I don't understand."

"Hic sunt dracones," gasped Jonas.

Emil's thin body went rigid like a banner snapped by the wind. "I recall that phrase." His voice began meandering toward Jonas. "A stupid old nierób once said that to me, long ago," said Emil, almost wistful. A small draft from the old man's approach fed the scent of breakfast sausage and spent cigarettes into Jonas' nostrils. "Let me speed you to the ending of his story, my young Jonas." Emil was now teetering over him. "He died. So sad."

With the flourish of an aged magician, Emil struggled to his feet, aided most of the way by trusty Fabian. "And as far as *dracones* are concerned," he said, shrugging the brute's hand away. "The only dragon *that be here* is me." Emil's face wrinkled within a massive sniff. "Because I am feeling generous, I will give you another month to pay me in full." Then added, with a raspy chuckle, as he turned away, "Hic sunt dracones."

CHAPTER 8

"Who was that?" Jonas spoke through the bag of frozen peas his mother had just handed him, along with his glasses. The skin flap beneath his nose had ballooned to the size of walnut, but thankfully the blood had finally stopped seeping from his inner lip. "They didn't act like bankers."

Sandy hunkered down on the floor beside her son, wiping the cold from her fingers into her jeans. Jonas' question was more than justified, but she did not want to talk about her father and his stupid pride. Instead of offering an answer, she stared at the vacant places in the room, imagining what was once there.

Emil and his men had taken everything.

Sensing that an answer was not forthcoming, Jonas rose to his feet.

"Wait!" said Sandy.

As Jonas glowered at her, Sandy noticed that there was something *different* about him. Not to mention the hideous state of his t-shirt and sweatpants.

She took a deep breath. "Let your inhaler work its magic before you start spinning out."

"Too late for that!" Jonas shouted and staggered. The blood rush from the sudden rise hit hard. "Oh, geez," he mumbled, sliding back down to the floor.

The vacant dust-swept room seemed to swallow all of Sandy's thoughts. Memories as ghosts and phantoms played about the room, manifesting happy moments in the shop. She recalled her father at work while she played with her dolls on the floor. She recalled her mother embracing her father after handing him a cup of coffee, nearly spilling it in his lap. She recalled a younger version of that creep Emil speaking harshly to her father, mirroring the manner in which he had spoken with her. Time and time again she failed to conjure an apt description for Jonas, and when she felt as if she had finally come upon one — poof — gone.

"I'm not a kid anymore," stated Jonas. "You can tell me what we're up against."

Sandy sniffed and contemplated her next words. "I'm not sure how to begin."

Jonas shifted the bag of peas, revealing the laceration beneath. "You can start with who Emil is," he said, pointing at his mouth. "And why they did this."

Emil. That name was the primary source of contention between Sandy's parents for as long as she could remember, from her birth until their death.

She cleared her throat. "Emil was an..." she was not ready for this. "What happened to your clothes?" she asked, pivoting the conversation.

"Mom. Don't." Jonas was not biting.

"Did you get into a fight with a woodchipper?" she said, plucking at his t-shirt. "And how did your feet get so filthy?"

"No," said Jonas, losing patience. "I got into a fight with a bunch of giants who were stealing my mom's clock repair stuff. Didn't turn out very well."

Sandy stood and folded her arms across her chest. It was time to take the first step. "Emil is a Polish mob boss," she revealed.

Jonas' brows knit with confusion.

"Yeah, I know," said Sandy.

"But, we're not Polish." Jonas pointed between them. "And grandpa and grandma weren't Polish."

"No, we aren't and your grandparents weren't either," she agreed. "But our lineage has nothing to do with it." Sandy took a deep breath. "You see, this block was once owned by the Poles. In fact, they still lease a lot of the properties in the city. Your friend next door — Darren — his family rents a house from Emil's nephew."

"Darren isn't a friend," corrected Jonas. "But go on. So the Polish mob used to own this shop —"

"No, not the shop." Sandy drilled a finger toward the floor. "Just the *land* it stands on. And when your grandpa purchased it and turned it into a business, that's when the trouble began."

Jonas adjusted his glasses. "Okay, so..."

"Unbeknownst to grandpa, back then, when you started to make money in this district, you would owe the mob a fee. A *security tax*. At least that's what the mob called it. Totally bogus, a scam. Claimed that they would run protection for you, making sure your business was safe and sound while you slept."

"How nice of them."

"Yeah, sure." Sandy's bitter smile slid from her face. "The day that daddy opened his little fix-it shop, the very moment he proudly hung his *OPEN* sign, Emil arrived. What began as a friendly chat devolved into a heated argument, which quickly spiraled into a war, and finally dissolved into what we are looking at today." Sandy gestured to the empty space. "This is what happens to the aggressively stubborn."

"Grandpa refused to pay, I take it?"

"Kind of goes without saying," replied Sandy.

Jonas flung the frozen peas aside and planted a hand on the floor. He strode to the front window and slipped the open sign from the sticky hook affixed to the glass. "How did the business stay afloat for so long?" he asked.

"Your grandpa never willingly *gave* money to Emil. But Emil found ways to *take* it."

"Ah." Jonas understood. "And after grandpa and grandma died, you inherited the debt. I always wondered why you didn't go to the bank and work something out."

"Your grandparents —" Sandy stopped herself with a chuckle. She looked to the ceiling as tears began to gather. "Your grandparents didn't die. You see, Emil... well..."

"Emil had them killed?"

Tears were streaking from his mother's tightly pinched eyes. "I started to pay Emil back," explained Sandy, wiping her face. "I didn't want us to end up like my parents. I was trying to pay the rest of the mortgage and at the same time pay Daddy's debt back." She shuddered. "I tried, Jonas. I tried. But it was too much. And now we've lost it all."

This was too much for Jonas. Buried somewhere within his current pathetic vessel the Leeds Devil screamed for penance. Amidst his mother's protest, Jonas ran from the shop, struggling desperately to bring out the inner power that he was unable to wield in this realm.

"I tried," said Sandy, staring at the place on the floor where she once played.

Jonas, unable to stand being in the shop for another second, needed distance from his woe. The pavement skimmed beneath his bare feet. Running was a poorly hatched idea, but he had to satisfy his intense anger somehow. If he wound up wheezy and doubled over at the end, so be it.

This new revelation rocked Jonas harder than Fabian's boot. In the end, his lip would heal.

For as long as he could recall, he and Sandy struggled to simply tread water, while the world seemed over the moon about pressing a prevailing thumb into their flailing backs. Jonas never asked for much, and that much had been denied.

Jonas had no destination in mind, just someplace far enough away...

"There he goes!" A voice cracked off to his right.

Or someone...

Jonas slowed.

"The Count is out on a morning jog, is he?" Darren was standing on his porch. His friends, fellow Scarberry seniors, surrounded him, each clinging to a mug of coffee, their flannel-draped shoulders trembling with laughter. Like a half-witted murder of crows, they had all risen in jumbled unison to see what had caught their leader's attention. "Do what do we owe the pleasure?" jeered Darren, lifting his cup in mock salute.

Darren set his coffee cup aside and leaned out over the handrail. "It's not every day that we're graced — Ho! What happened to your face?" He pointed toward Jonas while his offhand covered his mouth. "Looks like somebody woke up on the wrong side of the coffin!"

Jonas grazed a finger over the lump beneath his nose.

"Yeah! That's a gnarly goose egg ya got there!" One of the crows added.

"Forget his face," another heckled, "look at his threads! Did ya get into a turf war with a werewolf last night, Brokula?"

"No, no, wait!" Darren beamed, appearing on the edge of a violent surge of laughter. "That's the latest in vampire fashion, straight out of Transyl-brokia! Ode to Pover-tay!" He announced, lifting his cup over an eruption of laughter.

"It's fabulous!" One crow howled, losing his balance.

"It really is!" Another agreed, flicking tears from his cheeks.

Over the years these jokes had grown stale, and Jonas would normally just walk them off, but today they plucked a nerve. Instead of walking away, Jonas strode toward the porch with molten eyes, furious.

"Hey!" Darren shouted a warning. "Not another step, you dirt!" The crows bristled around him.

Heedless, Jonas continued up the walkway. The moment he had set off from the shop his asthma had begun to prime its pumps, and now it was just getting started, spinning clotted cobwebs all throughout the inside of his chest.

"Watch your step!" Darren called, noticing the flag in Jonas' gait. "Maybe if you owned shoes flat sidewalks wouldn't be such a struggle!" He placed his mug down and crossed his arms. "But seriously, don't come any closer."

"Yeah, stay away!"

"We don't want to catch what you have!"

By the time Jonas reached the base of the staircase his breathing had devolved into slivered gasps. His rage was full blown, but his traitorous body had thrown in the towel.

"Oh, man," moaned Darren through a scowl. "What are you doing?"

Clambering on his knees, seething and wheezing, Jonas managed another step. With every ounce of might, he tried to draw the devil from hiding.

"C'mon!" Darren sounded far away. "Get your lame carcass out of here!"

Lying face-first on the stairs, Jonas rolled to his right and tried to prop himself up on an elbow, but his head felt cast in lead.

"Maybe the dude just needs a pick-me up?"

"Yeah, Darren," another voice chimed in, sounding like Chad or Mark. Jonas could never keep those two straight.

"Looks like the little guy could use a bit of pep in his step!" Helplessly Jonas watched Mark or Chad angling a cup of steaming coffee over his head.

"Here, Choke-ula! Have some —"

"Chad!" someone shouted, causing the slippered feet on the porch to shift. "What are you doing?!"

"Nothing," replied Chad. "I was just gonna water this sick plant."

"Sasha, go back inside," said Darren.

Sasha. Somehow Jonas deflated further into the stairs. Sasha was Darren's younger sister, and above and beyond that, she was Jonas' dream girl. And in keeping within the lore of his love life, her timing could not have been more perfect.

"Is that Jonas, the neighbor boy?" said Sasha, sounding regrettably closer. "What happened?"

The once derisive voices suddenly stiffened with concern.

"We found him like this, Sosh."

"For real."

"I think he's drunk."

"We tried to help him."

Sasha was not taken by their act. "I don't think pouring scalding coffee on someone would ever be considered *helping.*" Jonas heard the porch creak when Sasha shifted her stance. "Darren, why didn't you help him?"

"Cuz he sucks."

Beneath the wave of renewed laughter, Jonas tried to rise, his rage now given way to embarrassment.

"He's not strong like you," said Sasha.

"Clearly," said Darren, side-eyeing Jonas. "Get him his puffer, then." He threw his head back, slugging the remainder of his coffee. "Come on, boys, let's see if Welker's is open yet."

The entourage departed the porch, hooting and laughing, making for Darren's car, sluicing past Jonas as if he was no longer there. It was all the same to Jonas. When you can't breathe, nothing matters.

"Jonas," said Sasha, her breath a mist beside him. Even in the cold she smelled of peppermint and lavender. "Where is your inhaler?" she asked, bringing Jonas' arm over her shoulder.

Jonas groaned, vaguely pointing over his shoulder as Sasha helped him stand.

After she swept a hurried look before them, Sasha's eyes returned to Jonas' pallid face. "Did my brother do that to you?" she asked, indicating his top lip.

"No," Jonas managed to reply, meeting Sasha's eyes.

"Jonas!" Sandy's voice cut across the snow-laden lawn. "Are you okay?"

"He needs his inhaler!" shouted Sasha as she struggled to maintain the slumping teenager's balance.

Sandy nodded with wide-eyes, and as she backpedaled toward her front door, caught sight of Darren making his way from the curb. "Hey Darren!" she called. "Help your sister!" Believing the teenager-next-door to be decent, Sandy spun around to focus on retrieving the inhaler, and nearly missed his curt reply.

"I'm good on that burden." Darren flicked a scornful nod at Jonas. Then the subsequent creak of his driver side door opening met Sandy's ears, drawing her to a dead stop.

"What did you say?" Her head tilted sharply like a serpent first noticing a mouse entering its enclosure.

But Darren had already entered his vehicle and ignited its engine, drowning all sounds in the vicinity. And in a moment of disbelief, Sandy watched Darren and his friends cruise by without sparing a second glance.

"What kind of..." said Sandy shaking her head, petering off. Then she swung her attention back to her son precariously propped on the staircase. "Sasha!" she shouted. "Just sit down and wait on the stairs, I'll be right back!" A trip to the hospital was something that she wholeheartedly wished to avoid. Although it was cold and Jonas was not dressed for the weather, Sandy preferred a few cold digits to broken bones. And she could have asked her to just take Jonas inside with her — the thought struck Sandy as she was exiting her house, rattling the inhaler in her hand.

By the time Sandy arrived, Jonas had regained a scrap of strength, seated upright beside Sasha without aid. The color, however, had yet to make a return to his face.

"Thank God!" said Sasha.

Sandy continued to shake the inhaler as she passed it to her son. He accepted the medicine and gathered it to his mouth. With the first dose Jonas' face passed from gaunt to fatigued, then after a second knock, a smile of relief bloomed as his chest swelled.

With Sasha's full attention focused on him, instead of saying something cool, Jonas extended a hand for a friendly handshake. She accepted, glancing at Sandy and quirking a smile. "See you around," added Jonas as Sasha retracted her hand.

"Yeah," replied Sasha. "Glad you're okay. That was scary."

Jonas bobbed his head. "See you around," he said again, leaving the stairs, wishing his brain was not set on repeat.

"Thank you, *Sasha*," said Sandy, cocking her head. "Your name is Sasha, right? We've been neighbors for forever and —"

"You got it right," interrupted Sasha. "And it was no problem, Ms. Porter." She waved goodbye. "See you around, Jonas."

Jonas sketched an awkward bow. "See you," he said, turning for home.

After returning to the shop, Jonas made for his bedroom, seeking a fresh change of clothes. Once free of his shirt Jonas glanced into the cheval mirror, and in the reflection noticed the mottled blood around the collar of his t-shirt. A resurgence of anger flared in the depths of his gut. He bit back his rage, re-opening the wound on his lip, seeping fresh blood into his scowl.

For all his life Jonas had felt as a burden, and the fact that someone else had noticed made the feeling even more real. Darren's statement only solidified that cold truth.

Hours ago he was tall and capable and had been recognized as a savior. But that was in another realm, another world.

In order to pull a pair of woolen socks over his frozen feet Jonas sat upon the floor before the mirror. The act required more labor than it should have. He tugged and tugged, and if he were stronger may have torn the seams for how he strained.

"This shouldn't be so hard," he complained to the mirror, giving up and throwing the sock against the wall. "If only there was a way I could carry those powers I had back over with me."

Things would be easier.

Downstairs his mother was in her office, rifling through a bureau containing her financial documents. Thankfully Emil had seen the sense in leaving that piece behind. Unfortunately the chair that had partnered nicely with the bureau had been snatched, so Jonas found Sandy at work upon her knees.

Shafts of straying light punctured the big picture window beyond the slanted shape of his foraging mother, highlighting the fresh emptiness. This room had once contained innumerable items that his family held dear. Knickknacks from his grandfather's generation, reminders of the man he had been. Every article, every framed photograph, every weird paperweight that held intrinsic value, was gone.

The filaments dancing in the sunlight over the vacant places beckoned a renewal of Jonas' wrath. They mocked him, showed him that he was nothing more than dead weight. Revealing how powerless he was without expressly stating such.

Jonas strode into the cavity. "Mom," he said.

"Yeah," replied Sandy, consumed by her errand.

"I just want you to know." He stopped to fight the burgeoning quiver in his voice.

"Yeah, honey," said Sandy with more focus, yet her eyes remained within the bureau.

He wanted to tell her that he was going to turn everything around, that he would make everything right. That he would do whatever it takes, that he would fight until the bitter end, travel to the gates of hell and back, but his throat hitched upon the first syllable. And in that moment he knew that he could only voice a simple truth.

I will never give up.

"I'm going to go take a shower."

CHAPTER 9

This time, the mattress rejected him.

Face first on his bed, Jonas seethed. "Take me back!" He battered the blankets with a tight fist. And the mattress' resiliency mocked his furor as each strike was harmlessly repelled. "I'm ready! I'm ready!" He screamed into the blankets bundled to his chin until his throat grew ragged. The hollows of his eyes had grown raw from his glasses' nose cushions rubbing against them. Arching back, Jonas stripped the frames from his face and side-handed them at his clothes hamper.

His innards roiled in a blind fury, and yet the devil had not stirred. On countless nights he had cried himself to sleep, but raging to sleep was untested ground.

Tunneling his chin into the softness, the exhausted teenager reached his limit. From the back of his throat he unwittingly exhaled, "You'll see..." The moment before sleep latched itself to his eyes and pulled him into dreamland.

"Jonas..." A clear, small voice, sounding distant, filtered into his ears. "The time has come."

The grainy soil parted when Jonas shook his head. "What?" Earthy particles clogged his eyelashes. "Who?" He blinked, but there was no one nearby. He was alone in a dank, dark crevice. The stagnant space carried the scent of a soggy basement, and its humidity clung to Jonas' skin as a muggy summer morn. An ambitious pinhole of light from the opposite end of the tunnel highlighted each fuzzy strand that enwrapped the overhead roots that he was staring through.

Wait, I know this place. I've seen these furry tentacles before!

He was back in the cavern he had shimmied through a few hours ago! He was passing along the spongy soft moss teeming with glorious spiders, of which he was far too elated to fear!

I'm back!

On elbows, knees, and belly, Jonas crawled toward the light. "I remember you," he remarked to the gigantic root that had nearly caved his nose. Rotating onto a shoulder, he navigated the space around the root, and to his great disappointment, discovered that his body was still terribly achy and weak. The magical transference between realms had made an error; he was still inside his normal, ordinary body. "What the heck," he mumbled.

After each push, the opening widened. The yawning vastness that lay beyond gifted Jonas a sudden sense of dread. He was no more than a fragile plankton adrift before an untamed sea.

If only I were strong again.

Upon the lip, he hesitated, careful to keep his head from passing into sight. He was fearful of the monsters that snatched their prey from above. His decision to cower brought to mind the way his mother had shied away from Emil's raised hand. Recalling the threat and the way it spread fear, ignited a spark of anger, and without sparing an overhead glance, Jonas clawed himself free of the hole.

After he shot to his feet, dismissing every ache invading his tired limbs, he cast his blurry eyes to the treetops and shouted, "Ritz!" And from his ankles to his hips, he felt a renewal of strength.

Then with clenched fists, he addressed the forest. "Hylda!" he screamed. Every blurry form within the forest vaulted into clarity, as if his glasses had appeared atop his nose. The gnarled trunks wrapped in vegetation, the boulders slathered in moss, and the leaves twirling downward, freed by the Ritts' obedient arrival, were observed with diamond-cut clarity.

The Devil had returned.

Maybe it's the air in this world? wondered Jonas as he followed Scary and Posh's bobbing heads. Their lank, black hair limply flowed behind them as they ran through the forest, leading Jonas to Guiltbrand. *Some of my strength has returned, but how long until I can tap into my power again?*

The forest ended where a meadow began. It was a sharp transition as they broke from the darkness and out into the daylight. Along with the piercing radiance, a series of horns lifted their voices, rending the air at a distance below. The

Ritts' sudden appearance on the horizon had presumably stirred the alarms.

From where they abandoned the treeline, Jonas noticed that they were approaching the fort from a different angle.

The gentle downward slope of the meadow yielded an easy crossing, which Jonas was grateful for. As he passed along the earth, the Ritts maintained a soaring vigil, scattering a boundary of shadows within his footfalls. From a distance they may have appeared as nothing more than a kettle of vultures.

As Jonas drew closer, the shouts from Fort Brimon's wall grew louder.

"He has returned!"

"Already?!"

"Open the gates!"

"The Devil has returned!"

"Someone alert Guiltbrand and the Council!"

"The horns have already done that!"

Chains grated as the portcullis hiked upward, and an escort of armored knights streamed forth to meet the Devil. Every member of the knightly contingent was adorned with a full-face helmet, except for one soldier whose wind-swept locks furled around his ears like a movie star. That amount of handsome could hardly be contained.

"Hail!" The helmetless knight saluted Jonas.

Jonas slowed. "How's it going?" he asked.

The handsome knight simply smiled as he stepped aside. "Welcome back, our Devil."

The moment Jonas' feet met the fort's flagstone pathway the gate closed behind him, cinching in place with a grunt of finality. Heads turned and fingers pointed as a ripple of excitement spread throughout the knights and archers.

This bailey stretching before him appeared the same as its north end, except a siege was not underway. Organized by rank, not by stature, the Brimon brigades stood at attention awaiting Jonas' arrival. It was a magnificent display of discipline and respect, but Jonas was not really in the mood for admiration. After hearing what Emil had done to his family, revenge was his current goal.

Two thirds of the way along the corridor of knights and soldiers Jonas caught sight of Guiltbrand and his entourage speeding toward him. The Sage's robes battered at his ankles with each excessive stride, and beneath beaming joyful eyes, his fingers were steepled and pressed to his lips, much like a wealthy child sweeping eyes across his Christmas morning haul.

Determination spurred Jonas forward. He was more than prepared for a green light for his vengeance on Emil, and within the span of a breath, Jonas found himself standing before the Sage.

Guiltbrand recoiled at the ferocity in Jonas' approach. "What great relief!" he proclaimed. "You have returned!" He supplied his upraised hands with wiggling fingers. The onlookers upon the walls burst into a frenzy. Jonas could see their frustration and disillusionment from his abandonment evaporate.

Streamers and banners were cast from the parapets and upper walkways, cascading down in striated patterns. Juvenile minotaurs and satyrs scampered on the scaffolding in deliriums of excitement, flinging flower petals and dead butterflies onto the street. Then from beneath a footbridge, a choir of hooded imps unleashed a discordant series of screeches that only acted to pump the crowds up even further.

Jonas was uninterested in the celebrations. The more he thought about Emil, the angrier he became, until he blurted, "Give me your worst monster!"

Snapping from elation to concern, Guiltbrand lowered his head. "I'm sorry, Jonas," he said as panic began stitching his eyebrows. "Care to repeat that?"

"I want the most dangerous monster you've got." Jonas replied.

A beat passed between the Sage and the Devil, then in a grand sweep, Guiltbrand regained his full height. "My friends! The Leeds Devil hath returned!" he declared. This brought a new surge of excitement, garnering roars of approval all throughout the fortress. After performing a quick bend, the Sage spoke in Jonas' ear, "Follow me. Let us speak."

Guiltbrand pivoted and signaled to his trailing sages that it was time to move along.

"Come along," said Jonas to the Hylda. And within the gait of his following step he felt half an inch added to his stature. Additionally the outermost bones in his shoulders had thickened.

The fort's perimeter widened the further Jonas traveled until he could no longer see either palisade. A cobblestone roadway appeared beneath their feet, siphoning their steps toward the village proper. An air of permanence infused the wide-open space, creating contrast between the makeshift fortifications they had departed. Hands that had been reinforced with iron resolve established these timber-framed houses. Centuries had come and gone leaving a distinct residue that Jonas could sense through the soles of his feet. A beating heart thrummed in the earth below and echoed throughout the air above. This place was not meant to be abandoned. This was a place worth defending.

The sages ahead of Guiltbrand pointedly curved their steps to the left, charting a course for the most magnificent building. A pair of towers that concluded into dangerously thin pinnacles vaulted over their heads, and crouched between the towers was an A-frame structure that connected the two, creating a series of triple peaks. Between the wooden frames of the building's outer wall a pristine white patina seemed to collect itself and evaporate in an endless cycle. It was an impossible display that Jonas believed must be some sort of magical working.

The sages were the first to press through the high arched double doors. Guiltbrand courteously stood to the side, allowing Jonas to enter next.

"Nach ihnen," said the Sage with a courtly bow. "After you," he clarified after Jonas' confused expression prompted him to do naught else.

One step shy of entry, Jonas looked down at the Hylda. "I'll be back," he said. Scary and Posh shared curious looks with one another. "I'm sorry guys, but I'm doing this part alone."

The Hylda obeyed, watching the Devil enter the building without them.

Jonas' bare feet met the marbled floors of the foyer, sending shivers down his forearms. To his right a fire kindled in a raised hearth that appeared as though it were comprised of cast iron. The modest amount of heat perspiring from the embers somehow washed his prevailing chills away.

Jonas gaped as he craned his neck at the stonework inlayed within the walls. One particular stonework relief depicted a werewolf and a minotaur thrusting spears into the chest of what appeared to be an archangel. When he stopped to gain better understanding of the piece, Guiltbrand cleared his throat, encouraging Jonas to follow him into the main corridor.

From the high vaulted ceilings to the saintly statues adorning the base of every column, this place appeared to Jonas as a cathedral. Granted he had never been to a cathedral, but he had seen them on TV, and this place resembled one. But whoever had designed this one seemed to enjoy illusions. After Jonas traversed the foyer, the architecture framing the generous corridor ruptured at odd angles throwing the floors out of synch with the portals. Though he purposefully walked forward, no matter how far he corrected, Jonas felt as though he was listing sideways.

"You grow accustomed to it," remarked Guiltbrand. He nodded toward one of the sure-footed sages ahead. "For the first few weeks after his arrival, Stefan required a cane."

Jonas grunted, parsing each step with care. Without intending, his left foot crisscrossed his right as he passed beneath another crooked threshold.

"Arduous as it may be," Guiltbrand continued, sensing Jonas' growing displeasure. "For those without certain *gifts* this grand hovel of ours is nigh impossible to negotiate. Most of your average folk regurgitate their previous meal for simply peering through the front hatch. The merest glimpse can stir a spell of wet heaving that will only settle once the afflicted dives headfirst into the nearest body of water. Luckily, for most, a smithy's quenching trough will do the trick."

"That's messed up," said Jonas.

"Indeed." Guiltbrand nodded. "We are not far. See where the hall terminates ahead?"

Jonas' eyes had not left the floor. "No," he replied, refusing to look up.

"Well, trust me," said Guiltbrand. "It does. And where it does, we will make a right-hand turn, and shortly thereafter we will find ourselves within the confines of the Sanctum of Susurrance. And therein you shall meet the Council."

"Neat." Jonas clenched his jaw, wanting to say more, but his right foot teetering off an invisible precipice distracted him. Before he could correct his fall, his right knee painfully overextended, sending him toppling sideways. The noise from the ensuing collision rippled in all directions. Seething, Jonas drove an elbow into the wall, snapping him up onto a knee.

"This is so stupid." Jonas swiped at his nose, rising from his crouch.

He felt foolish, but in the end, assuming the saddle-sore cowboy stance proved the best way to defeat this hallway. With bent knees and fixed hips, Jonas swaggered his way to the end, then swung a right turn.

The Sanctum of Susurrance was an expansive chamber with an endless ring of balcony seats skirting below the apex of a curved ceiling. Appearing as if it had occurred ages ago, a titan of a tree ruptured through the stone floor, its peak accusing the center rise of the dome, inches shy of scraping. The branches had been hewn flush to the trunk, crafting the tree into a cylindrical shape. All, save for one broad branch that cut a hard right angle parallel to the floor. Hitched to this sturdy limb was a row of swings, and as canaries in a cage, the Council sat upon the swings like children on the loneliest playground.

Guiltbrand was seated on the centermost swing. His feet dangled as he tilted his head and parted his lips.

"Enter."

Through mystic means, the Sage's whisper crossed the room easily. "Be mindful of your volume. This is a whispering chamber. Fragile components abound that cannot be perceived with the naked eye."

Jonas heaved a sigh and entered.

While Councils' eyes rested evenly upon Jonas, Guiltbrand smiled a deep generous smile. "Make your request known to us, Dev — Jonas," he whispered, amending his error, still reconciling Jonas' given name.

Each footfall was muted as Jonas cut toward the Council. The stone felt cold and superficially smooth under his bare feet. And with eyes shimmering through slits, Jonas began his appeal.

"I would like —"

Of one accord the Council sucked air through their teeth and slammed hands over their ears, recoiling as if Jonas had doused them with lava. One swing began to twirl in place while the occupant hissed a string of curses.

"Mind your volume!" Guiltbrand's brows crinkled hostile. "Only whispers are permitted in the Sanctum!"

"I'm sorry, but this —" said Jonas.

Another feverish intake of air came from the swings.

"Whisper! Whisper! Whisper!" The Council flung the words, sounding as a thousand voices.

Angrily Guiltbrand bounded from his swing. "You must whisper!" He pantomimed a lid fastening to a jar.

This seemed silly to Jonas. More rules for the sake of rules, and he had grown sick of the hoops and the jumping.

"I would like you to steer me toward..." Jonas ignored the sages clutching their chests as if his words contained bullets. "Your worst..." Two members fainted and dropped from their swings. Three shushed him, demanding silence like outraged librarians. And the remainder bucked and roiled as if their heads were about to explode. In composed contrast, Guiltbrand folded his arms, awaiting Jonas' final word.

"Monster."

CHAPTER 10

"You do not know what you ask for." Guiltbrand maintained a whisper though he appeared ready to throttle someone. He eyed the floor as if it may crack at any moment. "And *please*, I beg you, do not use that volume!" He brought his hands together and wrung them violently. "This is a *whispering chamber!* Please! Whisper!" A cacophony of hushed agreement flooded the chamber as the Council nodded feverishly.

Jonas said nothing. He grated his jaw and inclined his head the way his mother would whenever she was done with an argument. *I will not repeat.*

Guiltbrand took the passing silence as agreement and resigned his hands to his sides. The anxiety in the chamber began to drain slowly. "As I said before," he stated calmly. "You do not know what you ask for."

A pale-faced council member leaned forward, placing her elbows in her lap. The swing wavered beneath her, tempting a forward fall, but the woman quickly and safely adjusted her position. Instead of tumbling, she merely wobbled. "By *worst* monster." Her whisper fell light as a coffee filter. "Do you mean the most dangerous? Or do you mean, perhaps, the most disgusting?" She spoke with a calculated finesse that Jonas would have found grating on a better day.

"Yes." Another member sat up. Her cowl yet drawn, shadowing her features. "Context. Would. Shed. Some. Clarity," she spoke haltingly, following each syllable with a bob of her head.

A member whose cloak reflected a dark cherry complexion rubbed his chin. "What do you need this monster for?" he inquired, his voice challenging a volume above a whisper. Glares of displeasure swiveled and locked onto him. "Apologies," he whispered, hunching.

"Perhaps a couple Skorsa would do?" A youthful-sounding member asked, looking to Guiltbrand for approval. The Sage tersely shook his head. Not one to be dissuaded easily, the member bit her lip and amended the number. "Twenty-five Skorsa?"

Guiltbrand's eyes traced the slanted ceiling. "Need we rehash this conversation?" He rotated his shoulders toward Jonas. "I offered you a solution, last we spoke. And you turned it away."

"Things have changed in my world," said Jonas aloud, ignoring the pearl-clutching expressions. "My family is in real danger."

Guiltbrand wanted to scold, but he choked back the urge. "I thought that, *'You can't just kill your way out of every problem?'*" he said, mimicking Jonas with a squeaky falsetto. One member snorted a laugh and immediately covered her mouth. Guiltbrand continued, "What has changed? The circumstances?" The Sage picked at his goatee as if it were a necktie. "Or, perhaps, it is *you* who have changed?"

Jonas scratched at his eyebrow and looked away.

Fearing that he was overplaying his hand, and also fearing a reply at regular volume, Guiltbrand raised his hands in surrender. "Why don't *we* do the secret slaying for you." The Sage crossed before the Council, and every head followed his steps, hanging on his every word. While *you* stay here and fulfill your destiny?" He paused, allowing the Council to focus on Jonas. "Take care of both problems at once?"

"Because I want to be there," replied Jonas. "When my problem is solved."

"You want to be there..." Guiltbrand tapped his top teeth while the Council writhed in agony. "You want to see... Oh, enough!" he hissed at the Council, then rounded on Jonas. "It was a mistake bringing you in here."

"Yeah?" said Jonas. "Well, I'm done." He began walking toward the exit with his hands steepled under his chin. "This place is stupid." He pointed joined hands at the Council. "And it was a mistake coming to you first. See-ya, tools."

Shoulder tackling the front door, Jonas stumbled out into the daylight. He wiped the sweat from his brow, relieved to be free of that dumb building and its exhausting layout. He had stubbed his toes and fallen down at least a hundred times.

"Why?!" Jonas shouted, whirling on the cathedral. "Why build a funhouse for idiots?! What purpose could that possibly serve?" The Hylda nodded while Jonas stood with his hands on his hips. "And where is your most dangerous monster?"

After a few moments passed without an answer, Jonas decided to seek the next-most-important-looking building. Maybe it would offer a straight answer for his question, and hopefully it would not be filled with chucklesages twirling on swings.

With the Council now in his rear-view, Jonas began to weigh his options. If his current plan did not pan out, then where would he turn? Jonas chewed on the possibilities as the shadows cast by the Ritts battered him like an enraged nest of hornets.

While gazing at the rooftops Jonas repeated his question aloud.

"The Still," replied Scary, tugging at Jonas' knee.

Jonas started at the unexpected touch. "The Still?" An undeniable chill curled his spine.

"A Hush," Posh added astutely, as if clarifying for her counterpart.

"A Hush?" Jonas echoed, adding to the gooseflesh. He rubbed at his forearms and for a passing moment wondered if the village had a clothing shop.

A change of threads is long overdue, Jonas thought, sparing a few sideways glances.

"What is a *Hush* exactly?" asked Jonas.

"Not an option," said Guiltbrand, suddenly sweeping before them.

"Oh, come on. Not this guy —"

"Not unless these *creatures* understand a Hush as well as I do?" Guiltbrand's right eyebrow towered up, challenging the Hylda to continue.

Jonas bit his lip, imagining the Ritts carrying Guiltbrand to the sun.

"No?" Guiltbrand twirled his goatee.

Scary and Posh paid the Sage equal indifference.

"I see. Well," began Guiltbrand, ticking his eyes from Hylda to Hylda before resting on Jonas. "There is a certain... discretion one must undertake before entertaining a Hush. Things one must know. A Hush is not a stray cat that one simply adorns gauntlets before handling."

Scary's grip on Jonas' knee suddenly constricted. "Thrice thy query hath been cast..." she recited, looking to Posh.

"Know this for certain..." recited Posh, then turned to Scary.

"T'will be thy last," said Scary, finishing the rhyme.

Jonas turned to the Hylda, feeling left out of something important. "What?"

"Those are the rules," replied Scary, tilting her head. When Jonas looked to Posh, the Hylda simply bobbed her head in agreement.

"If I may?" offered Guiltbrand.

"No, you may not," replied Jonas. "What's with you, man? Why can't you just get to the point?"

Guiltbrand appeared taken aback.

"Let me make this easy for you," said Jonas. "I want the baddest hombre you can hook me up with, living on this side of whatever that river is called —"

"The Taub," supplied Guiltbrand. "The river is called the Taub."

Jonas glanced up at the sun and the circling Ritts. "The Taub, yes. How could I forget. Just point me in the direction of the nearest Hush. And I'll be on my way. And after I'm done with the business in my world, or realm, or whatever, then I'll come back and deal with as many Terrens as your heart's desire."

The Sage lifted an objecting finger. He wavered speechless, reluctantly lowering his hand. "Are you certain that you wish to entertain a Hush? They are seen as outcasts, and not to be —"

Jonas heaved an anguished sigh. "Does a Hush kill without a trace?"

"They may." Uncertainty creased Guiltbrand's forehead.

Jonas glanced at the invisible watch on his wrist.

Guiltbrand continued. "A Hush may kill from great distances, yes, without the use of a physical implement." He sneered at the Hylda. "Or an abyssal incantation."

"Sounds perfect."

"Does it not?" Guiltbrand frowned. "But the Hush does entertain allegiances. Be wary, a Hush may turn. They are unpredictable. Like wielding a double-edged sword forged without a handle."

"Still sounds perfect."

"The blade being the only option for your hands," stated Guiltbrand as he watched his plea for understanding dissolve into the breeze.

"I get it," said Jonas. "He's dangerous. If he's the best of the best, then I want him. So where can I find one? In some spooky hollow deep in a haunted forest? Entombed in an underground graveyard? Bound and shackled deep in the darkest dungeon?"

Guiltbrand shook his head. And after a dramatic pause, Scary stole the old man's thunder.

"Down the lane," she told Jonas, pointing toward a row of unassuming houses.

"Oh." Jonas gaped at the Hylda for a moment. "Thank you, Scary. That was very helpful." He turned to Guiltbrand. "See how easy that was?" He lifted a hand in farewell. "If that's everything, I'll be seeing ya."

Naturally, the Sage could not allow Jonas to leave so easily. "You have one night and one day to accomplish your... business."

"You seem confused," Jonas seethed. "This is when I go this way, and you go that way. We are done here."

The time had come to meet this Hush. Jonas strode in the direction Scary had indicated. From behind, he heard a heavy groan.

"It's not..." Guiltbrand called. "I want you to succeed! One night and one day is simply the length of time that a Hush may be away from this realm."

One day and one night... Jonas wondered as he gained distance from the Sage. If there was truth in Guiltbrand's words, would that be enough time? Probably not, but what is the worst that could happen?

This neck of the village that the Hylda had been leading him through was remarkably cute, in a foreboding and ominous sort of way. The product of what Scarberry High's Goth Club and Glee Squad would create if given free reign over a neighborhood's aesthetic. A few, very certain houses appeared to have been plucked straight from one of those miniature Bavarian Village dioramas and puffed to a livable human size.

"What kind of monsters live there?" Jonas asked, admiring a front stoop that emanated a mystic purple glow. "Hey, Scary," said Jonas. "Before we get to the Hush house, is there anything I should know? Like, what was that creepy nursery rhyme you two recited back there?" He raised his voice an octave, impersonating the Hylda speech. "Something, something, something — T'will be thy last."

"Precisely," replied Posh.

"Exactly that," added Scary.

Their combined answer failed to shine additional light on the subject. "Can you explain?"

"Ah!" Scary launched toward Jonas and thrust a finger at him, while behind her Posh drew a thumb-dagger across her throat while gagging.

"You dead now," Posh elaborated, "the Hush would have slain you for the three questions you only just asked. If you ask three questions of a Hush, he will kill you."

"For just asking questions?"

The Hylda pair nodded.

Scary had yet to lower her accusatory finger. "Thrice," she said gravely.

Jonas scratched his head. "So he's kind of like a genie? Only instead of three wishes, you get murdered for asking three questions?" He tipped his head and scratched under his chin. "Not really like a genie at all, now that I think about it, except for the whole rule of threes thing..."

As their trek continued, Jonas grew more anxious to meet this monster. In truth he did not have much to go on, besides the Hyldas' distinct indication that this was *the* monster for the job. And his penchant for asking a million questions was something that he would need to keep in check.

After the road dipped and shrugged a couple times, the Hylda hooked a left at a crossroad, and as bloodhounds narrowing on a scent, drew up short before one of the Bavarian style houses. A stone sidewalk supplied an easy footpath from the street to the front door. For being a terrifying monster, the Hush sure knew how to throw up an impassable barrier. Nothing screams, *"BEWARE — DO NOT ENTER"* like a charming cottage with spangled tulips and a wrap-around flower garden. If that was not enough of a dire warning, then the pastel birdbaths placed symmetrically throughout the front lawn would certainly dissuade even the most hardened warrior.

"You sure this is where the Hush lives?"

"The Still," Scary corrected. "He's called the Still."

"A Hush named the Still?"

The Hylda nodded.

"Glad we got that cleared up," said Jonas. "Shall we?"

Jonas assumed the lead as they tread single file across the garden path. Right as he lifted the brass knocker on the steel banded oak door, an odd fluttering sensation entered his gut.

Is this a premonition?

With eyes closed, he dispelled all stray thoughts, focusing on his mother.

This is it.

His stomach settled.

Once he took this step — this step of employing a Hush, an assassin — there would be no turning back. An unbidden grunt escaped as he dislodged the heavy ring from the knocker's goblin-headed inset.

When the Devil comes knocking...

CHAPTER 11

The creature that greeted Jonas at the door was not what he had expected. And at this point, he could only take things in stride.

"It's you," said the Still flatly. His voice sounded no older than Darren's, but this Hush exuded more maturity than your average upperclassman. Initially Jonas believed that it had been Elias who had opened the door, if Elias ever showed his face, and if his face were that of a teenage vampire. Jonas had been equipped with only the sharp vampire teeth, but this guy bore the teeth *and* the pointy ears.

"Come in, if you like." The Still stepped to the side and swept a cordial arm. Unlike Elias, not every move the Still made was imbued with lethality.

A crosshatch of daylight from a nearby window rolled onto the Still as he guided them past his staircase. The light had a strange effect on the monster's tunic, morphing the fabric's pigment into a softer shade.

Light activated camouflage, Jonas noted.

"What —" Jonas bit his tongue, wanting to ask about what he had just seen.

The Still spun around, his eyes narrowed, smoldering with danger. Clearly what the Hylda had told Jonas about asking questions was true.

"What... a lovely house." Jonas recovered.

The Still's intensity lessened, giving way to an air of cordiality. "It should go without saying, but you must always choose your words carefully around me."

"Yeah," said Jonas, embarrassed.

"No matter." The Still smiled. "You caught me during my knit time. And judging by the state of your raiment, I feel that perhaps a change may be suggested?" His eyes traced Jonas from the floor up. "Come along," he said with a note of relish.

The majority of the kitchen was comprised of hearth and oven. A sliver of a path circumvented the heating components, where Jonas could yet feel breakfast's coals radiating. Needlessly, but politely, the Still cautioned his guests regarding the hot surfaces while they carefully ambled past.

The room sprawling beyond the kitchen, by Jonas' best estimation was some sort of costume crafting space. Underneath a low ceiling, comfortable-looking chairs huddled, surrounded by racks and racks of clothes in varying stages of completion. Beside the most prominent-looking chair was a nest of tatting, stitching, and sewing implements. From one side of the room to the other, it seemed that distaffs and spindles had been set adrift on a sea of yarn.

"Dude can sew," remarked Jonas, taking it all in. He was in a space that dawdled that fine line between cozy and claustrophobic, and somehow maintained the cozier aspects. This Hush, this murderous maniac was also a closet fashionista.

Scoping Jonas with a raised thumb, the Still arched sideways on one hip. "I'd say, just by looking at you, that you're a few sizes down from the average Vorpalritt." The Still retrieved his tongue after a moment of hard calculations. "I think I may..." With a leap, he sprang from the room. Footsteps clobbered the staircase, indicating his direction, and further racket in the rooms above explained that the Still was madly intent on finding something.

"We don't have time for this," said Jonas to his Hylda. "Silly me for thinking that I could come back and retrieve a horror beast and just —"

"Found it!" The Still appeared beaming.

Jonas started for a few reasons. Firstly, he had not heard the Still's return flight down the staircase, which was distressing. Coupled with that, the outfit that he was threatening the room with was breathtaking. It was inspired, a garment torn from a high-end comic book that would cause a Hollywood Red Carpet to curl up and take notice.

"Hollywood," Jonas muttered. The brightness dimmed and died, abruptly the needle scratched the record. Jonas realized that this outfit was perfect for this world, but ridiculous in his own.

"Hollywood?" The Still's ears pricked up. "What is a *Hollywood?*"

"Nothing, never mind." Jonas chalked it up as another link on the endless chain of disappointment. "Do you —" He caught himself mid-question and rebooted. "I need something less... less like a dress. Less like a gown. Something a bit more, I don't know, more like this." With weakened spirit, Jonas tugged at his collar. "T-shirt and jeans."

"T-shirt and jeans?"

Jonas shrugged. "Trousers and a shirt."

The Still lowered the magnificent tunic, unimpressed.

"I mean no offense, of course," Jonas explained. "You see, I need your help to take care of some... bad people. People that have hurt my family. People that killed my grandparents." Where Jonas lacked in skillful tact, he hoped to make up for with honesty. "The Hylda told me that you're the one I'm looking for, and they don't lie to me."

"The Leeds Devil seeks my aid?" said the Still. "What you speak of does not pertain to the Leeds and Terren dispute."

"It has nothing to do with this world."

The Still smirked and Jonas detected amusement on his face.

"I told the Sage that I would come back," continued Jonas. "Once I took care of what I need to take care of..." Jonas held his tongue, not wishing to come across presumptuous. He understood that the Still had other activities to occupy his time. "That is, if you decide to come with me."

The smirk had yet to vacate the Still's face. "Are you *asking* me to join you?"

Jonas flared a toothy grin at the Hylda, entirely unsure how to proceed without phrasing his request as a question. And doing so would be a big no-no.

The Still snickered. "I'm making jest!" he said, draping the prized tunic across his forearm and taking a seat. "As you can surmise, my life can be rather isolated."

"Yeah, I can see that." Jonas took in the room in for a second time. "On the bright side, it gives you plenty of time for sewing and stuff."

A sharp laugh cracked from the Still. "Keeps me busy," he said as his eyes meandered to the clothing racks. "I like you, Devil without wings." He sighed and looked to the bundle of fabric in his lap. "Though I would rather not play a role in the Leeds Terren quarrel, because you amuse me, I will aid you in this personal endeavor."

Jonas brightened, rising to his full height and nearly cracking his head on the ceiling.

"Ah-ah." The Still halted Jonas' excitement, raising an objecting finger. "Pray, on one condition."

"Name it," said Jonas.

Not for the first time that afternoon the Still closed an eye and cocked his head, as if measuring more than the young man's silhouette. A shadow wandered and settled across the handspun mantle upon the Still's shoulders, bathing his upper half in a darker green hue. "Of all the coats, jerkins, and jackets I have crafted, this surcoat is by far my favorite." He lifted the dazzling piece by its shoulders. "I spun it many years ago when I was going through some... trials. And it has a certain *value* to it. And I have yet to come across a body that it would suit..." The Still trailed off as his pristine eyebrows nearly soared from his forehead.

Picking up on the not-so subtle hint, Jonas inclined his head. "It would be an honor to wear your awesome threads, man." From the corner of his eye he caught Scary's ordinarily blank expression flash giddy.

The Still rose to his feet. "May your enemies be trembling at this moment," he said, reverently passing the garment. "For if they are not, they shall be."

Jonas excused himself into a side parlor to admire his new outfit. And also to conceal his tears of joy.

The figure that stared back at him from within the floor length mirror was no longer a frail youth. He was imposing, intimidating. A Devil.

For as long as he could remember, his canines were a point of embarrassment, something to conceal with closed lips. But in this form his fangs tied the ensemble into ferocious perfection.

He wondered what Sasha would think of him *now*.

He took it all in. The immaculately trimmed surcoat dropped from his shoulders down to the folded collars of his newly acquired boots. By the sheer purity of the colors, it seemed as if the Still had extracted pure onyx at its ripest, right from the peak of midnight and injected it into his loom. The fathomless crimson, which gave the surcoat its voice, depicted patterns so intricate, so fine, one may be fooled into believing it had been spoken into existence by the whisper of an angel.

In a display of practicality, a single strap baldric had been slung across Jonas' back and chest, hitching perfectly into a heavy ring fashioned to a thick leather belt.

As he twirled and posed, lifting a heel to admire the expert precision that had been paid to the hem, a harsh truth suddenly revealed itself, unbidden. This would all fade once he returned home. After his boot soles cleared the magical sluice, he would be nothing more than Count Brokula.

As his heel returned the floor, his reflection contained the most real of illusions, for which he somehow coveted and obtained all at once.

The Still had insisted on tidying up before shrugging off. While Jonas and the Hylda stood on the Still's front stoop, waiting for him to finish, the little witches struggled to contain their approval of Jonas' new outfit.

Scary nudged Posh and tittered something in her ear, which caused the taller Hylda to cover her elongated mouth and rasp gleefully.

"Alright!" Jonas had seen enough. "I'm not going to order you to stop, but..." Never had the young man experienced this sort of attention from females. And it was made all the weirder when it premiered by way of a pair of murderous witch-creatures. "Could you tone it down?"

The Hylda shared an impish look and nodded. Luckily the Still emerged from his door, dispersing the weirdness.

"Shall we?" said the Still. He had changed into a striking set of light armor where the steel only glistened from his shoulders, wrists, and shins. Underlying the armor he had selected a tunic weaved in the textured fabric of his personal wardrobe. A mysterious composition of threadwork that granted chameleon-like color shifts.

"Lead on, *the* Still," said Jonas, following his new companion over the stonework lane. Hundreds of claws launched from roof tiles as the Ritts took flight. "We should come up with a nickname."

"A nickname?" puzzled the Still. His feet came to a stop midway across the lawn. "Wager it will rain?" he pondered, staring at the sky.

Aside from the circling Ritts, the sky was the clearest of clear skies, nary a scrap of cloud to be seen.

"Probably not," replied Jonas.

"What I feared." The Still chewed his lip. "I should probably refresh my birdbaths."

And then Jonas' thoughts turned to his mother's shop, and all that had been stolen. He recalled Fabian's boot and Emil's mocking glare.

"The birds will survive," he said with more severity than intended. Scary punctuated Jonas' statement with an unexpected hiss.

Somehow the Still's eyes narrowed without losing their sparkle. "I suppose," he agreed, playing his steps along the pathway as if he were balancing a tight rope. "Now what was that about a *nickname?*"

Following and not wanting to crunch the Still's heels, Jonas had to measure his steps. "Yes," he began. "I feel goofy calling you *The Still*. It's too formal."

"Oh," the Still replied over his shoulder. Thankfully his strides widened once his feet met the road. *"The Still* is what folk simply refer to me as," he explained. "The title's author is unknown to me, but I can only guess that he coined it from my ability to maintain a strict pose for days at a time. You see, the name bestowed to me at birth was —" He stopped and began rummaging over his chest and hips as if he had misplaced his wallet.

Jonas managed to swallow the urge to ask what was wrong.

"Isaac!" The Still announced in near anguish, gasping, sounding as one surfacing from drowning. "My true name is Isaac." The tension in his face eased with relief.

"Solid name, man," commented Jonas. "Isaac it is then."

With that settled, the Devil with his Plus One began the next leg of their journey in relative silence. In an amusing contrast to their solemnity, the wind carried the unmistakable sounds of a party set to raging. It seemed that Jonas' welcome celebration had continued to kick after he had departed, and now they were apparently kicking it into outer space.

Jonas could not help but notice that they were treading in the opposite direction of his regular inside-the-tree-cavern-portal. It was true that Isaac was not one for a party, but Jonas imagined that there must be another explanation for why they were taking the long way around. Without *actually* giving voice to a question his brain began tinkering out a means of discovering their destination.

"The portal I have been using is the other way," said Jonas.

"Typical," said Isaac. "I imagine the Sage directed you to an upended locust tree?"

"He did."

"There's a gate much closer that will not stain our clothes," said Isaac. Of a sudden he stiffened and barred Jonas' steps with an outstretched arm. "Alas, I fear that our journey has met its first *snag,*" he whispered.

Pounding footsteps stuttered from behind and came to a halt. Jonas whirled, and two knights dropped to a knee upon eye contact, assuming a pose of reverence. Even with their faces angled toward the ground, Jonas knew whom he was dealing with.

"Vera, Greta," he said, stepping in their direction. He was uncertain of what to say to compel them to stand. "Rise?" he tried.

At the same time the pair lifted from the ground as if practiced beforehand.

Both Vera and Greta cut youthful figures, having shed the hard contours of their armor. Upon their first brutal meet & greet, blades drawn and set to killing, Jonas had been under the impression that these knights were women. Like, full-grown women. But looking at them now dressed in free-flowing summer gowns, they appeared no older than your average Senior that graced the halls of Scarberry High.

"Devil," said Vera. "Would that you allow us a moment of your time?" She spoke with her hands humbly folded upon her chest. "Upon hearing of the Devil's swift return, Greta and I joined the festivities to see for ourselves. We searched and searched but could not find you! Then it was explained that you had immediately adjourned to the Hall of Sages." She tucked her chin and stared at the back of her hands. "It's such a relief to see you!" she cried. And then *actually* cried. In that moment it was difficult for Jonas to reconcile her as the savage fighter he knew her to be.

"Hey, hey now," said Jonas consolingly. "No need for tears. You two look great! I mean it. Like, really pretty. Way prettier than most girls in my world."

Vera looked up and sniffed back a few straying tears. "You mean it?"

"Yeah, sure," replied Jonas, glancing at Isaac. "Look ladies, I hate to cut this short, and it was awesome seeing you and all, but me and my pals are kinda in the middle of something." He slugged a thumb over his shoulder. "So, if you don't mind, we best be scooting..."

Greta's dress gave the impression that she was floating when she intercepted Jonas' departure. "Might that we spare a bit more of your time?"

This sort of attention made Jonas uncomfortable. "I guess," he said, grimacing at Isaac. The Still had grown visibly impatient. If he wore a wristwatch, he would be tapping it. "What is it?"

Shadows rippled across the hopeful faces of the knights. The Ritts' holding pattern had been tightening from all the standing.

The knights exchanged a look and Greta spoke. "We heard that you are seeking vengeance." The way Greta's lips curled around the word *vengeance* caused Jonas' heart to skip a beat. "And though it pains us to hear that you will be leaving us again, we would regret not telling you about a weapon that may prove its worth." Greta folded her arms and allowed her words to hang.

"A weapon whose power does not wane when it passes from our realm into yours," revealed Vera, her warrior side bleeding through. "A weapon unlike any other. And we know his whereabouts."

Jonas swiveled sharply to Isaac and arched a questioning eyebrow.

The Hush bore an expression of doubt. "They speak of Dafodhel," he said, shaking his head as if he had swallowed an insect. "They don't know where Dafodhel is."

Greta took a step back while Vera blanched, parting trembling fingers across her throat. Up until now the Still's presence had apparently gone beneath their notice. And with that awareness, Jonas perceived their disapproval plain as day.

"What manner..." Vera gasped.

"What madman told you that consorting with a Hush was *ever* a good idea?"

Jonas covered his laugh with a fake cough when Scary smirked a glance his way.

"It's like stowing a squeeze bomb inside a seat cushion!" said Vera backing away, plastering palms to her face. "Send him away!" Then remembering whom she addressed, quickly added, "Please?!"

"Not on your life," said Jonas cutting the distance. A smile graced the Still's face for the briefest moment, there and gone. "Forget about him." He pressed the knight, dropping his voice into a grisly baritone. "Tell me more about this Daffodil. This weapon that crosses realms without losing its magic."

Vera's jaw drooped. "Uh, uh," she stuttered, terrified, inches from the ivory curvature of the Devil's fangs. Between this new unholy attire that ominously sculpted his frame and the coal black cruelty in his voice, she appeared spellbound.

"Can it give the guy who holds it the same power?" Jonas scoured Vera's vacant expression. "Can I be the same Devil here and *there?*" he asked with urgency.

"Yes." It was Greta who answered. "Yes, it does."

Jonas growled and turned his head. "Are you sure?"

"She is," said Vera, thawing from her momentary stupor. "Dafodhel has that ability."

"Awesome," said Jonas. He appraised the knights for a moment before stepping away to face Isaac and the Hylda. "We're taking a detour."

CHAPTER 12

"They do not know where Dafodhel lives," asserted Isaac again.

Jonas knew nothing about the sword, other than it was magical, and the knights were too scared of Isaac to even spare a syllable in his direction. Also Jonas wanted him to be wrong. So badly. This sword, should it meet the hype, would solve all of his problems.

When Jonas came to a stop on a roadway, everyone stopped with him. "Alright," he said. "I can't take it anymore. Do you have proof that you know where Daffodil is?"

"It is in Moütz," replied Vera, her head twitching as if to say, *Hey, Jonas, can we have a sidebar?*

Jonas caught her subtext and tapped her elbow. "Give us a sec, okay?" he said to the Hylda. From behind, Jonas heard Isaac say, *"Moütz?"* as if the word tasted bitter. The knight led Jonas beyond eavesdropping range, up and over one of the grassy embankments that corralled the road.

"Have you asked the Still a question?" Vera questioned. "Just one, perhaps? An honest slip-up?"

Facing the roadway, Jonas glanced overtop the crown of the knight's head. The Hylda were unmoving, bodies aimed toward his heart. Meanwhile Greta had taken advantage of the break to sharpen a dagger, and deeper in the background, Isaac stood with his head cocked, admiring his fingernails.

"Nope," replied Jonas. "Had a few close calls, but I managed to shift gears in time."

Vera smiled as the moment's urgency drained. "That's a relief! Greta and I were worried…" She paused, savoring the response. "Now, I would never delegate orders to you, wouldn't dream of it, but is there a way we may carry on without the Still?"

Vera toed the protruding head of a boulder marbled in moss at her feet. Being a knight she was accustomed to fighting for what she desired, and it was obvious that the art of negotiation was outside her wheelhouse.

"You mentioned earlier that there would not be a debate," continued Vera, eyes downcast. "You are exceedingly *important,* and we cannot afford to lose you from a careless turn of phrase. So, Greta and I believed our concern was worth repeating."

"I'll be fine," said Jonas. "How far is Moütz?"

"Uh." Vera drew a step to consult her internal map. "Another five miles south," she said, and bolstered her reply by firmly tugging the collar of her chest plate. "Yes, roughly five miles. It's not far. But, Devil, about the Still…"

Jonas closed an eye. "I'm starving. Are you starving?" When his eye opened it was pegged to the sky. "Ritz! You three! Score us some rabbits and have a fire waiting for us in Moütz!"

"Devil," said Vera. "If I may? The Still —"

"I'll be fine," repeated Jonas reassuringly. He swept past the knight and bounded over the embankment. "These five miles won't walk themselves!" he shouted as he backpedaled among the group. "And I'm famished! Come on!"

The crunch of their footsteps rebounded from every jagged outcropping outthrust from the cliffside, and eventually the sound concluded somewhere in the quiet, solemn valley far below. A distinct boundary seemed to have been crossed a few steps behind them, where the road had come to an end.

The way that the hillside dipped beneath his feet reminded Jonas of a steep waterslide. He stood at the peak gazing down on a canyon that spanned endlessly for miles. Along the wall, through the mist, he could make out ladders arranged in places that crept upward from the basin to the natural awnings that jutted in places. A few stray ladders concluded partway through their ascent, while others managed to persevere to the top, leapfrogging the stone slab platforms.

A tingle lanced through Jonas' boots as he imagined stepping upon the topmost ladder rung. The sheer elevation of the drop caused his lip to twitch. Even as the Leeds Devil, he preferred stable terrain.

While Jonas gaped, Isaac walked the basin ledge, and the knights began unfastening their chest armor. The Still held a finger to his chin staring down into the depths, muttering beneath his breath.

"Here," said Greta, offering her backplate. Then she whispered in his ear, "You're going to want this." Somewhere inside his stomach the tingles from his boots coalesced with a tingly wave from his scalp.

"Thanks," Jonas obliged, accepting the steel plate. "But what are we —"

After retreating a few steps from the tremendous slant, Vera rushed forward and cupped her rear with her chest plate, attacking the slope as a sledding hill. The knight whooped along her course, right before becoming a speck.

Jonas side-eyed Greta. "Oh."

"Your turn, Devil." Greta's lips creased into a vulpine smile. "I will be right behind you."

The chest plate seemed solid in Jonas' hands, and the curvature along the base sparked an idea. He pressed it to his chest, preparing to dive down the hill as if it were covered in snow. "See you," said Jonas, right before charging headlong over the drop. Greta made a remark, but he was too far gone to hear.

Weightlessly he sailed, fearing that he had overshot his jump and would plummet to his death. Perhaps his companions would bury him somewhere within the ashy gray landscape oozing far, far below, between the tufts of mist.

Wonder who'd they tap to pen my eulogy? Before Jonas could envision the person who would perform his short life's tribute, his body aligned parallel with the hillside, flawlessly joining one to the other. The contours rimming the base of the chest plate cupped his lower torso, and unlike the cheap saucer sleds from home, the hardened steel prevented his stomach from feeling any divots or bumps.

Though absent the soft cushioning of snow beneath him, Jonas felt as though he were sledding at a terrifically fast rate of speed. He squinted against the swiftly rushing air, wishing for goggles. His eyes grew dry, but upon penetrating the fog, wind whipped corneas experienced a dose of relief from the moisture waiting within the mist. The wave of dampness scurried across his face, leaving his eyelashes thick with saturation.

The fog began to peel away while his body leveled, meeting the resistance of flat, solid ground. The ride was finally coming to a close, but his momentum continued at a frightful clip. Jonas centered his attention on an irregular brick wall that, he could have sworn a mere moment hence had been miles away, now rushed to greet him. To his immediate right he caught the refrain of a panicked Vera, and he assumed that was his cue to bail.

He rolled to his right, released the back plate, and collected his hands to his chin. The leading edge of the steel plate struck a tightly packed tuft of grass sending it on a harmless cartwheel. It was after this that Jonas discovered an impediment on his own, and of course this was not a gentle bump of wayward fescue. No, not to be, for his came in the form of a protruding wall of solid hearth stone. His casual tummy slide abruptly wrenched into a tumble and upon his second or third somersault, he glimpsed the wall at roughly another rotation's distance. Instinctively he clenched from his teeth to his tailbone, bracing for a cataclysmic death.

Whichever body part that would be dealt the blow, at this point, was a roll of the die.

Jonas had never been an athlete and had never played organized sports. Yet he always wondered what it would feel like to be that football guy who punches through the breakaway banner beneath the Friday night lights.

Now he did. More or less.

The delirious haze produced by his breakneck speed prevented him from noticing that the wall was fairly dilapidated, harboring roughly one heart piece in its dwindling health bar. And just like a boned-up Kool-Aid Man, Jonas pitched through the wall as if it were nothing but filter paper.

Time faltered as he tried to collect himself, shaking his head, pressing off the ground. Believing it to be all part of a haze, his upright rise was unexpectedly simple, as a pair of Ritts had assumed an elbow, lifting him without a sound. Jonas hovered, suspended for a single breath before the gargoyles returned his boots to earth.

"Thanks, boys," he said to the Ritts, slapping at a clod of dirt on his left thigh. "Or girls," he revised. The Ritts replied with a solemn nod and flung themselves heavenward.

The space left in the Ritts' wake was immediately assumed by a very concerned-looking Vera. "Are you harmed?" she exhaled, looking Jonas up and down.

"I'm fine," replied Jonas. "You should see the other guy."

Vera chuckled.

So saying, Jonas turned around to take in his surroundings. "Whoa," he said reverently. His tonal shift downgraded Vera's smile into a frown. "Is this Moütz?" he asked the knight.

"What remains of it," Vera answered.

"What happened?"

"Grass stains!"

Jonas whirled at Isaac's roar. White and gray powder intermixed the breeze as the Still parted the ashy landscape.

Vera gave ground, backing several paces.

The Still moved with dark ferocity, and Jonas etched comparisons between him and Elias. He could easily be convinced that they shared a common ancestor somewhere along one of the contorted branches of the Monster Family Tree. If Elias were a raven, then Isaac was a crow.

Isaac began to paw at Jonas' tunic as if it were on fire.

"Come on, man!" protested Jonas. "Give me some air!"

A forked vein appeared on the Still's forehead, pulsating with wrath. "Cease moving, Devil," he demanded. "I must inspect each stain. Understand that the deeper stains will need to be pre-treated with a rare and expensive salve."

"Fine." Jonas relented, allowing his limbs to tumble loose. He turned his attention to Vera while Isaac continued to probe. "So what happened?"

"The Terrens," replied Vera.

"They burned the village to the ground?"

"It was more of a city at the time." Vera chewed her thumbnail.

"Very uncool," remarked Jonas. His eyes descended on a burnt and tattered rag doll with one braided pigtail intact. "Did the people make it out alive?"

Vera's gaze became unfocused as she beheld the wreckage, for the moment she could not find words.

From behind, Jonas heard Greta sliding down the face of the canyon, the elation in her voice contrasting sharply with the scene before him.

"Most did not make it," said Vera once the echoes of Greta's laughter dwindled to vapor. "The survivors fled north to Brimon."

"Brimon?" asked Jonas.

A familiar presence emerged beneath Jonas, offering an answer before the knight could reply. "The border village we departed from is Brimon." Scary and Posh had elbowed Isaac out of the way, trying to get as close to Jonas as possible.

"Oh." Jonas withdrew from the attentive Hylda. "I forgot its name. My bad." The Hylda filled the gap, stepping past Isaac who did not follow. "Can you give me some space? Vera was talking to me."

"The Terrens razed Moütz," said Isaac. "As they do." He paused in a way that told everyone he was not done speaking. "Unlike the usual war strategies of old, the Terrens began their campaign far to the south, far from Serpentfel, far from their home. An admirably risky maneuver."

Vera both grunted and growled at once. "A desperate move," she spat into the ash at her feet. "There is nothing admirable about those craven swine herders!"

"Craven?" Isaac swiveled toward Jonas. His expression conveying: *get a load of this junk, huh?* "Say what you will about the Family Terren, but cowards they are not."

"Okay, okay." Jonas yielded space from the Still's advance. "I'll take your word for it."

"I was addressing the Terren exile," Isaac clarified.

Vera shifted her feet as if she was smoothing a bump in a rug. Jonas had fallen witness to many guilty expressions before, and her mug exuded nothing but pure unadulterated guilt. Some sort of secret lid had just been blown off.

"What did that imp just call you?" Greta had arrived, sounding murderous. "Did he just —"

"Greta," Vera chopped through the knight's fury. "Leave it alone."

Greta balked like a bridled horse driven aside. "An *exile?*" she hissed incredulously.

"We should get out ahead of this," said Vera to Greta. Then her eyes found Jonas. "It is true, I am Terren born. *We* are Terren born." She glided a hand over to Greta's wrist. "Perhaps now is as good a time as any to explain?"

"Maybe," replied Jonas. "Or, could we go over this some other time?"

The knights stared at the ground as if it would swallow them. Vera was the first to hazard a question. "You're not interested in an explanation for our deception?"

"Honestly, I'm more interested in that crazy awesome sword. That's why we're here, isn't it? And I have a month to make everything all right. And also..." He scratched at his stubbled jawline. That was a new thing, stubble. He did not know how many days he would need to burn in order to sport a majestic beard, but it would likely take longer than he wished to spend in this world. The beard would have to wait, his hunger, however. "There it is!"

"Impossible," Isaac gasped, crossing ahead of Jonas' finger. "You can see Dafodhel?"

"No, I wish," said Jonas with a laugh. "I see lunch."

As Isaac had been gazing into the distance, believing Jonas to have heightened vision, he had overlooked a Ritts duo turning a makeshift spit overtop a modest fire. A third Ritts was nearby, working through a pile of recently slain rabbits, performing intricate slices with his claws and peeling back the blushing meat underneath.

"Ah, yes," said Isaac, salivating. "How could I forget?"

Raw meat had never appealed to Jonas, preferring char over pink when it came to cheeseburgers. But for the first time in his life he felt compelled to give hare tartare a try.

Vera and Greta walked by the stack of pre-stripped rabbits and snagged one each, sucking them down like milkshakes. Once the essences had been drained, the knights began to peel the fur and dine, skipping the entire cooking process altogether. Isaac had done the same, but he was much hungrier, placing a bunny in each hand and alternating greedily between the two.

Jonas nibbled at an overly blackened corner of a rabbit strip, picturing himself plunging his teeth into a freshly peeled rabbit. Though the notion no longer grossed him out, he decided to simply enjoy the free meal and hold off on the raw stuff for the time being. After all, the Ritts had gone through the trouble of building a fire and a spit and everything. You can't just pee on hospitality like that.

Show some class, he thought. "Yeah, *class,*" he said. The others may have begged explanation if their slurping and gnashing had not smothered his words.

Scary pulled at Jonas' tunic and offered another cooked haunch.

"I'm good for now," said Jonas, pushing the meat away. "Thanks, Scary."

The Hylda would not be dissuaded, rising on tiptoes, persisting with adorably horrifying optimism.

"Fine," relented Jonas. He took the gift and pretended to chew and faked a swallow. "Yum, yum." He beamed down at Scary and discarded the hunk over his shoulder after she skittered away.

The burnt, forsaken ground stretching out from beneath Jonas' feet reminded him of his mother's ransacked shop. Memories, images, people, all of them gone. Lives built for generations only to be trampled and disposed of. Here and — *poof* — gone, before you know it.

The Terrens do what they do just as easily as he had tossed aside that chunk of rabbit meat that Scary and Posh had pressed upon him.

How many children lost their mothers and fathers? How many parents lost their children? Jonas' thoughts drifted to his mother once again. How many Moütz clock shops were now crispy piles of cinder?

The crushing blows dealt by the endless streams of unchecked corruption nearly brought Jonas to tears. The Terrens and the Polish Mafia may as well have been donning the same team jerseys.

A reckoning is coming.

"Vera," said Jonas. The darkness encompassing his tone froze the knight's jaw mid-chew. "Where is Daffodil?"

"Not far," she said, but came out sounding like, "Ocklar."

"Take your time and finish that mouthful," encouraged Jonas.

Beneath a nervous smile, she chewed and swallowed. "Not far," she repeated.

"Is that so?" Isaac flicked a blob of red goo from his index finger. "Pray tell."

Jonas ignored the Still. "Great," he said with zero enthusiasm. "Let's walk and talk shall we?"

The knights traded looks while wiping the juice and fur from their hands. Once their hands were moderately clean, Greta drew a line from the sun to the opposite horizon while Vera counted invisible pickets along the base of the canyon.

"The blade lies in this direction," revealed Vera after a great pause.

"Do you know the precise location?" asked Isaac without binding his disbelief.

Greta glanced at the horizon. "Not the *precise* location, but—"

"That's well and good." Jonas and the Hylda were already several steps in Vera's indicated direction. "How 'bout we start the *walking and talking?*"

"We do not know exactly where Dafodhel is," began Vera, quickening to a jog. "But we do know who has him."

Isaac strode at his normal pace. Presumably his sense of urgency had been expended sometime before their departure from Brimon. "Who, exactly?" he called.

"Yeah, who?" insisted Jonas.

"The Yéne who stalks the forest surrounding Moütz," replied Vera.

"Now that," said Greta hurriedly ahead of Isaac's scorn, "the defenders of Moütz are gone, the beast has become emboldened and has widened his hunting sphere."

"And what does that have to do with finding the sword?" asked Jonas, his tone reeking of Isaac's suspicion. "Please explain," he corrected.

"Everything," replied Vera with a nod, acknowledging Jonas' courteous shift. "Once we espy the Yéne, we follow him to his lair, and thereafter it is simply a measure of time before we slip in and reclaim Dafodhel."

"The Yéne's broadened hunting area will make him much easier to spot," added Greta. "Additionally —" She stiffened, causing the party to do the same, save for Isaac who used the refrain as a means to catch up. "The ash makes for easier tracking." Greta picked her steps toward a disturbed mound in the sea of sun-bleached powder. "He was here right before dawn broke," she said, kneeling to admire the enormous paw print. "Roving westward."

Vera sneered at Isaac. "Which means..."

"The lair should be somewhere this way," concluded Jonas, pointing along the course they had been tracking. "Well done."

CHAPTER 13

Jonas' feet dangled freely above an emerald sea of moss. Vera had led them to an old, long abandoned stone fortification that overlooked a lush gully. Not many trees had sprung from the terrain, and the ones that thrived appeared in juvenile stages.

From high atop the crumbly entablature, Jonas viewed the comings and goings of varying creatures and monsters. The forest was packed with action. Back home, whenever he ventured into a forest — which was rare — the most chart-topping prospects were butterflies and squirrels.

After taking his seat and refusing another helping of dried rabbit from Scary, Jonas noticed three wolves carving through the vegetation. They stalked forward with precision. Some distance beyond the wolves, inside a copse of elms, a family of thylacines were at rest, lounging. And bisecting between, a prolonged line of prehistoric-looking turkeys persuaded the bracken, unaware of the wolves.

Recently, in Biology Class, Jonas had learned some fascinating details about thylacines, or Tasmanian tigers. The thylacine had not been feline at all, and was actually the largest carnivorous marsupial on earth, but the fact that they had been totally wiped from the earth tagged the subject with a disheartening asterisk. When he had inquired of Greta about this, she had briefly explained that whenever the last monster from Jonas' realm died, then the line would somehow carry on in this one. She did not understand how it worked, only knew the result.

"How long do you think we'll be waiting for the Yéne to show?" asked Jonas, deciding that he would circle back to the *extinction* discussion later.

"We'll wait as long as it takes," replied Vera.

"Should not be too long," Greta supplied. The knight sat beside Posh to Jonas' left. "Those wolves usually hunt alongside the Yéne. I think he should return shortly." Delicately she returned her sword to its scabbard, careful not to register a sound. "Not too long, Devil," she concluded, whispering over Posh's head.

Jonas felt his scalp tingling once again. The way the taller knight had been checking him out recently made Jonas grateful for the Hyldas' persistence in latching themselves to his hips. He had enough going on.

"They hunt together?"

Greta nodded. "The Yéne resembles a wolf," she said. Jonas was grateful that she had turned the corner from intimate whisperings. "Well, mostly."

"Its deadly leap is much like a lion's, I believe," Vera speculated. "Lions and cobras," she added.

"Okay..."

"Yes," Greta agreed. "But its top half and tail are almost spider-like... no not spider-like... as I said, it's hard to describe."

"The Beast of Gévaudan," offered Isaac, entering the conversation.

Jonas offered a confused expression, encouraging the Still to go on.

"That is one famous example of a Yéne that had once entered your realm," replied Isaac. "I had hoped that you were familiar with the tale, but it appears I was mistaken."

"Coming from the guy who couldn't remember his own name..."

The Still yelped a laugh, startling a brightly colored junk drawer of songbirds into the sky. Below, the troop of turkey also took flight, abandoning the gully. The wolves, whose spines had only just aligned for a synchronized pounce, sagged wearily and gazed up at the Still, annoyed and defeated.

Vera and Greta hissed, urging silence.

"Fair enough," said Isaac to Jonas, smiling, ignoring the knights. "The message that may have shot over the folk in your realm's collective heads is this: You cannot kill a Yéne, you may only hope to contain it."

Jonas switched his attention to Vera. "You can't kill a Yéne?"

"If you do, then you would be the first," replied Vera, scowling at Isaac.

"That's why the plan is to observe," stated Greta, then locked snake eyes onto Isaac. *"Quietly."* The hatred within Greta's eyes made Jonas want to look anywhere else.

"The wolves are gone," said Jonas. Scary and Posh reacted instantly, using Jonas' shoulders to stand.

Each strand of the Still's attention was suddenly pulled from Greta. Hastily he tracked a line from his knee to the thicket, where the wolves had been sulking only moments before. "Fancy a game of cat and mouse?"

"You really shouldn't say things that make me want to question you," said Jonas.

"I felt like it was more of a yes or no sort of thing," replied Isaac with an apologetic tilt of his head. He seemed about to continue but was brought short by a distinct crackling of underbrush on the downside of the gully. "Never mind," breathed Isaac.

No one dared move.

Ever since Jonas' arrival to this realm, it seemed with brutal regularity, he faced ever more scarier things.

The Yéne was unreal. Jonas thought he was hallucinating. What Greta had mentioned earlier about the Yéne, moving spider-like, upheld grains of truth, but Jonas detected more shark in the twisting curvature of its spinal column. It was almost as if the monster was wholly composed of cartilage bound within tightly manicured fur. At first the Yéne came across as a huge wolf, two or three times larger than the gray wolves he had seen earlier, but the longer you held your eyes upon it, the more you realized how wrong you were.

Select ten apex predators from Earth and extract their most sinister essence, then distill that into a syringe and inject it into the biggest dire wolf that ever hunted an ice cap, and, in a nutshell, that is a Yéne.

The Beast of Gévaudan, Jonas thought. *I'll have to look that up.*

Soon the head of the beast was out of sight and only his tail lingered. The Yéne had stopped just outside the gully's final crease. The thylacines that had occupied that space had made themselves scarce not long after the wolves had fled.

"Wait," Vera warned, whispering sharp. "We follow when…" She held a breath, tethering her neck muscles tight, awaiting the Yéne's disappearance. "We no longer see him," she exhaled, several moments after the beast's tail had vanished.

The knights agreed upon the route, tracking the Yéne from the highest ridge, opting to maintain a healthy distance while still managing to capture a glint of silvery fur. It was a very fine line that they chose to tread.

Before shrugging from the ruins, Jonas had instructed the Ritts to sound an alarm should the beast grow wise to their chase. Jonas had found comfort in this failsafe until Greta remarked, "If the Yéne wants to kill you, he will. Alarm or not."

"But still," replied Jonas, "I'd rather see it coming, you know?"

Greta pondered the statement for a second. "Not in this case."

"Oh."

Gradually the sounds of midsummer died as they crept deeper into the Yéne's demesne. Creatures that thrived in darkness were all that dared make their homes here. A sign may as well been posted that read, "You're going to be really sad here." Even the trees adhered to the edict, appearing gaunt and gloomy, heads dejectedly bowed to the earth as if rinsed of their last shilling.

Aside from overwhelming despair, the acrid stench of decay began blistering their nostrils.

Isaac cursed then muttered, "We must be nigh."

Mere steps ahead of the Yéne, a great cave arose. Darkness seemed beholden to its cavernous maw, for daylight went inside and never returned. At its foundation, sun-bleached bones and skeletons lay scattered, as if they had been released within a torrential belch. A few among the dead had flesh yet clinging and had been left to rot beneath the afternoon sun.

I hope you have prepared yourself, young Devil... The clear, small voice that had greeted Jonas upon his return, in the dank tree cave, spoke inside Jonas' skull. *This is quite a leap for someone who has yet to take a life.*

Jonas smacked the side of his head, hoping to dislodge the voice.

"Get out of my head!"

Greta was before him with a dire look scrawled from forehead to chin. "You must be quiet my Devil!" she begged. "Please!"

"There's something speaking inside my head," confessed Jonas.

Isaac and the knights looked to one another, sharing expressions of grave concern. Briskly the Still conducted Jonas behind a tree, relocating him safely from sight and sound. The Hylda nipped behind and sprang to Jonas' side once the space afforded.

"Do not speak," said Isaac, urging Jonas to sit. "I can tell that you have questions."

"As do we," said Vera, flattening onto her belly, keeping an eye pinned to the Yéne's lair. "This had not been foretold."

"I need that sword," Jonas snarled, generating an unexpected wave of anger.

Vera and Isaac shared looks of great unease, while Greta blushed and fanned her face.

Jonas turned to Vera. "You got us to the beast's doorstep," he began, his arms pulsating with wrath. "Now tell me how to get the sword."

Vera gulped a dry swallow and eased her eyes overhead. "Easy," she said. "Bid your Ritts go and retrieve him."

"They will die," said Jonas, easing back. "Was that your plan all along? Just throw waves of Ritz at the problem until it's solved?"

"Not all of them will die," Vera explained. "And yes, that was our plan. How else could we succeed? The Yéne has no known weakness. We can only hope to overwhelm him with numbers and pray that one of your pawns succeeds."

"And to hell with the ones that don't make it?"

"That's what pawns are for."

"What if I don't see them as *pawns?*"

Vera's mouth moved wordlessly before the words streamed forth. "How-how do you view them?" She balked. "When the Lancethanes gave chase you discarded the Hylda like spent matches. You had started with every Hylda in known existence and now you have merely two."

"Spent matches?" Jonas spat. "I tried to help them..." The groundswell of conflicting emotions tripped a breaker somewhere in his brain. "I tried to help them, but they wouldn't let me..." Then an unseen hand flicked the breaker to life. "Did you just say, *every Hylda in existence?*"

"I thought it went without saying," replied Vera slowly. "Your influence would have drawn more out by now."

Jonas knelt and drew the Hylda to his sides. "Scary and Posh are all that's left of their kind?" he asked.

"I thought you knew," replied Vera.

"Oh, man," Jonas lamented. The witches embraced Jonas and touched their foreheads to his arms.

"Sacrifices are made all the time," Greta intervened. "For you to make everything right in the Riverlands, the Hylda willingly give their lives. It's all for the greater good, a return to Leeds rule. And they understand that. So do the Ritts. As flippant as the word *pawn* may sound to you, Vera didn't mean any dishonor by it. But in the end, that's what they are. And in another sense, that's what we all are." Greta balled her hands into fists. "Right now, you just have to ask yourself one question." She held the moment to peer upward at the Ritts circling through the forest canopy. "How badly do you want that sword?"

Now upon the ground, Jonas found that the cave mouth yawned much, much wider than he first inferred. This sudden change in perspective revealed further unwelcome details.

Foremost being, there was a drastic three-foot slope that dropped like a slide from the opening of the cave, and the bones and skeletons that were sprinkled all over the Yéne's front lawn were actually several layers thick, piled atop one another.

Every step, every inch that Vera and Greta took, leading Jonas as close to the lair as possible was jam-packed with worry. If he did not require a decent view of the cave's interior in order to better augment his orders to the Ritts, then they would not have dared tread so near. Wisely, Isaac had opted to hang behind and observe.

The idea was to get close, but not *too* close.

If only one of them had stowed a spyglass or binoculars in their packs, Jonas thought, side-eyeing Vera. *If only someone who had the knowledge of where we would end up —*

"Devil," whispered Vera, lying prone, urging him to crawl to her. She and Greta had stopped to sink down a few yards from the bone clearing's edge. The tall grass that had long ago gone to seed, bobbing and weaving in the breeze, was all that stood between them and their adversary. Their invincible adversary. "This is as far as we go," she said, shuffling awkwardly on her elbows to give Jonas and his Hylda more space.

"You sure you don't want to just crawl in?" said Jonas. "I mean, we might as well."

It took Vera a moment to realize that Jonas was being sarcastic. "Funny," she remarked with flat affect. "Whenever you are prepared." Her index finger sprouted up, indicating the Ritts perched above.

From the host, Jonas had selected ten. Five to distract and five to retrieve the blade. The rest had been instructed to standby and be ready if their brethren failed.

Jonas had performed a brief, silent ceremony beforehand for the chosen Ritts. After borrowing Greta's sword, he honored them, dubbing each of the ten as knights. It was all he could think to do. When Jonas tapped the gargoyles' shoulders with the cold steel, he struggled to swallow his grief. Meanwhile the Ritts, having understood their orders, regarded the whole ordeal with confusion.

Now in the present Jonas admired the solemn Ritts in the trees staring into the heart of the storm, claws grinding branches, awaiting their command.

The greater good, Jonas thought, recalling Greta's words. There was something hidden within that phrase that brought worry... the words did not feel right. But he needed that sword. *The ends justify the means.* He groaned internally as yet another platitude bubbled to the surface.

What am I becoming?

Crumpled to the left of the lair's opening an armored figure reflected a sparkle of daylight. From chin to belly a deep, bloodied crater had spelled his demise. Apparently the Yéne had deemed the poor soul not fit for consumption and left him to decompose in the elements.

"That dude." Jonas nudged Vera and indicated the steel-clad dead man. "He looks like a recent kill."

Through the reedy grass Vera caught sight of whom Jonas referred. "Ah," she said and nestled back down. "That is an

Oathsworne. In short, a keeper of Dafodhel. If not for him, Dafodhel may have fallen into Terren hands."

"Gotcha."

"When the Terrens descended upon Moütz, the Oathsworne spirited Dafodhel to the last place a Terren, or anyone else, would dare tread. That brave soul over yonder sacrificed himself, sprinting that dicey terrain and then pitching the blade inside the cavern right before the Yéne smote him."

"Why didn't the Yéne eat him?"

Vera shrugged. "The Yéne is said to be a finicky eater. He kills many but eats few." Once again, she indicated the Ritts. "On your word, Devil."

CHAPTER 14

Your sacrifices will mean something, Jonas transmitted to the waiting Ritts. *The time has come. The ones chosen for distraction, make your move now!*

When the Ritts took off, branches snapped. Their shadows combed the boneyard, each diminishing in turn as the five gargoyles alighted before the cave.

Jonas sent an order to the remaining five, instructing them to move once the distraction team entered.

The Ritts entered, darting into the darkness and then a snarl like none other emanated from deep within. The Yéne reacted instantly, like a tripwire. The gargoyles began squalling and shrieking, fighting for their lives.

An admirable strategy. The voice in Jonas' head reared around for another go, causing him to snarl.

"Quiet you," seethed Jonas, steeling his attention toward the second wave of gargoyles flashing for the depths.

Vera spared a moment to flick an admonishing glare his way, batting her mouth with a finger, encouraging him to take his own advice. The Devil placed them in further peril each time he spoke.

Jonas was not paying attention to the knight. His Ritts were being slaughtered before him and he was, once again, helpless to do anything. Inside the cave, he could sense that two were still alive. He imagined their bodies flinging about the low unyielding ceiling, trying their best to avoid getting snagged by a claw.

A guttural shriek sounded and Jonas felt another life lost. Only one remained.

The thief squad entered amidst their brethren's final appeals for life.

You should have dug a pitfall, said the small voice, adorning the backdrop of renewed screaming. The thieves had been detected immediately. *Drawn the beast out and caused it to fall. Although, on second thought, the Yéne is renowned for cleverness, so perhaps that may not have worked either. Alas! The pit could have doubled as your grave should the plan not have worked out. No use in allowing a good hole go to waste.*

"Shut up!"

Vera and Greta tightened their chest plates to the earth, twinning mortified looks. Surely the beast had heard the Devil's shout. Even above the screaming, dying Ritts. The Yéne was not ordinary.

Send more Ritts to lure the beast out, the small voice advised beneath the sounds of flesh puckered from bone.

"You lure him out!"

I cannot, the voice replied. *For I am already inside.*

"What?!"

Compel your Ritts to create a disturbance from without.

Jonas gritted his teeth, pulling three Ritts from the central host that had been placed well beyond the lair and instructed them to make racket outside the cave. His heart was breaking, hearing his Ritts crying out, dying, and he did not want to lose anymore. Three of their number somehow felt perfect and cruel all at once.

Circling an unhealthy distance from the lair, the trio obeyed, clamoring and carrying on, attempting to lure the Yéne out into the daylight.

A vulgar silence dropped within the cave. Instinctively, Jonas knew that the ten had fallen. Posh and Scary shimmied closer.

Upon an unexpected heartbeat, the shadows of the cavern winnowed around a great silvery coat, marred in viscera. The Yéne stalked forward, warily eyeing the fluttering Ritts, wolf ears set to swiveling. In a language that should have been foreign to Jonas, the Ritts hurled insults that he somehow understood. Well, mostly, from what he could gleam, one Ritts was congratulating the Yéne's mother on her vast stockpile of social diseases. Another cackled indecipherably while the last repeated "Glompback!" over and over.

"I should have dug a hole," intoned Jonas.

Outside of time and space, the Yéne pounced from earth to sky rending one cackling Ritts from existence. The other two billowed higher, beating their wings frantically to get clear of the beast's influence.

Send more! urged the voice, losing composure.

Jonas dropped his head. "No!" he screamed into the ground, tears flowing. "I won't lose another one!"

"Devil!" Greta shouted inside a whisper. "What are you doing?!"

Placidly the Hylda's hands fell from the Devil as he rose.

"Not one more!" Jonas accused the Yéne.

The beast focused eyes on Jonas, arresting the skyward lunge he had been preparing.

You fool! the small voice berated, but Jonas was not listening.

He broke from the thicket.

The Yéne's weight drifted to his rear limbs, gathering a defensive stance.

With near perfect timing, one of the Ritts spat, "Glompback!" from above, diverting the Yéne's focus. Within that glimmer of a distraction, Jonas faked a leap and pivoted hard to his left.

The Yéne balked but recovered quickly, wheeling to aim a strike Jonas' side.

You beautiful fool! The small voice sounded on the verge tears.

The beast's swipe caught Jonas just beneath his right hipbone. He conceded a single staggered step, and pressed on with added ferocity, enraged by the pain. The entrance widened frantically as he hastened toward it.

The voice piped up excitedly as the cavern cast a cool blanket of shade over Jonas. *Six paces to your right!*

Jonas spurred to the right and dove, curling his body while clinching the cloth grip of a sword. He resolved a squishy somersault atop the remnants of his Ritts' sacrifice, losing his footing in the mire of gore. Darkness shrouded Dafodhel's appearance but he discovered the blade's true length when he planted it upon the cave floor for stability.

Easy now! The voice warned. *Another strike like that and you're liable to take a chip from me!*

The voice in his head belonged to the fabled blade! Jonas tucked the revelation down, there would be time for introductions later.

Clasp my blade and hilt! Dafodhel advised.

Jonas obeyed, and as his hand glimpsed the blade's razor sharpness, the sword morphed into a dull wooden haft before he could sustain a cut. His other hand experienced the same transfiguration, and he discovered that he was no longer holding a longsword. Dafodhel had become a spear!

Drive the beast back! Dafodhel shouted. Her tenor reverberated deep into the cavern, beyond the walls of Jonas' head.

Past the shadow curtain, the Yéne strode toward the cave, his head recessed between ridged shoulders.

Jonas caught the Yéne unaware, thrusting the tip of the spear into the beast's face. With unnatural reflexes, the Yéne recoiled and reared, avoiding the blow. Violently his hindquarters rebounded from the skeletons while his front claws tore trenches in the soil beneath the layers of bone.

Move into the open! Dafodhel's voice had returned inside Jonas' head, sounding out of breath. *Face him and angle your back toward the forest!*

Taking the cue, Jonas tore across the crunchy ground, bone fragments jabbing at his boot soles along the way.

Time felt as though it stuttered around the Yéne's attack, lashing Jonas in the exact same spot below his hip, launching the dulled pain into pure agony.

He is cautious, observed Dafodhel.

Jonas stumbled back, favoring his side, cupping the rent flesh beneath his belt.

Return your hand to the haft!

Jonas did as he was told and dragged his attention back to the Yéne. "I'm losing blood," he said, releasing a shuddering breath. "Like, a lot of blood."

Dafodhel did not respond. The weapon seemed to be ruminating on other matters.

The Yéne appeared to be contemplating a stratagem as well. After a few breaths spent in scrutiny of this new prey, he plodded to the right and lunged unexpectedly, snapping his jaws at a fair distance. Jonas flinched and retreated a step.

He is attempting to herd you back into the cave, explained Dafodhel.

Jonas riposted, shooting back to where he had been standing.

The Yéne inclined his head.

Good. Now. Dafodhel took a measured breath. *When he feints like that again, I want you to retreat into the mouth of the cave. Make it look clumsy. Really sell it.*

"Shouldn't be too hard," remarked Jonas, slipping on a loose femur bone. The pain from his wound had grown negligible but the blood pooling under the arch of his right foot indicated a time restraint. If he did not staunch it soon, he would be in for a total collapse.

"Glompback! Glompback!" The Ritts continued spewing the insult.

The Yéne cast an eye upward and faked another charge. Jonas zagged to the left, pivoting hard, and clipped a toe on the gnarl of a knucklebone.

Well played! I daresay your feigned ineptitude appears masterfully rehearsed! Dafodhel praised the performance while Jonas tried not to die. He stumbled to the finish line, staving a horrible crash by using his spear as a staff.

The Yéne bought it; an expression passing on his pointy face that Jonas recognized all too well: disappointment and compassion blended together. The beast had believed the Devil would pitch a better fight, and it seemed that he had fallen beneath the beast's expectations.

Hold me as a cudgel!

"A what?!" Jonas faltered.

A cudgel! Like a club or a mace!

The Yéne approached.

"None of those things are similar!"

Dafodhel let out a pained breath. *Like a club! Knuckles together at the base!*

Jonas arranged his hands, feeling as if he were waving Old Glory instead of a weapon, the spear blade at the top balancing clumsily. He felt naked, exposed, totally unprepared for the forthcoming attack.

He will feint once and then rebound into a death surge.

"How do you —"

Trust me! When he springs back, drop to the right and rise, swinging me upward as if I am a water-logged oar!

If Jonas were going to request clarification, the Yéne determined that the time for questions had come and gone. The beast lurched forward, mimicking one falling out of sync, just as Dafodhel had predicted.

Drop!

Jonas closed his eyes and the last frame he saw before shifting his balance was the Yéne unfurling his jaws, siphoning weight into his rippling haunches. When Jonas' knee touched down, the unwieldy tip of his spear ricocheted off a bone.

Rise! Swing!

The weapon's haft increased in his grip while assuming a substantial heft. Yet this additional burden did not slow Jonas' rise in the least. His eyes flared open in time to see the Yéne leap. The beast's lips peeled back, readying a bite that would see Jonas' head and shoulders shorn clean.

Jonas had already begun his upward stroke with the notion that he was wielding a heavier spear. In a drastic shift, the spear had now, along its course toward the side of the Yéne's head, transformed into a sledgehammer.

The Yéne's hubris, as is the case for the powerful, proved his undoing.

Dafodhel caught the beast behind his left ear, submerging through fur and tissue, connecting wickedly with spinal bones. All the light within the beast's eyes flickered and failed. Jonas completed his hip rotation while tucking his shoulders beneath the trailing hindquarters, sloughing the Yéne's great weight to the earth.

The thrill of triumph drove him forward. He raised the hammer for another blow while the beast lay still.

Nay! shouted Dafodhel. *Run! Flee! The beast will recover faster than you think!*

Jonas ignored the weapon and brought the hammer down, aiming for the Yéne's heaving ribcage. He missed, as Dafodhel transformed into an everyday letter opener, leaving him twirling in place.

"Let me finish him!" Jonas screamed into his palm, tears of anger bursting. "He must pay!"

No! defied Dafodhel, rocking the inner portions of Jonas' headspace. *See! He stirs!*

The Yéne's elbows lengthened and his claws contracted, seeking something to shred. His head twitched while growls churned deep in his chest. With eyes pinned shut, the beast acted as one immersed in a stormy fever dream.

We must fly!

Wheeling to his right, Jonas caught the sense in Dafodhel's claims. Lady Luck had smiled on him for one bright glimmering moment, but now it was time to cut his losses.

"Devil! This way!" It was Isaac on the edge of the clearing.

Jonas turned and corrected his sprint, loose bones scattering beneath his swivel. He could feel his wound prying itself wider by centimeters.

"Do not stop!" urged Dafodhel from Jonas' hand. The weapon sounded in broken stereo after Jonas had grown accustomed to hearing the voice. "Fly from this place!"

The knights and the Hylda had fled to a thin flock of trees some twenty yards from the lair. They stood, waiting. Jonas wished that they had gotten further, but it warmed his heart to know that they had not completely abandoned him.

"Go! Run!" Isaac shouted, waving frantically at the shapes assembled within the threadbare copse. The Still maintained a purposeful distance ahead of Jonas, five or six steps at least, a feat unto its own for they both moved at a blistering rate.

A roar of lament and frustration picked up behind them.

Suddenly, hemming their escape path on all sides, wolves began to bay.

Amidst pounding feet and hurried breaths, Dafodhel had resumed her demands for acceleration while the walls began to pinch ever inward in Jonas' blearing vision. And within her shouts, an idea came to Jonas, then his eyes fell from focus. All this running was not doing his wound any favors. His steps ebbed and Isaac looked back, sharp eyes affixed with panic.

"Devil!" the Still yelled, slowing. Then the Hylda were there, tugging an elbow apiece. Further ahead Vera and Greta had turned as well, rolling shoulders with blades drawn, resolving themselves to fight.

The amount of blood loss had finally taken its toll.

Jonas' head swam, then somebody pulled the plug and drained it all empty, and he began to drop. Cognition flickered during his fall but he managed to catch himself on a knee.

"Stand and run!" The voice ruptured from Jonas' closed fist.

Bristling fur containing fangs readied for carnage were being drawn like curtains around the party. Vera and Greta were backed one to the other staring down the horde. Isaac whirled in front of Jonas with daggers in each hand. Scary and Posh hissed and hunched as if they were withholding some sort of evil secret.

"Why do you laugh?!" Dafodhel's voice quailed in disbelief. "All is lost!"

"Because," replied Jonas. "They don't know what I can do." And only sparing a single moment for Dafodhel's disbelief to deepen, Jonas, while the tunnel crammed itself shut, whispered, "Ritz... now..."

CHAPTER 15

The Ritts fell upon the wolves like a firestorm. Some were hefted from the ground to be torn asunder, while others were spared the sky shredding only to suddenly find their faces speared several inches into the soil, suffocating in dirt.

Within the circus of slaughter, Jonas faded in and out of consciousness. His instructions to the Ritts had been simply, *"Kill these wolves, then take us away!"* As he had been hemorrhaging vast helpings of life fluids, his attention had diverted from the minutiae.

Yelping into the dark of the forest, the remaining wolves scattered as they were picked off one by one.

A segment of the Ritts had landed and spread their wings around Jonas and his friends, shielding them. Then in a jarring rush that Jonas regrettably did not feel, the Ritts heaved the company up into the sanctuary of the sky.

Secured within the claws of two Ritts, one for each crook of his shoulder, Jonas dreamt of warm summer breezes through a screen door that looked out over a sweeping meadow, none of which he recognized. Meanwhile the gash set on his side wept through his tunic, piping the forest below in a crimson icing that left a delicious, trackable trail for predators... should any survive. But if the Yéne were to take it upon himself to pick up the scent, well, Jonas could provide cover for only so many possibilities.

A wholesome damp warmth enveloped Jonas' mouth, bringing him from sleep and catapulting him into real life. His eyelashes fluttered as he woke, and somewhere between the blinking barrage, the image of Greta's face appeared.

Jonas found himself upon a bed in a small room. The curtains upon the solitary window above his knees had been drawn, draping the huddled bystanders at the door under an obscuring shadow.

Greta leaned closer. "Ever since that time you cast me aside like a soiled undergarment," she whispered, her mouth hovering a treacherous inch from his own. "I can't stop thinking about you." Then rising on her arms, she flung her head back. "He wakes!"

The group that had amassed in the hall funneled into the room, and soon Scary and Posh were over Jonas, stealing Greta's place.

"I'm alright, I'm alright," said Jonas sitting up. A bandage had been tightly applied to his entire midsection, making an upward bend difficult. Greta backed up, smirking as the onlookers moved forward.

My first kiss! thought Jonas with shock and dismay. *Of course I had been unconscious for most of it.* The fact that he had been asleep brought relief. His thoughts suddenly belonged to Sasha as he lay back, experiencing odd pangs of guilt.

The room could comfortably accommodate three people for video games and pizza, but three would be the cut-off. Four would be pushing it. And right now, not counting Scary and Posh, he was staring back at a semi-circle of six astute-looking creatures. Their bodies were kinked sideways, pressed tight, overlapping one another to make the most of the limited space.

"How do you feel, Jonas?" the most human of the six asked. A disturbing enthusiasm radiated in her gaze.

"Fine."

"May we...?" she inquired, gesturing to her nodding colleagues. Scary and Posh, clutching a wrist apiece, began to make low hissing noises and Jonas could feel brush burns developing. "Take a look at your wounds?"

Jonas surmised that this overeager chorus line must be physicians of some make. Before answering, he looked for familiar faces. Vera and Greta were standing in the hall. Jonas assumed the sword clutched defensively to Vera's chest was Dafodhel in her resting state. Mature tree branches scratching at the window told Jonas that he was in an upper level of whatever weird building he had been dragged into. And he could sense his Ritts adorning the rooflines above. Isaac was nowhere to be seen, which was unsurprising. Everybody else near him placed the *strange* in the word stranger.

Jonas propped himself up. "Vera!" he shouted over the collective. The knight handed Dafodhel to Greta and cautioned her first steps, making it as far as she could into the crowded room. "Did Isaac make it out alive?"

"He did," replied Vera on tip toes. "But he wanted —"

A beak-faced doctor cleared his throat and punched his chest, silencing the room. The watch nestled in a shallow pocket on his vest dropped and dangled on a silver chain. The creature stepped back to snug it into place, and in doing so lost his spot in the pecking order.

The doctors had grown restless, fidgeting with clipboards and rubbing their chins... or the places where chins would often exist.

"Yes!" Jonas finally replied. "But can we go someplace bigger?"

"I wuth about to thuggetht the thame thing." A bespectacled reptilian raised a fin with tiny clawed nubs rupturing. "Let uth be off to the Obthervation Hall," he spoke with a singsongy lilt.

Jonas imagined a sterile lab full of microscopes and forceps and sharp dissecting tools. But on the other hand, "halls" were spacious places, not often cramped, which lessened the heebie-jeebies he was working through about the whole *observation* thing.

Snatching his arms free from the Hylda, Jonas scowled at the hairless patches worn by the nervous witches. "Just point me in the direction," he said, shaking his head at Scary. The Hylda tucked her chin, mildly crestfallen.

When Jonas swung his legs over the bed and hopped to his feet, one would think he had flawlessly performed a triple axel salchow for the reaction he received.

"Magnifithent!"

The room was aghast; each scholarly creature's mouth parts were gaping. A few spellbound moments passed before the tension broke and they pulled one another aside to whisper-hunch.

"I can even tie my own bootlaces," said Jonas, folding his arms and lifting an eyebrow.

One physician's head poked above the cluster. "Come!" they beckoned, gesturing for Jonas to follow with a furry tentacle. "Come with us, please."

After following the doctors through a meandering corridor that dipped and buckled, Jonas emerged into a large kitchen with roiling cauldrons feverishly stirred by long-eared goblins teetering on leaning ladders. The steaming liquids spilling over the sides collected on the tiled floor in gigantic drains. The spaces between the grates afforded Jonas a free view of the dull gloomy rooms below, where shapes scurried to and fro within the pale foggy light. If not for the physicians' brisk rate, Jonas would have stood staring for hours.

"What the heck is this place?" asked Jonas.

"It's the foremost structure in Brimon," replied Vera.

"I'm not asking for a history lesson here —"

"Hand me over, would you please?" Dafodhel cut in, agitated.

Vera obliged, relinquishing possession of the blade as the group ducked down a spiral staircase. An ancient brick shod turret acted as the center post for the flight, while the steps dipped and rose like a poorly crafted cat tree. Dafodhel had cleverly changed from a hazardous sword into a dull truncheon, complete with a wrist strap. Jonas was grateful for the safer option and wondered just how diverse Dafodhel's arsenal spread — visions of bazookas and sub-machine guns sprang unbidden to mind.

Firmly rooted floor planks greeted Jonas' feet at the end of the swirling staircase, and one physician craned his head back. "Almost there, Jonas," he announced encouragingly.

"Goody goody," said Jonas under his breath.

Dafodhel chuckled.

After passing through what Jonas could only describe as an art gallery whose primary focus was feathers and... snorkels? — the doctors then hurried through a hallway that caused Jonas to stumble. Feeling reminiscent of...

"Wait a minute..."

Scary and Posh pressed near, perceiving Jonas' unease.

"I have been here before."

Vera was giving him the same look she had given him a minute ago, when she had told him that *"it's the foremost structure in Brimon."*

The physicians clustered at a heavy door beneath an arch. After a few knocks, the door slowly gave way. As Jonas strode forward, he passed a solid gold inset with the words *Observation Hall* chiseled upon it.

The backs of sauntering doctors blocked Jonas' view of what lay within the generous-sized room. The most humanlike doctor stood just beyond the threshold, a toothy grin imprinted within her prominent gum line. Her intention was a welcome, but it read otherwise.

"Welcome to the Observation Hall, Jonas," she whispered. "Please keep your volume to a minimum."

This feels familiar, Jonas thought.

When the crowd finally parted, dispersing opposite of one another, they revealed the Council, beaming at Jonas. A colossal tree offering swings from its heavy branches trailed only a few feet behind. A tall, lanky man swept forward with an all too familiar air of authority.

"Nope," said Jonas, turning for the door he had just walked through.

"Please!" Guiltbrand pleaded. "We beg a boon!"

Jonas pretended he could not hear the Sage.

The humanlike doctor closed the door and placed her back against it. "Please, Jonas," she began, "we only wish to clarify some matters —"

"Please let me leave." Jonas felt the flesh of his grip expanding as Dafodhel began to transform. "I have all that I need." He stopped himself short and continued within his heart, *To make everything right.* Christmas was coming and his mother's present was not yet wrapped. *Only just recently acquired the funds.*

Tucked behind her overlong nose, the doctor's nostrils flared in panic. Dafodhel had assumed the shape of a mace and chain, a morning star pendulating ominously within striking distance.

"You should be dead!" shouted Guiltbrand, ignoring the Council recoiling at his outburst. "The Yéne's claws spell death to all!"

"Are they poisonous?" Jonas asked, turning toward the Guiltbrand.

"Technically, they would be venomous..." Guiltbrand trailed off, then re-focused in a whisper. "No, no, no. What I am speaking of dwells within the realm of the metaphysical... the mystical... the magical, if you will..." Guiltbrand stopped.

"Go on."

"Ah, yes," said Guiltbrand tugging at his collar and swallowing as if a lump of rock candy had been lodged in his windpipe. His last exchange with Jonas was still very clearly aligned within the Sage's memory. "The gash on your side was nearly healed by the time your Ritts delivered you to the village square. Which, I must admit, was a very clever —"

"So I heal quick?" Jonas interrupted. "That's not new."

"Yeth," replied the reptilian doctor. "But to shrug off a thwipe from a Yéne ith, well, it'th miraculouth. And the fact that you thtand here right now... well, the fact that you're actually thtanding ith outthide the realm of reathon."

"Uh huh." Jonas found this ordeal lackluster. He lowered Dafodhel and turned to face Guiltbrand and the lizard doctor. "Let me guess, you want to run some tests and draw my blood and hook me up to some machines? Something like that?" As Jonas strode toward the tree Dafodhel morphed and lengthened into a quarterstaff. "And wasn't this place called the Center for Stupid, or something, the last time I was here?" he asked, tapping the top end of Dafodhel against the trunk.

"Sanctum of Susurrance," muttered Guiltbrand from the corner of his mouth.

Jonas plucked at the topmost bandage above his pectorals. "Hm, I don't know if that sounds right. Are you sure?"

"You have us all wrong." The doctor with the tentacles decided to step in. Their mouth protuberance fluttered like battered curtains, continuing. "We only wished to usher you to this space in order to take a look at your wound. That's all. The recovery room was inadequate for all of us to use."

"Oh yeah? Then why was this chucklehead waiting?" Jonas inclined Dafodhel in Guiltbrand's direction.

"We were already here," confessed Guiltbrand, sneering at the accusation.

"I don't believe you," said Jonas. "Do you believe him Daffy? Scary, Posh? What do you have to say?" He looked to the Hylda then slowly lifted his head.

The occupants were speechless.

"I'm just messing with you!" said Jonas, spreading his arms wide. "Go ahead, take a look!"

The doctors eagerly sped across the Hall. The first physician to arrive began to carefully peel the ribbons of the dressing as if a trip-wired bomb lay within.

"That tickles," complained Jonas. "Just yank it off."

"As you wish, Jonas," came the doctor's reply.

Jonas felt tingly and raw in the wake of his rapid unpeeling. The site where the Yéne had scored a chunk of his flesh had completely healed into a teardrop scar. The doctors gawped, taking turns poking and prodding the new skin. Meanwhile Guiltbrand and the Council looked on with mutual interest.

The tallest of the physicians requested a chance to peer into his eyes, and not having a problem with that, Jonas lowered to the creature's level. Elongated toothpick fingers pried Jonas' eyelids apart. "Look up, please," the doctor instructed softly. "Okay... now look down, please." After a few aggravating moments, vines began forming in Jonas' vision and his eyes began drying, feeling like Scotch tape.

"That's enough," said Jonas, rising.

The doctor appeared mollified. "If you say so..." she mumbled, backing into the ranks.

His old body had undergone its fair share of examinations, and Jonas had grown weary of them, and now his patience waned. A hesitant horse-faced doctor made a cautious step, requesting permission with a toothy smile.

"I think I'm spent," grumbled Jonas rubbing an eye with the meat of his hand. The doctor retreated quickly, apologetically offering her hooves in surrender. "Now if that is all, I have a dinner date with a gentleman from Poland —"

"Merely one more account!" interrupted Guiltbrand. The volume of his outburst sent the nearby Council spiraling into agony. "Please spare us one last boon." Guiltbrand whispered, soothing his writhing counterparts. "Herta, if you would please?" The Sage addressed the humanoid doctor. During the exams she had returned to the physicians but had prudently maintained her distance.

"Uh!" Herta's face flushed pale at the mention of her name. "What do you — I mean, what is it —" she stammered. She looked desperately to Guiltbrand and her cohorts for deliverance, trying to duck the bull's eye on her forehead. Her pearlescent eyes climbed Jonas, growing more terrified the higher they travelled.

"What is everyone looking..." Jonas leaned back, craning his neck, scaling Dafodhel's new height. "Ah," he concluded. Dafodhel had changed into an overlong reaper's scythe. Her haft diameter had not altered, so from his perspective, he was still holding a quarterstaff. The blackened steel crescent hung over his head like a halo fit for an archdemon. "Okay... I think, judging by my *companion's expression*, it's time for us to leave."

Herta, lousy at stalling, nodded. If Guiltbrand were to bring forth another case, it seemed that whatever he drew would appear as a farce.

"You have seen Moütz, have you not!" Guiltbrand cried out in a last-ditch effort.

"What of it?" asked Jonas.

"The desolation! The undue death! The Terren cruelty on vaulted display!"

"I have what I came for," said Jonas. A wicked titter came from the overhanging blade, sweeping downward chills over his wrist.

"Brimon will suffer the same fate! Do you not see how dire this is?!" Guiltbrand flailed, failing to connect. "Think of the children!" The Sage wilted as he watched Jonas turn his back.

The Hall had finally assumed one of its monikers, falling deathly silent. The physicians and Council stood defeated, all their hopes were now draining along with the Devil's diminishing steps.

Prominent ears that were given to free rotation began to twitch at a noise from the back of the room, beyond the huge swing tree. Trickling meandering footsteps creased the stillness, and a brisk heel-to-toe was recognized by those nearest the escalating sound.

"Sage, Sage, Sage," a harried, frantic voice whispered.

All attention spun toward a little messenger creature. Even Jonas turned, his free hand upon the exit door's latch.

"What is it, Amos?" said Guiltbrand.

"The Skorsa!" Amos shrieked, abandoning decorum. His face dipped to the floor out of shame and also from the fact that he was quite winded and needed to catch some air. The Council who would freak out from a sound louder than a needle drop were instantly rapt. Amos continued at a poorly contained whisper, "The Skorsa have rallied!"

The sense of dread abruptly depleted as quickly as it had arrived. A combined sigh escaped from every Leeds-sworn, as they turned their backs on the messenger.

"But!" Amos was not finished. "Scouts are reporting Lancethanes south of the Taub! We are to be assailed! Brimon will be under siege! Under siege!"

Cloaks and robes and any hem of loose-fitting cloth whirled on Amos.

"This is our final hour!"

CHAPTER 16

"Found it!" Sandy announced in triumph, holding the parchment aloft. "Hey, Jonas!" she shouted, rising to her feet. The old house responded with quiet, not even a creak. She had been focused on her search for the house deed, and last she recalled, Jonas was off for a shower. That had been *minutes* ago, or so she believed, though she hardly remembered the sound of water running from the upstairs bath.

"Could have only been fifteen minutes, tops," muttered Sandy, making for the stairway. Suddenly her foot caught, hovering over the bottom step. "How can I begin this conversation, when I haven't sorted the details?" Putting the house up for sale could solve a few of their problems, but it may kick up a whole bunch of others. The foremost being that the Kowalski crime family would probably not respond very kindly to the missives. Also, Sandy held doubt that the Kowalskis would leave her and Jonas alone, even if she were to satisfy the debt.

In Sandy's eyes, the weight of the Kowalski thumb had robbed Jonas of a shot at a decent childhood. If she could liberate him of all this, then maybe he could enjoy the last remaining years of his youth in peace — far from this town.

Now just outside Jonas' closed room, Sandy's knuckles held a freeze-frame before the old wooden door. She still did not know what to say. Beyond the door nothing stirred. Sandy pressed an ear to the paint-flecked door, a few stray hairs caught upon the ruts when she pulled back. Beneath the floor, below her feet, she had heard the unmistakable sound of shuffled footsteps.

Sandy stepped back from her son's door, her throat suddenly parched. Who could be downstairs? She ruled Jonas out. He would have passed the office upon his route to the streets. Perhaps Emil and his men have returned? Maybe a banker had come demanding his due... on a Sunday? No, whoever was below would not be a nine to fiver.

Ever so lightly, she tiptoed toward the landing. Still wearing her winter boots, she managed the hallway with the delicacy of a shiatsu massage, and somewhere between her third or fourth step, a blood-freezing squeak erupted.

The person in the shop seized mid-step. Sandy gritted her teeth and winced. Miraculously she crossed the remainder of the crunchy hallway without sending up any more flares. Upon the staircase, she inhaled deep and held her breath, willing herself to be lighter, each footfall administered with the caution of a minefield. Soon she found herself on the landing, halfway, and still she had yet to hear another sound from the shop.

Slowly, ever so slowly, Sandy peered through the topmost corner of the doorway at the base of the stairs. She furtively replaced a stray lock of hair that fell loose from her messily pulled chignon, veiling a segment of her vision.

"Nobody's here."

The office door to her right was still ajar, with no shadows inside.

Rubber munched upon the salted road outside when a pick-up truck ambled by, and Sandy took advantage of the noise, whisking into her office to snag the letter opener in her desk's leftmost top drawer. It was not much of a weapon, but it was better than nothing.

From the office she could survey the entire shop floor. And indeed, just as before, it was vacant. She pressed from behind cover, striding into clear visibility, letter opener concealed at a kinked angle. She made a stop at the exchange counter, rising up on the balls of her feet to make certain no one was squatting on the other side.

A pent-up breath grated from Sandy's throat, sounding as more of a groan than a sigh. "Nobody's here," she repeated with finality.

Without sparing another second she hurried to the front door and twisted the deadbolt into place, then switched the street facing "OPEN" sign to the preferred "CLOSED" side. When Jonas had re-hung it earlier in the wrong direction, it had gone unflipped. An easy mistake, and perhaps the person who had entered had done so upon that false pretense.

If someone had been there at all, as there were no damp boot prints set to shimmer beneath the exposed fluorescent bulbs.

"Am I losing it?" said Sandy to the letter opener. "I'll keep you nearby, just in case."

Daytime came to a close. The winter sky had changed from their ordinary shade of gloom, opting for a darker shade. And when Sandy decided to adjourn to her room for the night, she had to fight the urge to knock and wish her son goodnight. It seemed that the poor kid had been sleeping soundly for the past six hours. At least that was what she assumed. What any sane parent would assume.

Sandy, for the most part, feared that Jonas would seek alcohol or drugs as coping strategies. He had been alone so often as of late. Through the years his stable of friends had diminished from meager to none at all, at break-neck velocity. Whenever she stirred the subject, Jonas would steer the conversation elsewhere.

Sandy hugged herself as she looked out through her ice-glazed window. A streetlamp's bleary halo along the lower base of the pane bled vanilla filaments throughout the glass. She tugged the cuffs on her shaggy wool sweater past her knuckles, resembling fingerless gloves.

Her thoughts wandered from one love to another before settling on the whirlwind romance that had brought Jonas into this world.

"Another Christmas without you," she said, chewing her thumbnail. "Sebastian."

Sandy shook her head and trained her mind back to the present. As happy as those memories often began, they always ended sadly. Always without him.

The bed sheets were cold at first, but the chill quickly vanished once she lugged the comforter to her chin. After clicking her lamp off, her hand slid down to the surface of the nightstand where the letter opener resided, atop the deed.

How could she pay the Kowalskis inside such a short span of time? For years she had been chipping away, keeping the hounds at bay, but that had left her funds nearly desolate every month. And now without her equipment and tools, her career as a horologist was kaput. She would need to figure something else out, and quick.

Oh, Daddy, she thought, *how will we get out of this?*

Selling the house and moving would get Jonas away from the Kowalskis, but on the other hand...

Sandy sighed. She had been over this a hundred times. No matter how hard she plotted and planned, every redemptive thread ended right back where she started. The scenarios began to swirl, growing tiresome.

Tomorrow...

Tomorrow she would come up with a plan. Tomorrow would be different. She would no longer repeat the mistakes of her past.

She closed her eyes, leaving a day that she would love to forget.

Sandy woke to quiet. When she rolled onto her back to stare at the ceiling, a stale coldness filled the air, pale light punched through the window.

"Time to get to it," said Sandy, rubbing her left eye. Today would be dedicated to strategy, but first, Mr. Coffee beckoned.

Not a sound escaped Jonas' room, and Sandy lingered at his door for a few moments. It was the first Monday of Christmas Break, so what did it matter if Jonas slept in for a few bonus hours? She thought about cracking the door open just a tiny bit, but her desire to let him rest outweighed her curiosity.

"Maybe your old mom will finally have a plan by the time you wake up, kid," mumbled Sandy as she began her trek toward the bubbling and churning coffee machine.

The kitchen was located on the second floor, a few steps from her bedroom. A brilliant remodel decision made by her father before the family had settled in. Of course this had all taken place when she was a little girl, so describing the kitchen décor as *outdated* was an understatement. Intermittent wood paneling consumed the walls, a checkerboard linoleum pattern pressed the floors with a yellow round-topped fridge tucked within a series of faux wooden cupboards. The kitchen was indeed functional, usable, and also very seventies. Just another line item on the chart of things to update, if only...

Sandy placed her trusty letter opener upon the headrest lining the breakfast nook. The backrest beneath displayed a galaxy of wear, heavy age lines spider webbed all throughout the lime green cushions, and the yellow spongy innards peeking from the deeper furrows only solidified the fact that selling this place would be an uphill battle.

"We're screwed," she admitted, rescuing her Scrooge Mc-Duck coffee mug from the dish strainer. With one hand she upturned the coffee carafe while the other strategically slammed the mug beneath the pour. Black liquid twirled laps to the top of Scrooge's top hat, while Sandy inhaled an aroma that never got old. Even the sound of a bird kamikaze blasting into the front window of the shop below could not ruin her moment of solace.

Then a second bird dive-bombed the window, and a few beats later a third decided to end its life in repeated manner.

"What the..." said Sandy, roving to the window. She gazed out as another strike resounded from below. "Heck?"

An old timer chipped at the ice that had accumulated overnight on his Buick's driver side window, while a newly minted father picked careful steps along the sidewalk, his toddler bemusedly straddling his shoulders.

As her eyes fell on a doddery old pick-up truck parked behind Darren's car, which she had never seen, a fifth bird torpedoed the window. The impact sent a shockwave up through her squishy slippers. She had missed the flashing of feathers before the strike, but the sound was undeniable. Those generous-sized storefront windows had been starling magnets since their installation.

Sandy decided to go and investigate, abandoning her coffee, taking up her letter opener. While ascending the staircase, a sixth bird offed himself.

"Geez," muttered Sandy, pondering the local avian population's state of mind. Perhaps a bit of funny juice had made its way into a nearby bird bath?

Sandy laughed the moment she reached the bottom of the staircase. "Tasso?" she whispered. It had not been birds after all, the man had been rapping at the window with a walking cane.

The good-looking man that had sold Jonas his new bed was standing outside, his back to the window.

Oh, no! Sandy thought with horror. She had brokered a deal that she could no longer uphold! Today was meant to be spent dispensing problems!

She felt as if a contortionist were practicing routines inside her guts, easing the door open with a pained smile.

"Hi there," said Tasso with a lean. "Hope I didn't wake you." In his hands was a dandy walking cane with a thick curved handle.

"Uh," said Sandy, realizing that she was wearing sweatpants accompanied by a hooded pullover that crudely depicted a swollen orange tiger cat, of which despised Mondays.

Play it cool, Cassandra, she told herself.

"Sleep?" she replied. "What's that?"

"Ah," said Tasso with a cordial laugh. "Yeah, teenage son, huh? Phew, I get it." He passed his cane to his left hand and hefted a thumb over his shoulder. "So I've got the Howard Miller waiting in the truck..." He trailed off. His eyes had fallen upon the sheer blankness that lay behind Sandy, color drained from his face. "Oh, man! Were you robbed?!"

Sandy shook her head. "No, no, no," she replied, struggling to conjure a solid lie. "No, well, kind of?" *So much for a solid lie.* "We're kind of experiencing a bit of... well, a bit of..." She took a step back and uncoiled her wrist to gesture at the room, revealing the letter opener still clutched in her hand. "Come on in. It's much too cold to be discussing this sort of stuff in the great outdoors."

Tasso entered but stopped. "The Miller shouldn't be kept out in the cold for too long. Mind if I bring it in right quick?"

"Sure, sure," replied Sandy with a shooing motion. "Do you need a hand? I can wake Jonas?"

An urgent expression appeared on the man's face. "Please don't!" he blurted. "I mean, I'll be fine. I got it in the truck by myself, I can manage the rest." He turned for his truck and slipped a hand into his coat pocket, striding as if he were escorting an invisible woman. "Oh," he said, pivoting on his cane to face Sandy in the doorway. "Cucumbers tagged along. Mind if the old boy joins us?"

"Of course!" Sandy smiled, rubbing her upper arm. "I'll just hold the door for you. But hurry, because it's really cold!"

"Say no more!" Tasso shouted, skating across the lawn.

For someone requiring a walking aid, the man was surprisingly agile. That assumed that the cane was not merely a fashion choice.

The rusty hinges on Tasso's old truck croaked, and a gangly amorphous blur spat from the widened opening. Perhaps Sandy was mistaken, or maybe it was the way the wolfhound's fur played on the snow, but Cucumbers appeared a few shades darker.

"Hi, boy," said Sandy, not needing to bend to ruffle the dog's head. "Good to see you too."

Cucumbers licked Sandy's wrist as he scrambled inside sniffing along the baseboards, tail stiffened for peak efficiency. Sandy had turned and did not notice when the dog thoughtfully eased for a few seconds atop the exact spot where Jonas, the day before, had been the recipient of a swift kick by way of a Polish man's boot.

"Hey, I want to ask you something," said Sandy to the man making his way up the sidewalk, a grandfather clock teetering on his shoulder. "That bed frame in Jonas' room —"

"Can we talk," groaned Tasso, "when this is safe inside?"

Sandy slipped from the doorway, clearing space, one arm stretched to prevent the door from closing. In a swift adjustment before crossing beneath the threshold, Tasso brought the clock to his chest in a bear hug and concluded the remaining steps in much shorter strides.

"Where should I put it?" asked Tasso, surveying the room.

"Anywhere, really," said Sandy. "Right there is fine. Should be far enough from the entryway."

Tasso's knees bumped the back of the clock as he baby-stepped the distance. "Here?" he asked, bending to set the clock down.

"Sure, yeah, that's good." Sandy folded her arms. "So, how did you manage to get my son's bed frame —"

"What happened here?" interrupted Tasso. "Have you phoned the police?"

"It's a long story," said Sandy. "It's a family thing."

Tasso strode for the office to peer inside. "Family thing, huh?" he asked, and followed with, "Will your family be returning your stuff anytime soon?"

"Well, it's not *my family,*" said Sandy coming up beside Tasso and slyly closing the office door. "Like I said, it's a long story. And obviously, I won't be able to fix any clocks for the foreseeable future. So feel free to snap your fingers or cast whatever hocus-pocus spell you performed that put that creepy bed frame into my son's room. But please, wait until he wakes up first, at least."

"When was the last time you spoke to your son?" inquired Tasso as Cucumbers sidled next to him. Beneath tufted eyebrows, the old dog's eyes shared the same concern as his owner.

"Yesterday," replied Sandy, her voice rising with concern.

"He was here yesterday." Tasso rubbed his chin, ill at ease. "But you haven't seen him this day? Did he not go to school?"

"It's... Christmas break..."

"Are you certain that he was here yesterday? Your son, I mean."

"Who else are we talking about?" said Sandy, beginning to feel irritated. "And why are you so concerned about Jonas?"

"Jonas!" Tasso tipped a harsh nod at Cucumbers. "That's his name, yes! You have yet to see Jonas today, correct?"

"He's sleeping upstairs," replied Sandy slowly. "Look, I'm sorry that I can't keep my end of the bargain, and I certainly wouldn't hold it against you if you took the bed and mirror —"

"The bed and mirror stay," Tasso cut in, pinching the bridge of his nose with eyes squeezed tight. "Some things you just cannot anticipate, eh Cucumbers?" Then refocusing his attention on Sandy, concluded, "Wake your son, for we have much to discuss."

CHAPTER 17

"**I**s everything alright?" shouted Tasso up the stairs from the employee entryway. After listening to shuffling footsteps overhead make their way down a hallway, a knock on a door, then a creaky stalled opening — a curse-laden clamor rattled the foundation.

The footsteps sped down the hallway and concluded in another chamber where Tasso heard further cursing and shortly thereafter what sounded like a telephone receiver violently disconnected and thrashed to bits.

Sandy surged into view upon the middle landing, frantic and feral. "They took him!" she seethed. She had donned a winter coat and jeans.

"Who?" said Tasso, backing up.

"Emil!" Sandy was before the man, emanating waves of hatred. "The Polish Mafia!" Her eyes flashed to Cucumbers when he imparted a whine. "Why are you just standing there?!" she shouted and whirled for the door.

In contrast, Tasso was a structure of calm. "Let's take it easy," he said. "How do you know that he was kidnapped by the *Polish Mafia?* Did they leave some kind of note or sign?"

"No!" said Sandy as she tugged a boot while balancing on one foot. "I just know it!"

"How?"

"Because they were here yesterday! They were the ones who took all of my equipment! And one of Emil's men must've showed up afterwards and abducted Jonas!"

"We shouldn't be hasty."

"We should be beyond the pinnacle of haste!" Sandy slammed her heel, setting the second boot. "I'm going to murder them!"

Tasso slid between Sandy and the door. "Whoa! Whoa!" he brought his hands up. "Breathe, Cassandra!"

The sudden use of her given name startled her. "How did you know —" Sandy snarled and twitched her head. "Never mind that! Get out of my way!"

"No," said Tasso with resolve. "I'm going to make tea and we will talk this out."

Today is a day for planning... Sandy recalled the day's intended purpose.

"No!" Sandy declared a dual argument. "Today is a day for murder!"

"What if the Polish Mafia had nothing to do with Jonas' disappearance?" pleaded Tasso. "And it was me, by the way, who stopped by yesterday afternoon, but no one was here so —"

"I don't care!" Sandy tried to muscle past, but Tasso continued to run interference. "They deserve to die for everything! Move now!"

Tasso leaned against the door. "You're making a mistake," he said. "What if I —"

"What if nothing!" Sandy tried to push, but the man would not budge. She shoved his chest and took a step back to glare. "Who are you anyways?! Why do you even care?! Just take your stupid clock and get out of here! The deal's over! And this has nothing to do with you!"

"That is where you are wrong," stated Tasso. "I am here, aren't I? We had a deal and this Polish Mafia — you said Polish Mafia, right?"

Sandy continued to glare.

Tasso took a breath. "These *criminals* are preventing our transaction. You see, I want that Howard Miller back up on its feet. And you're the only horologist that I trust within one hundred square miles." He cleared his throat and glanced down to adjust his scarf. "One thousand square miles. And now, you see, I have a vested interest in this affair."

"But they have my son!"

"They have your instruments and your accusation," said Tasso. "You don't know if they have Jonas."

"Regardless!" countered Sandy. "My phone has been disconnected, so I can't just call and find out. I have to *physically* go to them."

"And what if they have him? What's your plan then?"

That was a very appropriate question. "I don't know," muttered Sandy, stumped. Then after a very quick think, she had it! "You can magic him out! The same way you magicked that stuff into Jonas' room!"

"Who says I magicked anything anywhere?"

"You have a vested interest in this, you said it yourself!"

"But who says I have magic?" Tasso repeated his point, shaking his head. "That is not a solution. What will you do if they *don't* have him? Will they just let you walk out of there?"

"Maybe?" Sandy tried to push again. "I don't know! Guess I'll find out." She pushed again, and this time Tasso relented, holding the door for her.

While she walked the icy path to her minivan she fumbled in her coat pocket for her keys, plotting the quickest route. She no longer felt December's chill.

If those scumbags bent one solitary hair on my baby's head...

"What do you think Sebastian would say?" called Tasso.

Sharply Sandy inhaled, a bitter cold lapped the back of her throat.

"Come inside so we can talk," said Tasso to Sandy's back. The woman had yet to move. "The Poles do not have Jonas."

Not of her own accord, Sandy's right hand lifted. Cucumbers was beside her, encouraging her to return with him. She dodged away as if the dog were molten.

"How do you know..." she said, slowly turning.

"Inside, please," replied Tasso, inclining his head. "You're not going to believe me, but I assure you, I am not a keen liar."

"You're right," said Sandy. "I don't believe you." The mug of Earl Grey on the counter before her untouched.

Tasso took a sip of his tea. "Which part?" he asked, swaddled in the lurid green of the breakfast nook. After removing his winter coat and scarf, underneath he wore a tweed waistcoat over a button-up dress shirt. Very cowboy-ish, Sandy thought approvingly.

"I don't know," replied Sandy. "Like, all of it? It's a lot to take."

"You think I'm making this up?"

Sandy finally approached her tea. "My son is not on earth anymore. Kinda hard to believe." She slurped a loud pull from her mug and set hard eyes upon Tasso. "I'm going to need proof."

"You didn't need proof a half hour ago when you were ready to storm a mafia hideout," Tasso pointed out.

"That makes more sense," said Sandy. "When you take into account the events of yesterday, and my family's history with Emil."

"Fair enough," said Tasso rising. "If that is all that —"

"Wait," Sandy interjected, covering Tasso's hand. "You still haven't explained how you know Jonas' father."

"More like, know *of* Jonas' father," replied Tasso, sitting down. "Dealing with prophecies is a fickle business. Especially for a skeptic."

"How so?" said Sandy arching an eyebrow. "I have very limited experience myself."

Tasso laughed. "I don't take much stock in them, to be honest with you. But there are others who take each and every syllable of a sage straight to heart. It's a gamble, really. Sometimes the prophecy is spot-on and you can stand to make a windfall of a fortune. And other times, well, I think you can imagine the other direction."

Sandy raspberried a thumbs-down.

"Exactly," said Tasso, nodding. "But other times a prophecy can be misinterpreted ever so-slightly. Like how an angle coming off a structure can be just a fraction off-kilter at the base, but the higher you travel, the more obvious the error is at the top." The man looked away. "Apologies for the carpenter's metaphor."

"I can keep up," said Sandy.

"Right." Tasso met Sandy's gaze and continued, "So when people place hefty stakes in something unsubstantiated, they are putting a whole lot at risk. And I have seen it time and time again when these people think they're doing the right thing, but all they're actually doing is paving a road to disaster."

"But how often have you seen victory?"

Tasso looked to Cucumbers and both closed their eyes.

"Not often," replied Tasso at length.

"And what does this have to do with Sebastian?"

"Everything." Tasso rubbed his chin. "A prophecy is what spurred his departure."

Sandy slapped the table, threatening to rise with excitement. "You mean he lives?!"

Tasso shook his head. "His departure *from* the nether realm." The Joiner grew somber, seeing Sandy's hope dashed into fragments. "The reason for his coming here," he said, clarifying. "I thought you knew that Sebastian was not... that he did not..."

"Survive?" said Sandy, withdrawing as far as she could into the spongy backrest. "I figured as much. They never found his body."

"I am sorry, Cassandra."

Cucumbers placed his chin on the table, within petting distance. Sandy obliged, cracking a smile at the dog. "It's alright. I figured as much," she admitted with a sniff. "If he could have returned to me, he would have." A sudden spark ignited behind her eyes, and Sandy jolted. "Wait! Is Jonas in danger?!"

"I can't know for certain," said Tasso. "He may be safer there than he is here. My job as Joiner was merely to get him from point A to point B."

"Well is there a way for me to go to him?" asked Sandy with re-kindled hope. "Can you get *me* from point A to point B?"

Cucumbers lifted his head, straying away from Sandy's hand.

"I can," began Tasso, interrupted by a snort from the canine. "I'll get to that, Cucumbers. But you wouldn't survive," he said, gazing at the ceiling. "Only certain people may cross safely, unscathed — people from this realm are notoriously soft, when it comes to portal jumping. Understand that there is a toll for nearly everyone. A very slim few must give up something near and dear to them. For most everyone else, they simply die choking on blood, the toll paid with death."

Sandy shifted uncomfortably. "How do you know which kind of person you are?"

"Shoot," said Tasso. "Tends to be in the blood."

Sandy brightened.

"Passed from the father," revealed Tasso, causing instant deflation. "Sebastian, to wit, had to pay when he crossed over though." He thoughtfully smoothed the shadow of his moustache. "When you saw Jonas yesterday, did he appear intact?"

Cocking her head at an odd angle, Sandy stretched a moment to think. Tasso dabbed his tea bag inside his mug while Cucumbers leaned on his haunches and scratched an ear.

"No," said Sandy. "He was whole. I mean, he was intact, yes."

"All his fingers and toes?"

Sandy looked at the man through slitted eyes. "I'm pretty sure..."

"Wonderful!" Tasso clapped. "So he is a rare breed!" He slapped Cucumbers on the back, which set the dog's tail wagging. "You knew there was something about him," said Tasso to Cucumbers. He turned to Sandy, pointing to the wolfhound. "Always batting a thousand, this guy."

"Are you saying that Jonas went to that nether region and then came back?"

Tasso smirked. *"Nether region,"* he murmured as an aside to Cucumbers, then returned to regular volume. "Yes. And then he went back... again."

"Why would he do that?" Sandy spoke into the flat of her hand.

Tasso shrugged. "Who knows? Your guess would probably be better than mine."

"Can you help me cross over?" said Sandy, inching awkwardly out of the nook. "Can you help me get to my son? I'll gladly take the risk."

Tasso gaped at the woman standing over him. "Why would you want to do that?"

"Because," said Sandy. "I'm his mother."

Tasso scratched his eyebrow. "You won't come out alive. And what good will you be to anyone in that state?"

Sandy was adamant. "We can try."

"That's rather rash," replied Tasso. "Trust me, you will die. And besides, if you really want to check on him, you can just use that mirror I gave you."

The floor seemed to lurch beneath Sandy's feet. "What," was all she could manage.

"Yeah," said Tasso offhandedly, pausing to take another sip of tea. "It took some convincing, but I managed to work that into the deal, last minute. You're a good mother, me and Cucumbers could tell."

Sandy found herself with Tasso's loosely buttoned collar wrapped tight in her fist. "Show me," she demanded. "Now."

"No problem," said Tasso, unlacing Sandy's fingers one by one. "Just lead me to the mirror." He plucked her pinky and scooched out of the booth. "I probably should have mentioned the mirror earlier."

"You should have led with that," said Sandy, giving Tasso space to stand. From behind her back Cucumbers huffed in agreement.

"Whose side are you on?" said Tasso to the dog.

Cucumbers' eyes darted to Sandy then to the hall.

"Oh, right," relented Tasso. "The side of virtue. There's nothing more terrifying to a ne'er-do-well than an honorable man." He gestured for Sandy to lead the way. "Never forget that," he muttered under his breath, following dog and woman out of the kitchen.

Upon entry into Jonas' bedroom, Sandy noticed that the face of the oval cheval mirror was angled toward the ceiling, which she quickly corrected. And as the others entered, she stood to its side, barring her view from the glass. When she peered inside the mirror's ebon gothic frame, Tasso stood by himself, while Cucumbers was nowhere to be seen.

Sandy looked to Tasso and back into the mirror. In the room, Cucumbers was hitched to Tasso's side, but inside the mirror the wolfhound was not there.

"Where is..." Sandy pointed at Cucumbers. "Oh, there he is."

Then, in the mirror, a wolfhound appeared, standing at Tasso's hip.

"Why did it take so long for him to show up..." Sandy trailed off. "That's not Cucumbers." Cucumbers remained at Tasso's side in the room while the mirror wolfhound had strode forward, his snout nearly pressed to the opposite side of the glass, his breath leaving foggy apparitions.

"What manner of," said Sandy at a total loss. "I'm beginning to hate everything."

Tasso patted Cucumbers on the head, then urged him forward. "It's okay," he said.

Immediately after the wolfhounds touched noses, the mirror dog sprang back and reared playfully, stretching forepaws on the floor. Cucumbers beamed and wagged his tail.

"Can I borrow this?" said Tasso, snapping Sandy's attention. The man was dangling one of Jonas' dirty crew socks by the welt.

Sandy wrinkled her nose. "Yeah, sure," she said. "Knock yourself out."

"Here you go, boy," said Tasso, passing the sock off to Cucumbers. The wolfhound dutifully accepted the article, chomping down and trotting to the mirror.

The mirror wolfhound had been bounding willy-nilly, coaxing Cucumbers to play along, but when he noticed the sock his demeanor shifted. Inside the snap of a finger, he scaled from buffoon to business executive. As a noble knight called to swear an oath, the wolfhound strode to the forefront, his silhouette expanding, challenging the mirror's size with each step.

Ardently Cucumbers pressed the grimy fabric to the glass. And with the reverence of a courtier receiving a diadem, the other wolfhound placed his snout to the offered sock. Pain streaked the wolfhound's eyes as he drew in the scent. Not from the odor emanating, Sandy believed, but from something deeper, more primitive. There was an acknowledgment that passed between these gentle beasts. As if Cucumbers had just asked the wolfhound to begin digging a family plot.

"Is my son alive?!" blurted Sandy. She touched the mirror, half-expecting the surface to give a little and ripple outward. "My Jonas? Is he?"

The wolfhound flicked an eye at the woman's hand but did not shy.

Sandy looked pleadingly between the wolfhounds. "Will he find my son?" she said to Cucumbers. The dog lowered his head to release the sock and when his face returned, he immediately swatted her chin with his tongue.

"Is that a yes?" said Sandy through tears. She wrapped Cucumbers about the neck, gratefully embracing the overlarge canine.

"That's a yes," translated Tasso. "Or he'll die trying."

"Oh," said Sandy. "How dangerous..." she swung her head at the mirror. "Where did he go..."

"Where do you think?" Tasso removed a hand from behind his back to tap Cucumbers on the head. "Tracking a scent."

CHAPTER 18

Archers took the ramparts like dusk sweeping a field. Ground forces bulked up, helping one another affix armor and inspect weaponry. Blacksmiths billowed their forges creating the winds from legend. At the gates heavy armored knights tethered cords to their waists, latching the receiving end to great iron hooks upon the stonewall. Schoolmarms ushered children into sheltered bulwarks, followed close behind by the elderly. All of this beneath the falling of tradesmen hammers, playing a dirge while shouts filled with need swirled amidst the humid afternoon.

"No!" The Leeds Devil would not relent. "It's not happening! I'm not sticking around here any longer!" A growing entourage of pleading magistrates and common folk had accumulated at his heels as he tread the streets.

"You and Dafodhel could change the tides!" Vera offered, tugging Jonas' elbow. Scary immediately swatted her away. "We need you!" She shouted as a last-ditch effort.

"This is our hour of need!" shouted a man in a flowing caftan robe.

"Help us! This is the last bastion, the last Leeds village!" Another man piped in, his apparel comprised of simple hand-spun wool. "We'll be done for!"

A woman with an infant wrapped around her neck made her appeal, "Please, Devil!" She clutched at him and was rebuffed by Posh. Startled, the woman nearly fell face-first on the cobble.

From the corner of his eye, Jonas watched the woman stumble. "Sorry about that," he said, catching her. "But seriously, guys. I have to get home."

Dejectedly the crowd dispersed, and Jonas found the remaining steps to Isaac's front door much quieter. The Ritts alighted upon the roofline at the same moment Jonas' knuckles tapped the front door.

The door swung open.

"I'm almost ready," said Isaac, waving for his guests to come inside. "Nearly there." He straightened and quickly glanced at Jonas. "Just as I thought," he mumbled with a shrug as he glided away.

Dafodhel transformed into a manageable walking cane upon Jonas' crossing of the threshold.

"I'm glad to see you survived," said Jonas as he hurried into the kitchen. This time there were no flavorful scents to greet him, only stale air brought about by burnt toast. "I was worried."

From within his sewing grotto, Isaac called back, "Likewise." Then added, "I baked bread if you're hungry."

A lump of charcoal atop a checkered tea cloth was all that Jonas noticed on the central counter. As he scoured the tight kitchen, lifting lids and opening drawers, Isaac called out again.

"It's a bit crisp around the edges!"

"Oh," said Jonas. He approached the charred hunk with harnessed enthusiasm. "Great. Thanks."

"Don't mention it," replied Isaac. "And don't come in until I tell you, alright?"

"No problem," said Isaac, sucking a paper cut sustained from punching a thumb through the immolated crust.

"Give this a go." Dafodhel offered, diminishing into a bread knife. "This should *proof* more to your liking." The blade giggled as Jonas began sawing through the crust. "Proof... just a bit of bread humor."

"It's not really a joke when you have to explain it," said Jonas.

In an unexpected turn, the innards of the burnt lump were mysteriously pastry-like. Smooth and light and warming, with a touch of sweetness. Its texture leaned more towards cake than your simple loaf of bread.

"This is delicious," praised Jonas through a mouthful. "What kind of bread is this, Daf?" Jonas directed the question towards his knife but was hoping Isaac would respond instead.

"I do not know," replied Dafodhel. "Perhaps a baker may know?"

A quiet was all that stirred in the sewing chamber.

"Burnt bread," came the reluctant response.

"Come on now," scoffed Jonas. "I've had my fair share of burnt bread, believe me, you've never met my mother. And this is not burnt bread."

Isaac did not respond.

"I mean, sure it's burnt, anyone can see that," continued Jonas while the Hylda munched and hummed a tune. "But this tastes like birthday cake or something! It's so airy and, and, and..." Jonas snapped his fingers, hoping that Isaac would pick up the *Yes, and...*

But Isaac was not playing.

"Scrummy?" Scary answered, totally unsure of herself.

"Yes! Sure! Yeah!" Jonas snapped a finger and pointed at the little witch. "Scrummy! I like that!"

"Sounds suitable," agreed Isaac irritably as he entered the kitchen rubbing his eyes. He appeared uneager about the current topic. "Alright, come on in." The Still beckoned Jonas to follow.

Jonas entered the chamber and was rendered spellbound.

Standing prominently over the marsh of cloth and thread were two fully dressed wooden mannequins. One displayed Jonas' tunic, repaired and ready. The other weaved a vine of lustrous plate, tinged a vibrant shade of cobalt.

"You know how to make armor," said Jonas at length, carefully calculating the words so they flowed like a statement.

"I do not," replied Isaac. "But I do know a thing or two about repurposing."

Jonas approached the tunic and flicked a leather band embroidered between collar and sleeve. "These are new," he said.

There were several such strips adorning the tunic on the upper chest portion, spaced symmetrically from one other.

"You will find reinforcements beneath each," said Isaac, skimming the clutter to stand beside the armor. "They are latches, of a fashion." He plucked the tunic from the mannequin and passed it to Jonas. "Here, cover your shame."

Aside from the bandings about his stomach, Jonas was indeed naked from the waist up. A detail that had gone unnoticed until this point.

Jonas slid the tunic over his head, the fabric lightly grazing his newly chiseled frame. Not a draft pierced the layers, all tatters and holes had been seen to, flawlessly mended, not one single blemish. Word that a Yéne had scored a rip on the article would seem outright slanderous.

"This has healed better than my wounds," said Jonas, passing a hand over his right side. "At least I have a scar to remind me of my tangle with the Yéne. This doesn't show any signs of damage at all."

Isaac was aligning a spaulder to Jonas' left shoulder. "And here, this is how you fasten the armor to the tunic," he advised.

With a gratifying click, Jonas felt the armor snap into place. "Holy smokes!" Adjoined to the plate, his shoulder rolled buttery smooth. "Hand me the other."

"Of course," said Isaac, stepping back. "It's designed for self-service."

Jonas fiddled with the right shoulder piece and Isaac stepped forward.

"I can get it, I can get it," said Jonas.

"You may need to feel around a bit with your thumb..."

A satisfying pop came from beneath the steel.

"Nice!" Jonas beamed, slapping his newly armored shoulder before reaching for another piece of the set.

Isaac nodded with a strained smile, hands willfully locked behind his back as spectating proved to be quite difficult.

After a few moments lost to orientation, and only requiring Isaac to point out twice which end of his chest plate was up, Jonas stood complete in his armor. It was a rather simple suit, not heavy and unwieldy like the robot-looking knights depicted in history books. Merely his shoulders, wrists, chest, knees, and shins were armored. This granted plenty of space in-between for freer range of movement. Also the chest plate was smaller in comparison to traditional chest plates and was notched and secured in a way that allowed him to bend and move without snagging his belt.

"How does it feel?" asked Isaac with a curled finger to his chin. "Do I need to adjust the knee hinges at all? Try a few squat thrusts."

Gym class anxiety welled up uninvited. Visions cropped up in his mind of Coach Taylor screaming for him to shimmy up the rope while other classmates effortlessly climbed the unthinkable height. Then Jonas remembered that he was jacked now, and performing a couple exercises would be child's play.

"You got it," said Jonas, his response fortified with a thumbs up. He lowered to the floor and squatted like a frog, testing his dexterity by bouncing on his heels a few times. He planted his hands and shot his legs back in a movement he had never accomplished with such grace but had witnessed countless times in envy. And while he performed a few more thrusts for fun, not one contradicting squeak issued from the armor's joints.

"Immaculate," said Dafodhel.

Jonas and Isaac looked around, unsure of where the weapon was speaking from. Jonas had left her on the counter beside the bread, but she sounded much closer.

"The small witch," hinted Dafodhel. How they had overlooked the sword teetering in Scary's hand, was a mystery for all-time. The blade alone rivaled the Hylda's height. "Take me," she instructed, "before this monster severs a limb."

Delicately Jonas retrieved the sword from Scary, taking the flat of the blade between thumb and forefinger. "Why didn't you just change into something dull?" he asked Dafodhel, momentarily dazzled by his own reflection in the steel.

"Bah," scoffed Dafodhel. "I wanted to be taken up in this form. Anything less would have been tawdry. Now, see how we complement one other?"

"I do," said Jonas, then turned to Isaac. "Last time I was here, before we began our journey, you mentioned a gate that was much closer..."

"Yes," replied Isaac, handing Jonas a baldric. "Just snug this *over* your chest plate, I want to see how it looks." He roved a hand to his mouth and thoughtfully pressed a thumb to a vampiric fang. "That should do fine, actually. I was concerned that the ruddy brown of the leather may upset the steel's natural hue, and it does not."

Jonas angled Dafodhel into the frog attached to the baldric. "The closer gate," he repeated, securing the mythical blade to his hip. A war was arriving and Jonas wanted to be home before the crashing of blades.

"You are missing something," said Isaac, reminding Jonas of his mother when she was neck-deep in the clock repair zone.

"A shield?" offered Jonas.

Dafodhel gasped.

The Still's jawline grew viciously taut.

The Hylda flashed to Jonas' side.

The air in the space clamped down on Jonas' chest, beneath his armor.

"That," said Isaac with grim resolve. "Was your first query." The words were an antidote of sorts, dispelling the murder that had gathered in his eyes. "Two more, Devil without wings, and you will no longer walk among the living." He turned his face and wiped his nose as one who had just been punched, then casually added, "Nothing personal. And no, not a shield."

Jonas would rather take a road trip through the Sahara in his mother's minivan, or square off with multiple Yénes, than ever, ever stand before a Hush after imparting a third question. What he sensed in Isaac was crippling, horrifying, and beyond anything a nightmare had ever conjured. Without a shred of doubt, that was the scariest moment of his life.

"Not a shield," said Jonas, hollow. "Good to know."

"No." Isaac shifted his feet. "It will come to me." The spell had passed, yet the Still appeared agitated. Perhaps an imprint had been left by the dark magic, and he needed time to sort it out. "We should not be gone overlong, you wager?" he asked, spinning in place uncertainly. He shot to his sofa and rifled beneath the heaps of fabric. "We have only to avenge your family." He sounded as one checking off a list.

"Pretty much," replied Jonas.

Isaac lunged from the sofa to the circular window above. "There is bloodshed on the wind." A restless spirit had afflicted him.

"The Terrens have rallied their forces," stated Dafodhel. "The war has finally come to Brimon."

"What lovely timing," said Isaac, looking up from the blade to admire his own hands. "It seems we must take a detour on the way to the graveyard."

Jonas and the Hylda stood waiting on Isaac's front porch as he made preparations. But unlike the last time, the Hylda were not tittering with excitement. In fact, they had not made a sound since Jonas had voiced his stupid question to the Still.

"Hey, Scary," said Jonas. "Can you put that somewhere else?" Since departing the home, the Hylda's hand had been glued to the hind side of his thigh. The Hylda responded by sliding her hand to the crook of his knee. "That's better, I guess," Jonas conceded with a sigh.

War horns bellowed in stereo from opposing gates. This was very disconcerting, seeing as they were fixing to leave, unless Isaac held knowledge of a secret, hidden exit. The point of living inside a massive fortification minimized the threat of invasion, so it seemed reasonable that the only means of escape were through the north and south gates.

"That was costly," said Dafodhel.

"I know," he said, patting Dafodhel's pommel. "I've been wondering though. What would happen if you asked him a question?"

"A very good inquiry," replied Dafodhel after a moment of thought. "I do not know for certain, but understand, that is a theory I will never test."

"Huh," said Jonas, his shoulder armor rising and falling beneath a deep breath. "I kinda figured."

The door opened and Isaac stepped out, revealed in a different set of light armor, crueler in appearance, having sharp edges where a more functional suit would hold round. A knight's helmet with an open visor covered his pointy ears and dark hair, limiting his features to eyes, nose, and mouth. Abruptly holding his next step, he shrugged the hood of his mantle up over the top of his helm.

"Why are you smiling at me like that?" asked Isaac.

"Just glad to have you on my side, is all."

The Polish Mafia had no idea what was coming their way. But first, Jonas had to free himself of this world.

The first waves of Terren arrows pelted the north and south gates simultaneously, forcing the fighters upon the scaffolding to raise their shields. After that, the next wave stippled the courtyard, then after that, without regard for those not in the fight, rained down on the village proper. Any watchmen bold enough to lower their shield during the downpour did not survive. Which, unsurprisingly, was the reason why the Terrens managed to reach the gates without suffering a scratch.

"The Terrens aren't saving money on arrows," muttered Jonas, hugging the stone wall, trailing behind Isaac. Beforehand the Ritts had conveyed to Jonas the impending arrow assault, and in response he had ordered the gargoyles to rise higher into the sky. The Ritts were Terren defectors after all.

Jonas looked to the heavens. "Aside from the arrows, you have more tips?" he asked his Ritts.

"Avoid their blades and fangs," came a reply.

"Try not to trip and fall," added another voice.

"Gee, thanks," said Jonas. Isaac peered at him quizzically. "I'm speaking to my eyes in the sky." He pointed up. "Anymore pearls of wisdom?"

"We can clear a way for you." The voice growled resolute.

"No!" Jonas shouted, then internalized the next. *No! I won't lose anymore of you!*

"We should press on," said Isaac, indicating the north gate with an open hand.

"Gotcha," replied Jonas while inwardly instructing the Ritts to stay out of harm's way.

Knights on horseback sped past Jonas on their way to defend the gate. Riding vanguard was that helmetless knight who had greeted Jonas at the gate the day before, his flowing hair a glorious banner.

"Dude operates on a relaxed level of Hollywood hand-some," said Jonas to Isaac.

Isaac nodded. "Indeed."

Dashing at ground level, betwixt and between the horses' legs were a pack of unusual canine creatures. Fin-like appendages bilged from their spinal columns, among an array of other unusual traits. Regrettably the beasts flashed by at a rapid velocity, leaving Jonas with the faintest of glimpses. For now his curiosity would remain unsated.

The closer Jonas drew to the gate, the clearer the battle sounded. They were at the point where they could hear the archers groaning, the commanders dictating orders, and the dead... well, dying.

A platoon of wiry-thin bipedal creatures graced into view along the opposite wall, their direction the same as Isaac. Stealthily they crept, withholding weapons beneath mantles. Isaac caught the leader's eye, and after exchanging nods, pushed forward in concert.

Once Isaac and Jonas crossed beneath the scaffolding, twenty yards shy of the gate, the sneaky creatures signaled to hold.

"I don't believe they recognize you at the moment," said Isaac. "But I believe these chaps will prove most useful in gaining headway."

Jonas turned his face away from the creatures along the opposite wall. "Who are *they?*" he inquired, needlessly blocking his mouth.

"Demolitions," replied Isaac.

"Nice." Jonas lowered his hand to send a thumbs up.

The leader, from across the expanse, nodded at Isaac and tugged the collar of his mantle. Then as one, the demolition team rose and made for the gate, the battlefront.

"Wait," said Isaac, barring Jonas with an arm. "We should allow them some distance." His eyes blinked in clockwork rhythm, counting to an end.

A patchwork of knights, werewolves, and minotaurs hurried past, led by what appeared to be an elementary school field trip. Stone-faced women, hand-in-hand with frightened children and fledgling creatures pressed forward while fully armed knights cowered at their heels.

"Hey, Ike," said Jonas concerned, nudging the blinking Hush. "Are they using kids as —"

Isaac raised a finger for silence.

Rebuffed, Jonas turned to his Hylda. "If they are, that's pretty messed up," he said. His eyes hardened on the children as they disappeared into the smoke.

If the Leeds entertain this, what kind of game do the Terrens play?

"Now!" said Isaac, bringing Jonas to his feet.

One after the other, flames fizzled to life on the ramparts as archers ignited arrows. While distracted by the small fires, Jonas bashed his shoulder into something, causing the something to stumble in turn. Caught up in the sudden rush, he had not noticed the troop of burly hog-faced creatures that had joined his right flank.

"My bad," admitted Jonas.

The swine-like monster had been occupied correcting her steps to recognize whom she had collided with. Then suddenly the monster's rheumy eyes tripped with recognition, and from beneath her flat snout a smile began to spread. "Devil!" she bellowed. The curly blonde locks seeping from beneath her conical helmet bounced gleefully. "Girls! The Devil is with us!"

One of the swine soldiers dropped to a knee, while her kin carried on, and wrestled a horn from her neck. The leather strap dangled across her bulbous knucklebones as she navigated the horn beneath her snout, inhaled a tremendous breath.

"We mustn't stop!" shouted Isaac, pulling Jonas along.

No horn sounded.

Jonas glanced over his shoulder to see the swine soldier listing forward on both knees, a clutter of arrows projecting all over her front. The horn had become an afterthought as the dying creature sadly swatted at the fletchings, as if she could rid herself of the inconvenience. Jonas willed himself to turn away.

Before them, the war burgeoned. Brimon forces fought blade to blade, claw to claw, and fang to fang, twenty steps shy of the north gate. Dying creatures whimpered while the living fought desperately to avoid joining those below.

Isaac had not led them far before Jonas counted the elementary field trip among the dead. Some still clung to their mothers' hands.

A spear lashed out from the fray but was harmlessly defused by Jonas' chest plate. Though Jonas had not suffered an injury, the Hylda activated with a fury he had yet to witness. In midair Scary pounced on the weapon, toppling the wielder while Posh latched onto the Terren knight's face. What immediately transpired afterward, Jonas was not privy to. He had looked away as he sensed apprehension from his Ritts in the skies above. The spear thrust had sent a current of panic throughout his passing spirits.

It was then that Jonas noticed flaming arrows speeding from the fortress like fiery comets. "Shouldn't they be aiming higher —"

"Down!" screamed Isaac.

Jonas and the Still dropped to their chests. The Hylda, abandoning their prey, slick with gore, fell atop Jonas as a protective barrier. Meager though it was, Jonas appreciated the gesture. Then as the banter of flames passing directly overhead explained to Jonas just how close he had come to death, the world exploded.

To their right, a great yellow orb was rapidly expanding into a bubble the size of Chicago's Cloud Gate. Soon its surface halted taut, reaching maximum tension, and ruptured another explosion. Bodies blasted up into the sky, and upon their descent Jonas noticed all over the field more and more bubbles were blossoming, seemingly fed by flaming arrows.

Isaac had returned to his feet. "Up!" he shouted.

More arrows sailed and more blasts erupted in off-rhythm cadence. Knights and creatures alike fled from the orbs, and those caught up in the detonations were long gone. Future generations of forest folk will be discovering bones in their tree boughs until the end of time.

"Draw me!" Dafodhel shouted. "Are you daft?!"

Jonas obediently drew the weapon, hurrying behind Isaac. "Sorry!" he shouted. "I was preoccupied by —" Another orb burst to his left. "That!"

The fighting had ceased for the most part as both sides focused concern on the devastation wrought from the explosions. Isaac tucked behind a sunken wall from an abandoned bulwark and gestured for Isaac to hunker down beside him.

"We should be booking it!" Jonas said to the Still. "Now feels like a really good time!"

Isaac lifted a hand for calm then applied it to his chin. "Because," he said, peering toward a mantled figure twenty yards to their left.

"Hey," began Jonas, "that's one of those demolition dudes..." He trailed off as the creature broke into a sprint, aiming toward a squad of Terren archers that had settled at the peak of a hillock. Had they not been so preoccupied, rocketing arrows into the village, they may have noticed the creature.

"Wait for it," said Isaac, resting a hand on Jonas' vambrace.

The creature appeared among the startled archers and wheeled to his right, exposing his glowing yellow chest to the fort. With the most perfect of timing, a flaming arrow, fired from the fort, struck dead center on the creature's chest. The creature curled his body around the arrow, protecting it. And that's when Jonas discovered the origin of those exploding orbs.

"That's brutal," mumbled Jonas as the creature's skin expanded, stretching its limits. The archers broke and ran, save for three. One of the three took notice, but before he could alert the others, it was far too late. The fissure at the peak of the orb began to split and a blistering flash overtook the afternoon's daylight. A bone-jarring explosion ensued.

The explosion merely rattled Jonas' bones, but for the fellows on the ridge, their bones were powdered.

"Come! Now!" said Isaac, bolting to his feet. The detonation echoed into the valley.

As Jonas rose, something tugged the hem of his tunic. He swatted it away, believing it to be Scary. But the hand he struck was far more fragile than the Hylda's clinger.

"Devil," said a child.

Jonas whirled around. The ringing in his ears had finally receded enough to pick up lesser sounds.

A girl, no older than five, stood beneath him rubbing her eyes. Her skin was a pale gray and her teeth were squared like a horse. "I can't find my mother," she said. The bottom fringe of her dress was soaked, tinged crimson. Jonas wanted to believe the stains were nothing more than mud.

One hundred percent mud, please.

"Jonas, her mother is dead," said Dafodhel from her scabbard. "For some, like the demolition regiment, leaving the gate is meant to be a one-way trip."

"Hey!" screamed Isaac from no man's land. "Let's go! Our window is closing!"

"How she survived," said Dafodhel. "Why she survived… is not for us to know, but she is not supposed to be alive." The sword's voice matched her skin, cold steel. "We must abandon her. She was counted among the dead before the war horns first sounded."

The little girl surged into Jonas' left leg, hugging him tight. Tighter than his armor, for he could feel the buckles digging into flesh. Scary and Posh approached with questioning eyes, but Jonas waved them away.

"Stay here," Jonas ordered his Hylda. The skies continued to rain arrows, discouraging Jonas from summoning his Ritts. "I will be back." He set his jaw toward Brimon and drew Dafodhel.

"What are you doing?!" Dafodhel shouted enraged. "I won't aid you!"

"Become a pinwheel for all I care," replied Jonas. "This one is meant to live."

CHAPTER 19

Was it three or four years ago?

Jonas had been in sixth grade, so it had to be three years ago.

How time flies.

For whatever reason, Jonas' mind sped back to a Scarberry Junior High Field Day three years back. An end of the school year custom that gave the screws of humiliation one final crank right before summer arrived.

After his name had been announced for the Green Team, how they groaned. One would believe they had received a cancer diagnosis all at once.

Jonas understood that it was not a groan of disappointment, for in order to be disappointed one would need to hold prior expectations.

"Anybody else!"

"Not *him* again!"

"C'mon! Give Chokula to Yellow this year!"

He recalled the looks of disdain smeared across their faces. Their pain was his fault. As he walked toward his assigned team, they parted aside like a repulsed Red Sea.

"I'm sorry," he had muttered. "I'm sorry that I'm me."

But no one had heard him.

The whistle blew in the past, returning him to the present, where the tiny girl meant as a sacrificial shield was cradled in his left arm, yet alive.

The Leeds had retreated to the gate, and the Terrens fled to the topmost crest upon valley's hillside. Once the final combustible creature had blown, both sides stared at one another across a newly formed expanse. A collective breath of relief had been taken, allowing space for the licking of wounds. A respite fell, but for the most reluctant among the ranks, hoping to be let off the hook, their hopes would soon crumble.

Hollow breaths borne from over-exertion soon gave way to seething, ragged spit riddled exhales. Now recovered the fighters picked up screams and roars, they bashed their shields in challenge, signaling break time's end.

"I'm sorry," said Jonas. "I'm sorry that I'm me." But the war bugles had sounded, drowning his words. And then with the poorest of timing, he joined the fight.

An arrow pinged from his right vambrace. The arrow spent by a Leeds archer upon the battlement. An easy mistake, seeing as Jonas was running in the same direction as their foe.

"Can you transform into a shield or something?" Jonas shouted at his sword.

"I thought you wished me to be a cheap trinket?" came the surly reply.

An arrow skipped off the ground a few feet ahead, clearly trained on him. "That was before —" A truer aimed arrow struck Jonas square in the shoulder, luckily deflected by his armor. "That was before everybody was my enemy!"

"Sorry, Jonas," said Dafodhel. *"I may only prevail in the form of weaponry."* She held a pause between Jonas' beating steps. *"Sorry that I'm me..."*

Fortunately the Leeds ground forces, unlike their archers, were not interested in Jonas. He approached at their left flank, while the heat of the battle radiated central to the north gate.

These pesky archers are dead set on bringing me down! Jonas thought while bobbing and weaving in between the spent shafts, shielding the child with his sword arm.

These dudes just won't let up! He hoped that they would soon recognize him and stop trying to kill him. That was, until a shriek from the hilltop froze every hair on Jonas' arms. Which in turn froze every nocked arrow on the ramparts.

This was *the* shriek. The Lancethanes had arrived.

The Leeds army had been barely holding on, their last hopes dissolved. And now the drake-and-rider force would lay waste to whomever stood in their way.

Dread circulated throughout Jonas' insides. His legs were infused with lead and his hands began to shake, and momentarily he wrestled with the idea of playing dead.

Get a grip! He told himself. He glanced down at the child to see a brand-new look of terror on her face.

Some twenty yards ahead, the battle had rejoined. With admirable resolve the Leeds continued to fight, despite the Lancethane's arrival. The momentum granted to the Terrens by the downhill slope was undeniable, and when they clashed,

Leeds could not help but give ground. It would only be a matter of time before they fell back into the fort.

Leeds archers continued to spend arrows, their trajectory focused, narrowed, picking off the Terren rearguard. This meant that the skies were no longer plagued by arcing shafts.

Jonas could sense his Ritts holding back, their purpose suspended, forbidden, and it was eating them up. Soon their Devil would be joining the fight without them. He need only say the word and a pathway could be cleared. One order and this forsaken child would be inside the fort, alive.

Not another Ritts would fall, and this child, signed and sealed for Death's doorstep, was not headed there. Scary and Posh were the last of their kind and he would not be responsible for their extinction. Vera and Greta, Isaac, the Leeds children, the Leeds people, the Leeds' falling soldiers...

And my mother — are all going to make it out alive.

The dam was Swiss cheese, spouting buckets of water, and Jonas felt like the little Dutch boy staving the flow with his finger.

A disarmed Leeds knight stumbled into Jonas. A gaping wound to his midsection pulsated blood into his open palms. Jonas wanted to reach out to help, but he had no idea what he could do. On his knees, the knight looked up as Jonas passed him by. His misty eyes cleared for a moment, giving way to hope.

"Devil," the soldier muttered.

The north gate was well within sight. Jonas was nearly home free. Fortunately the tide had shifted long enough for him to skirt the central fight. Dafodhel, locked in his fist, was dry.

The heavily armored knights tethered to the fort were rushing back and forth, ruthlessly striking down any Terrens that broke through. An ape-like monster vaulted a series of Leeds fighters, landing inside the knights' killing radius, and was only given a moment to regret his decision.

A tremendous impact struck Jonas' chest plate, knocking him back. The Lancethane distraction had lifted, and the archers had retraced their aim on him.

Jonas heard a Ritts voice growl inside his head, *"Say the word."* The gargoyles did not care for sides, and only cared for him. *"Please,"* pleaded the voice.

Far below, Jonas sensed the gargoyles in the heavens above threatening to descend.

"No!" He shouted.

A single archer nocked and leveled his bow toward Jonas, the rest were occupied by other targets.

The archer's draw arm twitched and Jonas staggered. A flash of searing pain graced his left thigh and he feared that he had crushed the child upon his flinch. Jonas hurtled forward as the archer reloaded, crossing a significant amount of ground, feeling the wound knit as he advanced. His eyes were locked on the rampart and a wriggle upon his left vambrace told him that the child yet lived.

Jonas' left foot caught on a protruding scrap of armor, careening him sideways. Fortunate and unfortunate, for an arrow had been sent his way, this one targeting his skull. And that scrap of armor had belonged to the corpse of a Terren rear-guard, which signaled that the battle now knocked upon the Leeds' doorstep. Of a sudden, it seemed that every ounce of the luck Jonas had been sipping dried up.

Raise me and fight! Dafodhel shouted. *Call your Ritts!*

"No!"

You tried your best, there's no shame in it!

Jonas drew the child closer and turned for the gate.

There is no other way! Discard her and fight!

An arm's length from Jonas' back, the tethered guards pulled at their restraints, yearning for the fight.

"Fall back!" A commanding voice carried from the battle-front. "Back through the gate! Behind the walls! Fall back!"

The Leeds army was failing.

Amidst the commotion threatening Jonas from all sides, he remained fixated on that bothersome archer. The guy just would not give up.

Just give the order, said the Ritts, knowing who his Devil was staring down.

"No," replied Jonas quietly. "There is always another way." And with that he raised Dafodhel over his head and strode forward. "Do you not recognize me? Do you not recognize your Devil?!" he screamed. He had wanted to sneak through the battlefield incognito, but that archer had forced him to tip his hand.

The knights before Jonas reeled in awe at his sudden appearance, creating a crevice for him to pass through.

Trailing his steps, a chain reaction of hope had been ignited. The ground beneath the Leeds forces seemed to list as they garnered momentum. Unbidden, in a rush, thoughts of survival flashed behind the knights' eyes. Not only survival. With the Devil on their side they could finally rule the Riverlands! The commander, the one who had been calling for retreat, began screaming for his knights to turn and press onward.

The Terrens conceded ground. And framing a thunderous backdrop, behind and above it all, the Lancethanes screeched into the valley as if they had suffered a branding to their privates.

"Jonas!" A strikingly tall man in armor called from across the flagstone courtyard. "Your timing could not have been more perfect," praised the man. If Vera and Greta's race had a male counterpart, then this guy was a dead ringer for it. His smile revealed long and sharp canines, like a vampire, like Jonas. Aside from all that, there was something else about this guy that seemed blatantly familiar.

"Yeah, my mom is a clock doctor, so good timing runs in the family," said Jonas distractedly, scanning a safe harbor for the child.

"Among other things," said the man as a villainous troop of winged figures assembled behind him. They shared a resemblance to the man's race, except they bore wings upon their backs. Huge, menacing bat wings that made the Ritts seem a Huffy to a Ducati. "Do what you must," said the man, hard eyes glossing from the child to Dafodhel. "Then meet me at the gate." His smile broadened. "Sebastian would be proud."

"Sure thing," replied Jonas, half-listening.

The man gave a sharp nod, then waved his sword arm, motioning for the winged entourage to follow.

From the parapets, the war horns unified into one great warning bellow.

Whatever's drawing those horn men's attention must be pretty important, Jonas speculated, making his way deeper into the fort. *Wait a minute, did that guy just mention —*

The man's parting phrase suddenly struck Jonas, stopping him dead in his tracks; as if the remembrance were infused with paralytic venom. "Sebastian," whispered Jonas. His mind reeled.

How could some random dude in another dimension know my father's name? What the heck was going on?

"Cholira?!" a strangled female voice freed Jonas from his spiral. "Is that you?!"

The child began to squirm with arms outstretched. "Aunty?" she sounded half asleep.

Quickly Jonas approached the gray-skinned woman and half-heartedly deposited the child into her arms, still suffering from his daze.

"Oh my sweet Cholira!" the woman over-pronounced through her horse teeth. The family resemblance was irrefutable. "I thought I had lost everyone!" She skipped in front of Jonas, who had turned to head for the gate. "Thank you so much, Devil..." she trailed off, stepping from his path. "Devil?"

Jonas was blank, not listening.

"Dad..." he muttered, sheathing Dafodhel.

The horns upon the ramparts continued to blare, which made gathering his thoughts difficult. And something had whipped them into a frenzy.

I wish these guys had a snooze button, thought Jonas.

A riot of clicking hooves startled Jonas aside as a mass of excited juvenile satyrs and minotaurs capered past.

"The Skorsa have arrived!" they shouted in joyous rapture, leaping as they ran. Giddily they jostled one another like teenage girls gifted VIP badges.

"Skorsa?" said Jonas. A funnel storm of questions roiled in his skull. "Good thing Isaac isn't around..."

"The Skorsa are the winged braves we met mere moments ago," offered Dafodhel. "They are awaiting us at the gate."

"Ah." Jonas nodded. "Those guys."

The fledgling minotaurs and satyrs, in their infectious excitement, had accumulated into a horde, and were now advancing upon the scaffolding. This gave Jonas a clear-cut run to the gate, and in a pleasant shift, as he drew up before the man who had mentioned his father's name, the Skorsa Captain, the horns finally ceased.

The captain greeted Jonas with a solemn nod. He was leaned against the gate's leftmost stanchion, casually chewing a twig of some fashion. The other Skorsa were nowhere to be seen.

The battle had moved, raging a bitter tapestry upon the hillside. Despite the difficult incline, the Leeds forces pressed the Terrens back onto their heels. Though numbers had favored the Terrens, their losses were blaringly obvious. And soon the tally would threaten equivalency. Yet not one Terren had cut and run, and all of this transpired beneath the Lancethanes' watch.

"Hey, so, I was wondering —"

The Captain interrupted Jonas with a lifted finger. "Witness," he said, removing the twig from his mouth. Then with twig in fist, brought his thumb to its pinnacle and severed it twain.

Jonas caught a shimmer on the far reaches of his sight. He turned from the Captain to see the Skorsa soaring toward the battle. The Lancethanes took up a warning call as the Skorsa shadows overtook the Leeds rear flank. Alas, the warning arrived late.

The Skorsa struck like vipers. And as the twig, the Terren line fractured. Overwhelmed and in a panic, the attackers fled, discovering their downhill advantage was now poison to their limbs.

"That is enough," said the Captain, looking at Jonas but speaking elsewhere. "Do not get carried away." The Skorsa retracted their claws, rising into a circling pattern over the hillside. Then the Captain's eyes focused on Jonas. "When you think you have won the day, defeat lurks behind excessive tenacity. Be careful not to over-extend yourself. Even when you believe victory is assured, never underestimate your opponent." The Lancethanes released a foreboding roar in a lower register, their echoes punctuated the Captain's point.

The Terrens had disengaged and retreated, having lost the high ground.

The Leeds youths perched upon the walls screamed their throats raw as the world that stretched before the gates released a sincere breath of relief.

The field commanders upheld the same belief as the Skorsa Captain, signaling their forces to fall back. Tomorrow would arrive soon enough. Today they had proclaimed that Brimon was not a prey so easily consumed.

Suddenly Jonas sensed the requests of his passing spirits; his Hylda begged permission to join him, while his Ritts conveyed ravening hunger — requesting freedom to hunt.

The captain shrugged from the post. "Did you see that?" he asked, standing close.

"How could I miss it?" replied Jonas. Internally he sent an affirmative nod to his Hylda and Ritts, granting their requests. "Your Skorsa saved the day."

The captain cocked his head. "*My* Skorsa?" He laughed. "No, no, that is not what I'm talking about," he continued, scratching the side of his nose. "It was not the Skorsa who won the day, Jonas. It was you. Can you not see that? You did not even need to join. And I can hear some half-witted troubadour now — *'All it took to turn the tide was knowing that the Devil alone was on their side.'*" In the wake of the playful melody, a somber look came upon his face. "That's power."

The realization came as a gut punch. "All because of me?" said Jonas. A vision of his humiliated former self picked for the Green Team floated into his mind.

The Skorsa approached from the courtyard. Their steps fell light, as if their feet were liable to take flight at any moment.

With the visors on their helms lifted, the Skorsa's faces looked very much like their Captain. For all Jonas had witnessed thus far, the Skorsa may have resembled a housefly or a blobfish. Gross for sure, but not surprising. Nevertheless, Jonas was relieved to discover that they were not hideous mutants.

"All because of you," agreed the captain, taking a knee and bowing his head. "The Skorsa — at your service."

Jonas barely felt Scary and Posh arrive. The Hylda clung to his side, taking in the kneeling Skorsa.

"*No Valorous...*" murmured Posh.

The captain brought his head up but said nothing.

"Please, stand," said Jonas, clearing his throat. "You can stand. Earlier you said that my dad would be proud of me..."

"I did," said the captain.

"How, how do you know my dad?"

"How I came to know your father?" The captain inhaled. "Why, I knew him from my birth. You see, Jonas, my name is Siegmund Raguel Terren. And I am his brother, your uncle."

CHAPTER 20

The conversation was far too important to be held out in the open, under the gates, with victory horns set to blare. It was difficult to speak and even more difficult to listen. And Jonas really, really wanted to listen.

As Uncle Siegmund led the way toward his encampment, the Hylda pressed tight to Jonas' sides. As usual, Isaac had made himself scarce, lingering somewhere off-stage, out of frame. The Skorsa humorlessly marched behind, treading light, hardly disturbing a pebble.

Songs of victory swept the streets, fed from the crenellations above to the soil below. And it felt to Jonas as if it would have no end.

Whenever the onlookers caught sight of the Skorsa, they would cheer all the louder. The most daring among them would even reach out to clap a winged warrior's shoulder. One bold fox-faced monster wearing a baker's apron stepped inside the retinue to drape a companionable arm around the neck of a stone-faced Skorsa. Jonas immediately feared for the baker, but the Skorsa returned the gesture, swinging an arm over the fox creature's scrawnier shoulders, bestowing a rough but friendly jostle.

Jonas avoided eye contact with the crowds, fearing recognition. He did not want to stop for anything or anyone. His uncle, a half-head taller and walking lockstep beside him was a truly fearsome man. Based upon his uncle, Jonas' imagination began weaving a needlepoint of his father's appearance.

Was he taller? Thinner? He wondered. *Could he have been scarier? If that's true —*

An astute-looking goblin standing atop the backrest of a park bench flailed wildly, upsetting Jonas' train of thought.

"Aw, c'mon…" he muttered, helplessly watching the goblin cupping his twisted little mouth to broadcast his whereabouts to the surrounding village.

Siegmund turned at the goblin's crowing and noticed his nephew's deflation. "Embrace it!" he declared, charismatically pumping a fist at the crowds. "It's who you are! Try as you might, you can't hide it!"

"I'm not into being in the spotlight," said Jonas pivoting to be heard, nearly tripping on Posh. "And I want to know more about my dad!"

"There will be plenty of time for that, Jonas," said Siegmund smiling. "Just enjoy this victory."

Word of the Devil spread at an ungodly rate throughout the village. Crowds had emerged and joined the network, and with the army filling in behind there was nowhere to hide. Jonas had not felt so tightly packed like this since belly crawling in the cavern beneath the uprooted locust tree.

"Draw me." Dafodhel spoke directly into Jonas' mind.

"Whoa, that seems a bit drastic," replied Jonas. "I think I'll just take my uncle's advice and —"

"I simply wish to see what is transpiring."

"Oh, yeah. Sure."

On the sly, not wanting to scare anyone, Jonas wrested Dafodhel from her scabbard ever so slowly.

"Raise that blade!" said Siegmund taking notice of the weapon. "Skorsa! Present arms!"

The Skorsa drew their swords as one. The synchronous display elicited gasps from the commonfolk, then they exhaled an uproar of elation.

Siegmund drew his sword. "This day is ours!" he cried, his onyx blade reflecting torchlight. Night seemed to have fallen quickly.

Time flies after you meet an uncle you didn't know you had in the middle of a battle you tried to avoid, thought Jonas as torches sizzled to life along the promenade ahead.

"Celebrate!" Siegmund continued. "But prepare! Prepare for tomorrow!" This warning was received with a consensus of further cheering and spirited dancing.

"My tents are up ahead," said Siegmund to Jonas. "Notice how that pathway doglegs to the right toward the village's southern gate? Advance in that direction and you won't be able to miss them."

"Wait, where are you going?"

"I'm going to prevent this horde from interrupting us any further," replied Siegmund, then added with a wink, "Nephew." He hitched a step and spun around with arms open. "Where's the nearest tavern, eh?" He pulled an on-looking Sylvan to his side and crushed his leafy trunk in a cheerful headlock. "First round's on this guy!"

It was odd, sitting in the quiet — in his *uncle's* tent — contemplating the emptiness of the shadows. All his life, Jonas had seen creatures there, from the corners, just out of sight. He had not been losing his mind. They had been there all along.

They had really been there all along.

Jonas hunched forward with chin resting in palms, facing the opening. The tent was spacious, ring shaped with two tables hobbled on one side where stacks of decaying maps overflowed. A lonely armor stand stood on the opposite side, empty. A one-piece spear crafted from marbled stone hung over Jonas' head, clasped in hooks that punched clean through the tent fabric.

Scary and Posh patrolled the tent, swapping shifts in measured increments, ensuring that Jonas did not go a moment without their presence. Evidently his mad dash through the battlefield had rattled the Hylda pretty good.

"Hey Daf," said Jonas, leaning back to let his dangling hair scratch the tent fabric. "How do you think I'd look with a beard?" He decided to dispense his gloomy thoughts and focus on happier stuff — like the arrangement of facial hair. "Or maybe a really big, puffy mustache that could curl at the ends?"

"From my limited understanding of such things, the men I have known to grow beards did so out of necessity," replied

Dafodhel. In her default sword form, she had been laid across a wine table that was positioned between the two principal chairs at the rear of the tent. One of which Jonas occupied. "Makes no difference to me how you appear when we slay your enemies. As long as you don't appear a clown or any other farce."

Jonas rocked forward in his chair; the front feet consumed several inches by topsoil. "Careful, Daffy," he said through a grin. "You're giving me ideas again." He stood to rescue his chair with his back to the front opening.

"Ideas, eh?" Siegmund's voice punched through the tent's front flap. "What ideas?" Then the man entered, his armor radiant in the torchlight.

Jonas laughed, trying to cover for his startled jump. "Me and Daf were just talking about clowns." He stood, knotting his hands together.

"Sounds important," said Siegmund, motioning for the exit. "Should I leave you to it?"

"No," replied Jonas at a loss. "No! It was —"

"Joking!" said Siegmund, making for his armor stand. "Only joking, dear nephew." He began to disarm, slipping buckles and loosening knots. "And who is *Daf* by the way? One of your skulking little Hylda?"

"No," replied Jonas, gesturing toward the wine table. "Daf is the sword. Dafodhel."

"Ah," said Siegmund. If he was astonished, then he hid it well.

"You've heard about Dafodhel, right?" asked Jonas.

"I have," said Siegmund. "A powerful blade that only intertwines itself with the affairs of others when it suits its own ambitions."

Suddenly Dafodhel was treading Jonas' ear canals. *That is a baseless accusation!*

Siegmund settled his sword into a row of hooks projecting from the armor stand and strode toward the vacant chair beside his nephew. "Even now," he said, stretching his torso against the backrest. "I'll bet it is speaking into your thoughts, dismissing what I just divulged." He locked eyes with Jonas for a moment. "I'm right, aren't I?"

"Yes," replied Jonas.

"Why tell him that!" Dafodhel huffed.

"It matters not," said Siegmund with a wave, addressing the sword. "It certainly has its *uses.*" He rocked to his feet and rubbed his hands together. "Anyhow! Nephew! You must have a slew of questions rattling around inside your head!" Siegmund made for a tall bucket fashioned from wooden ribbons. "Care for a splash of wine?" he asked.

"I don't," began Jonas uncertainly. "I don't, no, I mean, I'm not old enough to have alcohol." He understood that the laws back home did not extend to this realm, but to be perfectly honest, he was just not interested. And currently he was taken aback by his uncle's blatant disinterest in Dafodhel. Up to this point, everyone who had come into Dafodhel's close proximity had, by varying degrees, freaked out.

"Alcohol?" Siegmund straightened at the accusation. "Oh, no, this wine is unfermented." Innocently, he displayed the raised letters on the glass bottle, reading *abstemious*. "I refrain from poisoning myself, if it can be helped." He sloshed the purple liquid as if that would bring truth to his claim.

"But, earlier, didn't you lead a gaggle of monsters into a pub?"

"Gaggle..." remarked Siegmund. "Nice. And yes, I did divert that mob into a public house, to your benefit, but I did not imbibe of its spirits." He claimed a pair of wooden cups on his way back to his seat. "Do you wish to smell my breath as proof?"

"No, no," replied Jonas laughing. "I believe you. But, if it's all the same, I'm going to pass on the grape juice."

"Suit yourself," said Siegmund, setting Jonas' cup aside.

Insects hummed beyond the fabric, but within the tent stillness fell. The great captain stirred once to cross his legs and cradle his drink with two hands as if it were providing warmth.

At length Jonas breached the quiet. "My father," he began, taking a breath. "Your brother."

Siegmund considered Jonas with a faint smile.

"Is he really dead?"

Siegmund closed his eyes and drew a long pull from his cup, appearing troubled. "What do you know of the Prophecy?" he asked.

"Not much," replied Jonas. "Just that I'm the Leeds Devil or the Evil Seed or something, and it's a really big deal..."

"That's all?" Siegmund growled. "Guiltbrand can be just as useless as nips on a chest plate." He flicked a finger to Dafodhel. "Has your sword offered any guidance concerning the Prophecy?"

Jonas shook his head. "No, she hasn't," he said. "It's been pretty much everyone else saying, '*You're our Devil and you're supposed to rescue us.*' That kind of stuff, over and over."

"She?" inquired Siegmund. "The blade sounds as a woman to you?"

"Yeah," replied Jonas. "Doesn't she sound like that to everyone?"

"I would not know. I have never heard it speak." Between a blink, Siegmund's eyes flashed to his own sword at rest upon the armor stand. "My weapons have the decency to remain silent. The fact that the famed Dafodhel sounds female is a peculiar detail." Siegmund swapped which leg crossed the other and sat back. "Nevertheless, your rudimentary understanding of the Prophecy is disconcerting to me, to say the least. Guiltbrand, for all his faults, is actually an accomplished seer, believe it or not. There is no other living Sage whose predictions that I would stake my own life upon. Truly." Siegmund bit down a smirk and added, "Although he is a bit of a *clown.*"

Jonas smiled at his uncle. "He is a clown. But he's not as bad as his Council."

"Indeed," said Siegmund with a raised eyebrow. "Which is quite often the case." He reached for his bottle to refresh his cup. "Now, about enslightening you on the Prophecy — are you sure you don't want a drink? No? Fine by me." Siegmund proceeded to fill his cup to brimming. "A decade or so ago, our esteemed Guiltbrand divined or discovered or, more than likely, stumbled upon a most dire report. Prescient, impending, and of exceeding import. Mind you, at this time, Guiltbrand was employed by my parents — your grandparents — Leopold and Priska Terren." Siegmund held, waiting for Jonas to stop blinking. "That's correct," he continued. "Guiltbrand, along with many others, are Terren defectors. Myself included."

"So, wait," said Jonas tapping his armrest. "We're all Terrens in this tent? And there are Terrens on that hill, aiming to kill us?"

"Correct."

"And the Terrens are the baddies who have been looting and pillaging the countryside unchecked?"

"Also correct," stated Siegmund.

"So who're the Leeds?"

"Allow me to explain and everything will be clear," said Siegmund.

"Okay. Thanks for getting me up to speed," said Jonas. "Continue, I guess."

"I will not bombard you with a history lesson," assured Siegmund. "We have both seen the visage of war this day and I'd wager you're just as ready for the comforts of a soft cot as much as I am." Siegmund raised his cup and took a sip, observing his nephew reply with a shrug.

"Meh," said Jonas. His father's identity had been shrouded in mystery for his entire life, so sleep was hardly a blip. "I'm good."

"Very well then," said Siegmund nodding. "It is *I* who is longing for the comforts of the soft cot. Now, back to it. More than one decade has passed since the night that Guiltbrand and his Council entered the gates of Serpentfel, wailing, rousing even the dead from sleep. I will never forget that awful sound. In that moment, from my chambers, I believed that someone was grape-stomping a children's nursery — for the sounds of lament that rent the air. Never before had a premonition stirred that level of anguish from the diviners. Right then it became painfully clear to me — this did not bode well. And I was not wrong. Though, for once, I wish I had been." Siegmund's chin found his chest as he concluded, "For after that, this whole world changed."

Jonas teetered forward in his seat. "What did it say?"

"That Sebastian's first male offspring would become a Devil for the Leeds family, ushering the Terren family's demise. The child would be an Evil Seed, and no matter how much kindness would be extended to him during childhood, in the end, he would always grow to be a Devil. There was nothing that could be done to stem the child's nature." The age-lines beneath Siegmund's eyes lengthened as he gazed into the lamplight. "I'm paraphrasing of course."

Jonas, at the edge of his cushion, interjected, "Couldn't my father just refuse to get married or something?"

Siegmund continued as if Jonas had not spoken. "And once the Seed matured, his powers attainable, the disposal of his unseen shackles would be imprinted upon his wrists." He blinked. "I'm sorry, did you say something?"

"Yeah," replied Jonas. "My dad could have become a monk, right? Just not have had kids. Easy enough." Jonas swiped his palms together, dry washing them. "Problem solved."

Siegmund smiled, glancing upward. "Clearly, you did not know your father."

"And whose fault would that be?" said Dafodhel.

For a moment Jonas was unsure as to whether the blade was speaking into his thoughts, but the murderous expression that glimpsed his uncle's face revealed otherwise.

"The blame is shared," said Siegmund. "The Hells know how I blame myself. What I could have done, should have done. Was there something I could have said to my brother to change the course of history? Perhaps. One can torture oneself in the stretches of the night, endlessly thinking and thinking, losing days' worth of sleep without reaching a solace that does not, nor will not, ever exist."

Dafodhel sighed.

"Regret is a thorn," stated Siegmund, sneering at the magic sword. He turned toward Jonas. "You look so much like your father, it's uncanny."

"I've heard I have his teeth," said Jonas with a wink.

Siegmund laughed into his shoulder. "That, and many other traits."

"So what happened after the Sage made his prediction?" inquired Jonas. "I assume my dad fled the kingdom?"

Siegmund nodded. "It was ill-advised. But, yes, Sebastian decided it best that he remove himself completely. Despite the fact that he was the heir of Serpentfel."

"He was your older brother," said Jonas.

"He was."

"And how did he cross over?"

"Unlike you," said Siegmund, pausing for a sip. "Your father was unable to cross between realms freely. He had to give up something important in order to satisfy the crossing."

"What did he give up?"

Siegmund chuckled. "The same thing I gave up," he stated with contrition. "His wings."

Jonas reeled. "Wait, wait, wait —"

Two figures burst into the tent, disrupting the conversation. Posh followed close behind, being much shorter made her entry nearly invisible.

A Skorsa and a knight drew to a halt before Siegmund, and Posh joined Scary at Jonas' side.

"Apologies, my prince," the Skorsa spoke first, sweeping to a knee. The knight remained standing. "There is a matter that requires —"

"Father!" The knight cut in with greater urgency.

Her voice was familiar to Jonas, but the scattered lamplight made it impossible to discern a face.

Siegmund rose, focused on the Skorsa. "Phinehas, please stand." He strode for his armor rack, ignoring the knight. "What is happening?" He turned with sword in hand. "Has battle rejoined?"

"No, my lord," replied Phinehas. "Nothing of that —"

"Father," the knight boldly approached Siegmund. "This is an event you need see to believe." Though she stood at arm's length, Siegmund refused to acknowledge her.

"Phinehas, I was engaged in a very important discussion. If the Lancethanes are not pouring through the gates, then what could be of such import at this hour?"

"If it were not vital, I would not be here," replied Phinehas. As he spoke his eyes darted to the knight, expecting another interruption. "It is something to be seen in order to be believed, I assure you."

The knight nodded at the Skorsa's answer.

Siegmund's features relaxed. "Will my blade be required?"

"Not necessarily," said Phinehas, "but I would bring it anyhow. There is no sanctuary to be found where we tread."

Turning his back to retrieve his scabbard, Siegmund addressed the knight. "Vera," he said with unmasked ire. "Why must your disobedience be the defining theme of our relationship?" He then looked to Phinehas. "Lead on," he said, then set hard eyes upon Jonas. "Nephew, come along if you so desire."

"Never thought you'd ask," replied Jonas, already hitching Dafodhel to his baldric.

The cool night air carried the scent of early autumn. Phinehas had revealed their destination lay upon the hillside overlooking the day's battle.

Being the son of a clock doctor lent the expectation that Jonas carried a timepiece. But he did not, and before he could help himself, he asked Phinehas if he knew the time. The Skorsa admired the dark ribbons ranging the skyline before answering, "Probably several hours shy of the witching hour."

Jonas nodded as if he understood. "So, like midnight?"

"I don't know what that is." Phinehas was not one to pretend.

"Uh." Jonas searched for an apt reply but decided to drop it once the moment crossed into awkward territories. "Fine night for a stroll, eh?" he said instead.

Politely Phinehas obliged the statement with a nod.

Vera had yet to speak a word. Not even a sly glance or a friendly hand squeeze, or an apology for withholding the fact that she was his blood relative. Nothing. She acted as if they were total strangers. In all fairness, aside from Jonas' brief exchange with Phinehas, the walk had been carried out in silence.

"Hold up," said Jonas, breaking the aforesaid silence. "Maybe we should get some camo or something?"

"What?" said Phinehas.

"When you said, 'The hillside overlooking the battle,' I didn't think that you meant 'The heart of the battlefield,' like where tons and tons of people were killed. And also, I think it bears noting, if we continue walking in this direction, we'll soon find ourselves inside the Terren encampment."

Vera cleared her throat. "Yes," she said. "You're correct."

"Oh, hey Vera!" Jonas turned to the knight. "How's it going? Didn't see you there. Long time no see!"

The contrast between the amused Jonas and the sullen Vera was beyond obvious, even in the darkness of night. "Hi, Jonas," she said flatly, in the hopes that would shut him up.

"Scouts should have alerted the garrison of our presence by now," said Siegmund.

Steeply Vera inclined her head, regarding the peak of the hill. "One might think."

"That would mean —" remarked Siegmund, setting into a run.

Phinehas took to the sky while Vera, Jonas, and the Hylda chased Siegmund. The hill's incline was so severe Jonas' heels never once touched the soil. And while his calves received a thorough workout, the moonlit shadow of the effortless Phinehas scrawled the ground ahead, and in that moment Jonas appreciated the value of flight.

The ground leveled, rolling off into a plateau that stretched far beyond sight. Shortly after assuming the apex, Jonas and Vera caught up with Siegmund and Phinehas waiting in a massive clearing, beaming at one another. When Vera leaned back to crack a triumphant laugh, Jonas jumped.

"So what's the big deal?" said Jonas, patting his heart. He assumed that the Terren encampment lay further ahead, perhaps just beyond the trees.

"Can you not see it?" Siegmund was practically glowing. "The Terrens have abandoned the high ground."

"Okay..."

Suddenly Vera had Jonas by his shoulder armor, violently shaking him as if he were comatose. "What's not to understand?!" She shouted. "We beat them! We defeated the Terrens, you beautiful oaf!"

CHAPTER 21

Sandy woke to the sound of a dull thud. She needed a moment to make certain that it was not another aching pulsation wrought from her stress headache. Aspirin proved helpless in its grip, and before sleep had rescued her, she had endured its nagging for hours. The thud struck again, beneath the floor, and this time Sandy had awakened enough to recognize the sound; a visitor at the front door.

"Give me a break," said Sandy, flinging her collection of blankets aside. "Who could be knocking at this hour?" It was then that she noticed the patches of daylight at rest upon her wall. Looking to her bedside alarm clock, espied the hour hand threatening the *nine* and the minute arm beneath the *four*.

"It's almost 9:30 already?" she moaned in disbelief. She had been sleeping, but she did not feel rested. When she stood, she endured a dizzy spell that vanished after a few deep, controlled breaths. "Let's get this over with."

She slipped down the hall, hoping it was Tasso.

Maybe he left something behind.

The pounding ceased. The knocker may have given up and gone home. Sandy had a lot going on right now anyways. Over the last two days her entire world had been jammed into a blender, set to liquefy.

When Sandy reached eyeshot, relief flooded her veins as the glass door revealed the visitor's departure. Now she could focus her energy on the problems that had already been dealt to her hand. Her slippered feet spun on the floor, deciding that a return to bed was the first step toward peace of mind. As hopeful as that notion was, Sandy had to laugh.

Peace of mind, what a joke.

"Ms. Porter!" The muffled voice beyond the door induced angry goosebumps. "Hey! Ms. Porter!"

"Dang see-thru doors," Sandy snarled.

A girl near Jonas' age wearing a knee-length winter coat with fuzzy leopard print trim at the fringes was the person responsible for the racket.

It was the neighbor girl, her name suddenly escaped Sandy's memory. The recent distress made her brain feel like a useless lump of lead. *Sophia? Sarah?* Sandy rummaged through her mind, hoping to make one stick. *Samantha?*

"Hi, Ms. Porter," said the girl, waving. "It's Sasha, your neighbor. I was just coming by to check on Jonas."

Sasha! Of course! Sandy thought, then voiced, "Shouldn't you be in school..."

"This is the first week of Holiday Break," said Sasha with a quirked mouth.

Sandy nodded. "Ah."

"There's no school until after New Year's..."

"Yes, yes of course," said Sandy. "I'm sorry, Sasha, where are my manners? Come in, please, get out of the cold."

"Thanks, Ms. Porter," said Sasha entering, rubbing her hands together. "We skipped over fall and went right into winter, didn't we?"

"We did, yeah," agreed Sandy half-heartedly. "Can I get you some coffee, tea?" She gestured toward the employee entrance, trying to hurry the girl through the newly emptied space. Empty aside from the grandfather clock that Tasso had delivered the day prior. "The kitchen's upstairs."

"Tea would be great," said Sasha, crossing the room at Sandy's quickened heels. "Wow, are you guys moving or something?" Then commented beneath her breath, *"That's a really neat clock."*

Sandy did not look back. "No, uh, we're *downsizing* a bit for now."

"Oh," said Sasha, hurrying to keep up. "Are you remodeling too? My dad just remodeled our kitchen over the summer and he had to get rid of *all* the old stuff. It was more of a pain than he thought it would be."

Sandy paused on the landing and looked down at the girl. "Doesn't your family rent their house?"

"Not for a long time," replied Sasha, shaking her head. "My parents made some kind of deal with the landlords when I was little. Not really sure how all that stuff works, but I know that we have a mortgage now."

"Your landlords were the Kowalski family, right?" said Sandy, continuing up the stairs as Sasha responded.

"I think so, yeah. They had funny accents. I think they are from Russia? I don't know." She shook her head. "Every Christmas, for as long as I can remember, old man Emil gives me a cute little crocheted animal. Last year's was a mouse."

Sandy's breath caught. "Emil has been giving you Christmas presents?" She prayed her disdain was not bleeding obvious.

"Yup," replied Sasha. "Every Christmas. Never fails." Her nose wrinkled upon entering the kitchen, taking in the décor. "You're planning a remodel up here too, I hope?" she said, handling her words with the skillful care of a well-meaning troglodyte. "If you want, I could ask my dad to help?"

"I don't think your father and I have that kind of relationship," replied Sandy. "But thanks for the offer." She approached the tea cupboard and pried the cabinet door open with a fingernail to its bottom. The knob had broken long ago. "I have Earl Grey, English Breakfast, and…" she trailed off, picking through the packets. "And that's all we have in stock at the moment. What'll it be?"

"Earl Grey, please," replied Sasha. "Hot."

Sandy furrowed her brow. "Of course," she said. "Wouldn't dream of serving iced tea while there's still ice on the windows."

After fixing Mr. Coffee with a blend of cheap coffee powder, and setting the kettle to boil, Sandy encouraged Sasha to take a seat at the nook. The invitation was declined, and Sasha went on to explain that her legs were feeling restless.

"And that's why I'll only be able to sit once I've gotten some things off my chest," said Sasha. "I know that I've lived next door my whole entire life and this is the first time we have had an actual conversation, and well, yesterday was..." The girl began to nervously twine her scarf. "Well, it was not the best introduction..."

Sandy was not in the mood for courtesy. What had happened to Jonas yesterday was awful and required a truckload of apologies. But Sasha was not the one to deliver them. She was innocent.

"So, I would like to apologize for my family not being very neighborly," said Sasha, staring at her shoes. "And I would like to apologize for how my brother acted yesterday." Her eyes lifted to meet Sandy's. "And I came here this morning because I wanted to see how Jonas was doing..."

"Well you're too late," Sandy blurted. "Jonas is, is..." She scoured the room for inspiration to spice up her fib. Her eyes fell on the small painting above the sink depicting a red tractor ardently tilling an uphill field. "He's off visiting his uncle." Her lie was halfway to truth, though she had no clue at the time.

Sasha's countenance sank. "Oh," she said. "Will he be back before school picks up again?"

"I hope so," replied Sandy. "I mean, yes, he'll be back." The kettle's sudden squeal tensed her shoulders. "Tea's up!" She rounded on the stove, relieved by the interruption. "Do you prefer milk or sugar?"

"No thank you," replied Sasha. "I like my tea with just hot water."

"Excellent," said Sandy. "A purist."

Sasha welcomed the steaming cup with both hands. "Thank you," she said. "My mom says my tastes are boring, that I should branch out and explore more. But honestly, I prefer reading a book beside a rainy window to pretty much anything else."

"You paint a nice picture, Sasha. I can relate to that." Mr. Coffee chortled from behind, catching up to Mr. Grey. "I don't accept your apology," Sandy stated off-handedly, reaching for a mug. "Because you don't owe me or Jonas an apology."

Sasha smiled at that.

"I only wish," continued Sandy, "that Jonas were here."

"Yeah," said Sasha. "I'll bet he's glad that Darren will be going off to college next summer."

"Why's that?"

"Because," began Sasha. "He's been pushing Jonas around forever."

"Wait, what?"

"Ms. Porter." Sasha winced. "Jonas didn't tell you *all* that happened yesterday, did he? I was afraid of that..."

Sandy folded her arms. "No, he didn't."

"Oh, man," said Sasha. "I've always wondered why you've never come over to confront my parents about Darren. Well, that explains it." Sasha crossed to sit in the lime green nook. "You never knew."

Sandy reddened. "Makes sense why you came over to apologize then. Exactly how long has Darren been mistreating my son?"

"Since they were little," admitted Sasha sadly. "Ever since Jonas' *teeth* grew in."

"For crying out loud." Sandy rocked her head back. She collected her mug and joined Sasha. "Jonas has never said anything, but I have a feeling your brother will eventually meet his match someday."

"Yeah," agreed Sasha, "and they'll go off and get married and leave the rest of us alone."

Sandy laughed, snorting hot coffee. "Dang! Ouch!" She snagged a napkin. "That hurts!"

Sasha covered her mouth with a mittened hand. "That's an awful feeling!" she said between laughter. "I'm sorry!"

"I'm fine, I'm fine," said Sandy, tossing the soiled napkin into the trashcan. She sat back down and checked her nostrils with a squeeze. "Now," she said with a sniff. "Where were we?"

"We were talking about my dumb brother," replied Sasha. "I want you to know that he's never been violent or hurt Jonas, or anything like that. But I'm always badgering him to knock it off and stop picking on him, but he just shrugs it off and keeps doing it." She closed her eyes and frowned into her tea. "It would take a divine act for him to change."

Sandy cleared her throat. "I'm relieved that Darren never assaulted Jonas, I feel like I would have noticed *that*. I only wish all this had been brought to my attention sooner." She chewed her lip. "But enough about your brother." Sandy was dying to know more about Sasha's relationship with the Kowalskis. But she needed to bring the subject up without sounding forced. She decided that it would be better if Sasha brought it up first. "So, Christmas is coming up, huh?"

Sasha rose in her seat, appearing offended.

Oh, no, was that too weird?

"I didn't know you guys had a dog," said Sasha.

Sandy whirled around, fearing Cucumbers in the doorway. Gratefully the wolfhound was nowhere to be seen. "No, we don't," replied Sandy flustered. She smoothed a curly lock that had toppled over her right eye. "Why, why do you ask?"

"I swore I just heard a bark from down the hall..." Sasha spoke as she craned an ear.

The silence that stretched for a few seconds netted nothing.

Sandy pulled a loud slurp from her mug. "See, you must be imagining —" A sharp yelp accompanied by a distinct whine interrupted whatever Sandy was saying. Luckily Jonas' closed door had hampered the full volume. "Oh that!" she said, thinking fast, grinning and flinging a casual gesture over her shoulder. "That's just Jonas' alarm clock."

"His alarm clock whines like a dog?"

"Yeah," lied Sandy. "I bought him a robot dog clock when he was just a little guy. Picked it up at a clocking conference in Columbus. Kid never outgrew it. Loves it. Kisses it every night before bedtime."

"That's cool," said Sasha sliding from the booth. "Can I check it out?"

"Oh, no!" blurted Sandy, slapping the tabletop as if killing an insect.

Sasha slid back down uneasily. "Okay..."

"I'm sorry," said Sandy, steepling fingers to the bridge of her nose. "It's just that Jonas is very particular about who goes into his room."

"Ah."

"Teenagers, right? You get it. Anyhow I actually have some things to take care of this morning, if you don't mind..."

Sasha nodded. "Yeah, I get that," she looked into her mug, swirled the remainder. "It's been nice chatting with you, Ms. Porter. I didn't mean to intrude this morning."

Sandy pulled herself to a stand and splashed the sediment from her cup into the sink. "It has been nice catching up hasn't it. We should do it again sometime?" Her eyes flicked to the doorway, half expecting a mirror world wolfhound to bound through.

"I'd really like that," agreed Sasha. "And speaking of clocks, there was something else that I wanted to talk to you about."

"Oh, yeah," said Sandy, walking toward the door, gently coaxing the teenager to follow. "And what would that be?"

"I've been thinking about applying to M.I.T." Sasha rinsed her cup at the sink without a lick of urgency. "And, ever since I can remember, I've been interested in how things work. Taking stuff apart and putting them back together. Mr. Holzonger says I have a real knack for it."

Mr. Holzonger being the beloved shop teacher at Scarberry High. Everyone knew him and loved him.

"Does he?" Sandy was hovering at the door, furtively glancing down the hall. "Just leave the mug by the sink, I'll get to it later."

Sasha removed the hand towel draped across the oven handle. "He does," she replied. "And I was wondering —"

Another yelp came from down the hall.

Sandy ground her teeth. "Sasha, I must really get back to things..."

"Does that clock have a snooze button?" asked Sasha with a laugh, replacing the towel. "Yes, yes, sorry." At last the teenager strode for the door. Sandy stepped aside to let her go ahead. "So, I was wondering if you could show me a thing or two about horology."

Right off the bat Sandy wanted nothing to do with an apprentice. For a few reasons, but firstly, and most importantly, all of her equipment had been recently confiscated. "That's going to be kinda tricky, Sasha."

"I know, I know," said Sasha. "All your stuff is in storage. But I was thinking that I could bring one of my grandpa's old pocket watches by and you could show me how it works, and how it all goes together. Maybe take it apart and teach me some lore?"

"Lore?"

"Like, its history."

"I know what lore means, Sasha."

As they crossed the shop floor, Sasha began winding her scarf around her neck. "So what do you say?" she asked, coming to a bouncing halt at the threshold.

"I don't know," began Sandy. The hand-sewn scarf secured about the girl's collar reminded her of Emil's gifts, which instantly brought a brilliant scheme to mind. Perhaps over time, after taking Sasha under her wing, she could gain some critical intel on the Kowalski family. Maybe uncover something that may change the game? Also, how could it hurt?

"Actually," began Sandy, feigning hesitance. Then exclaimed, "Yes! Why not?"

"Awesome!" Sasha clapped on tiptoes. "Can I come by tomorrow? Same time?"

Sandy shrugged. "Works for me."

Once the door sealed shut, Sandy was gone before the cold breeze could snug to her ankles. If Sasha had turned to see the cinnamon-haired woman sprinting as one with her underwear set ablaze, she could not even pretend to care.

Frantically Sandy spilled into Jonas' room, desperate for news of her son. The mirror presented a statuesque wolfhound, her snout locking onto Sandy upon her moment of entry.

"Oh, hi," said Sandy gasping for breath. "What have you, oh man I'm winded." She was bent over, sucking the room's stale air. "Have you found my Jonas?"

With a stately tilt of her head, the wolfhound transmitted a look of grave concern.

It was then that Sandy realized that this dog was not the one who had been tasked with tracking the scent. That wolfhound's fur had been a drab overcoat gray, while this wolfhound's coat maintained a healthy strawberry blonde.

"What is it? Where's my boy?" she pleaded, approaching the wolfhound's image. "Tell me! Is he alive?"

The dog looked down at the grass before her forepaws.

"You can't speak." Sandy thumped her forehead. "But I know someone..." She pointed at the wolfhound's chest. "You just wait right there! Don't move, please!"

Sandy barreled into her bedroom, bunching the area rug into a heap beneath the open doorway. "Phone! Phone!" she scanned the room. "Where?"

Busted, broken, and laying in a puddle of fragments beside the scrunched rug was her red rotary phone. A frayed gray tail, exposing the inner workings of the snapped phone line extended several inches from a shattered hunk of red plastic. Her violent outburst yesterday had been completely forgotten. Hope rose up in her chest when she recalled that the office phone was yet intact, then immediately deflated. Though the phone may be intact, it was presumably intact within a dank, dark Polish owned storage unit.

Far from reach and far from use, she thought, abandoning her room. *I have no other option.*

Gratefully the noble-looking hound was waiting patiently in the mirror, a disconcerted look clinging to her face.

"I'm going to Tasso's shop," explained Sandy, then clarified, "The Joiner."

The wolfhound cast a sideways glance at the mention.

"Can you meet me there?" Sandy begged. "That's possible, isn't it?"

The wolfhound responded with what could only be interpreted as a nod of agreement.

"Perfect! See you..." The wolfhound had already sprang from view. "...there," concluded Sandy to her reflection, alone.

CHAPTER 22

Sandy rocked to a halt, nearly mashing the brake pedal through the floor, and aimed an aggravated growl at the blue sedan beside her.

Customers.

Tasso was hosting customers in his Antique Shop.

Over her many years driving past Tasso's goofy shop the parking lot had always been empty. Countless times it had been a wasteland, a crater of inactivity, always empty!

"On this day of all days, of course he would be entertaining carloads of knuckle draggers," Sandy fumed. "Gosh!" She strangled her steering wheel. "Why can't things ever be easy?"

Once Sandy took a few measured breaths and clenched and unclenched her hands, she abandoned her minivan and crunched to the shop front door, pressed inside. Every polyp of snow that was caked to her coat and boots was vaporized instantly from the absolute inferno inside. She had forgotten how hot Tasso maintained the building. She wondered if Tasso kept exotic reptiles somewhere, or perhaps it had something to do with his trade and all the aged wooden furniture. Or maybe it was less practical, and he simply enjoyed the heat.

Voices generated from the hallway that lead to the repair shop, the space where Tasso had first introduced Jonas to his bed. As she made her way, she noticed that the sale floor was absent of shoppers. It seemed that everyone parked out front had congregated elsewhere.

The repair shop had been converted into a classroom with generous-sized tables spaced evenly apart, lined in orderly rows. Rocking horses, in varying degrees of completion, inhabited each table. And behind the horses were adult students, mostly of the senior variety, with tools in hand gaping towards the entryway where Sandy stood.

Tasso, at the front of the class, noticed the sudden departure of his student's attention and followed their gaze.

"Sandy, what are you —" He shook his head. "Class, please continue doing what you're doing. Remember to hold the chisel parallel, Mary Lou... I will be right back." He crossed the floor and motioned for Sandy to exit, then turned back to his class buzzing with hungry-eyed gossip. "I'm sorry for all the interruptions today. This isn't a normal thing... this isn't how things usually go. Please, I will be right back."

"Other interruptions?" Sandy asked right after Tasso closed the door.

"Yeah, in the middle of class Cucumbers started freaking out," replied Tasso in a whisper, thumbing upstairs. "Had to confine him to quarters."

Sandy squinted. "How long ago would you say he had his little freak out?"

"Maybe twenty minutes ago?" Tasso shrugged. "Long enough for the class to settle down and return to normal. Then you waltzed in and —"

"Hey! Hey!" Sandy snapped her fingers.

"Don't snap your fingers at me!"

"We don't have time for this," said Sandy, lowering her hand. "Is there a *mirror* in Cucumbers' quarters?"

"Why are you saying 'mirror' like that?" whispered Tasso offering meager resistance, allowing Sandy's tow. "Can't you see that I have a prior engagement underway? Those people are paying me good money for —"

"The dog came back," snapped Sandy. "The mirror dog. Well, not the same mirror dog..."

"A different wolfhound?" said Tasso, breaking from whisper. "A regal-looking female?"

"Well, I can't tell a dog's sex based on a glance, but yeah, sure, she seemed really dignified."

Tasso's color drained.

"What?" said Sandy. "What?!" She repeated with greater intensity.

"It's not good," revealed Tasso, returning to whisper.

The staircase was a blur beneath their feet. The second level held two rooms across from one another, divided by a generously wide hallway, a patterned rug shot through its center. Sandy followed close behind the Joiner, her footsteps muffled by the cushy rug. The temperature upstairs was milder, but she continued to sweat, nonetheless.

Tasso pressed a firm hand to the left side door and cranked the brass knob, forcing entry as though expecting resistance.

"That's... that's," voiced Sandy in awe, stopping shy of the threshold. "That's a lot of mirrors. Are you collecting mirrors for a funhouse, or something?"

There were hundreds of mirrors strewn across the massive living space, standing like misplaced orphans. Most had their reflections concealed by sheets. And none were of the same shape or size, and the uncovered few held their faces indifferently toward the floor or ceiling. It seemed not one held conviction to look a person square in the face.

A circular area rug spread out from the center of the room, and perched atop was an austere Cucumbers. He refused to meet Sandy's eye. The dog held a hunched, troubled look, far removed from his regular demeanor. The kind of look that barely managed to keep *bad news* pent up. Sandy felt akin to an army wife readying to answer *the* wartime knock.

"Why are all those mirrors covered?" asked Sandy in an attempt to stave the report.

Tasso adjusted a central mirror, bringing an overcast image of a regal wolfhound to view. "Those mirrors are liars," he stated distractedly to Sandy, then turned to the mirror wolfhound. "What is it, Donann?"

The wolfhound, seated afore a vaguely sunlit forest, had been peering thoughtfully at Sandy, and gradually swiveled her neck to the mention of her name. Cucumbers released a huff and crept closer to the mirror.

A series of growls and yips were exchanged between the wolfhounds, concluding with Donann unleashing a tight-lipped grunt. Cucumbers backed away sullenly. Sandy deduced that Donann was weary of repeating herself and sought Cucumbers as the new bearer.

"Out with it, Cucumbers," said Tasso with eyes on Sandy. "Donann has other matters to attend."

Donann glanced at Sandy, nodded, and bounded from the mirror.

Cucumbers drifted toward a standing mirror angled toward the floor. He nosed the top frame, tilting the face upright. Dejectedly, the dog looked to Tasso as if to say, *Must I?*

"Go on," said Tasso.

Cucumbers' lip curled into a weak snarl, more of a groan.

Sadly the dog strolled right into the mirror, absorbed by the glass as if it were an upright pool of water.

If Tasso had not caught Sandy when he did, she would have suffered a split lip at the very least. The shock had yanked the floor out from beneath her. "How?" was all she managed to say.

Tasso propped her to a stand with his wrists hooked beneath her armpits.

"We're Joiners," he stated as if that satisfied her question.

A lanky wolfhound had just disappeared into a mirror.

Sandy spun from Tasso's touch and stood in the place where Cucumbers had been moments before.

"Where did he —" She whirled in place, searching the mirror, the room with frantic eyes. "Where?" she asked again, bundling her hair in fistfuls.

Tasso smirked and pointed toward the mirror that Cucumbers had disappeared within. Sandy noticed a wiry gray creature no taller than a road cone peering mournfully at the grass. Easily overlooked, the creature nearly blended with the landscape. She withdrew her hands from her head, hard squinting at the little fellow as her hair cascaded. "Is that?" she asked Tasso, going to her knees before the mirror. "Cucumbers?"

"Cucumbers can assume a handful of forms in different worlds," replied Tasso. "He likes being a wolfhound best though."

Inside the mirror Cucumbers' features were concealed by a drawn mantle and scarf, with eyes that refused to rise higher than the turf. The prevailing characteristic that Sandy detected was a deep, sunken sadness that the wolfhound had borne before entry.

"What else are you hiding from me?" said Sandy.

Tasso laughed. "Come on, Cucumbers," he said. "What did Donann tell you?" He begged the gnome-like creature, clumsily skirting Sandy's question.

Cucumbers brought a fist to his scarf and coughed. "She said that Clovers," he began, then paused. He spoke with a voice deeper than someone of that stature presumably owned.

Tasso leaned into Sandy and whispered, "Clovers is the dog tracking Jonas."

"I figured as much," said Sandy, and gave the Joiner a gentle shove.

Cucumbers wanted nothing more than to draw all of this to a close. "Clovers tracked Jonas' scent north of Moütz," he relayed quickly.

Tasso inhaled, cursed under his breath.

"To the lair of a Yéne." Cucumbers concluded, his eyes returning to the ground.

Tasso muttered a different curse. "A Yéne is a giant wolf-like monster that has never been slain," explained Tasso. "No one has bested one, and they do not take prisoners. There is no reasoning with a Yéne." Then he turned away to shake his head. "Especially at the gates of their lair."

"Why would my son go there?" asked Sandy surprisingly calm. "To a Yenny's lair?"

"Something compelled him," replied Cucumbers. "But that is all that we know. Clovers was not keen on getting closer."

"So Clovers did not find my son's body," said Sandy rising to her feet. "No actual evidence that he was..." Sandy's voice faded.

"Yeah sure, if you're looking for forensic proof, then yes, Clovers did not find any such evidence. But from what we know of Yénes," said Tasso, drawing a heavy breath, continuing softly, "we highly doubt that Jonas came out on top. I'm sorry, Sandy."

Sandy pushed Tasso and staggered back. "You have no reason to be sorry. My son is still alive. I can tell, I can feel it."

"Sandy, I don't think —"

"Not until there's proof," said Sandy straightening. "Not until I see my boy." She rounded on the mirror. "Where did Clovers say he was heading next?" She regarded the vast supply of mirrors surrounding them. "Can we reach out to him with one of these?"

The mirror showed a reluctant Cucumbers. "Jonas' trail originated in the nearest occupied village," said Cucumbers. "Clovers will be going there next. It's not easy to say these things, Sandy, but Clovers is no longer seeking your son. As far as he is concerned, the search is over. I am truly sorry."

"What if he runs into Jonas when he's in that village?"

Cucumbers looked away.

"Sandy," said Tasso, laying a hand on her shoulder.

"No!" Sandy rebuffed the gesture. "I'm not giving up so easily." A warmth brushed her hip and suddenly her right hand rose, not of its own accord. Cucumbers had abandoned the mirror and had returned to wolfhound form. Kind eyes beneath bushy eyebrows conveyed endless compassion.

"Oh, stop it!" said Sandy, snatching her hand back. "You're all wrong. You think, because you can travel into other worlds and can change shapes and can build magical mirrors, that you know more than me? I'm his mother and I can feel that he's still alive. Even through the galaxies and beyond, I can *feel* it. Jonas is fine, you'll see."

Tasso and Cucumbers traded looks scribed in worry.

"You'll see," said Sandy. "Jonas and I will be enjoying our Friday night fries and chopsticks before you know it."

Tasso opened his mouth, but did not speak.

"They taste better that way," Sandy clarified. "Plus it's fancier."

"Listen, Sandy," said Tasso. "You're right. There is no proof that Jonas is gone, and there doesn't seem a way that we can convince you otherwise. And there really isn't anything we can do right now." His eyes flicked to the door.

"But you have a class waiting for you downstairs." Sandy clapped and held her hands together. "Also, you're wrong. There is one thing you can do for me."

"Anything."

Sandy pivoted, pointing toward the mirror that Cucumbers had just exited. "Get me to that world."

Tasso scratched his chin. "That's not going to happen."

"Please?"

"I'm sorry," said Tasso.

"You're a *Joiner*, right? Isn't that your job? To get people from one plane to another."

"It's more complicated than that," replied Tasso. Cucumbers supplied the statement with bark of agreement. "I join a lot of places and worlds, and I don't really want to get into all of that right now. And, honestly, I don't really keep the greatest of tabs on the people and things."

"You should," said Sandy. "Excuse me." She stepped aside as Cucumbers sauntered past her, deeper into the room.

Tasso folded his arms. "You're not wrong."

"He's not dead," insisted Sandy. "You'll see."

"I hope you're right," earnestly Tasso imparted, then looked beyond the woman. "Cucumbers, you coming pal?"

The wolfhound emerged at a measured gallop, jarring Sandy on his way out.

"Hey," said Sandy recovering. "What gives?"

If the wolfhound had heard her complaint he made no admission, shuffling down the hallway with ears pinned forward.

"Rude." Sandy bit her lip and glanced back into the room. A crumple beneath the sole of her boot drew her up short. She focused her attention to the floor and noticed a red ribbon peeking from the toe of her boot. She stepped back to discover a scrivener's scroll. In the dimness, it appeared aged and weathered, scrunched inward from her footfall. "You weren't here before," said Sandy.

Plucking the ribbon free from its bunny knot and tucking it in her hand, Sandy unfurled the scroll, began to read.

After the third line, she allowed the ribbon to fall.

CHAPTER 23

"Némer," said Jonas, lying on the grass staring up at this world's arrangement of constellations. He had given up searching for the Big Dipper. None of the stars were the same.

"Yes, that is his name," said Siegmund. "The name of the man who killed your father."

Siegmund had suggested that they spend the night under the stars, in the clearing. The decision to stay had been unanimous. Additionally, the statement made by sleeping where their enemies had only just lain was the stuff of legend.

"Pray do not forget Leopold, the lord of Serpentfel shares equal responsibility."

Jonas nodded. "My grandfather."

The skies darkened into deeper shades while Jonas had been regaled on the tale of his father's demise. Although the horizon had begun weaving hints of daybreak into view — dawn seemed forever away — and penance even further.

"Tell me again," said Jonas verging on a growl. "How Némer did it? How he killed my dad?"

Siegmund cracked a twig as he shifted. "Stabbed in the back —"

"While he crawled away," said Jonas, finishing the statement, blinking back tears. "And Némer got away with it."

"And he got away with it," echoed Siegmund.

No matter how many times he would ask his uncle to tell him this story, the ending would always be the same.

The even breaths of Phinehas and Vera at slumber defied silence, supplying rhythm to the calm. Internally, Jonas reeled, reconciling reality. And just how much of this had his mother known?

Probably not much. But still...

"Uncle," said Jonas.

Siegmund stirred and yawned, implying that he had dozed off. "Yes, Jonas."

"Does my mother know any of this?"

"Doubtful," replied Siegmund. "Sebastian was slain on this side of the rift."

"Ah," said Jonas. He felt bad for keeping his uncle awake, but he had loads of questions readied in the chamber. "Uncle?"

Siegmund groaned.

"Can you tell me something happy?"

Something resembling a chuckle came from his uncle. "Good night, Jonas."

Suddenly Jonas found himself in Scarberry High's boys' locker room, the scent of springtime and sweat clung thick in the air. Jonas knew he was dreaming. He was aware that it was a dream, though his suspicions wavered.

This almost feels like it's real.

As he strode past the vacant showers, he could not help but notice that every showerhead was set to full blast, kicking up a tapestry of fog. Some guy had cranked every knob, then immediately made himself scarce.

"Weird," remarked Jonas, looking down and noticing that he was not wearing pants. The momentary alarm was quickly reconciled by the fact that of all the places within the school, the locker room was the place where you could be totally naked. Also, he was dreaming, and this kind of stuff was typical. Insecurities and hormones coupled with average teenage grief, and stuff.

The running showers had created a foggy film that masked every mirror over the hand sinks. A string of letters scrawled on one of the mirrors drew Jonas up short. Not easily spotted, but there, nonetheless. It was a fun thing his mom used to do when he was younger; scribing a phrase on the bathroom mirror while he was showering, so when he hopped out a message waited for him.

"Chin up," said Jonas, reading the dripping letters written in his mother's script. He checked the mirror to his right and noticed that the mirrors continued endlessly, like an infinity box. When he turned back to the mirror, the phrase had been overtaken by fog.

"There has to be more," breathed Jonas. He took off down the corridor, scanning mirrors, hoping for more messages. He ran for what felt like a mile before a golden blur within a sink brought him to a skidding halt. A medium sized box of French fries had been jammed into the drain, and when Jonas reached for them, a pair of chopsticks appeared in his off hand. The cheap kind, affixed to one another. Jonas could never snap that kind apart without destroying them. His mother had the meticulous hands of a master craftsman, so freeing the sticks had always been her department.

"Fries and chopsticks," mumbled Jonas to himself. "The Friday night fare for the distinguished gentleman." He missed his mother beyond words in that moment. His throat tightened in a way that he had not felt in ages; the way it would right after she'd drop him off for pre-school.

One more hug, Mama.

Pantless he stood before the mirror, wolfing down fries, trying to keep it together. Suddenly the mirror de-frosted, reflecting back old helpless Jonas, pitifully weeping through a mouthful of fries.

Someone down the corridor clipped the showers, dispersing the fog, save for a thin cloud hovering at ankle height. Though clarity had been restored to the room, the mirrors refused to clear. Jonas passed from mirror to mirror, wiping and swiping with the heel of his fist, demanding a different reflection. The foggy film prevailed, refused to go away. All of his efforts had been a total waste of time, only succeeding at marring the glass with greasy fry-fingers.

In a fit of unforeseen rage, Jonas smashed the nearest mirror with his forehead. The glass became powder, then a gust of wind blurred his eyes. He blinked and blinked but his tears would not come to do their job. Then a face that was not his own appeared within the breeze-woven mist. The face appeared similar to his own, like the *Devil*, not the frail boy that attended Scarberry High. But it was not Jonas, nor the Devil, peering back.

With each blink, grains of sand crammed into the front corners of Jonas' eyes. "Who are you?" he asked beneath great discomfort.

The phantom pointed to the broken mirror, a cavernous hole yawned back. Above the opening on the tiled baby blue wall the phrase "WHICH WAY, MISTER OWL" was scrawled in red and black; the two colors alternating.

"I don't know what to do!" exclaimed Jonas to the phantom. "I can't save Mom and the Leeds people all by myself! I'm just one guy!"

Slowly at first the hole began sipping the remaining fog. Jonas felt the breeze at his bare ankles climbing its way up. Then the pull became stronger, seizing cracked tile from the floor, and any stray towels or clothing, and sucked them toward itself with heavy gale force. Jonas could hardly maintain his footing. The phantom was undeterred, holding Jonas in a contemplative stare.

"Help me!" pleaded Jonas, reaching for the phantom.

The phantom stretched his hand a hair's breadth from touch. "You are never alone," he said.

Jonas' feet slipped and he felt his body upturn, upend, and — not for the first time — sever ties with gravity. As he began corkscrewing wildly into that hole, he woke in the hilltop clearing.

"Need a moment?" said Siegmund, eyeing his nephew warily.

The Hylda were lying at Jonas' feet, regarding him with concern.

"I'm alright," said Jonas. He was upright but did not recall moving. "I'm okay," he breathed, patting his forehead, somehow tender from bashing a dream wall.

Siegmund sheathed the knife he had been sharpening and went to a knee to offer Jonas a leather waterskin. "Thirsty?" he asked.

Jonas drained the skin, squeezing it for all it was worth, then handed it back.

"Quite thirsty," commented Siegmund.

Jonas felt dozens of eyes upon him, and when he looked around, noticed that his Ritts inhabited the nearest treetops.

"Hey," said Jonas to the dour gargoyles. "How goes it?" He accepted a hand from Siegmund and stood.

The Ritts remained passive.

"Talkative as always." Jonas turned to the Hylda and smiled. "Where are the others?"

Siegmund scratched his chin while Scary and Posh shrugged. "They returned to Brimon at daybreak," he revealed, squinting at the Hylda. "Hours ago. I thought we'd spare you a few extra scraps of rest. And we also spared some scraps of breakfast that your Ritts provided this morning; just some berries and nuts." He nodded toward a stump. "Vera said that you weren't too keen on uncooked meat so we didn't save any of the rabbit."

"Appreciate it," said Jonas. "If you don't mind, I think I'm going to go for a jog."

"A jog?" said Siegmund.

"Yeah, you know, to clear my head," replied Jonas backpedaling and swiping a handful of berries. The Hylda rose at once, angling to join. "I'm going to do this one alone," he expressed kindly to the Hylda. "I'll be back soon."

Scary whimpered.

"I'll be right back," Jonas assured her.

From inside her scabbard on the ground, Dafodhel transmitted a message to Jonas alone. *"Do not cross the river."*

"Make sure you don't cross the river!" called Siegmund, duplicating the magic sword's advice, unwittingly.

Though he had been doing a lot of running as of late, more than his body had ever done before, the idea of jogging as a casual activity had never even been the ghost of a possibility.

Have I finally outrun my asthma? thought Jonas. *Eh, maybe? I've skipped a ton of levels using this new hot bod as a cheat code.*

No matter how he spun it, the fact remained; he was jogging. And doing so without his bronchioles shriveling into prunes.

The forest air flowed as a nourishing broth for his lungs, caffeinated his soul, and spurred him forward. He lowered his head and dashed.

Without any idea where he was headed, it may have been unwise to run at such a break-neck speed. But it was great fun.

He slowed to leap onto a boulder to take in the view. As striking as his surroundings were, Jonas' eyes did not lift from the boulder. A distinct turquoise striation ringed the center of the great rock, reminding him of the conjoined warning; *don't cross the river*. It also brought to mind his plight. Like the rock, Jonas felt cracked in half, torn between aiding his mother and rescuing a kingdom. Fortunately for the rock, it did not have hooks embedded, pulling it apart. Hooks that fought tooth and nail, tearing it between paths, between worlds.

"Did I cross the river?" said Jonas scratching his head, taking in the area. The boulder he stood atop was mitered to the edge of a gentle slope that ended in a shallow gully.

I'll bet a Taub tributary flows here and pools during the wetter seasons, speculated Jonas. *Which would explain the gully depression.*

Jonas leapt to the ground and began seeking the tributary source. If found, then he could trace where the river ran, and know for certain whether he had crossed. If that proved true then he would need to hightail it back to Dafodhel and Siegmund. In truth he was not overly concerned, but peace of mind was rare.

"Just where are you, little guy," he mumbled.

A threatening rumble issued beyond the hillside, and Jonas paused before continuing his search. The deep, throaty quavering held before sharply transitioning into horrid snarling, screeching. Jonas started, going to ground.

Shivering trees and snapping branches marked the location of a fight taking place, spitting distance from the gully's shoulder. It sounded to Jonas as more of a cat fight than a sword-to-sword battle; hisses laced with spittle, deep guttural moans, choked growls, high pitched mewls.

Curiosity tugged Jonas toward the hillock, but he fought the urge. The fight would end soon, and besides, it was none of his business. He decided to leave it alone, turned his back, resumed his search.

After all, thought Jonas. *Finding my bearings is way more important than checking out a monster fight.*

"It's not like you've never seen monsters fight before," said Jonas, wading into a plot of mixed vegetation to pluck a purple clover-like plant. The soft hue of the petals seemed to shift when he twirled it between his thumb and forefinger. "Never thought I'd ever say something like that —"

Then the sound of children wailing brought a change of heart. The mysterious clover was dropped, forgotten, lost to its flora maze.

The hillside drifted downward, spanned beneath a sparse track of trees. Hunching beyond the trees was a rock mound with a cavernous opening at its base. A solitary figure stood afore the cave, assailed by half a dozen lions, savagely feinting and lunging. The fighter was tall and ape-like, torn at the forearms, and her breath came ragged, reluctant. Huddled behind her inside the cave, three children clung one to the other.

Valiantly, for the last several minutes, this mother ape had been defending her young. Now she wavered, dying, heaving the last of her strength.

Jonas cursed himself for not acting sooner. But he would make up for it. He reached for his sword but his hand replied, *"It's empty, dummy — You left your sword behind, remember?"* He clawed in desperation at his other hip, only to find zero sum — all while rushing headlong into peril.

Jonas centered a shoulder through the hindquarters of one lion, catching the beast completely unaware. The force of impact crumpled the lion and sent it sprawling before the mother ape. All attention swung to Jonas, and the lions' moment of concern over their fallen kin quickly shifted to murderous rage.

These lions resembled their earthly brethren — the lions of the Serengeti, but they were not the same. Much like many of the monsters in this world, they probably shared a common ancestor in Jonas' world, but somewhere along the way these guys had hopped onto a darker timeline. For one, Jonas noted: their eyes were red. A caustic red, a red that seared right into your soul. He assumed that this was probably because they were really mad at him. But if this was their resting gaze, then Jonas would not have been shocked.

These are some intense dudes, thought Jonas before speaking.

"Why don't you felluhs take five and chill." He spoke with a surprising amount of confidence. The lions flinched when he jerked a step toward them, which drew a wry smile from the wounded mother ape. "Go on, get out of here!"

Their display of weakness, the way they had huddled back, ushered the memory of his mother into his mind. The way she had flinched from Emil's raised hand.

Then the lions rallied. They had sensed his lapse in attention and assumed an advantage. Jonas gave ground, backing toward the cave, precisely what these apex predators had hoped for.

The largest, more sinister of the lions prowled toward Jonas, and two lions from the pack peeled for the cave.

"Aw, dang it…" said Jonas crestfallen, retreating. The lions were on the verge of checkmate. "Can we talk about this? Maybe get some coffee and really get in to what it is you guys want?"

"We want sustenance," the leader drawled.

Jonas' temples throbbed. "I mean, what you *really* want. Afterwards, in the future, like, what is your ultimate life goal?"

"Afterwards? The future?" The leader stalled his approach. "After we consume one's flesh and use one's bones for —"

"Yes!" Jonas cut the lion off. "Exactly that! What's the next step for your pride?"

Meanwhile the mother ape had fallen along her intercept of the cave mouth and grasped desperately for the pair of lions that sought to make a meal of her offspring. Her hands yet moved, but that was all.

"I suppose we shall find a shady place to nap," replied the leader, gesturing for the cave.

"I didn't want to do this," muttered Jonas.

The leader proffered a dim smile. "I didn't catch that." A predatory semi-circle began to form around Jonas. "At the very least, one should make one's final words loud enough to be heard."

"You seem to be speaking at a decent volume," said Jonas, flicking his eyes upward where a shadowy mass had gathered.

Go on and save those monkey babies, said Jonas to the Ritts.

The brutally silenced squeals from the mouth of the cave were not those of infant apes.

"Clarify oneself..." said the baffled lion, his voice tapering. "Oh, my." His eyes snapped upward only to fall back down, trailing the sundered flesh of a lion plummeting to earth. An enraged host of Ritts had assailed his pride, and were greedily tearing them to pieces. "Flee!" shrieked the leader. "Flee!"

The pride flung themselves into reverse, as if repelled by powerful magic.

"You get a five second head start!" Jonas shouted at the retreat.

A harsh Ritts voice entered his head, *"May as well give them five minutes."*

CHAPTER 24

The ape younglings had been struggling to roll their mother over until Jonas stepped in and helped. The creature was entirely dead weight.

Jonas had very limited first aid skills, which began and ended with sticking a band-aid to a scrape, so he really was not bringing much to the table. But still, he felt compelled to do something.

"Oh, Papa," one of the children said, burying her head in the great ape's shoulder.

"Papa?" said Jonas confused. He took a step back to allow space for grieving.

Goes to show what I know about that kind of thing, thought Jonas, biting his lip. But this begged the question, *if this is dad, then where's mom?*

A horrified scream erupted overhead, boiled and concocted in a crucible of pure suffering. Jonas looked to the rocky outcropping that formed the helm of the cave and saw a broad-shouldered gorilla-type monster raging out.

"Oh," said Jonas. "That's Mama." He had watched enough National Geographic to know that you should always steer clear of bear cubs, cause mama is never very far. And mama does not check IDs.

The mother Sasquatch let fly a warning howl and set off on a crash course for Jonas. With deltoids the size of Mars and hands like backhoes, the monster cleared the slope nigh instantly.

"Jonas! Where are you?" Dafodhel's voice sprang into Jonas' head. *"You should have returned by now."*

"Now's not the best time!" Jonas replied mid-sprint, snapping an eye behind him. "Oh boy! Oh boy!"

"What's the matter?"

"Nothing," said Jonas under his breath, then shouted, "It's all a big misunderstanding!" He lowered his head and continued to sprint, thankful that his Ritts were still occupied by the lion hunt.

Those little Bigfoots — or Bigfeets — had lost enough today, and as crazy big as this mother 'Squatch was, she would not stand a chance against his Ritts. For her preservation, Jonas made the snap decision to just book it and hope she'd give up.

Seconds went by without a backward glance, and soon the spacing between the trees tightened. A set of oddly intertwined trees that formed a "V" shape forced Jonas to twist a vault between them. The canopy overhead was so tightly woven that only a thin layer of light pierced through.

After springing to his feet and clearing the scratchy pine needles from the back of his neck, Jonas hazarded a look back.

"Phew." Jonas heaved a sigh. "No way Big Mama is going to keep chasing me in this tightly packed forest." Then he whispered, "Go back to your family."

He took a moment to admire the V trees and just how solid, so firm, and so secure they were. *Perhaps I should take my own advice...* Suddenly the V trees exploded into splinters, bursting like a spaghetti filled balloon. The mother Sasquatch was not one to give up so easily.

Jonas tucked a roll to his right and avoided becoming roadkill. The base of his heel had contacted the Sasquatch at some point on her body which initiated a tilt-a-whirl reaction. She wheeled, backhanding the base of an oak to correct herself, then straightened to her full height.

"It wasn't me," pleaded Jonas, backing away. "I didn't kill your husband... or whatever it is you call that monkey guy..."

The Sasquatch's eyes filled with intensity. She swiped at a string of drool swinging from her bottom lip, and as she caught her breath, her excessively heavy chest pendulated back and forth.

"So *that's* how you tell the difference," mumbled Jonas, halting his retreat. "Do you understand me?" He turned with hands upraised.

The monster crouched menacingly and roared a reply. And if a word could be plucked from the noise, it sounded like, "NARUF!" Which Jonas loosely translated to "No."

Darting between the trees, Jonas booked it even harder. The Sasquatch gave chase, sundering the forest between into particles. Branches lashed out as trunks hurtled by, and the woodchipper at Jonas' back only seemed to be gaining.

Suddenly the soil beneath Jonas became syrup. He quickly discovered that he had entered a bog. At the moment he used a sapling as a handhold to yank himself free from the quagmire, Dafodhel piped in, *"Where are you?!"*

"Not a good time, Daf!" replied Jonas. The boggy goo had wormed behind his armor and wedged deeper with every movement. Jonas scurried up a berm to find a worn dirt foot-path spanning left and right. The rush of the water grew in clarity, and just beyond the path Jonas caught sight of the Taub.

An innate sense of relief spread throughout him. *If only I could cross over —*

"Jonas!" Dafodhel sounded desperate. *"I'm straining my magic to its limits to reach you! If you can still hear me —"* Her voice faded.

Briefly Jonas contemplated his direction before he was spurred to the left by the unceremonious arrival of the Sasquatch to his right. She skidded out onto the path, locking eyes on her target and pulled a rasp-throated cackle deep from her guts.

This lady ain't letting up.

Jonas took off again, hoping to shake this monster once and for all. Miraculously, not much further down the path, a bridge entered view. He had commanded his Ritts to chase, but not kill those lions, and he feared their return. If they saw the predicament he was embroiled in...

Oh, boy, he thought. *There'd be quite the discussion.*

Suddenly, Dafodhel's voice cut in, *"Cross the river."*

The bridge was wide enough for two semi-trucks to cross side-by-side without their tires scraping.

"Why is this bridge so wide?!" said Jonas in alarm, pounding across the unyielding surface. *Where's one of those scary rope bridges from the adventure flicks when you need one?*

The open ground swept upward on a steady incline, sandwiched between opposing forests. Jonas sped faster, aiming to widen the gap just a smidge. Maybe she would hesitate upon entering Terren territory, and just give up.

Jonas did not need to look back for his answer. The unmistakable sound of bare feet slapping across the bridge told him the full story. This old gal did not give a single care about the Terren and Leeds dispute.

To the trees! Jonas thought, pinning a hard left, leaving open ground for the tangled brambles of the forest. He claimed a last-ditch idea, and if it did not pan out...

Amidst the cool shadows his legs did not let up, and his eyes clocked in overtime.

The Sasquatch howled. It seemed for the time being, she had lost track of her quarry.

This forest was more densely woven than the last, and in some places the trees thronged tight as conspiring scoundrels. It would not be long before she picked up his scent again, so Jonas took this opportunity to begin weighing options.

He bobbed his head at the trees. "Too thick, too skinny, too high." He sought the perfect tree, a tree with a built-in failsafe.

I need branches that will support my weight, but will break at the slightest touch from Kong back there —

Suddenly, his eyes fell upon a winner. "Perfect!" he shouted louder than caution advised.

The Sasquatch bellowed, keyed in on her target, renewed the hunt.

Jonas alighted the first forty feet with ease, then stopped to stare down at the Sasquatch's progress. Silence could spell any number of things, but he hoped that it meant she was scratching her head. And sure enough, in disbelief, she remained at ground level, staring at the broken branches in her hands. The base of the tree had been stricken of bark, and all the branches within leaping distance were gone.

"Go home! Go back to your family!" Jonas called out, lacking vitriol.

The fur around her collar bristled up, which must have been the Sasquatch version of a light bulb going off. With arms spread wide, she hastened to the freshly shaved trunk and wrapped it in a tremendous hug. A decent amount of debris rained down from the impact, a few nuts came loose and pelted the back of Jonas' head. The tree shook with such fervor that it may have garnered an earthquake's envy.

"A thicker tree," said Jonas, nearly biting his tongue, holding on for dear life. "Next time, a thicker tree." But before he could draw up another scheme, a far-off shriek brought the ride to a close.

Lancethanes!

Jonas shuddered, or perhaps the tree had yet to stop shaking.

From a higher elevation further away another shriek answered the first.

Nope, Jonas was shuddering. He peered between his boots to the forest floor and was relieved to see that the Sasquatch had finally ditched him at last.

But still, the thought of climbing down did not appeal. Not when he had an alternative.

Ritz! A searing itch sparked across his back, forcing him to jerk and slap. With one arm it was difficult to render a proper scratch, especially donned in armor. Presuming the culprits were harmless, perhaps a razor thin branchlet that had pierced his tunic or drops of bog that had slimed their way up his back, Jonas moved on and continued his message.

Come collect me!

He peered up through the branches where he hoped to see his faithful gargoyles. A response had not arrived, and Jonas began to despair that, like Dafodhel's magic messaging, he had ranged beyond their influence.

"Where are they..." he mumbled. All he had to do was get back across the river. Then worry began to set in.

What if that giant gorilla is waiting for me? What if she's using the Lancethanes as the perfect distraction, and as soon my feet touch the ground, she snatches me and pops my head like a grape?

"Jonas."

Jonas looked up to glimpse the most glorious sight; one of his Ritts upon the branch directly over his left shoulder, the rest alighting with cool assurance elsewhere.

The Ritts extended a sinuous arm. "Collect you."

CHAPTER 25

Jonas surged upward through the forest canopy, a Ritts for each armpit. Soon the entire Ritts host joined his rescue flight, darkening great patches of ground below.

I could get used to this, he thought, entering a stream of feathery pale clouds.

Heights had never been his favorite, but when you no longer fear the falling, and the abrupt ending, then what could stand in your way?

Passing from dark to light, Jonas suffered momentary blindness. Once his eyes adjusted he began scanning the ground for the screeching Lancethanes.

That remarkable itch had returned, now blistering both shoulder blades.

Without warning, the Ritts beneath his right armpit was struck by a tremendous force, lost its grip, and was sent spiraling to the ground. Jonas, now carried by a single Ritts, forgot about the itch. The sudden shifting of weight caused the Ritts to dip low in the sky, fortuitously avoiding a blurry silvery shaft meant for its chest.

That's a Lancethane's lance! Jonas screamed in his head.

Upon a plateau in the distance, Jonas espied a Lancethane readying another hurl.

"Please release me!" Jonas shouted, sensing the drop survivable. His mind manifested a swan dive. "Then fly back to Siegmund!"

The Ritts obeyed.

Somehow Jonas met the earth at the nape of his neck, and like a liquid glancing from a spoon, rolled his landing without suffering injury.

How did I just do that? Jonas stared at his hands as if they would burst into flame. He turned toward the sky. "All of you! Back to Siegmund!" he screamed at the Ritts host. "Cross the Taub to safety!"

The majority of the Ritts heel-turned their trajectory for the river, but a few held to offer protest.

"No!" said Jonas. "I don't want any more of you to die!"

"But that is our purpose!"

"You are more than that!"

A Lancethane spear rocketed overhead, finding its mark. As Jonas watched the poor Ritts on his death spiral, he grew incensed. Across the skies he retraced the spear's path, locked eyes with the Lancethane responsible.

The drake and rider stood upon a platform lodged to a cliffside, a decent span from the riverbank. From where Jonas stood he perceived the Lancethane was not alone, though a few rolling hillsides between obscured the remaining view.

"You can stick around," said Jonas to the lingering Ritts. "But steer out of range, and the fastest of you —" An idea suddenly solidified. "Fetch Isaac." With that he made for the platform.

Jonas' senses were on high alert as his body navigated the route. He remained focused, anticipating a spear. Then a spear rocketed through the air well over his head, and he flinched from sheer instinct. Without losing speed, Jonas peered back and noticed a handful of Ritts circling, avoiding the missiles. They had yet to cross the river and were well within Lancethane range.

"Please go back!" urged Jonas. "Across the River!"

The Ritts obeyed with a skyward burst, then drafted a hard angle over the Taub.

Wonder why those Ritz disobeyed —

A spear interrupted, off-target by a leap, splashing into soil. The enemy was not far, thirty yards roughly. Jonas tucked behind a rocky outcrop just in time for another spear to come his way. The hard ping against the crag sent shards scattering in all directions.

Smack! Yet another struck true.

"Geeze, those things hit *really* hard."

Thud!

"Whoa! That one pierced the rock!"

Smack!

"Okay, maybe I'll wait..."

Smack!

"Alright, it's now or —"

Thud!

"Not one move, Devil." The voice chilled Jonas' insides.

"...*never,*" concluded Jonas to himself, bringing hands into plain sight. "I surrender," he said to the armored rider. Below, the drake's lizard mouth pulled an impossible sneer.

The Lancethanes had surrounded him while he cowered behind cover. His stupidity had reached a new milestone.

What were you thinking?! Thought Jonas, ashamed.

He had given over to anger, and in doing so, forfeit everything. He could only imagine what he'd catch from Dafodhel, were she present. He sensed that his Ritts were fully aware of the situation, and were more than willing to step in.

"Stay back. I'll figure something out," crestfallen Jonas assured them, as a dismounted rider secured his wrists in shackles. *"Go back and tell my uncle what happened."*

The Lancethanes led him in the opposite direction of the river, away from his Ritts, and away from his... *friends.* He transmitted a brief message to his Hylda.

Sorry that I'm me.

The Lancethanes had been silent for the most part, save for the occasional grunt. Their armor and gear did not jangle nor make much of a sound. And Jonas did not bother asking questions; he knew where they were taking him — off to meet his living grandparents.

After they had reached the pinnacle of the hill, one of the Lancethanes had ordered Jonas to run, and when he did, the great lizards matched speed with a controlled gallop. Unlike knights and cowboys, these riders did not bother with spurs.

Which, without a doubt, was a plus when sneaking up on buffoons hiding behind boulders.

A handful of Lancethanes had remained behind to keep watch on the terrace platform. This left six for Jonas' escort: two positioned in the front, two to his sides, and two manning the rear. The front and rear guards maintained a strict watch over the land and skies. When a rider would focus eyes elsewhere, the drake beneath would pick up where he left off. Through his sadness, Jonas admired the clever, effective strategy.

For hours they travelled over hill and dale, roadway and pasture, meadow and forest. The landscapes changed with the frequency of a slideshow. And soon, at the heel of a great hill, a hum could be heard clearly, unmistakably.

Their course passed beneath an open gate with steel forged letters across the top that spelled out "SERPENTFEL." The Lancethanes fanned to Jonas' left and right, leaving him as vanguard. And as they drew near the central city, excited voices, numbering hundreds, melded with the hum. With each step it became clear to Jonas that the voices and the hum were one and the same.

When Jonas reached the crest of the uplands, he turned his head from the setting sun and discovered that his escort had abandoned him. He shielded his eyes, walking a pristine marbled footpath, totally solo. Unsure of what to do, he decided to continue the road. The accuracy of a thrown Lancethane spear punctured any notion of deviating.

Everything this city wrought was captivating, from the buildings to the banners, the shrubs and the animals, it was all coated in elegance. And the entire populace was a far cry from destitute. Whatever weird and disgusting city he had imagined Serpentfel to be, the splendor before him did not check off any of those boxes.

This place is clean. The atmosphere had momentarily freed him from his despondency. *No, that doesn't even begin to describe this place. What's that word for when something is completely germ-free?* He snapped his fingers, trying to recall the word. *Ah, it'll come to me.*

"My lord." A spritely young man swept a discreet bow before Jonas. Behind him a company of similarly dressed individuals declined to a knee. "We have been waiting for you," he said curtly. When he stood, it was difficult not to notice the angelic wings affixed to his back, fully flexing as if they had been restrained for hours. "Come with us, please."

"Do I have a choice?" said Jonas downcast, defeated.

The young man shook his head. "This way, my lord," he stated, indicating Jonas to follow. "We do not want to make a scene, do we?"

"No," replied Jonas, raising his hands, the shackles together. "We don't."

The generous-sized underground cell was pristine, miraculous. Serpentfel's level of cleanliness was top notch. The floor was scrubbed and polished to a gleam, and Jonas could even make out his murky reflection between his shackled, outstretched legs. The walls were of a similar material, but in much better condition; not metal or ceramic tile, something between.

The winged escort had taken Jonas on a wide out-of-sight path around the city. Eventually it concluded before a gigantic set of heavy stone doors that had been cleverly fashioned to appear as grave markers. Beyond the ruse, a staircase flowed endlessly downward.

The captain had explained that Jonas would be making his stay in a chamber that had been tailor-made expressly for his containment.

"Not to worry," he had pointed out. "We went so far as to employ ill-tempered drakes for the testing of the structure. You won't be going anywhere for a while, and nothing will be able to get in or out without our say. It should go without saying, but I'll say it anyhow; endeavoring an escape will prove a tremendous waste of your time and energy."

Jonas' wrists, ankles, and neck had been shackled to the wall with an expertly measured amount of slack; just enough to lie down, but not enough to stand.

Hours in the cell whittled away. This was the first time in days that Jonas had been left alone to his thoughts. No Dafodhel invading his mind, no Ritts requesting permission, and no Scary requesting a hug.

He mind wandered from the friends in this world to his friends in the other.

What friends? Jonas smirked. They had abandoned him the summer before eighth grade. When his mother's customers dwindled, and rumors of scarcity became cold fact, the scorn made a stench that even his best friends could not bear. At least what had remained of them. Marge, Hannah, Derek, and Kenny were the last to jump ship.

Derek came to mind, his face undone by distress. "I'm sorry, man," he had said, biting a quivering lip. "I just can't be seen with..."

Jonas forced himself to think of other things, returning to the present.

The cell was not as calm as it should be, but quiet. Blatantly quiet. A hard, harsh quiet. The kind of quiet that greets the beginning of a very long, severe punishment.

See where your anger has gotten you, Jonas thought in Dafodhel's voice.

"See where your anger has gotten you," he agreed.

They are going to kill you, you know, said Jonas' version of Dafodhel. *Once they gleam you of all useful information, they're going to discard you like a spent match. Like your father.*

"But I don't know anything useful," said Jonas.

You know more than you believe.

"Maybe they'll just keep me here forever?"

And risk your escape? As impossible as that may seem, it is still probable. You are very powerful, even more so with your passing spirits at hand. Why not command them to rescue you. Just to see what happens?

"I would never put them in harm's way like that."

The false Dafodhel laughed. *Why ever would you? Why would you ever use something for its intended purpose?*

"I'm tired."

I'm tired. The made-up voice mocked.

Jonas curled into himself. "Just be quiet."

The series of locks released one after the other in a methodical succession.

Jonas lifted his chin from his cold iron collar. His first visitor had managed to catch him dozing.

A studious woman entered, reminding Jonas of an intense librarian. A grating sigh escaped from her throat. Her gaze hovered all around the room, never once falling upon the prisoner.

"Let's get to it," she said. The scent of blade oil carried in the breeze upon the door's closure. "I can only imagine the nonsense Guiltbrand filled your head with. That the Leeds are the rightful stewards of the Taub? That the Terrens are a murderous cult exclusively seeking power? Prattling endlessly that you are the child of his prophecy and your destiny lies with the Leeds?" Her vampire-teeth receded within a terse smile. "That you are their Devil." Finally her eyes came to rest upon Jonas.

Jonas swallowed and looked away.

"Forget all of that," she said, revealing a clipboard from behind her back. "Even though Guiltbrand's prediction was debunked well over a decade ago, the Leeds yet cling to it, steadfastly, as lunatics are wont." She admired an abnormally large ring on her left hand. "Surely you perceived the foolishness for what it was."

Jonas looked away.

"Of course you did. You are your father's son."

And they'll kill you, just like him, whispered false Dafodhel.

"Just be quiet," said Jonas.

The woman's mascara lines twitched. "What was that?"

"I wasn't talking to you." Jonas turned her way. "When is my execution?"

"To the point." The woman's hands returned to her back. "Man after my own heart. In brief, the Terrens greatly prefer law, in stark contrast to whatever the Leeds adhere to. You say what you do, and you do what you say, yada, yada — you get my point. Anyways, your arrival has brought complications, to say the very least, to a kingdom on the verge of their greatest achievement. And right now, it's *my* job to help *you* decide how best *we* mitigate this... impediment."

"Wouldn't killing me mitigate everything?"

"You seem rather stuck on this whole *killing you* thing?" The woman produced the clipboard again. "Dark, very dark," she said shaking her head. "There are several outcomes that the magistrates have outlined for you." With a snap of her wrist, the clipboard came to a sliding halt between Jonas' legs. "If you'd be so kind as to give that document the most stringent of perusals, I fear that you will be disappointed to find that four of the five paths do not conclude with a noose abiding your neck."

Calmly, sadly, Jonas hunched as far forward as his restraints allowed. "What does King Leopold make of all this?" he asked, nodding at the paperwork.

"This is a republic," stated the woman matter-of-factly. "King Leopold and Queen Priska are nothing more than figureheads."

"That doesn't answer my question."

"Oh, but it does." The woman's fangs protruded ominously. "I wish that I could say that I had better things to do, and leave you to ponder your fate, but that would be a lie. The entire realm is on bated breath awaiting your decision." Her eyes became slits. "So I will wait for you, in this magnificent cell, until that happens."

"There are worse places," said Jonas.

"I was being serious," the woman insisted.

Jonas leaned back against the wall. "Okay, sure," he said, flipping the top sheet on the clipboard.

"Also, that's a pathetic argument," said the woman. "*There are worse places.* Makes you sound like an infant."

"I've been told a lot of things since I first dropped onto this stupid world," began Jonas slowly, "and that *might* be the sincerest advice anyone has given yet. Maybe, probably. So tell me, if I'm not the Leeds Devil, then what am I?"

The woman shrugged. "You tell me. Just because somebody calls you a devil — over and over and over — doesn't make it canon does it?"

Something shattered inside Jonas. This simple truth rendered him static. "Then what am I?" he repeated at a loss. "How did I become this?" He indicated his body with a feeble nod. "I was a short, practically blind weakling, and now I'm *this.*"

"I'm not going to stand here and define you," said the woman. "In my life, I have learned that the things that are quickly obtained are often the most easily lost."

Jonas exhaled a series of shudders. "Who are you?" he asked.

The woman took an uneasy step backward and thumbed for the door. "I'm going to give you a minute alone," she said. "Collect yourself."

"Who are you?" said Jonas.

Behind the quickly sealing door, she replied, "I'm just a legal clerk."

CHAPTER 26

"Tremble but do not quail, besmirch the surface again, certain not to fail." Sandy recited the scroll's riddle spell from memory. "With eye upon thy desire, bleed this scroll, that is all I require."

Her brain hurt. The last time her brain had cramped up this badly was a few years back while working on a nineteenth century Black Forest Cuckoo Clock that flat out refused to swing. No matter what parts she replaced and swapped, or tuned, the contraption preferred the life of a wall brick.

"Bleed this scroll," she said for the five hundredth time, rubbing dry, tired eyes. "That is all I require." The final lines of the scroll's riddle eluded her.

She was at her wit's end. She had not left Jonas' bedroom since returning from Tasso's shop, having determined that the best place to cast a spell would be near the oval mirror. After all, an Irish wolfhound had appeared on its surface, out of thin air, twice. Now she lay on her back on Jonas' creepy bed, knees upwardly bent high over the skeletal frame of the footboard, staring at the ceiling. Her feet had stopped tingling long ago.

This mirror had to be a conduit. It *had* to be more than just a looking glass. She had seen it work, the *how* was the linchpin to it all. The image of Cucumbers strolling through solid glass was an encouragement, but likewise an impediment.

"What about this mirror in particular," said Sandy, "would allow a bundle of atoms to contact it, then be consumed by it, and then be spat out onto *another* plane, *another* dimension, on the other side? It doesn't make a lick of sense! That's not how doors work, and that's not how mirrors work!"

She understood mechanics, and pendulums, and physics — not quantum physics and quantum mechanics — this, this was teleportation!

"Yes, teleportation!" she exclaimed, sitting up, tugging her legs from the footboard. "Rubbing shoulders dangerously close with time travel and wormholes, and all the rest of that hypothetical sci-fi space stuff. Mankind is so far behind any of this sort of knowledge. Unless it's all magic." Sandy tapped her top teeth. "That would mean that I'm just spinning my wheels, burning mind fuel, applying logic where logic and reason hold no sway."

She raised her wrist to check her watch. She had been at this for hours. What did Jonas call it, when she was trapped in thought and lost all track of time? With a groan, she gave up trying to remember that one. A fluttery grumble accompanied the groan.

"I'm hungry."

She eased her way over the rib cage, coming out safely on the other side. When she stood blood rushed to her head, and invisible needles assailed her numbed feet, and for a moment her legs felt as if she were listing aboard a ferry.

"It's only three o'clock," she muttered, counting the hours. "I've only been laying for a couple of hours, not that long."

Why do I feel like I just got pulled from a coma?

Her feet led her to the bedside window where she pried the curtain open. "Wait, it can't be..." The streetlamps had been lit against the clawing darkness of nightfall. "It's 3 a.m. not 3 p.m." A dull thud resonated inside her head. "I've been laying here for twelve hours."

For twelve hours she had been contemplating the scroll's riddle without making much headway. This was devastating. She must have been sleeping at intervals, because there was no way that she had been that deep in her *state of diagnosis*.

That's what Jonas calls it, my state of diagnosis.

"Points for figuring that one out, Cassandra," she moaned as she left the room, heading for the kitchen. "Too bad you can't crack this puzzler to end all puzzlers."

Within the kitchen an amorphous shadow lingered near the dining nook. Sandy ignored it, believing it to be a figment conjured from her exhaustion, and would dissipate once she flipped the light switch.

It did not.

The shape spun at the sound of the click, released a yelp.

Sandy, in turn, clutched the scroll to her chest and jabbered something like, "Who-do-you-what-do-you-want?!"

"I'm so sorry Ms. Porter!" The shape was Sasha. She had been freeing the bench of its lime cushions, intent on finding something. "The door was unlocked!"

"That doesn't give you the right to —" Sandy was furious, now with her bearings in order. "It's like three o'clock in the morning!"

Sasha straightened like a startled hound. "It's like seven-thirty," she revealed with a hard-angled brow. "Post meridiem."

"Wait." Sandy's eyes went from her wristwatch to the digital readout on the microwave. "What." Apparently her wristwatch's battery had died at three PM.

"Yeah," said Sasha. "I lost one of my favorite mittens and thought that I had left it here by accident. I was outside knocking for a long time. And your phone must be disconnected because I called it and that pre-recorded voice told me as much." She returned a cushion to its rightful place and shrugged. "I announced myself a bunch of times after I came in. Figured you guys stepped out."

Sandy folded her arms. "So you decided to just help yourself?"

"I'm sorry," said Sasha in a way that made Sandy believe her. It was not your average teenage *"I'm sorry that I got caught"* that she had fielded from Jonas hundreds of times. This girl meant her apology, or she was a really impressive liar. "I'll get out of your hair, Ms. Porter."

"No, no," said Sandy, puffing a quick exhale. "You can keep looking for your glove, it's fine. Just next time wait for permission. Permission!" She shouted, spinning a slippered heel out of the room. "Be a dear and see yourself out!"

"Oh, hey, I told my Uncle Emil about..." Sasha gave up, the woman had already gone.

Foremost, Sandy needed to retrieve her letter opener from atop her bedroom's nightstand. Then afterwards, she must be careful not to stab herself. This was *very* important. She had maintained the blade toward the hallway floor as she sped for the oval mirror.

"Tremble but do not quail," began Sandy ceremoniously, the scroll outstretched. "Besmirch the surface again, certain not to fail. With eye upon thy desire, bleed this scroll, that is all I require." With a quick slash, Sandy opened a slit on her forearm, then tossed the letter opener aside. "My desire is Jonas and if all you require for permission is..." She dabbed a finger onto her scarlet wound and traced a single diagonal line onto the mirror's surface. "And besmirch you *again...*" Returning her finger to the blood well on her forearm, she refreshed and drew a second line. Stepping back, Sandy admired the X she had made in blood upon the mirror, satisfied that she had at last deciphered the riddle's preamble.

Often the most difficult answer requires the basest solution. Akin to the lesson she had learned from that Black Forest Cuckoo Clock. After hours of testing, the clock had merely required a simple leveling procedure. And this riddle's key was much the same.

She fixed her eyes to a framed photograph upon the wall. "With eye upon thy desire," she continued, smiling at the image of tiny Jonas decked out in his t-ball uniform. *Gosh, Jonas hated baseball,* Sandy thought. *But how I love this picture.*

Without glancing away, Sandy tamped the scroll to her cut. "Bleed this scroll, that is all you require."

Now please, take me to my son.

She kept her eyes glued to the photograph, should the spell need time to take effect. She wished for a bang or a crack, some sort of acknowledgment. She waited and waited, standing there, holding the scroll, her dry eyes dampened with tears. After a minute, she looked down.

"I thought that was all you required," she said. "I don't get it." Her previous tries yielded the same result. This time she was left with a gaping wound and a blood-streaked mirror. "Thought I had cracked it."

In frustration, believing to be out of options and out of time, she punched the mirror with her scroll hand, shaping the bloody X into an asterisk.

"Hey, Ms. Porter —" Sasha's feet scuffed to a halt. "I... found... my..." She gaped, raising her mitten in suspended animation.

"Get out, Sasha," said Sandy to the floorboards. "Sasha, please." Sandy's voice hardened. "I won't ask again."

If not for the quivering of her index finger, Sandy would have believed the girl completely petrified. "Ms. Porter, who is that man in the mirror?"

* * *

"Mom?" said Jonas dumbstruck, staring.

Upon a tile on the wall, a roving image of her had suddenly appeared. He lunged against his restraints, the clipboard sent skittering.

"No way."

To be caught off-guard was one thing, but this was beyond reason.

The tile was fifteen feet away, no bigger than your standard microwave screen. But make no mistake; Jonas recognized the face in that pallid blue reflection. It seemed that his mother was not alone, someone loomed in the background. As Jonas zeroed in on the figure, the cell door squeaked, budged open.

Startled but unafraid, Jonas returned to the wall, resuming prisoner pose.

The shackles had scored his wrists, thin rivulets of blood had channeled into his resting palms. The unexplained burns from the night the shadow beast had ruined his bed had nearly receded, but now he was overlaying wounds, stacking scars. Coincidently, these Terren-forged shackles nearly matched the original marks, in scope and size.

"Have you come to a decision?" The legal clerk entered alone, yet Jonas detected further presence. "Which road will you take?" she asked, stooping to retrieve the clipboard.

"I have made up my mind." Jonas lied. He had only read the opening paragraph on the top sheet — a nettle of tiresome legal mumbo jumbo that nearly rendered him catatonic. He wanted out of this cell as soon as possible.

The current episode of *Sandy Porter in Prime Time* at play on the wall was something he wished to continue unnoticed. Though he believed that his mother could not do much from her side of the tile, he was unsure what sort of games the Terrens could play from theirs. Best not underestimate the side with the dragons on leashes.

"How fortunate," said the clerk. "I will alert the council that the prisoner has reached a decision."

"Cool," said Jonas, raising his wrists. "Can I come with you?"

The clerk scratched the side of her nose. "I am obliged to say no," she replied. "There will be a public signing, but that will take time to assemble. For now, you will remain here." She raised her chin with a faint look of approval. "We had not anticipated such a hasty turn around."

"Well get used to it," said Jonas, settling back. He peered to his left, opposite his mother. "Good day to you," he said.

The clerk folded the clipboard across her chest and adjusted her wrist. "Good day," she said disconcerted. "I will return once the necessary arrangements have been made."

The woman turned and vacated the cell, much to Jonas' great relief. However, the presence he had sensed upon the clerk's entry lingered. The room did not reverberate the same when his chains rattled, as if an invisible dampening barrier had been placed.

Or, maybe, just maybe...

"You can reveal yourself," said Jonas. "I know you're in here, whoever you are, invisible person-thing."

Set above a pair of slender muscular shoulders, an arm before the back of a head appeared. The person-thing was bent over, sloughing a heavy gown. At first the entirety of the form was hazy, but once his surfaces became known to the room, the colors of a disfigured human shape grew apparent.

"I was just about to reveal myself anyways," whispered a very familiar voice.

"Isaac!" said Jonas, rising, collapsing to his knees. His bonds allowed only so much. "It's good to —"

The Still called for silence, covering his clenched smile with a finger. "The guards!" he warned in a tense whisper. "Ask me nothing and keep your voice down!"

Jonas' chains drained to the floor. "Alright," he whispered. "You can be invisible. That's pretty awesome, man."

Isaac joined Jonas on the floor. "It is," he agreed. "Now take this, you will need it for the signing." A cold cylindrical object passed into Jonas' palm. "Keep this hidden at all times. Do not even look at it. Tuck it up under your vambrace, and when —" He broke off, started at the door. "Just know that I am with you, Devil without wings, until the end." And with that, the Still melted into air.

"Thank you, Isaac," whispered Jonas, his spirit lifted. "Thank you."

Now that a victory point had been scored in his favor, it was time for that old shoe to drop. He wondered what sort of disaster may unravel, turning his attention to his mother's tile. To his dismay, she was gone, but the view of his vacant room stayed.

"Huh, maybe she's grabbing a bite?" Jonas shrugged as his fingers puzzled Isaac's gift. He dared not ask what it was.

That would be stupid, recalling Isaac's flash into murder mode. That pivotal moment had revealed his friend's true nature. If only he had been given such keen insight on Kenny and the others. *Would have saved me a lot of grief.*

The Still's murderous nature should have been an obvious deterrent, the reddest of red flags. But not for Jonas. He favored the shunned castaway. Logic and reason, concerning the Hush, may as well be spices on a forgotten spice rack, for how often he seasoned his mind.

The locks on the door released and a guard appeared, adorned in the formal garb of the winged welcoming committee. "Hungry?" he asked.

"Sure," replied Jonas.

The guard strode across the cell with an arm behind his back. Today's offering was braised fowl and potatoes. Carefully he set the wooden serving plate on the floor, producing a clay cup filled with water.

"Enjoy," the guard stated with a flat affect.

"Much appreciated, and uh, hey," said Jonas, hitching the guard's exit. "Do you know how long it will take for the assembly to... um... assemble?"

"That I do not know," said the guard, and resumed departure. "I'm not one to speculate." He looked to Jonas as he placed a hand to the door's heavy strap. "Enjoy your meal."

In a cruel twist, the guard had methodically placed the meal just beyond Jonas' fingertips. He strained, tugging his shackles. The scent alone was enough to drive him mad. As he was about to scream, an invisible toe slid the plate a heroic inch in his direction. It was just enough to curl a finger to its rim and pull it inward.

"Thanks, Ike," said Jonas, grateful.

"No problem," he replied. "Oh, and I forgot to mention: do not compel your Hylda to move any place — don't ask me why — I know you'll want to ask me why. Just be content to know that it will make sense later."

"Geeze," Jonas sighed. "Okay." In truth he had not planned to reach out anyhow. He held no desire for further harm to befall his passing spirits.

"It's just very important."

"I got it."

As Jonas was hunched forward shoveling food into his mouth, a scene played out on the tile. In a desperate state, Sandy had returned to view. Jonas slugged his water as his mother screamed and punched the glass. Her panicked face had overtaken the tile's entirety, then was downwardly torn from sight. The scene ended with several figures hauling her out the door, out of sight.

Jonas moaned in satisfaction, scratching his chin with the rim of the empty cup. He leaned back to pat his belly, spared a glance for his bedroom.

Nobody home.

As if an alert had been sent when his emptied cup met the floor, the cell door swung wide. A troop of winged guards swiftly flooded in, their long mantles curled at their heels when they hastened to a stop.

The spritely Terren captain stepped from among the ranks, snapped his fingers, fracturing a pair of guards from the contingent. Immediately they set to work unlocking Jonas' neck restraints. The precision by which they moved gave the impression that this routine had seen practice.

"Where are you taking me?" Jonas asked.

The guard captain's eye twinged. "We are escorting you to another place of holding," he replied. "One with a bathing facility. Although you may not look the part, you are a Prince of Serpentfel, and at the behest of the royals, you are to appear as such for the ceremony."

"Peachy," said Jonas. Meanwhile Isaac's gift required a new hidey-hole. Preferably a place that was not actually a *hole*, should this apparent clothing swap take place before the guards.

The captain flexed his wings, signaling his deputies to leave. "Shall we?" he said once they were alone.

Jonas nodded.

"I had been told for years," began the captain, sneering. "That you were one to be feared. I want you to know that I always thought the Prophecy to be a total crock. But now that I've met you, I know that it wasn't completely false. It managed to get one thing right..." His words suspended as he turned a heel, but Jonas was not listening.

On the tile that displayed his bedroom, the shape of a man stretched into view. With each step the man grew in size and clarity, but he needn't take any further steps for Jonas to claim recognition. That pair of hiked up Dockers tightly belted just below an aged shriveled sternum, that stumbled gait, that reckless swagger, that loosely hung lower jaw — belonged to the man that Jonas had set his sights upon.

Emil.

Jonas unleashed a snarl that startled the captain from his yammering.

The captain was oblivious to the source of Jonas' quickened ire. "Yes," he said with a satisfied grin, believing his dialogue had produced the spark. "Anger is certainly a predictable response to such harsh truths."

CHAPTER 27

The guards had escorted the prisoner to a bathhouse, grand and palatial. The rate for patronage was unimaginably expensive, and for a regular Terren citizen obtaining a reservation was nigh impossible.

When the upper crust patrons were bidden kindly evacuate, the edict was met with tight-lipped obedience. As Jonas passed them, upon his entry to the bathhouse, their restrained hostility was given outlet. He was not listening to the insults, he did not feel the dirt kicked at his shins, nor did he wipe the spit from his face. If he could not save those he loved, what was this power good for?

All he could see was Emil closing his bedroom door. The vision played on repeat, over and over. Before he was fully aware of it, his armor had been stripped and the clothing beneath peeled away. Isaac's hidden object fell from his vambrace, and he could not even pretend to care. When the guards demanded an explanation, he was not listening, he was elsewhere.

He tried to soothe himself, lying to himself, proposing that maybe his mother was still at dinner with a friend. But he knew that was fiction. Emil was in his house. The *what* and the *why* did not matter. That was the cold reality.

At this very moment Emil is in my house, doing God knows what.

He was instructed to remove his smallclothes, and he acquiesced much slower than the escort wished. Suddenly Jonas became aware of an intense pain lancing his jaw.

"Hey!" The guard captain screamed, slapping Jonas across the face again. "Hey!" Although he had detected Jonas' return, he gave a final slap for good measure. "What is this?" He thrust a shining object before Jonas' eyes, nearly cracking the bridge of his nose.

Jonas eased back. "I don't know," he replied, as the object came to clarity. The torpedo-shaped item held a familiar aesthetic, but Jonas had never witnessed its like before. Felt it in his hands, but had not seen it, *until now.*

A bolt of pain scorched Jonas' jaw, his ears hummed anew.

"Where did you get this?" The captain parted the torpedo, revealing a blade. "You did not have this when we apprehended you! What were you planning?!"

"I don't know!" said Jonas. Isaac had secreted the dagger into his vambrace but had neglected the itinerary for when it should be drawn. He had only instructed Jonas to keep it hidden. "I've never seen it —"

"You bumbling prat! You've ruined everything!"

Jonas faltered, holding his head. "What?! You're?!"

All along, Dafodhel had been the secret item in his vambrace!

"See?" said the captain, turning around to face his guards. "This is what we have been fearing. This is what we have been told to fear, what we have been preparing for." He swiveled, and Jonas flinched to raucous laughter. "The Evil Seed, the fearsome Leeds Devil of Prophecy. What a joke, what a mistake." The captain gestured for the guards to depart. At the threshold he sniffed, looked back at Jonas, his bearing as one about to speak.

"Why didn't you tell me before?" said Jonas, crumbling to the wall, addressing Dafodhel.

"Tell you what before?" asked the captain, his interest piqued.

Jonas looked up as if noticing the winged man for the first time. "Nothing," he replied, turning away. "Just keep that stupid knife away from me. I don't want to see it again."

Smirking, the captain approached. "Oh, I don't know." His eyes dropped scornfully upon Jonas. "This needle may just weave its way back into your tapestry." He paused. "Make sure to scrub that pretty face of yours. Wouldn't want to go before the entire court with all that egg dripping from it."

For the eye of every newcomer, the grand cathedral in Serpentfel was a thrilling spectacle. The structure was massive, able to easily fit ninety skyward stacked cottages beneath its roof, and the footprint alone could accommodate three stadiums, not including the courtyards, gardens, and observatories spaced along the outer walls.

Lilac marble enwrapped the exterior walls, diamonds encrusted the roof-top shingles, and the doors were an impossible lustrous black onyx. Where the seven foundational markers had been placed, seven pinnacles roared up to the heavens. And Jonas would have noticed all this, should his eyes have risen higher than the boots of the guards ardently striding ahead of him.

Jonas was rushed through the grand cathedral doors. A carpet inlaid with scarlet gossamer traversed the corridor, eventually giving way to the central audience chamber. The six fountains carved from stone, the armor stands and statues lining the way, and the skull of a dragon slain long ago went unnoticed. For the trek, Jonas had stared into the carpet, hiding his face, hiding tears.

He was escorted to a table sunken into the center of the vast circular chamber, every seat filled. Hundreds, possibly thousands took up audience, staring down at Jonas, three hundred and sixty degrees of scorn. A chest high embankment that rolled before every seat, built as fall prevention, blocked the sight of their full bodies. When a heavy door closed from somewhere overhead, the sliver of midday light upon Jonas' table vanished.

The bathhouse clothes he had been gifted were stifling, unfriendly. When folded they appeared as your garden variety tunic and tights, but unfurled they were unlike anything he had ever seen.

The Princes of Serpentfel are fashion masochists, he thought, wincing at the Terren faces surrounding him.

Instead of an open collar, this tunic choked from collar to chin, acting as a serrated turtleneck. The boots were excruciatingly tight and pinched places that should not conceivably pinch, as if they had been form-fitted for toddlers with hooves. Also, there was a cape.

"We welcome you," boomed a voice. "Jonas Reuel Terren, Prince and heir of Serpentfel."

Jonas looked up to see a pudgy, beardless man standing among an austere panel of older Terren men and women. Five in total, their silver robes setting them apart. The chest high embankment opened a gap before them, exposing their full forms.

"Your arrival had been foretold," the beardless man continued, "and now that you have made your appearance, you have proven at least a few fragments of the Prophecy credible. But we are not here for a debate." He widened his stance and raised his hands in a cordial display. "I daresay, we are here to broker a deal."

The chamber could not rise fast enough to roar their approval. Jonas plucked the fabric stuck to his neck and sweat beaded his brow. After what seemed an eternity, like thunder diminishing in the distance, the excitement petered out.

"Before you lies five choices, the choices five," announced the beardless man, sweeping a gesture toward Jonas. "Three which come at great cost, one which grants your destiny, and one that..." Reverently the man inclined his head. "Demands the ultimate sacrifice."

Gasps thickened the air all across the chamber.

None of this matters, thought Jonas.

In that moment he desired a cure for his family's blight of poverty. Vengeance had fallen to the wayside. Everything had grown complicated and convoluted and confusing, between the monsters, the Riverlands, and prophecies. At this very moment his mother needed him more than ever. His body was powerful, perfect for righting all the wrongs...

Yet, I'm still just as helpless as ever.

"The first choice," a different voice intoned. This one of a husky feminine quality. "Swear fealty to the Terrens and assume your seat as a Prince of Serpentfel. Be generously granted all that such a station offers." The leftmost member of the panel was standing, speaking. She continued, answering the unvoiced question. "All prior sins committed against the realm, permanently and mercifully expunged."

Sections of the chamber buzzed in disagreement. One man went so far as to stand and holler that Jonas was the greatest threat to ever exist, which was agreed upon by everyone in his nearby vicinity. One excited woman, in solidarity with the man, hurled a string of insults that would have melted a swear jar.

"The second choice," proclaimed a nasally male voice in a higher pitch than the woman previous. "Relinquish all thy powers over the Passing Spirits: The creeping Hylda and the soaring Ritts. And be thusly granted a generous estate enduring the boundaries of the Terren domain, far from Serpentfel." He paused to allow the dissenters and supporters a chance to vent. "However," he cut into the dwindling voices. "However, thou shalt hereby be stripped of all title, inheritance, and claim to the throne of Serpentfel. A Prince thou shalt be no longer." Then quickly recited at a lower, muffled volume; "All prior sins committed against the realm, and the crown, permanently and mercifully expunged."

The room was divided. One side frothed with indignation and the other supplied uproarious approval. Those who managed to catch the tail end of the Chamberlain's statement flung accusations of treachery and deceit.

Jonas felt as a stone in a river, only wishing for time to pass quicker to hasten his erosion into nothingness.

"The third choice," stated a clear female voice. The chamberlain looked a true vampire, tall, regal, sinuous. Minus the thick Transylvania accent. "Relinquish all powers over Passing Spirits, the ones aforementioned, and in return receive a summation of gold equivalent to the estate mentioned in the Second Choice." Only the squeaking of seats could be heard as the torch was passed to the next speaker. This chamberlain, unlike her predecessors, exuded a tidal wave of authority.

"The fourth choice," rumbled a deep, rust-coated male voice. Sounding as if he took breaks from puffing a cigar to swallow fistfuls of gravel. "Stop controlling the Hylda and the Ritts," said the chamberlain. "And be given a harem."

This was met with a whirlwind of confused energy. Stammered queries abounded throughout as confused heads swiveled, and neighbors beseeched one another for explanation. This fourth proposition produced far more questions than its predecessors. Jonas pried his eyes from the table just in time to catch an encouraging wink from the Chamberlain right before he took his seat.

"The fifth and final choice," said a voice of equal male and female make. Curiosity edged Jonas' eyes upward. This chamberlain's trunk was slender as a gymnast yet bore the neck and shoulders of a linebacker. "Should you deny the provided choices, or take overlong in your decision-making, then by default, you have opted for the final choice: execution by decapitation." The chamberlain concluded while tipping a generously sized hourglass on its head.

Silence pervaded, holding the storm at bay. A storm that, for more than a decade, had been gathering for this precise moment. From the beginning, two teams had been drawn, the Terrens and the Leeds. The Prophecy had lofted a ball into the air that both sides had been frantically running beneath, striving to catch before the other. Initially the Leeds had been given the first shot, and failed, forfeiting to the Terrens. And the Terrens had skillfully moved into scoring position and now stood upon the goal line.

"How much," said Jonas as the chamberlain was readying to repeat the fifth charge. "How much is that gold worth in American dollars?"

The female chamberlain who had outlined the third choice, and wielded weapon's grade authority, rose to her feet. "The current conversion is estimated —"

"Is it more than fifty thousand dollars?" said Jonas, interrupting her.

The chamberlain folded her hands, waiting for the mumbling to subside. She alone seemed to be the only one who had not taken offense. "More," she replied as her face cracked with a smile. "Much, much more."

At this point, the fifth chamberlain took a seat while the third remained standing.

"I like that," said Jonas glumly. Through an act of magic, his voice had boosted loud enough for all to hear. "But I want you to leave the people of Brimon alone. They think that they can beat you."

"How much longer do you wager they can hold out?" asked the chamberlain while hundreds of spectators eagerly adjusted their seats. "You deduced that our retreat was a fabrication? It is true that we believed the taking of Brimon would be hard-fought, but what you inspired among their ranks was wholly unanticipated."

Jonas wearily pinched the bridge of his nose. "I have no idea how long they can last. Please leave them alone. You can do whatever you want with the river, claim ownership, or whatever." He looked up to meet the chamberlain's eyes. "They're beaten. You don't have to kick them while they're down."

"Oh, the Taub will be ours," sniveled the second chamberlain, rising to his feet. "It is only a matter of time. But in order for us to lay proper claim, the Leeds family must be extinguished. Profitable trade will commence again and the barricades will be lifted. This continent will prosper once again." The chamberlain's voice rose to an excited, squealing octave and every audience tier reacted with wholehearted applause.

"The days of my childhood, standing on the shores, watching the ships pass by on their way to lands unknown, returning with exotic spices and new-fangled toys... those days are coming again! And coming soon!" exclaimed the chamberlain, at full throat, wildly punching the air.

The house was on their feet at this point, fiercely clapping and nodding approval. Dust ripples drifted down from the ceiling, knocked free by the tremendous vibrations below.

"Why?" said Jonas. "Why do they have to die? Can't they just surrender?" His sadness began giving way to anger. "Can't you just leave them alone?"

The second chamberlain cocked his head, an intense spasm played across his lips. "By law," he said sedately. "One cannot stack such acts: treason, murder, contempt — to name a few, without paying the ultimate price! And they have amassed quite the pile at this point, my young prince." The chamberlain folded his hands beneath his belt and released a sigh. "For shame, they use women and children as shields. I mean..." He turned to his fellow chamberlains, displayed flat palms. "Come on."

Laughter belted from every corner of the chamber at once, as if the man had delivered the cleverest of punch lines.

"You're all monsters," said Jonas.

"Now he finally gets it!" the fourth chamberlain's deep voice rumbled, re-igniting the hysteria.

As Jonas waited for quiet, staring in disbelief at the faces of rictus rapture, he thought with all sincerity, *Is there any Royal House in this world that isn't filled with idiots.*

"Fine, fine," said Jonas, relenting. "If I take the third option, can I score only half the gold, and in return you promise to leave the people of Brimon alone? Like, do whatever you want, but just spare them?" *That amount of gold would satisfy Emil for sure, placing my mother in the clear...* Then his thoughts went to his newly discovered uncle, who yet lived on this world, in Brimon. And Jonas was not about to leave any of his family in the lurch.

"This is not a negotiation," said the high-pitched chamberlain, dashing Jonas' hopes.

"Select one of the five," added the first chamberlain.

"And be quick about it. We don't have all day," concluded the gravel-voiced chamberlain, thick burly arms folded over his planet of a chest.

Beneath an eve and against a balustrade, free from the chamber's wandering view, Isaac's head flickered to sight. Jonas feigned interest, tugged at his turtleneck, and casually winced in Isaac's direction. He did not want anyone detecting the Hush's sudden arrival.

Isaac appeared for the briefest glimmer, his index finger upraised, indicating that Jonas take the first choice; take his place as prince.

There was no easy solution facing Jonas and time was not his ally. Emil had stated that his mother had thirty days to pay, but maybe time passed slower on this side of the rift? Maybe the thirty days were up?

One of the things Vera had told him in earnest was that this whole mess, this conflict, this entire war was about family. His arrival had marked the beginning of the end, and as hard as he pondered, trying to work out a way for everyone to survive, he fell short.

If he agreed and became a prince, how much influence might he wield?

I'd be nothing but a figurehead, like my grandparents.

Try as he might, he could not deceive himself.

It's a tempting offer.

But what sort of loopholes and trickery could be found in the fine print?

Sure, I'd be a Prince. Which would be pretty cool, but it'd probably leave me shackled in a different way.

The silver sands of the hourglass had nearly depleted.

The first Chamberlain cleared his throat.

Of the five options, only two seemed straightforward. And one of those choices would render him headless, so that left...

"The third choice," said Jonas, lifting eyes to the hourglass. From the shadows Isaac released a groan of pure lead. "I'll take the gold."

CHAPTER 28

"I would've followed you anywhere..." whispered Jonas in his cell, frail once again. Off to his right lay a fist-sized pouch over-stuffed with gold.

After renouncing his claim to the Hylda and Ritts, his body had diminished, returned to normal. The overly tight princely clothing suddenly became a dozen sizes too large. He practically swam in them, until they were stripped and replaced with a prisoner's rags.

I was so big.

After signing the agreement with ink and sealing it with a drop of blood, twin vampire bats had been escorted to the table. Along with the bats, that moment brought with it the sound of creaking seats, as each and every spectator leaned forward. At spear point, he had been encouraged to stand and lay across the table. His hands had been separated from the shackles only to be stretched out to the sides and shackled anew.

One chamberlain had made an announcement, going on about the bats being symbolic of the passing spirits, and as soon as he had concluded, the bats clamped painfully down onto Jonas' wrists. One bat on his left and one on his right —

one for the Ritts and one for the Hylda, each feeding greedily as if nourishment had been withheld for days.

The moment those bats plunged their teeth into his skin, clarity of vision fled from his eyes. And he had yielded a pound of muscle for every ounce of blood the creatures slugged. Had he known that his powers were so intertwined with his passing spirits...

Maybe being a prince of Serpentfel wouldn't have been so bad after all.

As he lay upon that cold slab of a table, his powers draining, he had reached out to his Hylda. Posh was far too overcome with sorrow to speak, and all Scary could muster was, *"I would've followed you anywhere,"* before their connection severed forever.

The cell felt colder and deeper, and he could no longer sense Isaac's presence. He had called out to his friend several times, "I can't see very well anymore, Isaac. If you're there, can you say something."

Before Jonas' blurry return trek to the prison, the guards had cleverly swapped his shackles for a spare bootstrap. His wrists had withered far too much for a proper fit of iron. Why restraints were yet required was beyond comprehension, but it seemed rules were rules, and this kingdom just loved rules. And aside from the leather bootstrap, Jonas had no other such bonds. This meant he could now walk freely about his cell, and once the guards had vacated, he immediately visited that tile upon the wall. The tile that had at first held his mother's reflection.

Then it was Emil's... Jonas thought. Devil no longer, yet his soul darkened at the thought of that man.

He gazed into the tile, and to his great disquiet found his bedroom empty. Then he noticed the door ajar where light from the hallway spilled. His mother was pretty stingy, not one to leave lights on, so maybe she was still home elsewhere?

He walked away from the tile and sat down to wallow. The vampire bats had left his wrists sore and slightly swollen, and his head throbbed from staring into that tile. And to top it off, the outer fringes of his in-drawn breaths had begun to tighten. The remedy, his rescue inhaler, was within sight through the tile, but so far out of reach.

Abandoned, alone, and once again without a friend in the world. In *any* world. Funny enough, the Ritts and Hylda had given him a sense of belonging, a sense of purpose. Though he was their commander, or whatever, they had developed a bond.

We had grown so close, and it seems they felt the same. Jonas' head sank to his chest. He recalled a moment at the end of his ordeal when he had reached out for his Ritts. *Too late. Missed my chance.*

"And I would've led you everywhere," he voiced through blurry eyes.

"Led who to where?" The guard captain breached the quiet. "Whom do you address?"

Jonas squinted at the shifting woolly tapestry that was the captain.

How long had that guy been standing there? thought Jonas.

"My Hylda," replied Jonas. He did not see the sense in lying. "And Ritz."

The captain scoffed. "Do you have any idea how many good Terrens laid down their lives in the search for those blasted demon bats?" He spat and ranged closer. "Not to mention those we lost just trying to secure them ahead of the Leeds."

"I don't —" Jonas tried to reply but was quickly bitten off.

"That hourglass was empty!" the captain ranted. "When you gave your answer! I kept careful watch!" He vaulted in front of Jonas, his raging mouth locked into focus. "The final grain of silver sand had settled upon the lower pile right before you gave your sniveling response!"

Jonas braced for a slap, but it did not come.

"And you went for the third option! I never would have guessed that you would sell out!" A shadow seemed to pass over the captain's face as he thoughtfully settled a backward step. "You could have been a Prince," he stated. "You could have retained the royal family legacy, lived a life of ease and luxury, a life to kill for. Or you could have been the owner of a grand palatial estate, living out your days in peace and tranquility. And then there's the *harem.* I mean, really? What's the matter with you?" The captain leaned closer than was comfortable. "But you chose money."

That's when the slap came.

Jonas reeled, the pain exquisite.

"Pathetic," said the captain, rising to his feet. "Who would have believed our fathers were so inseparable?"

"What's your problem, man?" Jonas asked, rasping a wheeze. "And who's your dad?"

The captain notched an eyebrow. "Short of breath all of a sudden, eh?" he said dryly. "My father is the Lord Commander of the Lancethane Legion. Your father *was* the Crown Prince of Serpentfel." The captain's left hand scoured his left hip. "And my problem is that I'm fed up with this Prophecy that our kingdom has been dancing around for years, wasting time, wasting resources..." Abruptly the captain attached his hands to his hips in a pose of authority. *"The child born will be the Leeds Devil — The Evil Seed,* which if you change the letters around, spell one another. Except 'Evil Seed' has only one 'D.' But no one cares about details like that, especially when they're hysterical. Then years later, after Guiltbrand defected, another seer stepped up and declared that the Prophecy had been deduced incorrectly. And surprise, surprise, everyone believed that new prediction.

"*The child shall be the Leeds Scourge* — and floating somewhere within that raw sewage alphabet soup, you can scoop out the word 'courage.' And everyone went crazy, clinging to the belief that you were our final hope for our reclamation of the Taub." The captain, now positioned over Jonas, brought his left hand out from hiding. "Then they nabbed a dream demon to reach out to you, and employed a Joiner to bring you to us..." His eyes crawled to the unsheathed dagger in his hand. "But things became complicated, and you were more of a problem than we anticipated. Your actions shook a lot of our landsmen's deeply held beliefs. *'Maybe he is the Devil,'* some whined, *'If we can't believe in prophecies, what can we believe in?'*" The captain ceased his impersonation, settled murderous eyes on Jonas. "You caused a great deal of panic, a great deal of problems."

Jonas did not welcome the look upon the captain's face. "I thought I told you," Jonas wheezed. "To keep that dagger away from me."

The captain dragged the blade across his own chin, scratching at the developing stubble. "My father will be proud of me," he drawled. "For it was Némer's son who slew the *Evil Seed...*" He toyed with the dagger, flipping it and stabbing the air.

"Your father is Némer?" gasped Jonas. "You're going to kill me," he coughed. "Like your father did to mine?"

"My father did not —"

"Jonas!" Dafodhel's voice rushed inside his mind. *"Get back!"*

With knee-jerk obedience, Jonas scrambled backward against the wall. A tremendous sickly crack was heard and the son of Némer fell. Dafodhel, in the form of a quarterstaff, bounced once upon the cold stone before coming to a curt stop. Then like the removal of a shroud, Isaac appeared.

"Take up your arms," said Isaac. With his boot he rolled the quarterstaff toward Jonas. Bundled against his chest he held Jonas' armor.

"Let us leave this place!" urged Dafodhel.

"But how, Daf?" said Jonas, retrieving the quarterstaff. She shifted into the form of a crescent blade, and he began to work her over the bonds constricting his wrists.

"Through the mirrored tile!" replied Dafodhel. "You are slight enough to fit!"

"I can pass through that?" said Jonas, disillusioned.

Isaac seemed to manifest beside him. "*We* can pass through that," he stated, placing a hand on Jonas' shoulder. "And the blood spell cast by the vampire bats won't hold you in this form forever."

CHAPTER 29

Unlike Jonas' previous crossings, this one was made with his eyes open. And it was easy, much like crawling through an attic crawlspace, or passing from one room to another. As the entirety of his body was nearly into his bedroom, Isaac gave his boot soles a helpful push, boosting him clear over the mirror's bottom lip.

Jonas crept to the open door with ears perked while Isaac easily slid into the room. The house was totally quiet. After he determined that they were alone, his glasses were his second priority.

"What are you searching for?" inquired a muffled Dafodhel from inside Jonas' closed fist. She had taken the form of a standard push blade. Locked in his other hand was the pouch of gold coins — the Terrens' good faith offering. He hoped that this would be enough to satisfy his grandfather's debt, or at the very least smother a good portion.

"My glasses," replied Jonas, twisting the knob on his nightstand lamp. "I tossed them over there..." He turned to orient himself then went to his knees and began to rummage behind a stack of comic books.

"Are glasses like spectacles?" asked Isaac.

"Yeah, pretty much," replied Jonas, hurling a sweater over his shoulder.

"Then I do believe that the Hush has already found them," said Dafodhel.

Isaac meandered like a zombie, his palms in front of his eyes. "How do these improve your vision?" he asked, clenching and unclenching his fingers. "Or is this how you see the world otherwise?"

"Oh, awesome," said Jonas crossing the room.

Isaac removed the glasses and winced. "We need to get your powers back soon," he said. "That is quite an uncomfortable way to live."

Jonas froze with his glasses an inch from his nose. "I can get my powers back," he said in disbelief.

"Indeed," said Dafodhel. "But first things first. We must assuage this evil that has set upon your mother."

"Or at least find out whether this evil, *this Emil*, actually has set upon her." said Jonas, wriggling his nose under the fit of his glasses.

"This evil Emil, "said Dafodhel as if she were catching on to something.

Jonas curled his lip. "Yeah, they're pretty much the same thing," he said, beelining for his inhaler. "You'll see." He arched his back and drew a deep pull of medicine. And right after a clear breath, he swung a zip-up jacket across his shoulders and hopped into a moderately clean pair of gray jeans. And suddenly from toe to collar, as if for the first time, Jonas seemed to notice the Still.

"And if anyone *sees* you dressed like that." Jonas paused to think up diplomatic phrasing. "Uh, let's just say, that maybe it would be best if you wore something more... or maybe less..." His mind stalled and he gave up. "We don't want someone to call the cops on us before we get where we're going." It was sad to admit, but Isaac's attire would draw a lot of unwanted attention. Of this Jonas was certain. Isaac gaped in dignified horror as Jonas offered a solution: black jeans and a black hoodie. They were the best options that he had in stock.

"Enough!" Dafodhel snapped, transforming into a silver longsword that projected toward the hallway. Jonas buckled beneath the weight and Dafodhel wisely returned to her prior form. "Don the raiment and let's be off!" As abrasive as the sword could be, she was correct nearly all the time.

Isaac's face knit into a hard scowl. "Yes," he said. "Let us find your mother." The manner in which Isaac's tunic had masterfully accented the curvature of his inhuman torso was now blotted, draped in thick cheap cotton.

Before they set off, Dafodhel instructed Jonas to disrupt the blood smear on the mirror to extinguish the spell. He obeyed, swiping the stain with a stray sock.

Downstairs proved as empty as the upstairs, with nearly every light left on along the way. A sure sign that Sandy had left in a hurry. Whether of her own volition, the three travelers could not tell. But a knot had formed in Jonas's guts, twisting, telling him that she was in danger. If only he could go back to who he once was. The Devil or the Scourge.

As they scoured the shop for a scrap of evidence, Jonas whispered an apology.

"Sorry that I'm me."

Isaac was out of earshot, plotting a search of the office.

Dafodhel, on the other hand, heard every syllable. *"You have claimed that statement once before."* The push blade seemed to tremble in Jonas' hand, her voice bleached of usual callousness. *"Right before you spurred the most heroic rout I have ever seen on the field of battle. A resurgence not seen for —"* She cut herself off, seeming to need a moment to collect herself.

Daf, thought Jonas to the sword. Her words had brought calm resolve.

"Perhaps there are witnesses to your mother's abduction?" Dafodhel suggested. Expressing that amount of emotion was unacceptably out of character for a weapon torn from legend.

"That's an excellent proposal," said Isaac, beside Jonas.

Jonas agreed that was a great jumping off point, but he wilted at the notion of door knocking his neighbors after dusk. Also, a good deal of them had taken advantage of the Holiday to vacation down to the sunny South. By Christmas, most folk were already sick of the abysmal cold.

Once outside, Jonas ignored the briskness of the winter night and the din of Christmas music emanating from the Pinault's next door.

I'll avoid Darren for now, thought Jonas. *Maybe we'll uncover something before we need to knock.*

He strode opposite the Pinault's, keying for his leftward neighbor first, hopeful for warm glowing rooms with shadows at play inside.

"Dang it," groaned Jonas. No such luck. All that glowed were the Christmas lights framing their roofline. The driveway was desolate, nobody home. "Looks like the Thomases flew away for Christmas."

The homes across the street were just as dark and any others further down the lane were not going to harbor help. No one from that distance would have borne witness with any crucial detail.

That left the Pinaults. Jonas recalled the other day's humiliation, helplessness. The cruelty of Darren and his friends. The threat of doused coffee, their passive reaction to his shortness of breath. Darren's scornful admission when his mother requested his help; *"I'm good on that burden."*

The Jonas of old would have crumbled at the thought of approaching Darren's doorstep, especially when the wounds of disgrace were still fresh. But now these reminders, those memories, galvanized Jonas' bloody-lipped determination.

"Hey!" It was Darren. The unmistakable noise hooked Jonas' attention. "Yeah you!" Jonas whirled around. "I'm talking to you, ya skinny freak! We saw you come out of the Poorer House!"

Darren was not addressing Jonas.

That means...

"Oh, no!" Jonas took off for the Pinault's. "Don't ask questions! Darren! Don't ask him anything!"

The well-lit porch peeled into view as Jonas rounded the bend. He recognized a few of Darren's friends from the other day, plus a dozen other teenagers who were not part of Darren's circle.

Every room within the three-story house was ablaze with light, including the circular attic window. The driveway, the adjoining curb overflowed with cars. Checkered beams of light poured down from the windows and washed over a pair of beer kegs standing guard astride the front steps. Mariah Carey pumped from inside, sweating through the walls. *"Santa, won't you bring me the one I really need?"*

A party raged mid-swing, and well over half of Scarberry High's graduating class had showed. It was not difficult to infer that the Pinault parents had gone away for the Holidays.

Jonas caught sight of Isaac standing outside the outer rim of light, his hood drawn, facing the porch. Shrieks of anguish abruptly severed a commotion that had nearly attained full height.

"Oh, no," repeated Jonas, watching Darren crumple inside a mass of panic-stricken teenagers.

Isaac looked to Jonas. "He asked from whence I came," he explained. "That lad is no good. He is devoid of empathy."

"This is exactly what I wanted to avoid," said Jonas. *"We* need to ask the questions. *We* need to find out if anyone at this party saw my mother today." Gently he pressed Isaac at his shoulder. "Go wait over there, out of sight, okay? That guy you just messed up is a royal prick, but we can't have him taking a dirt nap right now."

The Still did not budge. "I am not leaving your side."

"Fine," relented Jonas. "But stay behind me, and don't make eye contact." From the corner of his mouth, Jonas whispered, "and try not being so dang scary."

A muffled laugh escaped beneath the Still's hood.

As Jonas and Isaac approached the porch, one by one the teenagers took notice, but Darren's close friends did not. They were beside him, begging him to remove his hand from his face.

"C'mon, man," said the guy Jonas recalled as Chad. "Let us see what's going on with your face. You might need stitches, or something."

"No!" bawled Darren, contorting his body. His face greased with tears that glistened in the cheery Christmas light. "I'm fine! Just get away from me! Just give —" Darren noticed Jonas. "What do you think you're doing here?!" He clambered to his feet, his uncovered eye darted frantically. "No one invited you!"

"Darren," said Jonas. "Don't look at him. Look at me."

With his free hand Darren slapped at his tears, then accused Isaac with an angrily pointed finger. "What's your problem, man?" he demanded, choking back tears. He was yet in the throes of agony. Then to Jonas' horror, suddenly Darren crumpled again, sucked an anguished yelp and collapsed, gripping the other side of his face.

Jonas rushed to Darren's side, expertly avoiding his kicking feet. "Stay back!" He commanded the encroaching porch, then focused his attention back down. "Where's my mother?" he asked, shaking Darren's shoulders. "Have you seen her today?"

Darren howled, his eyes stitched in torment.

"Where is my mother?!" Jonas began to lose composure. Hastily he pocketed Dafodhel and gripped Darren's wrists. "Where is she?!" he demanded. "Where is Cassandra Porter?" Jonas was losing grip of his anger. Last time he went ballistic, he wound up captured by dragons. He backed off to take a breath.

Then Isaac was there. "Reveal her whereabouts," he hissed. "Or I will end you."

Darren's body froze tense, his eyes shuttered open. "Sasha went next door a few hours ago to see your mom," he explained trembling. "She said that Uncle Emil was going to meet her there to buy a clock, or something, like, a big clock." He looked to Isaac and opened his mouth to continue.

"Don't speak to him," said Jonas. "If you do, you'll die. Only speak to me."

With both hands covering his face, Darren gave a tremulous nod. "Then afterward I saw your mom leave with Uncle Emil and his friends." He licked his lips, concentrated on something in the sky. "Now that I think of it, I never saw them leave with a clock. They only left with your mom."

"Where did they go?" Jonas pressed.

"Uh." Darren's eyes refocused. "Not sure. Maybe to his office at the storage place?" He shrugged and sucked a breath, which ushered a resurgence of pain. "Sasha might know," he groaned and rolled to his side.

"No she won't," revealed a voice from the porch. "She left with that Emil-guy and his hulk pals. Those dudes are *massive,* like I wonder how much those dudes can bench."

Darren bolted upright. "Colin, what did you just say?" he asked, removing his hands from his face. The porch drew back with a gasp. "Did you just say that Sasha isn't here?"

"Dude," said a guy beside Colin. "Your face."

"Forget my face, Trevor," Darren continued, "Sasha left with Brokula's mom?"

"Yeah, dude," confirmed Trevor, taking a casual sip from his red cup. "Hours ago. Looked none too happy about it either."

In a panic, Darren surged to his feet. "Where are my keys?" He rounded on Jonas, revealing a bloody roman numeral "I" etched deep into his left cheek, and a "II" on his right, symbolically denoting each question he had asked the Still. It was a grim and dark countdown, and a "III" spelled out upon his forehead would have spelled his end.

Jonas side-eyed Isaac. *I see what you did there*, he thought, then reached up to clasp Darren by his shoulders. "We're coming with you."

"Of course, of course." Darren, glanced warily at Isaac. "Luckily I parked on the street, in case I needed to make a snack run or something." He reached out and snapped his fingers, fetching the attention of his crew. It seemed a bit of his spirit had returned. "Hey! Where are the keys to my Neon?"

"Check your pockets, bro."

"Ah," replied Darren, rummaging inside his coat. "Right on."

The trio set off for the street while Darren pointed the way. Snow began to fall, the thick dense sort that sticks to your eyelashes. The lamp lit street would have seemed a Christmas painting come to life, if lives were not hanging in the balance.

"There she is," said Darren, indicating a black Dodge Neon huddled within a streetlamp's cone of light. Darren entered first and unlocked all the doors with the push of a button. Jonas sat shotgun and Isaac sat in the back middle seat, his feet upon the hump. When Darren checked his rearview mirror, he shuddered — not from the cold.

"Where is your friend from?" he asked Jonas, trying to sound casual. "I've never seen him ."

"He's family from Romania, visiting for the Holidays," replied Jonas. "There's an old family debt he's here to help with."

"Family, eh?" Darren's eyebrows shot to his hairline. "I see the resemblance," he said, poking at his teeth.

"You know that your Uncle Emil is not a good guy, right?" said Jonas, conducting the subject away from Isaac.

Every muscle in Darren's arms tensed. "Yeah," he agreed. "I've been trying to tell my family that he's no good. From when I was a little kid, I could never remember a time when he wasn't gifting my sister with toys and cash and candy. And he ignores me completely. The old dude always gives me this look," Darren turned to Jonas with a deep grooved scowl. "Like this, like I'm gum stuck to his loafers."

"So he showers Sasha with tons of stuff and totally leaves you out in the cold?" asked Jonas.

"Pretty much," replied Darren, angrily slapping his turn signal. "Most I get from that old fart is a sneer."

"Why's that?"

"Darren shrugged. "I have my suspicions," he said with narrowed eyes. "You know he's Mafia, right? Like legitimate Mafia. But not the spaghetti and concrete sneakers kind you see in movies."

"Yeah," said Jonas. "He's Polish."

Darren slapped the top of the steering wheel. "Right," he said. "Polish." He paused and his demeanor darkened. "I think he's angling to sell my sister to rich folks overseas. Like human trade stuff. I've been doing this research on it in the library after school, and I think he's been buttering her up for years, making her feel like she owes him something, you know?"

"I wouldn't," said Jonas. "But I can imagine it's difficult to say no to someone who has been extremely nice to you for your whole life."

"Bingo," said Darren, tapping the side of his nose. "Recently he's been giving me weird vibes. Like, he's actually *speaking* to me, but it's the same line of questions every time." He hunched forward and cursed under his breath. "I hate red lights," he groaned, then continued. "He asks me how my grades are, and if I'm actually graduating, and then he wants to know when my college starts up in the fall — as if my schedule would change. He's never paid this much attention to me before. Which got me to thinking, is he counting down the days 'til I'm gone? Like, am I what's standing in the way of his plans?"

Jonas glanced at Isaac. "Possibly," he stated. "No matter what, we have to find them. You said that we're headed to a mini storage?"

"Uh-huh," replied Darren, nodding. "It's by the lake. Only it's not so *mini*. You've never been?"

Jonas shook his head.

"Well, let me tell you," said Darren with a sigh. "He has quite the compound. On the outside it looks like your run-of-the-mill storage place, you know, where people stow their stuff when they're moving, or rich dudes use 'em to hide their swanky cars if they're going through a divorce or something. But that's all just a front for his *other* operations. And I hear the cops are in his pocket, so he has pretty much free rein, or whatever."

"Neat," said Jonas. "And how do you know that he's gonna be there when we come calling?"

Darren looked over at Jonas. "What's with you, man?" he asked with fascination. "I mean, since you showed up tonight, you've been *different*, like in a dangerous way. I'm kinda scared of you right now." He lowered his voice and leaned toward Jonas. "Not to mention our passenger in the back seat," he whispered, dabbing a finger to the wound on his right cheek.

"For your sake," said Jonas. "Pretend he's invisible."

"See?" Darren drew away. "That's what I'm talking about."

"How do you know he'll be there?" repeated Jonas.

"Jeezum Crow," Darren shivered and muttered. Then he spoke louder, "because the old codger lives there, man. His *whole* family lives there." He rolled his neck, working out a crick. "You know he used to own my house? And for all I know, he still might own it."

"What do you mean?"

"I mean," replied Darren, "when Sasha was nine or ten, my parents worked out some kinda deal. The deed was given over to them, but the whole thing played out weird. Not like my parents would *willingly* sell Sasha off or anything like that, but maybe they got fooled into it. Like in the fine print or something." He rubbed his left cheek. "And I don't think any money changed hands. Which gives my whole *selling off my sister to the highest bidder* notion... more... more..." He thumped the steering wheel, trying to conjure the word.

"Credence," supplied Isaac.

Darren flinched as if someone had flicked his ear.

"It really does," agreed Jonas. "There just may be *something* to your running theory." His fingers graced over the sleek impression of Dafodhel waiting in his pocket. Jonas' Plan B. "Are we there yet?"

CHAPTER 30

Darren turned left onto a dead-end road. From the lonely intersection, the lake could be seen bedding down, her shores encased by cottage lights. The snow swept road leading to the storage facility was lined with mailboxes and iron wrought gates, insinuating mansions lurked beyond the twisting shadow veiled drives.

"Those are all owned by the Kowalskis," explained Darren. "Every one of 'em. This road is theirs." He squinted and adjusted his seat. "And here is the place," he said, drawing out every syllable.

Hundreds of storage units crowded up to the road and stretched back so far that they nearly invaded the lake. Darren's car skidded as it slowed, turning inside a significant space in the razor wire fencing, which so happened to be the entrance. The big snowflakes twirling all over the place made it tough to see.

As luck would have it, knee-high ice walls contained the driveway, preventing Darren from drifting too far out of bounds. And moments later the car swooped before the central office, a dingy brick-shod building in dire need of an update. Though the parking lot was empty, several lingering tire track impressions indicated recent activity. Also the lights were on.

Darren killed his headlights and plucked a shiny, metallic item from inside his coat. "Let's find out what's going on, boys," he said, fitting his hands with brass knuckles.

"You won't need those," said Jonas, leaving the car. "I have something better." He lifted his sack of gold into the lamplight.

Darren's mouth hung open. "What is that?" His eyes played from the pouch to the front door where Isaac held waiting.

"My Plan A," replied Jonas, turning for the office.

"Is that a ransom?" Darren asked, hopping the curb and jogging to catch up.

"I hope so," said Jonas. "And Darren." He heaved the front door open. "Let me do the talking."

A cloud of snow chased them inside, swirling in desperation against a stifling wall of heat. In the lobby a u-shaped desk greeted the customers, offering pamphlets and mints for a nickel apiece. The walls, floors, and counters shared the same shade of olive society had phased out forever ago. A disgusting drop ceiling leered down at them, stained in places by greenish gunk. Where its panels had once been a crisp white, were now browning from decades of secondhand cigarette smoke.

Isaac stiffened as he rounded the desk. "Voices," he said, signaling to follow.

At the end of the corridor, underneath the flickering fluorescent lights and across the overworked carpet, an open room waited.

Voices expanded from dull to clear, quiet to loud, the further the trio strode.

Harsh voices in a foreign tongue.

Up until this point, for all Jonas knew, Darren could have been feeding him bologna. But now, confined within the tight boundaries of this gross corridor, he could hear plain as day, the decrepit rasp of his weaselly foe. Fifteen steps and counting, he would soon be face-to-face with the solitary force that had been preventing his family from prosperity, from happiness. From flourishing. From making something greater. From becoming greater. A force that had snuffed out his grandparents and now cast a repeat performance showcasing his mother as the star.

But not tonight. No longer, thought Jonas, striding into Emil's office. One way or another, his family would be rid of this impediment, this millstone, this *monster*.

"Well, if it isn't the dragon boy," said Emil unsurprised. The old timer's face was swollen, his eyes submerged into blackened craters. "Hic sunt dracones, am I right? That's what you said to me?" He creaked back in his dated office chair.

The office was deeper than it was wide and decorated in the same lame aesthetic as the rest of the place. The four mustached men seated before the mafia lord's desk inclined their heads toward the interruption.

"Are you here for your dear matka?" Emil folded his hands beneath his chin. "Do you need her for-to tuck you in for bedtime?" The old man puckered his mouth and tilted his head.

His men found this hysterical. "Still afraid of the dark, little dragon boy?"

"*Quite the opposite,*" said Dafodhel within Jonas' head as he crossed the room.

"And if it isn't the little Pinault boy," said Emil, clicking a pen and grinning. "What's his name?" he surveyed the men. "Darryl? Derek? Dylan?"

Mirth filled the men's eyes. One offered "Delilah," to back-slapping laughter. And another pitched "Darcy" to further peals of delight.

Jonas slid the coin pouch across the table, stilling sound.

The room took a sharp inhale and then lurched greedily.

"What is this?" Emil spoke with wonderment. He separated the opening with thumb and forefinger and peered inside. "How did you come across such a bounty, little dragon boy?"

Jonas peered into the darkness gathering in the depths of the room. "You wouldn't believe me if I told you," he replied.

Emil rummaged elbow deep in the pouch. "Humor an old man," he said, retrieving several coins.

"We came across a pirate shipwreck on our way here," said Darren. Jonas flashed a mystified look in his direction, but Darren continued, unable to help himself. "Who cares, right? It's worth like millions. So just hand over my sister and the *dragon boy's* mom." He paused for laughter, but there wasn't any. "And we'll be outta your hair. No problems, no more questions and we all get to go home and have a Merry Christmas."

"Father," said the youngest and smallest of the mustaches, "these coins look like they came from an ancient empire."

"Stefan." Emil addressed his son. "How much do you think they are worth?" Then the room kicked into Polish, casting the English speakers into the dark.

Meanwhile Darren slowly deflated in the background. At school this guy was the central hub of popularity, and being ignored flat out like that was humiliating.

After less than a minute of harsh debate, the men of the Polish mafia came to a satisfying conclusion. The three giants and Stefan settled back in their chairs, restlessly twiddling thumbs and grinding teeth. Emil returned the coins to the pouch and cinched the drawstring.

"We accept this payment," he said, weighing Jonas' reaction with indifference. "Your debt is paid. Now go. Fabian and Stefan will see you out." He fanned the air. "I do not want to see you ever again."

"Wait," interrupted Darren, watching Fabian and Stefan file out. "What about my sister? She's coming with us too, right?"

Emil placed his pen aside and folded his hands. One of his men cracked his knuckles, sighed heavily. "No," replied Emil. "But you may bid her farewell. She is asleep, but we can wake her for you." He nodded at the remaining men. "Erek, Elek, please escort young Dorothy to his sweet sister." The two men rose chuckling.

"Now, if you would all please vacate my office," said Emil to Jonas. "Follow my men." He focused on Darren with dead eyes. "Have a pleasant Christmas."

"But, but!" stammered Darren looking to Jonas and Isaac. Jonas offered a reassuring hand to Darren's shoulder as he exited. "My sister!" he said in disbelief.

"Maybe you should have searched that shipwreck better," said Erek, clasping Darren by the elbow. "Now, let us go before I get angry."

Outside the blizzard had not calmed.

Jonas and Isaac shielded their eyes from the stinging snowfall, following their Polish tour guides deep within the labyrinth of storage vessels. The lake revealed more and more of its body the further they walked.

"You're keeping my mom inside one of these?" asked Jonas, blinking away a snowflake.

Fabian grunted.

"I'll take that as a yes," said Jonas bitterly. "Fabian is it?"

Fabian grunted again.

"The other day," said Jonas to Isaac. "At my mom's shop, Fabian here — the giant here with the flashlight, decided that it was a good idea to kick me in the face while I was on the ground."

"Did he now?" said Isaac, grim.

Fabian scraped a step at the mention of his name. "We should be there soon," he said, hovering his beam over a particular unit. "I think that is the one, eh Stefan?"

"Aye," replied Stefan. His voice grated on Jonas' nerves just like his father's. "What can I say? Our hospitality is, how you say, *legendary?*" He laughed until he burped.

Jonas noticed that Stefan's selection of steps had fallen much more wayward than his partner. It appeared that the Kowalski heir had been hitting the nog hard this evening.

"Hey," said Stefan, slugging the side of Isaac's arm. "You remind me of someone." He released a phlegmy cough into his hand. "Hey, Fabian! Who does this cienias remind you of?" He reached his snot hand into his peacoat to withdraw a flask.

Fabian snorted. "Many people," he replied, greatly disinterested.

They were now standing before the unit that held Jonas' mother captive. The faint tinkle of snowflakes brushing against the roller door was the only sound Jonas heard. He could hear naught else.

"No, I know, I know," said Stefan, hammer fisting Isaac's shoulder. "I know who he reminds me of! Hey! Hey!" He grabbed at the Still and spun him around. "Look at me when I talk to you! Did your mother not teach you manners?" Stefan doubled over and released a gut-wrenching belch. "Ho! Some of mother's pierogies disagree with me!" he chortled, holding his sides.

"Stefan," said Fabian. "Let's be on with it." He shook his head.

Stefan muttered something in Polish as he began working the lock. Once it snapped its release, Fabian reached down and gripped a nylon tether. "Oi, leń," he called out humorlessly as the door began its upward climb. "You have visitors."

"I know English isn't your first language," said Jonas as his eyes traced a path to a huddled mass in the farthest corner. "But I think you mispronounced *rescuers.*"

Stefan shoved Jonas square in the back. "You're right about one thing," he said while Fabian applied the same move on Isaac. The two stumbled into the cube, caught completely off guard. "English is not our first language," Stefan concluded with a snicker.

Jonas had to hand it to Fabian — the dude was lightning quick when it came to the closing of rolling doors. But unfortunately for him, Isaac was practically lightning.

Beyond the crinkling of cheap steel, Fabian spewed strings of curses, struggling to bring the door to a close. Stefan chided the man in Polish, laughing the entire time.

"They are pipsqueak!" jeered Stefan in English. "Big strong Fabian! Fabian so strong! Fabian break brick with forehead!"

"Shut up and help me!" snarled Fabian.

Soon four booted feet were planted beneath the door. The men growled and groaned, heaved with all their might.

"How!" Stefan grunted in frustration. "How can these scrawny cienias do this?" He dropped to a knee to lend more weight. With a shock, he discovered that it was only Isaac whom they battled. "What did you eat for breakfast, child?!" Suddenly Stefan discharged a tremendous belch. "Ho! I felt that in my ribcage!"

"Don't let up, you fool!" shouted Fabian. "Keep pressing, they must cave soon!"

"This is idiotic!" laughed Stefan. "Why not shoot them and just get it over with?" The younger man craned his head beneath the door, brandishing a revolver. "Hey! Scrawny boy! Are you ready to meet your maker?"

A hush fell when Stefan breathed his last, fading from existence, as a long-drawn exhale transcribed by the wind. And suddenly there was only one pair of feet on the other side of the door. Isaac ripped the door from the lone man's grip and sent it furling into the rafters.

"Mój Boże!" Fabian staggered backwards as the Still advanced. He lost his balance and fell. He scrambled toward the nearest storage unit, fumbled in his coat for a key.

"That *dragon boy*, as you so cleverly named him," seethed Isaac, "is a friend of mine. A friend that I would gladly follow to the depths and back again. Thousands of times over."

Fabian had given up on the key. He sat beneath the lock, resigned to his fate.

"You see," continued Isaac. "Unlike the populace in any realm, above and below, my friend here was the first to ever show me courtesy. He did not treat me as an outcast, as he probably should have. And for that reason alone, he earned my undying allegiance."

"W-why," stuttered Fabian. "Why are you telling me this?" The man bucked against the wall, released a howl that concluded into a raking fit of coughs.

"He brought out my true name," said Isaac sadly. "The name given at birth, so long, long ago."

Fabian's coughing had been reduced to shudders, or shivers. The temperature had suddenly dropped below arctic and the snow whipped around as if an icy cluster bomb had detonated.

"And then I hear that you struck my friend." Isaac's tone returned to malice. "While undefended."

The heaping pile of mafia muscle recoiled. He recognized this scene. "What are you going to do to me?" he asked and wretched forward, gurgling bile. With the immense pain cranking his guts, Fabian almost did not feel the Still's knee restructuring the bridge of his nose with a driven knee. Almost. He wailed and clasped his face, tumbled onto his side. His limbs thrashed in desperation, making the worst snow angels imaginable.

"Stop!" Fabian tried to stand, but the snow was too slick. The man was defeated. "Stop doing what you're doing!" He lifted his hand to stay a second blow.

"You first," said Isaac.

The moment hung suspended, Fabian too afraid to speak, and Isaac wishing that he would.

"Hey, Isaac," said Jonas from behind. "I want you to meet my mom." He hobbled through the blizzard bearing the weight of a taller red-haired woman. Dried blood caked the side of her face and she favored her left side. The color had not quite drained from her face, but enough had been spent.

"Pleasure," said Isaac with a nod.

Sandy returned the gesture with a faint smile. "Mr. Owl," she croaked, invoking Jonas' nickname from childhood. "You made a friend."

"We have to get her to safety," said Jonas to Isaac with controlled urgency. "And someplace warm."

Without hesitation, Isaac assumed the weight of Sandy's right side. "Let us be off," he said. "I recall the way back."

"Good," said Jonas. "Cuz I don't."

As the three plunged into the wall of white, Fabian could be heard mumbling at their backs. Most of his words were indiscernible grunts and curses, then suddenly he raised his voice. "It is blizzard and my nose is broke!" he shouted. "I can't see!"

A step to Jonas' left, buried in the snow, a faint needle of light poked up toward the sky. In an act of kindness, he planted a foot and wheeled, kicking the fallen flashlight toward Fabian. It concluded inside a clump of snow, illuminating its rest like an x-ray.

"Thanks!" shouted Fabian on all fours. "Oh, and cienias!" He called out to Isaac. "We will finish our chat another day, huh. You think I will forget what you did to me, eh?"

A weighty exhale released into the wind.

"Of that, I hold many doubts," intoned Isaac.

In a tremendous stroke of luck, Darren had not only left his car running, but he had also left it unlocked.

"Here," said Jonas, easing Sandy into the passenger seat. "Watch your head."

It's the sort of luck that gets rewarded by a catch.

"Your friend Darren is nowhere to be seen," revealed Isaac.

Jonas was on his knees working the seat recliner. "He's not my friend," he said distractedly. "Oh! There we go." Sandy's posture settled into a comfortable position. "Much better." He smiled at his mother, and had she been awake, she would have smiled back. "We'll return soon, mom," promised Jonas, closing the door carefully.

"Do you hear that?" asked Isaac, tugging his hood back. "Sounds like someone in pain." Toward the lake, peppered in screams, a distinct rattling filled a pocket of vacant space.

Somebody locked inside a storage unit.

"I think we found Darren," said Jonas, turning away. "They played the same trick on him."

"Indeed," said Isaac taking a step, arresting the next. Jonas did not follow. Upon noticing the baleful expression that his friend directed toward the office, Isaac added, "I will see to him."

Jonas held out his hand. "There's something I need to do."

Isaac clasped the offered hand and pulled Jonas into an embrace. "May your enemies tremble," he said. "For if they are not, they will be."

CHAPTER 31

When Jonas was much younger, in years gone by, his mother had purchased generic Lucky Charms. Not the store brand, that stuff was too pricey — it was the even cheaper knock-off, hiding its shame on the floor shelf, inside a plastic bag. *"Awesome Stars"* they had been dubbed, a floating wizard adorned the front, sprinkling magic dust in his magical wake. They were pretty terrible, but at the time Jonas did not know any better. The non-marshmallow bits were grainy and flavorless, becoming soggy the moment they touched milk. And the ratio of grainy bits to marshmallows was way off. For instance, Lucky Charms stands at a 3:1, and this stuff resided around 5,000:1. Give or take a few vitamin enriched whole grain oats.

Jonas' mind wandered as he penetrated the offices of the Kowalski crime family. It meandered to those sunny Saturday mornings, a mouth filled with cereal, viewing cartoons. Far from this bone-chilling winter, far from all this harm wrought from debt, and far from the bruises on his mother's neck.

He would sit and devour that cereal as if it were the greatest thing to ever grace the innards of a paper bowl. But there was a specific order in which he went about it. In truth, he really loved the marshmallows, loved them so much that he would save them for last, skillfully maneuvering his spoon betwixt and between, consuming the plain bits first. Like a prospector sifting gold. And all he had to show for his hard work were a mere a dozen pale marshmallows, grinning back at him, afloat in their milky bed. But nothing, *nothing*, tasted better than those one and a half spoonsful.

And for his whole life he had been force-fed nothing but the grainy gross bits, but now...

Emil sifted through paperwork and did not look up when Jonas entered. Shadow creatures lurked in the recesses of the deep room, looking on with great interest.

"The birthday boy is not answering his talkie," stated Emil. "Perhaps this cold weather has frozen the batteries." He continued going through folders, eyes downward.

The reticent pause had been the old man's first hint.

"Do me a favor, go out and check on —"

The second hint was the dull thump of Stefan's flask striking the desktop and sliding against his forearm. The old man started, then recoiled when he realized the object. His mouth hung drastically lower than Jonas imagined possible. After a few moments of pained silence, the old man finally collected himself.

"I should have known," said Emil taking in Jonas before him. "I should have known that this business would end poorly. Please, take a seat."

Jonas remained standing.

"As you like." When Emil nodded, a single tear spilled out over a swollen eye. "Today was a joyous day. A joyous occasion.

It was my Stefan's twenty-first birthday, and I did not go to your mother tonight with any intentions of abduction," he stated, circling his left eye with an index finger. "But she lashed out, and that is not something that goes unpunished. At my age, when you are in charge, you must not show a sliver of weakness!" His concave chest puffed, and he bestowed it a hearty thump. "And we could not have her go crying to the police. You must understand, I had no choice. If she would have just allowed us to take that clock. But, no! She had to put up a fight! And my dear sweet Sashaczka, my little myszko, she did this!" Emil highlighted the other eye with an angrier circling pattern. "I did not know what to do! She would not hurt a flea! Then she looked at me with such hatred!"

The monster's façade began to crumble. Carefully Emil dabbed at both eyes with a yellowed hanky, more tears overflowed. Then he conjured a revolting snort, miraculously returning his posture to normal. With a peaceful expression, Emil leaned back in his chair, as if coming to terms with God.

"I should have known," he said, interlocking fingers over Stefan's flask. "I should have known," he repeated, shook his head. "The moment you threw that gold down, just like the way you threw my sweet Stefan's birthday gift at me just now." His fingers played across the glossy surface emblazed with a *twenty-one* in fancy script. "He was my only son and heir, and he is no more?" He choked back a laugh. "I should have known. It's written all over your face, plain as day. He is no more." Then he choked on a whimper. "In all honesty, he would have made a poor leader. He was too taken with childish things, always buying fancy new cars, chasing girls, you know." With startling speed, Emil bashed a hard finger against his right temple. "He did not have the right mind! His gifts were else-where! You see, my sweet, sweet young Stefan was no thinker. But Sasha! Ah!" The wrinkles upon Emil's forehead shot up to the moon. "My Sasha was to be his bride when she came of age. She! She! She was the thinker! That girl has a great mind for all things. Building, designing, logic, reason — I could go on and on."

Darren's theory shot close but fell short. Sasha was indeed being groomed as a bride, just not for a pervy European Prince overseas. A coin toss may have determined the worse of the two fates. Playing humans as pawns has always been a sickening practice.

"Sasha was my true heir," said Emil. "I should have known when you threw that gold at me! You see, Stefan is my only son, the baby of the family. Our miracle! He has six sisters — all of which should have been his brothers. All the other baby boys my wife bore did not survive the birthing canal. And last night I had *the* dream. A dream that I had not had in a very, very long time. The same dream that would come to me right before my wife suffered a miscarriage." Emil eased forward in his chair, growing more serious. A shadow seemed to cross his worn features. "It was an ill omen. A curse. In the dream I would be approached by a winged man — a man whom you Americans refer to as the *Mothman* — and he is *very* real and he has teeth," Emil paused to point at his canines, "just like yours. And he would say nothing to me, just as you are now, and look at me, just as you are looking at me now."

"In which form should I take," said Dafodhel inside Jonas' mind. *"When we slay this fiend?"* She sounded eager whilst the flames of Jonas' vengeance flickered. No longer was Emil a fearsome mafia boss — the self-proclaimed *dracone* — but an old, old man who was but a spectator to his legacy's demise. A whimpering, pathetic spectator.

"My wife," continued Emil, "is fifty-six years old, and gave birth to Stefan in the middle of her thirties. We can no longer have children, and it occurred to me all at once, *Whoosh!*" He flung a hand over his scalp. "When you walked in, that no, we cannot have any more children, but we can certainly lose them."

"Do not fall victim to this pitiful farce," urged Dafodhel. *"Recall your mother in that box, nearly frozen! Nothing but the clothes on her back, not even a chamber pot in sight. He was not planning on releasing her, Jonas. If he held the upper hand would he show you such mercy?"*

No, he would not. Suddenly, upon his shoulder blades, the infernal itching made a return. He snarled a response to the flare. *But we are not like him. We don't control other people.* A tinge of guilt coated those words as he reflected on the Hylda and Ritts.

The change on Jonas' face struck Emil terrified, believing the shift of anger directed his way. "Take the gold back!" said Emil straddling the edge of panic.

"Draw me and end this!" Dafodhel raged in Jonas' pocket, swelling in warmth. *"Allow me to take my true form! This useless bag of teeth does not deserve pity!"*

No! Jonas screamed the thought, his forehead counseled in a hand. The itching had grown unbearable as his winter coat prevented a proper scratch. *I'm not killing anyone!*

"You don't need to do it," said Dafodhel with unnerving calm. *"Simply aim me toward his throat and I will perform the remainder."*

Look, I know you mean well, but this guy is beyond defeated. And if I could go back —

Emil flung the pouch across the table. "Take the gold! Just take it back! I do not want it anymore!"

Dafodhel had accrued more heat. *"You would resurrect this vermin's offspring from the grave?"*

Jonas tore himself free of his coat, no longer able to withstand the harsh prickle. *I didn't want his son to die! If I could bring him back I would!* As he was about to dig nails into the itch, Dafodhel became molten cinder. "Ah!" Jonas called out in pain, dropped to a knee with such ferocity that his glasses fell from their perch.

"Take the gold and leave what remains of my family alone!" Emil was beside himself. If he were decades younger, he would have fled. "Leave me, please! And don't invade my dreams again! Take this gold and take the curse with you! Tu es Dracones! Your family owes me nothing! Tu es Dracones! Is that what you wish to hear?"

"Don't you understand who you are!" Dafodhel was not cooling. *"You are the commander of shadows! The death bringer! The harbinger of doom!"*

No I'm not! Jonas screamed in his head, drew the flaming Dafodhel. *Hylda and Ritz forgive me!* Upon uttering that plea, Jonas felt the tiniest spark of a connection cross between worlds, and for a frail, fleeting moment sensed Scary give a nod.

The dim-lit office ignited with radiance, like a fuel-soaked pyre.

The shadow creatures lurking in the depths shielded their eyes and recoiled. Emil, who was far too frail to launch from his seat, instead rocked backwards, spilled out on his head. The pistol he had concealed beneath the desk hurtled from his hand, lost to the darkness.

Searing heat radiated from Dafodhel, flames lapped from pommel to tip. She had become a brilliant broadsword, lighter than air, more menacing than a guillotine. When she spoke her flames billowed. "Look at what you have become!" she announced in awe.

Jonas felt both heavier and lighter. His heels rose as his chest sunk. He turned his head, and in the flickering light, beheld an elegant, terrifying set of wings sprouting from his shoulder blades. The itch finally relieved.

"You are a true Valorous!" exclaimed Dafodhel.

The room drew taut when he rose, somehow smaller. Moments before he could not see behind Emil's desk, and now he could see the old man, sprawled on the carpet, crawling, reaching for something beyond his fingertips. Framed overhead and out of Emil's view, shadow creatures barnacled the walls and ceiling.

A skeletal crunch issued from beneath Jonas' first step. He looked down with miraculous clarity to discover that he had tread upon his glasses. He also noticed his bare toes had pushed clean through his socks and old winter boots, having elongated several sizes in keeping with his increased stature.

This is all adding up! he thought. At long last he had become the Leeds Devil in this world! Then he shook his head, contradicting the claim. *No, not the Devil. Never again the Devil.*

Jonas made his way to the fallen Emil, and as he reached down to help, caught sight of what the old man had been striving for. A snub-nosed revolver, much like the one his son had carried.

Fear suffused every crevice of the old man's face. Dafodhel's brilliant light hid nothing. "I just dropped it, is all," explained Emil, his lips churned as driven waves. "It was gift from son."

"Liar!" Dafodhel shouted.

The sword's accusation landed caustic. Emil wept into his hands. "I am liar," he moaned. "Always lying. Emil so evil. That was not gift from son." Then his voice lilted sharp, his hands darted from his face, revealed a ghoulish grin. A second revolver flashed upward, aimed square for Jonas' chest. "This was gift from son."

Jonas brought the blade to front. The bullet ricocheted, terminated elsewhere. A secondary shot rang, setting his shoulder to char. The flashing burst of the muzzle brought a dizzying deafness. Off-balance he staggered to his right, weaved his wings to shield his side, expecting a third round.

Yet this did not come about.

Emil stared upward with glassy eyes, his breath arrived ragged, noticing the creatures for the first time.

The scent of burnt gunpowder had overtaken the stale air.

Jonas had not struck from a place of anger. "Shadows take him," he said.

And suddenly Jonas and Dafodhel were alone.

"Jonas?" Darren called through the blizzard, standing astride his car.

Jonas had exited the office building, his winter coat draped over his shoulders as a mantle, unable to fit as it should. His jeans had been over-stretched, exposing inches of ankle. By sheer luck, he had come across a pair of adult-sized winter boots idling in a tray beside the front door. Dafodhel was now the thinnest dirk, tucked snug into his back pocket. And to his great advantage, his wings retracted beneath his skin, divulging manageable bumps. How they developed, grew, and existed, Jonas deferred that explanation to the realms of magic spells and wizards.

"Hey! Don't come any closer!" Darren bristled.

"Chill out, man," said Jonas, striding to the passenger side of the Neon to look in on his mother. Her shoulders gradually rose and fell with the tides of sleep. Peacefully she slept, but not comfortably. To his great relief, Sasha was swaddled in a heap of blankets, laid across the back seat. She was asleep and breathing and seemed in much better condition than his mother.

"Where's Isaac?" Jonas peered toward the lake.

"Jonas?" said Darren, approaching cautiously as if the stranger before him were coated in toxic sludge. "Is that you?"

"Yes, yes, it's me," replied Jonas.

"I knew it!" said Darren beaming. "The teeth give it away every time!" He rushed forward and struggled to gather the now-taller Jonas into a hug. "I don't know how you got so huge, but I've seen some stuff tonight that would make me believe in God and angels and devils and... and... flying pigs!" Jonas felt warm tears dribble down his arm and froze before they fell. "And I'm sorry, man! I'm sorry for being such a jerk! For being such a scumbag!"

"It's cool," said Jonas, crowbarring forearms, releasing Darren's hold. "It's cool, man. All's forgiven."

"Okay, okay," said Darren backing and swatting his drippy nose. "And your friend, Isaac? Yeah, he killed a guy. Like, I heard it through the door. And after he forced the storage locker open and let me and Sasha go, he just took off after the other giant. He's not, like, he's not like a human *person*. And I haven't seen him since. I just got Sasha settled into the back seat when I swore I heard gun shots, and I was thinking of just peeling out of here, then you came out of the office, and well... here we are now."

"They didn't hurt your sister?"

"No." Darren shook his head, looked away. "She had a kerosene heater and a little bed. She was sleeping when they tossed me in, and she hasn't woken up since. Had to carry her all the way back." He folded his arms across his chest and nodded toward the road. "I don't mean to be a Nagging Nancy or anything, but the Neon's tire tracks are already filled with snow. We're going to be marooned here if your cousin doesn't get back soon."

"We'll make it," said Jonas. "He'll return." He gazed through the thick plumes of exhaust pumping into the skies. The car rattled as the engine sighed. "I hope."

A few more minutes stretched out with no sign of the Still. Darren grew anxious.

"Isaac!" Darren shouted into the cavernous night, drenched in white. The impenetrable barrier of fallen snow swallowed every syllable. "Isaac!"

Jonas turned, snow crunched beneath his heel. "Hey," he began politely. "What did I tell you about talking to that guy?"

Darren tucked his chin. "My bad," he admitted. "What's his deal though? What'll happen?"

"Keep doing that," replied Jonas. "Asking questions. If you ask him three questions, then he kills you. I think you have one more to go, then..." Jonas etched a line across his throat, symbolizing a dagger slice.

"That's," said Darren at a loss. "That's just, wow. Dude must not get invited to parties very often."

A nightmarish silhouette materialized just beyond the chalky veil. "Ha!" Jonas could not help but laugh. "There he is."

Sharply the figure cocked his head to the sound.

"Isaac!" called Jonas with cupped hands. "This way!"

The Still ripped a dead sprint, snowflakes spiraled in his wake. "You must be off!" he said, stopping against the car trunk. His breath came normal, showing little sign of exhaustion. "I will find my way," he pleaded. "Please! Depart!"

"Alright," said Jonas. He recalled Guiltbrand's declared time limit for the Hush. *One night and one day.* "Take care of yourself."

Isaac nodded. "Good to see you're back."

"Likewise," said Jonas to Isaac, then turned to Darren. "Let's go!" He spun a thin dagger in the air as he bounded to the passenger rear door. He slid inside the car while gently easing Sasha's head onto his lap. The girl stirred but did not wake.

When Darren pitched the headlights on, the falling snow tossed the lights right back. "This snow is thicker than peanut butter," said Darren, flinging the car into reverse.

"You mean pea soup," corrected Jonas.

The car struggled out of its K-turn. "You eat what you like," said Darren through chattering teeth, released the clutch. The tires spun, not grabbing much, then an unexpected jolt sent the vehicle forward. "And I'll eat what I like!" he stated in triumph. "Here we go! Slow and steady wins the race."

CHAPTER 33

J onas' head fell back upon his pillows, cupped hands cradled his head. He was exhausted, in a good way. The best kind of way.

The day had begun with a snappy prison break, and it had ended with the longest, slowest, trundled car ride home. For Darren every moment was nerve racking, but for Jonas it was awesome. The view from the driver seat was barred, scary, impossible to penetrate. In dire contrast, the view in the back seat was... it was...

Jonas exhaled, drained a lung. "Amazing," he admitted. Sasha slept the duration of the ride home, but she had awoken several times, and Jonas had pretended not to notice.

"She fancies you," Dafodhel had said. *"I can sense these sorts of things. Do you fancy her?"*

I thought you could sense these sorts of things? Jonas had answered.

"She is very beautiful," Dafodhel had said.

She is, Jonas agreed, sparing a sideways glance toward Sasha. *She's also out of my league.*

Dafodhel had nearly shrieked when she laughed.

In the present, Jonas smiled and rubbed his face, recalling the last moments spent with Sasha.

While he had carried her up the Pinault's winding staircase, he had ignored every glance she had sent his way. He had faced ghouls, goblins, demons, wolves, drakes, and a fabled Yéne. He had re-routed a war, commanded witches & gargoyles, bested a kingdom, and slew an evil mafia boss. He had been dubbed a Devil, a Scourge, an Evil Seed, and more recently, a Mothman. But for some unknown reason, he just could not look her way. Somehow that feat was much more difficult, as if he would find a way to screw that up. As if something residing within her simple glance might reduce him back to square one. Back to an old world that he hated with passion, one that hated him in return.

He had carried her to her bedroom, tucked her into bed. As he departed, neared the threshold, she had said good-night to him, and he had replied with a cool *see-ya later*.

Jonas wanted to stay in this new world, a world overloaded with possibilities. Brimming, overflowing. A world where his mother would be able to get her clock shop back up and running.

Or not! Heck she could do whatever she wanted! Go fly kites all day or read books in front of a fire, or travel to far off lands of mystery! They could eat fries with golden chopsticks on top of mountains! All of the above and more!

His mind wandered all over the place. Well, it was more of a skipping, leaping sort of *wander*. Not sure if that's how wandering works, but he was excited, and for the first time ever, Jonas Porter looked forward to tomorrow.

EPILOGUE

About one month later...

Statues dated by moss and decay, kept watch over the gravestones, like shepherds with wills of iron. Leading up the hillside, the evening's shadows tethered to the graves that had been toppled in sloppy, mismatched fashion. Just beyond the graveyard, the trees swooned along the outskirts, their symphony of leaves cut silent. The wind died.

"Your mother wanted to come," said Tasso, turning to his right. "Sorry about that."

"She understands," replied Jonas. "That's just how she is."

"It would be such a risk, having her attempt a crossing," said Tasso. "Maybe someday, eh?" He glanced to Isaac who was walking on the Joiner's left. "I'll get my hands on another scroll and show her how to *actually* use it."

"Yeah, someday," said Jonas, scanning the flat top of the hill. "When the Riverlands are not warring."

"For the best, I'd say," chimed in Dafodhel in Jonas' hand as a quarterstaff.

"Which grave did that Graveyard Joiner tell you was the one?" asked Jonas. "And also, how many different kinds of Joiners are there?"

"Too many," replied Tasso. "She said we couldn't miss it, once we got to the top..."

"Found it!" called Isaac. He had apparently left Tasso and Jonas to scout on his own. Or he already knew which grave marker belonged to Sebastian Terren. "I remember the Leeds' outrage from the sudden emergence of this statue," he explained as Jonas and Tasso came around. "It was presumed that some rogue Terrens had pitched it up under cover of night. Your father's grave had been unmarked until that point."

"Whoa," said Jonas.

Tasso shook his head. "Looks just like you, kid."

"In truth," agreed Isaac.

A grim, winged warrior gazed up, challenging the sky. From his waist down, the statue was yet cast, unfinished stone. But his face and wings had been meticulously crafted, complete.

"Circumstances must have spurred the craftsmen's haste to raise it," speculated Isaac. "That's how I reconcile the fact that it remains incomplete."

"Your father was a polarizing figure," said Tasso. "Still is, as you know."

"Rumor has it that he was buried where he fell," said Dafodhel. "Struck in the back."

"I recall that was a night where the Leeds rejoiced and the Terrens breathed a sigh of relief," said Isaac. "The prophecies had muddled everybody's minds, forgetting that Sebastian was a living, breathing creature."

Jonas had drawn a knee to brush the leaves from the blank grave plate. "I was told that Némer killed him, and that he and my dad grew up together."

Dafodhel grunted. "Half of that is proven truth," she said. "Your father and Némer were childhood friends and trained together in the arts of battle and defense. But whether Némer killed your father, no one is certain. Your uncle wholeheartedly believes that Némer is your father's murderer."

"Némer denies it," added Tasso. "To this day, I would wager. And both sides have their running conspiracies as to whom actually struck that fated blow."

"Who do you think killed him?" said Jonas standing, directing the query toward Tasso and Dafodhel.

Tasso idly scratched at a sideburn. "I don't know, Jonas," he spoke with reluctance in his voice. "Wish I did, and I don't like to speculate. But what I do know, is that when your father was chased back into this realm, he did not use one of my inventions to do it."

Jonas elevated an eyebrow.

"I keep a ledger," continued Tasso, "a record of every crossing that takes place using any of my furniture." He scratched at his chin. "And your dad didn't cross via Tasso Creations LLC."

A spark flickered in Jonas' eye. "Do all Joiners keep logs like yours?"

Tasso laughed. "Highly doubtful." He straightened, seeing Jonas' reaction and added, "I'm sorry."

"What do you think, Daf?" said Jonas turning to the staff.

"Siegmund," replied Dafodhel with ice cold certainty. "Your uncle Siegmund killed your father."

Jonas' eyes and mouth widened, astonished. Meanwhile Isaac continued crunching on the fries he had carried with him. Tasso coughed into a fist.

For the last few weeks Jonas had been visiting his uncle in secret, checking in on things. Siegmund had been keeping him abreast of the war, and also, as a special favor for his nephew, had been making inquiries on the whereabouts of his passing spirits.

"You, you think," stammered Jonas. "You think my uncle is capable..."

"Most assuredly," replied Dafodhel curtly. "You should always be wary of those who seek power for power's sake."

"I sought you out," said Jonas, more so for his uncle.

"That is much, much different." Dafodhel trembled in Jonas' grip. "You sought me to end a legacy of oppression. And your power came to you unawares. You did not know that for every command given to the passing spirits would grant an incremental dosage of power." Dafodhel grew more and more agitated. "Every command-initiated growth, in drips. But you did not know this! You did not command and command and command until you became what you are now. No, you accepted the power given to you, as a gift. As one worthy."

"And my uncle?"

"Your uncle desires power!" Dafodhel shot back. "Craves it. His motivations are envious, covetous, selfish!" She exhaled, shedding a bit of ire. "I know you care for your uncle, but I feel like you should be aware of his nature."

Jonas turned to Isaac but did not voice his question aloud, merely conveyed it with his eyes. "Your uncle is not one to be trusted," replied Isaac. Jonas blinked in surprise. The Still notoriously avoided politics. "What's his surname, and what side is he currently in bed with?" said Isaac with a shrug, popping another fry into his mouth. "It's not rocket surgery."

Jonas rolled his eyes and plunked them back down onto his father's chiseled face. "He wouldn't..." he began, then finished quietly, "didn't murder his own brother."

A few moments were spent in silence, save for the sound of Isaac scraping the bottom of his super-sized fry order.

"So, Jonas," said Tasso at length, clearing his throat. "What's next?"

"He's a true Valorous," said Dafodhel. "Has the wings of a Seraph, commands the shadows, and is able to cross between worlds as he pleases."

"For sure," agreed Tasso. "There are many stars that have fallen out of alignment that only a true Valorous may be able to reach and correct. On all sides of the mirror." He inclined his head toward Isaac. "And there will be no evidence left to track, with a Hush by his side." An amused look passed over the Joiner's face. "The row of For Sale signs along Kowalski Lane has not gone unnoticed, and oh, how the rumors are swirling. I've overheard the elder folk in Rocking Horse 101 espousing some wild theories."

Jonas laughed. "What theories?"

"You know," replied Tasso, casually rolling his wrist. "Some say it was mafia beef within the family. Others that it was an outside syndicate — Italians, Russians, Yakuza — something along those lines." His voice tightened as one about to reveal juicy gossip. "But a few rumors trickled out claiming that it was a shape shifting demon that claimed Emil and Stefan." He bobbed his eyebrows. "A family curse that finally came back to settle its due."

"That's not far off," said Jonas with a smirk. "But if it's all the same, I'm sick of bungled prophecies and the expectations of warlords. I was advertised as a Devil to one side and was written off as a liability to the other. Don't get me wrong, I want peace in the Riverlands as much as the next guy, but honestly, I'm a bit worn out from the tug-of-war."

"When ya get sick of juggling," said Tasso, "it's time to leave the circus."

Jonas dabbed an approving finger at the Joiner. "Right, right," he said with a laugh. "After the cup-check I gave the Terrens, they are wary of another invasion. And both sides fear that the other has my allegiance, so for now I'll just sit back and watch."

"It seems rumors abound wherever you go," commented Tasso.

"Is that not the way of things?" said Dafodhel. "Greatness does not require boasting."

"Let's not get carried away now," said Jonas, looking up to the statue. "Hey guys, give me a moment alone." He handed Dafodhel off to Isaac, ignoring the staff's groaning about greasy fingers.

"You got it, man," said Tasso with a reassuring nudge as he passed. "I'll see you back at the homestead. Don't be too long, your mother's making her famous chicken noodle soup. And I'll bet Cucumbers has driven her bonkers by now."

"Dude loves chicken," said Jonas with a smile. "Make sure to save me some."

"I'll do that," replied Tasso. "And I'll also save you a seat beside Sasha."

Jonas' ears reddened. "Bye, Tasso."

Dusk was beginning to seep around the edges, and daylight was just about to throw in the towel. Jonas took off his jacket, despite the late summer chill. The moon was only just lugging itself over the horizon when, in the not too far distance, a choir of lonely imps began reciting a dour melody.

"Well, Dad," said Jonas, spreading his wings. "I wish we would have met. I wish you hadn't died the day I was born." The imps' song grew closer. It seemed their journey's end lay in the graveyard. "I wish a lot of things," continued Jonas, unconcerned by the creatures' encroachment. If anything, the sad tune siphoned feelings that Jonas had buried away. "How about we make a deal, dad? What if I promise to never give up? Never give up — no matter what's going on, no matter where I am — I will always be trying." He stretched his wings, mirroring the statues' pose. "How does that sound? And wherever you are, if you're listening right now — how about you promise to be proud of me?" His throat constricted. This imp dirge knocked loose some emotions that he was unaware existed. "Because, guess what? Because I know you wouldn't have given up on me. And you'll be proud of me."

To Jonas' right, torches borne by small hands had formed a circle at the base of hill. The song was nearing its end; the harmonies dwindled into an outro, the imp voices died off one by one.

When his stomach growled, the sudden silence brought the gurgle to the forefront. "I gotta get going now," said Jonas looking down. "I'll say hi to Mom for you." He furled his wings, turned his back. "Remember our deal," he said to his father's stone image. "And always remember...

I will never give up."

ACKNOWLEDGMENTS

Ryan Krebs, Hiram Ring, and Scott Telle:
In spite of being asked to check out this manuscript over
the Holidays, you guys managed to find the time to pour over
it anyhow. Can never thank you felluhs enough.
These books would not even be nearly as good.

My thanks to Sarah Chorn for her guidance,
perspective, and brilliant edits.

Gina: You're the love of my life.
Can't see happiness without you.

And to my Mother (the best of mothers):
Look! No Swears!

ABOUT THE AUTHOR

M. Warren Askins lives in the Northeastern United States with his wife and the greatest dog.

In truth, 'tis much simpler to traverse 'round the thistles and thorns...